CHARLOTTE Nash

Charlotte Nash began stealing her mother's Jilly Cooper novels at the age of thirteen, and has been enthusiastic for romance ever since. She started writing after medical school, and her enduring stories of courage and love are now published around the world. She writes from a cozy cottage on the east coast of Australia, surrounded by family and chickens. *Crystal Creek* was her third novel, now republished in this international edition.

Visit charlottenash.net for all the books and to sign up for her newsletter (comes with exclusive previews and giveaways). She loves to hear from readers through:

@CharlotteNash79
AuthorCharlotteNash
@saxen49

Also by Charlotte Nash:

THE WALKER-BELL STORIES
Ryders Ridge
Iron Junction
Crystal Creek
Great Haven (in 2018)

STAND-ALONE ROMANCES
The Horseman

WOMEN'S FICTION WITH ROMANTIC ELEMENTS
The Paris Wedding
The Lucky Escape (in 2019)

Crystal Creek

Charlotte Nash

First published in Australia and New Zealand in 2015 by Hachette Australia (an imprint of Hachette Australia Pty Limited)

This international edition published in 2018 by Flying Nun Publications, http://flyingnunpublications.com/

ISBN:
978-1-925775-04-4 (paperback)
978-1-925775-05-1 (MOBI eBook)
978-1-925775-08-2 (EPUB eBook)

A catalogue record for this book is available from the National Library of Australia

Cover design by J.D. Smith

For Bek

Author's note

I'm excited to welcome you to this international edition of *Crystal Creek*, the third book in the Walker-Bell series, stories that blend contemporary romance with family, secrets, and medical drama, featuring the Walker and Bell family siblings and friends in small towns across Australia (though don't worry if you haven't read the first – you can jump in here).

If you're not familiar with Australia, think of Queensland (capital: Brisbane) a bit like Texas – big, warm and proud. Townsville, where this story takes place, is a tropical coastal city hundreds of miles north of the capital. There's a bit of colorful language, but also lots of space to hide from old hurts. Or to meet a man in a uniform, and other kinds of trouble …

Enjoy!

Chapter 1

"And what is your differential diagnosis?"

Christina Price stood against the wall in the stark hospital hallway, in the middle of the most important exam of her life. She tried to take a deep breath, but her ribs were panic-stiff, the clack of the nearby nurse's keyboard too loud. Her phone vibrated in her pocket yet again, distracting her. She had to *think*. "Uh, cirrhosis. And liver cancer," she said.

The examining doctor peered over the top of his glasses. "You need to expand on that."

She squared her shoulders, fingering the knot of scarred skin on her right palm for motivation. She'd had fifteen minutes with her patient. Surely she could think of something else.

"Um, there could be a primary liver tumor. Or a metastasis from another site." She tried to picture the anatomy in her mind, but her attention kept sliding back to her phone. It had been ringing for the past half-hour, and only one caller would be that persistent. Something bad must have happened.

The consultant tapped a pen on his clipboard, bringing her back to now. "Where else could a tumor be?" he prompted.

Her thoughts moved like sticky mud. "The pancreas?"

The consultant made a note and sighed. "Go back to your second idea. Which neoplasias could have metastasized to the liver, in this patient?"

A nurse with a phlebotomy trolley rattled past. Christina averted her eyes, trying to remember the page from her textbook. "Ah, stomach, breast, ovarian, ah ... lung and kidney."

"In *this* patient."

The blood drained from Christina's face. Oh God, had she just suggested breast and ovarian cancer for a male patient? "Umm ... lung and kidney."

"And what about your physical examination findings? Did you find evidence to support your diagnoses?"

"Um." She looked at her notes, her handwriting blurring. She knew this stuff. Why couldn't she remember? Her phone buzzed again.

"Like in the abdomen?" prompted the consultant. "Ascites?"

Christina shook her head. She hadn't remembered to check, and her thoughts were too hopelessly muddled now. Her face was burning, her stethoscope pulling the fine hairs on the back of her neck. She knew she'd done terribly, as she had all term. Really, as she had for the past two years, especially on the ward. At the beginning, she'd thought getting into med school was the hard part; it had certainly taken her long enough. But it turned out that she was hopeless at practical skills. *See one, do one, teach one* was the motto, but Christina could never pick things up that fast. All the other students seemed so much more confident. Maybe it was because they were younger.

"All right." The doctor checked his watch. "Please summarize your findings."

The thought of failing tore something in her soul. She forced a deep breath; maybe she could still recover.

"Grant Reading is a fifty-five-year-old man who initially presented with jaundice and, um, right-upper-quadrant discomfort ..."

When she finished, she realized she'd failed to ask Grant about any family history.

The consultant grunted, plainly unimpressed, his hands clasped behind his back. "That will do. You may go."

That was when reality crashed in. She hadn't recovered. Not even close.

Christina turned away, limbs sluggish with despair. She pushed through the ward's big double doors and trudged down the stairwell, then along the corridor towards the student common room, checking her phone as she went. Her heart froze when she saw five missed calls from the care house number. How bad was this going to be?

Other surgical students had collapsed on the old couches. Christina skirted them, and sank into a hard chair by the window, plucking at her shirt, which had stuck to her cold-fear sweat. She braced herself for the coming conversation.

Lena, one of the care staff, answered on the second ring. "Christina, I'm sorry, I know you have exams, but there's been a problem today."

"What kind of problem?"

A pause, as if Lena was considering where to start. "Your mother – she went missing."

"What? How could that even happen? She's partly paralyzed."

"She came back a few hours later. But she's been drinking again. I'm so sorry. One of the carers was sick and we were short-staffed."

Christina cursed, though it wasn't Lena's fault. Across the common room, she could hear a group of students from her class – Toby, Sean, Sarah and Katie – commiserating, giddy with post-exam relief. Katie was talking over everyone else, going over details no one wanted to discuss, until Toby threw his notes at her. Soon they would go out to drink beer and celebrate. Christina had never been part of that circle. Her life was taken up with responsibilities and obligations.

"I'll come now," she told Lena. "But I have to be at work in an hour." She ended the call and grabbed her bag, doing the math in her head. Thirty minutes to drive to the care house, time talking to her mother, another thirty to get to work. To revive herself, she splashed water on her face from the kitchen tap.

"How'd you go?" called Katie. "Hey, Christina, I said how'd you go?"

Christina glanced warily at Katie Prior, who was dressed impeccably in a crisp pale-blue shirt and black pants, her artfully streaked blonde hair pulled into a perfect bun. Katie was the only student who knew where Christina had come from. Her older brother, Sebastian, had been in Christina's high-school class. And the less said about both those things, the better.

"I don't want to talk about it," Christina said, heading for the door.

"Bye!" called Katie with a laugh.

Toby followed her into the hall, panting as he tried to catch up. "Hey, wait. Was the exam really that bad?"

"That bad," said Christina, not slowing even as she felt rude. Toby had tried to help her study, his efforts always interrupted by work or her mother. He was quiet and soft-spoken, the kind of study partner she'd have liked if she could. "Sorry, but I have to go."

She didn't look around. All she could think about was what might be waiting for her at the care house.

She pulled her ancient Corolla into the care house driveway twenty-five minutes later. Lena met her at the door, her dark eyes apologetic, her uniform blouse rucked from the day. She went to speak, but Christina cut her off. "Don't apologize again. Tell me the whole story."

When Lena was finished, Christina was aghast. She turned towards the lounge, the weight of what had happened sinking in. Four months ago, when the residential care package had first been granted, Christina had thought that the days of dealing with her mother's destructive habits were over. The care package was supposed to allow Christina to step back, to be only her mother's guardian – ensuring her finances were sorted, making medical decisions if needed. Not giving lectures.

She paused before she went in, carefully putting up her mental barrier.

Rita sat in one of the electric-lift chairs, a *New Idea* crooked against her weaker arm, her blonde hair shot with gray and tucked behind her ears as she stared at the pages. No matter how hard Christina pulled her emotions back, she always felt the gut strike when she saw the sunken cheeks, dotted with spider nevi, the red flush across her mother's palms – all medical signs of the addiction that had taken over her mother's life and nearly destroyed Christina's. She could smell the sour fumes in the air as she sat down in the opposite seat.

"What were you thinking, Rita?"

"What, no *Mum* today?" Rita said with a slight slur, not looking up from the pages.

Christina ignored this. "Where did you go?"

"Nowhere."

"This nowhere have slot machines?"

"So what if it did?"

Christina rubbed her forehead, wondering how much of this month's disability payment was gone. "How did you get there?" she asked quietly.

"I walked."

"No, you didn't."

"I took the bus."

"No, you took the house car. You took the keys and you drove."

"Why are you asking, if you know so much?" said her mother, folding her good arm across the other one, and keeping her attention on a spread of Kate and Wills.

"Jesus, Mum. You have fits. Your arm is paralyzed. You're not allowed to drive. And you were drinking. What would have happened if you'd hit someone?"

"I wasn't going to hit anyone. I'm a good driver."

"You know you can't drink with your medication."

"I had one beer. That never hurt anyone."

Christina's heart sank. Her mother's denial was powerful. Intractable. One beer had never been enough.

"I just wanted to get out, spread my wings," Rita said now, plaintive. "Eating up the miles, free as a bird. You understand that, don't you, Chrissy? You always loved road trips. You're my one baby, the only one who understands me. We were always so alike."

Christina abruptly stood. *So alike.* The words struck her emotional barriers like heavy fire, reviving her worst nightmares – of failing, of ending up where everyone had said she would: poor and dependent, just like Rita. She paced to the window and looked out into the backyard. The grass needed mowing and a paling had come loose from the fence. She had to remind herself that there had never been any road trips. That was her mother's fantasy. But it was harder to dispute the claim that they were alike, especially when she was close to failing out of medical school.

"Aren't you going to sit down and talk?" Rita demanded.

Christina didn't look around. "I have to be at work soon."

She found Lena in the kitchen, counting out the residents' medication into weekly pill boxes.

"This can't happen again," Christina said. "The keys have to be secure, all the time."

"Of course. The director is reviewing the procedures tomorrow. We'll call you."

Christina sighed. Lena did her best, but the house was always short on staff, and the agency that ran it had three other houses on their books.

"Lena, if this happens again – call the police. I mean it. She'll hurt someone."

Christina hurried out the front door, cursing as she checked her watch. She was twenty minutes late to work, where she shuffled around the hospital emergency room with her survey question sheets until nine thirty, doing the research legwork that a doctoral student hadn't wanted to do themselves. The department was quiet for a Friday evening, the rush of cases not due for at least an hour when the end-of-week partying turned serious. She scanned down the cases on the computer system, looking for suitable candidates, and managed four in three hours. Not her best effort.

By the time she reached home, her feet were throbbing and her back ached all the way down into her tailbone. Her rented room was upstairs, in a share house behind the freeway, which emitted a constant low roar. Even as she walked up the driveway, she could hear music. When she pushed open the back door, she found her housemates in the kitchen amid sizzling pans and a radio cranked to eleven. The air smelled of tacos, and charred onions.

She avoided them, climbed the stairs and pushed her door closed, which at least muted the music. She sat on the bed and tugged off her shoes, stretching out her toes on the threadbare carpet. Breathing in … and out. This wasn't forever. Things would get better. She just had to get through the next eighteen months, finish her degree, and her life would change.

But she'd never had less confidence in that vision.

It wasn't just the exam. Maybe it had been seeing Katie Prior, reminding her of home. Or maybe it was Rita's reference to road trips, evoking so many other broken promises. Or just that when her mother had gone into care, she'd thought her life would improve, too. … No, focus, she told herself. Breathe.

Her lecture notes were stacked in piles across her desk, her ancient laptop on screensaver. The muscles pinched between her shoulders as she pulled out her phone, deleting Lena's missed calls and messages.

Wait. What was this? Another missed call earlier in the day, from a number she didn't recognize. Frowning, she dialed voicemail.

"*Oh, Christina,*" began a vaguely familiar voice. "*I'm so sorry but Dr. Winterbourne's had some unfortunate news. I'm leaving you my home number. Please call me when you can. It's …*"

Christina's insides twisted. It was the receptionist at the family practice for her next rotation. The one she'd organized weeks ago. She dialed the woman's home number, not caring about the time.

"Is Dr. Winterbourne all right?" she asked as soon as the receptionist answered.

"No, it's terrible." The woman's voice shook. "He has cancer. Quite out of the blue, and they're still running tests. He's about to have surgery. I'm really sorry, but there's no chance you can start on Monday week. We have a locum coming in, but he'll be flat out. I'm sure you'll find something else."

When she'd hung up, Christina let the phone fall into her lap. How awful for Dr. Winterbourne. She'd only met him twice, a kind elderly man with a shock of white hair and half-frames on a chain. She couldn't imagine him facing surgery, or chemotherapy. Then there was the fact that she'd lost the placement. Don't panic, she thought. But she knew that by now all the practices would be full. Space was at a premium, and all the students were expected to organize their own placements. Music pulsed under her feet, starting up a corresponding throb behind her eye.

She thumped the bed with her fist, and allowed herself five minutes of cursing, releasing her frustration. Then she curled into a ball on the covers, thinking madly. She'd overcome so much to be here; there had to be a way through this. She just had to find it.

Late the next morning, dark circles under her eyes from a

sleepless night, Christina slumped at her desk amid the crossed-out and discarded sheets of the medical school's approved practice list. She'd called every number; they were all full. The medical school's receptionist refused to take any more of her calls. They were seeing what they could do, she said.

So Christina stewed in miserable suspense. She did her laundry while listening out for the phone, carefully hand-washing her thin work shirts to coax another week out of them. She went to a meeting with the agency who ran her mother's residential care, numbly listening to their reassurances that it wouldn't happen again. She'd heard that before.

And still no one called. As the clock crept towards five, Christina began to imagine what the school would say. Her grades were poor. Classes missed. Maybe they would make her repeat the year. Or maybe it would be worse: they would tell her there was no longer a place for her in the school.

At one minute to five, when she had given up hope, her phone finally rang.

"I have a solution," the school's placement coordinator began, without preamble, and with a distinct tone of relief. "There's a place available right near your home address."

"How is that even possible?" asked Christina, the reprieve running warm in her veins.

"Another student dropped out. You'll need to do the tutorials by remote, of course, but there'll be another student doing the same thing, so you can buddy."

Christina frowned. "But home's only a few minutes from the campus. Can't I do the tutorials there?"

A pause. "I mustn't have been clear. This place is in Townsville. On the base."

"What?"

"The home address we have for you is in Townsville."

Christina froze. She'd listed the Townsville address when she first applied to the medical school, after someone had told her a regional address would give her a better chance of acceptance. Never had she imagined it was still on file.

"Christina?"

"I haven't lived there for more than ten years," she croaked.

The coordinator cleared her throat, plainly exasperated. "Look, I've spent all day on this and exhausted all other avenues. You're welcome to keep trying yourself, but this is the best I can do. The school expects you'll have to travel for rotations now and then. If you can make it happen, I'd advise you to take it."

"Where in Townsville?" Christina asked reluctantly.

"A clinic on the army base. It works just like a regular practice. They often take students. I understand you'd have to organize accommodation. The school can help with the transport. But don't think too long. Let me know tomorrow morning."

Christina felt as though the stuffing had been knocked out of her body. She'd promised herself she was never going back. Not to the town she'd escaped from … and where Harriet still lived.

But after an hour, then two, distractedly stacking her notes and books into neat piles, straightening her bed and listening to the rumble of her housemates downstairs, she had to face facts. What else could she do – tell the school she wouldn't go?

Christina rubbed a hand across her mouth, considering. She didn't even know yet if she'd passed the current rotation. If she didn't, some kind of remediation might follow, throwing out the rest of the year.

But what if she passed?

She twitched aside the curtain and looked down on her Corolla under the streetlight, its sun-damaged bonnet covered in dropped leaves. No way would the car make it eight hundred miles to Townsville; she wouldn't reach Brisbane's city limits before it overheated.

Grimly, she pulled out a notepad, wrote down her tiny bank balance, and began a list, just to convince herself this couldn't work. *Take leave from job,* she scribbled. *Pay for flight.* That would use up most of the balance. But at least the school had said they could help. The bigger issue was: *Find somewhere to stay.*

Christina chewed her pen.

This should be where it ended. Harriet was only one option. Which she couldn't contemplate, could she?

Exhausted after staying up late studying the night before, her mind still swirling with thoughts and calculations, she went to bed, hugging the blanket close around her.

When the first lorikeets shrieked past her window Christina gave up on sleep and woke her computer. Results would be posted by now. She dragged the blanket over her lap as the school portal loaded.

The practical mark was first: forty-nine per cent, a terrible mark if at least a conceded pass. Christina groaned; that would earn her another caution on her record. Any more and she would repeat. She heard her mother's voice in her mind: *We're so alike.* With a surge of panic Christina flicked to the written exam result.

Ninety-two per cent.

"Oh my God," she whispered, reloading the page just to make sure, double-checking her name. She'd actually done it. Despite everything – her mother, her housemates, her job – she'd managed to do one thing right. The first time she'd ever earned more than a scraping pass.

In disbelief, she ran her hands over her crowded bookshelf, where two and a half years of notes were carefully arranged in folders alongside her textbooks. She'd done all of that in the past two months, converting her disorganized scribble into meaningful summaries, desperate to turn around her performance. Hard work. It hadn't been for nothing.

That boost made her decide to call Harriet.

She waited until eight. The number was still in her memory,

but her fingers trembled as the phone rang, and rang. Perhaps her aunt had moved, or changed her number? Eventually a machine picked up. *"You've reached Harriet Reed. I can't take your call …"*

When the beep sounded, Christina had to force out the words around fifteen years of anger and regret. "It's Christina," she said. "I, um, have to come to Townsville. And, um—"

Click. "Christina?" Harriet's voice was suddenly alive on the line.

Blood rushed to Christina's face. She could still picture her aunt as clearly as on that last day in Townsville: an imposing woman, broad in the hip and shoulder, with a stern stare that could soften into the kindest smile. Her mother's face, but unmarred by years of drink. But the relationship had soured all the same.

"Yes," she managed.

"Long time," said Harriet. "How are you?"

Christina tried to speak and found that tears had gathered in her throat.

"Well, I didn't expect to hear from you," Harriet said, her own voice cautious. "What's this about you coming up?"

Christina gripped her blanket. "My medical school rotation placement fell through. The only one I can get is on the base up there …" She very nearly hung up. She couldn't ask.

"How long is it for?"

"Two months."

A tiny pause. "Well, you're lucky you called today," said Harriet briskly. "I was about to leave on a trip. I asked the neighbors to look out for the place, but if you want the job instead …"

The shaking in Christina's limbs subsided. "You're going away?"

"Thought it was about time. Thomas died last year."

"Oh. I … didn't know," said Christina. Thomas was Harriet's husband, a man Christina hadn't known and yet who had so changed the relationship between them.

Harriet, never keen on sympathy, made a dismissive noise. "We had a long time to prepare. But the house is there if you want it."

"Where are you going?"

"Oh, Kokoda, if it works out. Then who knows? I've always wanted to see Italy. Be gone a couple of months. So, are you taking the house?"

"Yes," said Christina, not believing her luck.

"I'll leave the key in the usual spot."

Christina put down the phone, her aunt's words still ringing in her mind. *In the usual spot.* As though she were thirteen again, and coming home from school, to Harriet and a new life, one that would end too soon.

And now, after all that had happened, she was going back.

Chapter 2

Eight hundred miles north the next morning, Captain Aiden Bell shook salt water from his short dark hair and dropped his dive mask onto the boat deck as Travers, his best mate and diving buddy, straightened up from inspecting the outboard.

"Is it fucked, then?" Aiden asked, checking his watch.

"Yeah, it's fucked. Won't start."

The runabout barely moved on the water, the sun two thumbs above the horizon, the ocean a flat gray slate. They were only a few miles offshore, near a bommie perfect for an early-morning dive. The unmistakable knobbly peak of Castle Hill marked the way back to Townsville. Aiden stripped his wetsuit to the waist as he appraised the situation. Two main problems. He was due on base before eight, the fervent pace of his latest assignment requiring constant attention. And that would have been easy, if the outboard hadn't just died. That was problem one.

Travers muttered, muscles tensing in his broad shoulders as he cranked the motor again, the air tense. This was problem two. Aiden let the silence stretch out as he stowed their fins and tanks. Whatever it was Travers had dragged Aiden out here to hear, Travers would have to spill soon.

Aiden had begun the day with a bad feeling, a tiny ripple of foreboding that was pressing into the back of his skull. The feeling had intensified as Travers remained silent and evasive through the half-hour trip out, ten minutes of prep, a forty-minute dive and now ten minutes screwing with the engine.

They had a long history together; they'd met as teenagers, fresh off the bus at boot camp. Since then, they might have served in different corps but they'd been through more together than most friends did in a lifetime. They were brothers. They'd seen each other at their worst, knew all each other's secrets. After the past two years … Aiden didn't think there was anything worse to know. But now, sensing Travers struggling to find words, he wondered how bad this could be.

He checked his watch again. "You going to let me look now? Travers?"

Travers finally gave up and slid down onto the runabout's curving side. "Shit."

"Let me look." Aiden stepped around him, fixing his attention on the engine, his mind running through potential problems. "You checked the prime, right?"

"Yeah. It did this last week too. I knew I should've brought some beers." He fell silent again, frowning.

Aiden focused on the motor. "You want to tell me what you did last time?" *You want to tell me what's up?*

"It just came good. I should've had it checked out."

Aiden grunted. Another five minutes ticked by as he inspected the engine. When he could bear it no more, he glanced around. "In about twenty seconds, this motor's going to be running again. So for all that's holy, Travers, spit it out."

Travers laughed. "Don't know what you're talking about. I just wanted to dive."

Aiden threw up his hands. "Fine then." He turned back to the motor.

"I'm getting out."

Aiden paused, mid-reach to the engine cover. Slowly he turned back. "Out of the army?"

"No, out of the boat. Of course, out of the army." Travers

made a face. "My shoulder operation has been scheduled. Once it's done, that's it."

Aiden sank down on the bench opposite Travers, hoping that if he sat, his stomach would stop falling. He'd known this day was coming. Travers had little option left. But after sixteen years in the military together, the sense of loss knocked him sideways. "That's big news," he said carefully.

Travers fixed his blue eyes on Aiden. "I'm okay with it. Really. You don't have to worry."

"I'm not worried." No, it wasn't worry. It was much deeper than that.

"I'm still going to be kicking around," Travers went on. "So you're not going to get out of me dragging you away from that office of yours."

"What are you going to do?" asked Aiden. Travers was from a military family; his father, his father's father. He'd already been removed from active service to a medic's position. This was a much bigger deal than he was letting on.

"This." Travers flung his arms wide. "Diving. Easier on my joints, and I have a lead on some work with the university. Underwater survey, that sort of thing. Start with that, then move into salvage. It'll take a bit of setting up, but I reckon it's solid."

"Sounds like a plan," said Aiden. Relief chased the anxiety away. But a different emotion came heavy on its heels. His best mate was leaving the job they'd started together. Nothing would be the same again.

This time it was Travers who checked his watch. "Well, reckon you're about five minutes over on that engine fix ETA. Typical brass."

Aiden threw a mask at him as he stood up. "As opposed to the grunts, who screwed it in the first place. Didn't think they taught engines in sniper school."

"Bet you don't even know what's wrong with it."

"Safety fuse is gone. Going to bridge it, then we'll be sweet," said Aiden. And just to prove it, twenty seconds later, the outboard roared to life.

Travers laughed. "I knew I kept you around for a reason."

"Yeah, to save your ass from the MPs."

A moment passed, the outboard chugging. Aiden sat on the crossbar, his attention on the coast, now painted in golden early sunlight. "Travers …"

"Yeah, mate?"

There was so much he could say, but none of it was needed now. "If you're going to go into diving, you need a better boat."

Just after eight a.m., Aiden walked into a familiar maelstrom. The Solomon Islands recovery operation had only been official for two days, but he already felt right at home. The command center occupied temporary buildings at the back of the base, a warren of interconnected offices that faced an open bitumen square flanked with sheds. The place smelled of diesel and dust, and hummed with the activity of a new operation.

Aiden's office opened into the main hall, where boot steps and the constant murmur of voices kept him company. He didn't get far into his messages before one of the voices appeared in his doorway. "Bell, you good for this meeting?"

Two minutes later, he was in a conference with the major in charge of the operation. The walls were covered with satellite photos and projected timelines.

"Where are we on the equipment?" asked the major.

"All slots filled, except two," Aiden began, immediately in stride. "We need another two backhoes. But the drivers are a bigger issue. I'm still trying to find personnel. And the readiness of the equipment isn't confirmed."

"How long?"

"Give me twelve hours, I'll have it done."

"Good man," said the major.

Aiden's pulse was racing as he left the room. Shit, twelve

hours. And as the ops officer he had another pile of orders for an upcoming exercise to review. Okay, he could take those home. And the reports from the fires out west last month? Those too. He'd have enough paperwork to start his own bonfire.

"Here's the figures you asked for, sir."

Aiden glanced up to see a clerk holding another sheaf of papers. "Thanks, Corporal."

He plowed on. When he stopped at two to shove a sandwich in his face, he checked his personal mobile and saw two missed calls from his sister. Damn, he'd promised to call her back twice already.

"Dani," he said. "I know, I know, I saw your calls."

"Aiden, it's fine." She laughed, that lovely warm sound. "I know how busy you are. Just as long as you're still coming to the wedding."

"I haven't forgotten." His baby sister was marrying a cattle farmer she'd met working out west. As hard as *that* idea was to process, it was harder to know that it was all happening without his having seen her in an age. Separated for most of their adult lives, they were serendipitously both now working in Townsville, he on the base, she as a surgical registrar at the hospital. But despite their proximity, they hadn't yet managed to meet.

"You must have everything sorted," he said.

"Pretty much. I wouldn't mind going through a few things with you, though. I'm suddenly nervous about some of my choices!"

Aiden leaned back in his chair, a smile spreading across his face. "And you think *I'm* the person to ask? You've seen what I wear to work. Your bridesmaids will end up in camouflage."

"But you always back me up," she said, laughing. "I need you. Dad's become impossible. Every time I mention it, he starts reminiscing about when I was three. It's sweet, but irritating."

Aiden cleared his throat. "How about dinner ..." he

scrolled through his calendar, "Wednesday week? You said that was your night off, right?"

"Good memory. All right, yes." She sounded excited.

"I'll swing by the ward and pick you up after your shift?"

"Perfect!"

Aiden was soon deep in a tactical movement plan as trucks rumbled past outside. "Corporal," he called, spotting the clerk near his door. "I need a copy of the exercise area map. And can you find out if the CO is back from HQ yet?"

Two minutes later, boots stopped at his door. "Well, that was fast—" Aiden broke off. Standing in the doorway was a gray-haired man with a major's crown insignia on his chest and crosses stitched onto his lapels.

Aiden was instantly on his feet. "I'm sorry, Padre, I thought you were someone else."

"I get that all the time," said the padre with a warm smile, stepping forward to shake his hand. "Probably they wish I was. How are you, Aiden?"

"I'm good. Been to Perth since we last met."

"I heard. And now you're here. It's like a reunion."

"More than you know," said Aiden. "Travers is here, too, at the clinic these days." Their eyes met for a fraction of a second, silently acknowledging what had happened just eighteen months ago, when they'd all been posted in Victoria. Aiden searched for the right words. "It'll be good to catch up before things get serious," he said at last.

The padre nodded, then glanced around at the piles on Aiden's desk. The corporal was hovering near the door. "You've a lot on your plate. I'll see you in the mess."

As the corporal handed over copies of the map he'd asked for, Aiden listened to the padre's departing steps. He hadn't seen Major Dunning in more than a year. After the morning's boat trip revelation, maybe it was a sign.

"Sir?"

Aiden snapped his attention back to the room. "I'm sorry,

what?"

"There's one more thing. Word is there's a fire ban ..."

Aiden groaned. "You're not serious? We can't have a preparation exercise without rounds."

"Yes, sir. No firing anywhere until it rains. You have a briefing with the CO in ten minutes."

Aiden cleared a space in his piles of paper. There were signs and there were signs. And this one meant he had to go back to the start.

Chapter 3

At four thirty the next sultry Sunday afternoon, Christina stood on the sidewalk in front of Harriet's two-level house. It looked like many others in the south-west suburb of Aitkenvale: white weatherboard upstairs, brown bricked-in downstairs with neat white shutters, surgically trimmed grass rimmed with gardens of tropical plants that flourished in the dry spell.

The air smelled of hot smoke. Sweat trickled between her shoulder blades as she dug for the key in a pot plant saucer, pushed open the door and stepped apprehensively into the hall.

The change in smell was instant: from heat and dirt to spices and lemon, the first conjuring memories of Harriet's cooking, the latter of her habitual cleaning. For a few years, that scent had signified the happy end of a day.

The hall tiles were the same cream, and Christina stepped across the lounge's worn carpet, remembering when it had been laid. Harriet had enclosed the lower half of the house in the last year Christina lived with her. It was supposed to give them more room, a second kitchen, bathroom and guest room downstairs. Harriet had joked that they never needed to go upstairs again; she'd even moved her display cabinets full of models and army memorabilia downstairs. The house had barely changed in the fifteen years since Christina had lived there, other than several archive boxes now stacked alongside the cabinet, "Thomas" written in neat letters on their sides.

In the blue-tiled kitchen, she found a handwritten note on the bench – just an emergency contact number and two lines. *Christina, The old truck's in the garage – a bit rundown but she still starts. Take her out to keep her going. Harriet.*

Christina's steps quickened to the internal door that opened to the garage, where she gave a surprised laugh. Harriet still had the same battered old white pickup. Affectionately dubbed the Belmont, it was the same car Harriet had used to teach Christina how to check oil and radiators and change a tire, skills her aunt believed every woman should have. It had been old even back then; now, it must be ancient. The keys were in the ignition, two bottles of oil and a funnel pointedly left on the bonnet.

Christina emptied the letterbox before returning to the house, where she stacked the mail on the kitchen bench. Pacing through the rooms once more, she tried to free herself from the tendrils of her long-ago life here. There was her old room, still with the same green bedspread, the same small desk. Back downstairs in the kitchen, she sat at the table and put her head in her hands, awash in her conflicted feelings about being back here. Eventually, she sighed, tamping down the memories. Then she straightened her shoulders, unpacked her bag in the guest room, and claimed the kitchen table with her books. She had practical things to get on with. There wasn't time for regret.

Her rotation began tomorrow. She would have teleconference tutorials at the hospital every Monday afternoon. Travelling here had cleaned out her savings, so she also needed to find some kind of work, otherwise she'd be going hungry until she went back to Brisbane.

That was how she ended up back in the garage, scrutinizing the Belmont, which looked in worse condition than her Corolla. The truck was an unexpected blessing, if indeed it still ran. Christina was a veteran of menial, low-paying student work, so she knew exactly what kind of job she could find on short notice. Pizza stores always needed drivers.

She made a final circuit of the house. The big glass cabinets in the lounge room still held models of aircraft, large and small, in camouflage and silver paint. Vintage WWII planes, alongside helicopters and jets. The shelf below supported tanks and rows of painted soldiers. Those were new. Maybe Thomas had collected them. She stepped back, wondering if the boxes were his things, packed away now he was gone. The name had been written with great care. In fact, the whole room was neat, which was why Christina's eye caught on a pale corner of paper sticking out from under the bookcase.

Teasing it out, she found a photograph and was suddenly confronted with Harriet, gazing directly into her eyes. Harriet had always commanded attention, and even in the small photo her green eyes were striking and intent, out of step with her soft smile. She had taken the photo herself, a selfie before selfies had been a thing, the arm holding the camera disappearing into the foreground. Unusually, her blonde hair was loose, and she'd raised her other hand to stop it blowing into her face. Otherwise, she looked exactly as Christina remembered, as if it had been taken fifteen years ago. It was difficult to tell where, but maybe a beach – that could be a palm tree in the corner. At first she barely noticed the man standing behind Harriet, in sunglasses and slightly out of focus. So, this must be Thomas. Harriet's reason for leaving Townsville all those years ago. For abandoning Christina.

Quickly, Christina flipped the photo upside down on top of the boxes, just a pale square on the brown cardboard. She was here for only one reason, and it had nothing to do with the past.

Monday morning brought hazy blue skies, and sun hot enough to blunt Christina's senses as she negotiated the entry procedures for the army base. Damp circles had formed under her arms by the time she'd cleared the pass office. As she drove through the warren of streets to the health center, following the pass officer's directions, she half expected to find a bunker. The reality was less dramatic: the building looked like a regular suburban clinic, but for the defense posters on the noticeboard, and that everyone was in uniform. An imposing man in whites with a body like a linebacker was standing in a treatment bay, going through the wall bins, and two men were talking behind the desk, a tall, lean one in camouflage fatigues and the other a rounded older man in a sports jacket.

Christina dug in her bag for her stethoscope as she approached, trying not to tangle it in her visitor's pass.

The man in cams glanced up. "Christina Price? Captain May, I'm one of the clinic doctors," he said, extending his hand, which Christina shook awkwardly over the counter. He gestured to the man in the sports jacket, who smiled and also shook Christina's hand. "And this is Dr. Vaughn. Follow me."

And like that, they were off. Captain May then walked her through the three emergency bays, and the consulting and procedure rooms. The clinic was arranged in a horseshoe around the front desk: waiting area on one side, curtained bays and ambulance doors in the middle, consulting rooms back down the opposite hall. Waiting in the chairs were several men in uniform. Captain May pointed out the equipment and facilities, and quizzed her on her experience.

"What rotations have you already done?" he asked as they returned to the desk.

"Mental health and surgery." Christina jogged to keep up.

"Good, good. Perfect prep for here. You'll be all over procedures already. Now, the nurses and Dr. Vaughn are civvies – that's civilians – while the army provides myself and our medic." The captain nodded to the solid man in whites, who had now hauled a huge kit bag onto a gurney and was extracting manikin parts. "But you'll find we operate pretty much the same as any other family practice, except we're less busy. You can sit in with our appointments if you want, but the best way to learn is to do things yourself. See the patients before we do, and present the case. Take the bloods, et cetera. These are the case files. Where would you like to start?"

Christina mouthed in doubt, thinking about her last exam case. "Can I sit in with you?" she asked.

"Try a different answer."

Clearly Captain May believed in tough love. She forced herself to reach for the top file. "I'll see this patient."

"There you go. Use the curtained bay there, and come and see me when you're ready."

Christina took a deep breath and strode towards the waiting area, her shoulders tense. "Daniel Browning?" she read off the file.

A lean young man in fatigues rose and followed her to the curtained bay. After introducing herself and explaining what she was doing, she asked how she could help.

"Actually, I'm just here for a follow-up," said Daniel. "I'm being discharged. I'm here to collect some blood test results."

Relief. "Oh. Okay then. Just follow me." She could feel the medic's eyes on her as she handed Daniel off to Captain May. She moved on to the next file. This patient had the flu; she took a history and listened to his chest, but when she presented his symptoms to the doctor, Captain May simply wrote out a chit for time off. Two more patients followed, both with colds, and with the same outcome. All the time, the tall medic was in the next bay, sorting through equipment, and Christina knew he was listening in and watching her. She tried to ignore it. At least she was getting an easy lead-in.

Just as she was about to take the next file, Captain May emerged from his room, trailing a new patient. "Christina? I need you to take some blood for me." He handed her a pathology form.

"Sure," she said, but her insides buckled. Failure, here we come. After leading the patient to a curtained bay, she found the phlebotomy trolley and wheeled it over, her cheeks already flaming and fine shakes in her fingers.

She read through the form, trying to remember which colored tubes she needed for each test. If only that were the hard part. She'd never managed to successfully take blood from a patient during her surgical rotation – she either couldn't find the vein or missed it, and someone else always had to take over. On a few occasions, the patient had been left with a terrible bruise and given Christina a reproachful stare.

Grimly, she laid out the alcohol wipe and several vacuum tubes in a kidney dish. She found the vacuum system needles and twisted one into the holder, which slipped in her gloved fingers. A sweat bead trickled down her back. The patient's arm was thick and she fumbled with the tourniquet.

The medic was still watching, his tall solid presence shredding the last of her composure. She probed the veins in the crook of the patient's elbow. They were thicker than any she'd seen before, great ropey pipes of blood. Surely she couldn't miss?

"Hey, you all square with that?" The medic had leaned in, peering at what she was doing.

"Um, I'm okay," she said, hoping it would be true. She chose a vein and grabbing the alcohol wipe. She would do it this time. But when she picked up the needle, her hands were shaking. All she could remember was the last patient she'd tried this on, a little old lady whose arm had been bruised for a week.

"Whoa there. Let's just stop a minute, okay?" The medic came around and pulled up a stool. He loosened the patient's tourniquet and pointed to her equipment. "You're missing a couple of things. Talk me through what you're going to do."

Christina glanced at the patient, her chest tight with humiliation. But the man seemed unfazed; maybe he was used to useless student doctors. She found her voice, hoping it wouldn't shake as well. "Tighten the tourniquet. Look for a vein. Sterilize the area. Insert the needle. Put in the ... No, loosen the tourniquet a bit. Then push each vacuum tube in."

"Then?"

"Um. Let off the tourniquet. Remove the needle and compress the site with – ah." Christina rummaged in the drawers and pulled out a cotton ball, then peeled off a length of tape to hold it down with.

"Better," said the medic. "Now, we have heaps of time. Which vein are you going to choose?"

Christina indicated the one she'd selected, but the medic shook his head. "Nah, that one's okay, but this one's better," he said, rolling his finger over another vein nearby. "Feel how it springs back? Feel it. Yeah, good. Next, swab over the site. Okay. Now, you want to hold the needle like this." He demonstrated the angle. "When you're in, you'll feel the give through your fingers. Then brace your hand against his arm. Like this."

Christina watched him closely. She'd never had anyone go through the steps so slowly. Unsteadily, she grasped the needle, then guided it into the vein.

"Oh my God," she whispered, knowing that this time, finally, it was right. She glanced at the patient, who hadn't even flinched.

The medic grinned, passing her the first vacuum tube. "Now, don't shift the needle when you fill this. Brace your hand. All right, good."

When they were done, the patient climbed down and the medic disappeared with the pathology bag. Christina tidied the trolley, her momentary elation receding. What did it count that she had done it once, with someone guiding her through every step? She wheeled the trolley back to its home near the first bay. And there she saw Daniel, the first patient she'd seen today, looking distinctly bored.

"You're still here," she said, sticking her head through the curtains.

"Yeah. Just waiting on paperwork. There's a lot of it."

Christina hesitated, curious about the downcast tone. He only looked about twenty. "You said you were being discharged soon. How come?"

"They found out I have Crohn's."

"Oh," she said. She slipped into the bay and sat on the chair across from him. Crohn's could be a horrific disease; she'd seen patients with it during her surgical term. They developed ulcers in the digestive tract; sometimes the condition became so bad they had to have surgery to remove parts of their gut. "What job were you doing in the army?"

A smile ghosted across his face. "I was in the engineers. Lots of explosives," he explained when she looked confused. "I was posted to the new unit here, but not anymore."

"What are you going to do now?" she asked.

Daniel licked his lips, his brow furrowed. "Dunno. This is what I've always wanted to do. Guess I'll just go home."

"Where's home?"

They spoke for a few minutes more. Daniel was from Victoria, his father was in construction, his mother a chef. He thought his father might have work for him in the business, but he wasn't sure he was suited to it.

At that point, the medic stuck his head into the bay. "Browning? Captain May's ready for you."

Daniel slid off the bed and headed away down the hall, waving as he went. The medic watched him go, then turned to Christina. "That was a great question to ask him, you know."

"Which one?" she asked, wondering how long he'd been listening.

"What he was going to do next. It's hard getting out of here, make no mistake. I'm Travers," he added, offering his hand.

"Christina."

"I know. You're one of the med students. Now, we're going to talk about that blood test."

Christina's stomach twisted into a knot. "What about it?"

Travers was pulling the phlebotomy cart around. "You're

going to do one on me. No, I'm serious. You have to learn it right. I don't know what shit they're teaching you at medical school, but in here I'll show you how to do it properly. And what about cannulas?"

"I'm awful at them too," admitted Christina. "I almost bled a little old lady out one time."

"Then we're going to do them as well. Everyone you see here's going to have easy veins. It's not the same when someone's crashing on you. So, work out how to do it on these easy veins, get the drill in your head. Then when you get a hard one, you've only got to concentrate on that one little part, okay?"

An hour later, to her amazement, Christina had successfully placed a needle three times, and was trying to line up a cannula with the impressive veins in the back of Travers' hand.

"So you're from Brisbane?"

Christina looked up. "How did you know that?"

"I read your file," he said, his face deadpan.

"I have a file?"

He grinned. "Nah, Captain May mentioned it. Go lower," he corrected. "Good. You want to avoid that kink in the vein. So how did you end up here? That's excellent," he added, as Christina slid the plastic cannula over the metal introducer and into the vein. A flash of blood appeared in the plastic end.

With a surge of confidence, Christina taped off the cannula, screwed on the drip connection and tested it with saline. "My placement fell through. I couldn't get one anywhere else at short notice ... and I grew up here."

"Lucky you. Not going to be joining up, then?"

"I hadn't considered it."

"Pity," said Travers, flexing his hand and shooting another tube of saline into the drip. "This is good. You'll be a pro by the end of the week. The other student hasn't even turned up yet."

Christina wondered briefly who the other student would

turn out to be. She hadn't had a chance to ask the placement coordinator. But when they had finished and she stepped out into the waiting area, she saw a familiar face standing by the front desk in a crisp white shirt and sharp black trousers, a stethoscope slung around her neck. Her heart sank. Katie Prior had arrived.

Katie turned towards her with a smile. "Christina! They told me you were coming here too. This is great!" She dropped her voice. "Keeping me waiting, though."

Christina glanced at the clock, which showed eleven a.m. "I think they're in appointments now."

Katie shrugged. "It's okay. It's only the first day. Plenty of time. Oh, hi," she said, as Travers appeared. "I'm Katie Prior."

"Corporal Darren Travers." He looked between the two of them, his eyes resting longer on Katie. "You two know each other?"

"From med in Brisbane," Christina said quickly.

"Okay." Travers smiled as he turned back to Katie. "How are you with taking blood?"

"Pretty good," she said. "What are you doing over there?" She pointed to the gear on the bed in the spare bay. The next moment, Katie had co-opted Travers and he was showing her the equipment. Christina hovered awkwardly, then picked up a new patient file.

When she returned to the front desk two patients later, Katie had disappeared.

"She's sitting in with the appointments," said Travers, as Christina was looking around. "You want a go with the ECGs? We have time before the next rush."

Christina didn't see Katie again until the afternoon, when she emerged from Dr. Vaughn's room. She rolled her eyes at Christina and whispered, "Tell me it's time to get out of here."

Christina glanced at her watch. "Tutorial's not for another hour."

"Bugger." Then Katie's eyes shifted focus past Christina's shoulder, to where Travers was cleaning up, calculation in her expression.

"What?" Christina asked.

"Nothing." Katie fixed her smile back on Christina. "How'd you get here today?"

"I drove."

"Great! My brother dropped me off. Can I get a lift?"

Christina winced at the reference to Katie's brother, Sebastian. So he *was* still in Townsville.

Half an hour later, Christina handed in her pass at the gate, Katie on the bench seat beside her. The first tutorial at the hospital's teleconference room – with an intimidating tutor called Professor Green – rushed past; afterwards, Katie piled into the Belmont again.

"So, where can I drop you?" asked Christina.

"How about we go to your place? I'll get my brother to pick me up later."

"Ah, I'm not sure, Katie. I'm staying at my aunt's place, and I've got to be at work at seven." Anything to avoid seeing Sebastian Prior.

"What work?"

Christina blushed. "Pizza delivery. At Carlo's. In town."

Katie laughed. "Will your aunt give me a hard time?"

"Actually, she's not there." And suddenly Christina couldn't think of any good reason to refuse, at least not one that didn't involve asserting that she wanted to be left alone.

"Wow, nice place," Katie said when they pulled into the driveway. Christina drove into the garage; even before she had killed the engine, Katie had jumped out of the Belmont. And as Christina came around to unlock the internal house door, Katie was looking through the contents of Harriet's workbench.

"I figured you didn't have family up here anymore," Katie said as they entered the kitchen. "Must be great to have the place to yourself. My parents have a house on the north side. I might come back up here after graduation, who knows. Better lifestyle for an intern, right?"

Christina made a noncommittal noise as she dropped her bag on a kitchen chair, and poured Katie a glass of water. Katie sipped between the chatter, idly picking through the stack of mail. Christina found it irritating the way she poked around without asking.

"That's my aunt's," Christina said finally.

Katie dropped her hands with a disarming smile. "Sorry. I fidget a lot. I'm trying to stop." She leaned on the back of a chair, her voice suddenly serious. "Listen, Chris. I know you had a ... bad time growing up here."

Christina's stomach clenched. "Oh, it wasn't—"

"My brother used to talk about you a bit, so I heard some things. And I was in a tutorial group in first year with a girl in your class at school. Melissa Yates, remember her? Anyway, I know you had a foster family through high school because your mum's an alcoholic and you have to take care of her now. Right?"

Christina shifted. "Um, yeah. But she doesn't live with me. I just make sure she's looked after."

"Oh," Katie said. "Well, still that's really tough. So I totally understand if you keep to yourself, or you're angry or whatever. I'd be crazy mad if I had to look after my mum. What a drag."

Christina wished Katie would change the subject, but realizing other people talked about her was a shock. What exactly did Katie know about her mother's drinking? Did she know about Harriet? Or about what had happened with the foster family? Absently, she rubbed the scar on her palm.

"Anyway, getting into med is a huge achievement," Katie was saying. "That's why I think we should hang out. We can be study buddies, help each other. And you need to have some fun. You're wound far too tight, if you don't mind me saying so. It's not healthy. What do you say?"

Christina couldn't reply straight away. Her first instinct was to push Katie out the door. She didn't have time for fun. But she couldn't help being curious about this offer. Finally, she just shrugged. "Is it okay if we work here?" Christina asked, pulling her laptop out of her bag.

"Wow, where did you find that old brick?" Katie said, laughing.

Christina lifted the laptop's chunky screen, ignoring the jibe. Katie might work on the latest MacBook Air, but Christina had bought the brick with her own money.

Katie slid into a chair. "Right. This is going to be *great*."

Chapter 4

The next morning, Christina suppressed a yawn as she pushed through the door of the clinic. It wasn't yet eight, but the outside air already had the balmy quality Brisbane wouldn't achieve until November.

The previous day, Katie had hung around for several hours and then asked for a lift to the pizza store, saying that she wanted to see where Christina worked and that her brother would pick her up from there. Unrested, and unfamiliar with Townsville by road, Christina had anxiously wrestled with a map book all through her shift, which finished at midnight. But at least she hadn't seen Seb.

When she got home, she'd spent an hour totaling figures for her mother's pension and expenses, as the yearly accounts were due for review at the guardian oversight office. Between the care costs, rent, medications and magazines, money was always tight. She also had to work out how to account for the gambling. *Entertainment,* she'd listed with a wry smile. Afterward, she'd lain awake in bed, wondering if her mother would attempt another solo excursion to drink and play slot machines.

So back in the clinic now after only a few hours' sleep, she worried about staying awake. Only one patient was waiting, a dark-haired man in grubby fatigues, who limped into the curtained bay. She glanced at his name on the chart.

"So, Samuel … what happened?"

"Sammy's cool," he said, hoisting himself onto the bed. "Hurt my knee." He pointed at the offending joint.

Christina couldn't remember where to start with knee examinations. Buying herself time as she eased up his cam pants, she asked, "How did it happen?"

Silence. She glanced up to see Sammy looking sheepish.

"I won't tell anyone," she promised. "Or at least no one outside of here."

"I was on the obstacle course yesterday. Got my foot caught in the ropes and went ass-up. Hurt like buggery."

"Sounds bad," she said, trying to remember what to ask next.

"Nah, *bad* was trying to get me down again. I was twisted in there pretty good."

"And what's happened since then?" she asked, to keep him talking.

"I had ice on it all afternoon, and put my foot up."

Finally, Christina had to confront the examination. At that point, Travers stuck his head in. "How's it going?"

"Fine," she said quickly.

"Just remember to go slow. Think about what you're doing."

Look, feel, move, she recited under her breath. That was the basis of all examinations. Now, if only Sammy was like the diagrams in her anatomy book, with all the structures drawn on the outside. Working slowly, she performed the tests she could remember. The knee was clearly swollen, but she couldn't find an effusion, a collection of fluid in the joint. Time seemed to stretch painfully, and sweat prickled across her forehead as she concentrated.

"Are you all right there?" Sammy asked.

"Of course," she said brightly, mortified that he'd noticed her discomfort.

She asked him to lie face down for the next test; relieved of scrutiny, she pressed on. The ligaments also seemed fine, until she moved the joint from side to side.

Sammy hissed. "Yep, ah, that's it."

Medial collateral ligament, thought Christina. It had taken her twenty minutes, but that didn't diminish the surge of triumph. She'd actually worked it out. Asking Sammy to wait, she reported to Captain May.

"Okay," he said, absorbing her report in three seconds. "If that's your diagnosis, what's your treatment?"

Her jubilation trickled away. "Um. I don't know."

"Well, let's break down the problem: symptoms and pathology. What symptoms does he have?"

"Local pain … so I guess analgesia?"

Captain May nodded. "Let's come back to that. What's going on in his knee?"

"An overstretching of the ligament, or a tear, which is creating inflammation. So … I guess an anti-inflammatory?"

"What dose?"

Christina bit her lip. "Um …"

Captain May stood. "Let's go see him."

In the end, Captain May ran through the history and exam in a fraction of the time Christina had taken, and asked all the questions she'd forgotten. Christina took notes, ashamed she had missed so much. When he'd finished, Captain May looked at her with uncharacteristic sympathy. "Don't worry – I was a physiotherapist before I did med. You'll do better next time."

Reassured, Christina's embarrassment had eased by the time Captain May turned back to Sammy. "It's still pretty early – this only happened yesterday, so go back to ice and elevation for another day and see how it goes. You'll need a chit – no PT. That's physical training," he added to Christina. Captain May then discussed painkillers and anti-inflammatories. "Remember to take a look at the size of the patient," he added to her as he wrote up the script. "Sammy's a big guy, so don't be mean with it."

Christina was refining her notes at the front desk when

Travers appeared next to her. "Buggered knee?" he asked, watching Sammy's exit through the clinic's front doors.

"Yeah, medial collateral."

"Was he infantry?"

Christina glanced up. "I didn't ask. Why?"

"He looks like infantry. We've all got buggered joints. Look, see?" He pulled up his white trouser leg to show the scar of a knee reconstruction. "Knees, ankles and shoulders, often in that order. Had my ankle done too. And now I'm waiting for my shoulder op."

"How did that happen?" she asked. Travers seemed so strong and fit in his crisply ironed whites; she'd never have guessed there were damaged joints underneath.

"Running around with heavy packs. Going down on the ground and getting up again, over and over. We push our bodies pretty hard. Something has to give."

"How long until your surgery?"

"Three months. And when it's over, I'm done. I just can't carry the loads anymore. That's why I'm a medic here. Can't go out field, and I never will again."

Christina had seen that look before, on Daniel's face yesterday morning. "And what are you going to do next?" she asked.

"Very good," he said, grinning. "Now, let's run through that exam again. You'll love my knees. Snap, crackle and pop."

Two days later, Christina was riding on a sense of achievement as she drove home from her delivery shift in the warm Townsville night. Earlier that day, she'd taken blood from three patients without any trouble, and she still couldn't believe how quickly her fear had transformed into confidence. She was far from expert, but she'd begun to sense what mastery might feel like, and being able to help each patient while inflicting less and less pain filled her with satisfaction. She silently thanked

Travers for his patience.

She was even starting to think that coming back here hadn't been such a bad idea after all. She wound down the window, the breeze pleasantly cool on her face. Carlo had given her the early shift, so it was still only nine thirty; when she got home, she would spend an hour starting her essay.

As she wound her way south off the esplanade, The Strand, she spotted a large building with wrought-iron balconies and Federation cream posts, an orange neon sign over the door. Realizing where she was, Christina eased her foot off the accelerator and pulled over. She stepped out and clunked the Belmont's door shut, leaning heavily against it as she took in the pub across the street.

She didn't know what to feel, looking at it. She couldn't count the number of times she'd come here looking for her mother, to ask her for money for food, and sometimes to lead Rita home when she was too drunk to walk by herself. Christina had always walked in with a cold sense of resignation, and out filled with shame and worry, knowing how others talked about Rita.

Now a few Thursday night patrons wandered past, crossing the street towards the pub. Christina sighed, thinking she ought to stop dwelling on that past and go home, when she heard a squeal of brakes.

She had just enough time to see a man in the middle of the road, staring at the Belmont. He was gray-haired, tall and bulky, with a thick chest and strong stride, which was abruptly derailed as a truck collected him side-on.

"Oh, shit!" Christina sprinted towards the accident, only pausing briefly to make sure she wasn't run over herself. The man tumbled to rest in the gutter, bleeding from a scrape on the temple, his body limp. Several people stood around helplessly. The truck driver scrambled out of his door, his face ashen. Then Christina saw that the man was trying to rise.

She was on her knees next to him in an instant. "Hey!" she said, putting a hand on his shoulder. "Don't move, okay?

You've been in an accident."

He grunted, dazed, a drop of blood tracking down his face. At least he was conscious. Christina looked up at one of the hovering men. "Call an ambulance," she said, "and give me that jumper." She turned back to the man on the ground and padded his head as best she could while trying not to move his neck. "We're calling an ambulance, okay? I'm Christina. What's your name?"

"John," he managed, his voice ragged, his eyes unfocused. His nose was clotted with blood, and looked broken, although from the roughness of his face she wondered if it was an old injury. He had stubby eyelashes and a strong jaw, and hard lines around his mouth. He jerked his head, blinking as if trying to clear his vision.

"Hey, John, how about you try to stay still, just till the paramedics check you out. Are you in pain anywhere?" she asked, trying to distract him.

He reached to touch his nose.

"Yeah, I bet that's sore. Anything else?"

"My leg," he gasped, as if suddenly registering. "Oh, God, my leg."

Christina kept a hand on his shoulder as she looked down. In the long trousers it was hard to tell, but one foot was definitely turned out more than the other. Her stomach filled with chilled water. It looked bad, way beyond her skills. "The paramedics are going to sort that out for you too," she said, trying to sound calm. "They'll be here in a minute."

"My chest hurts," he said between short breaths, his ribs heaving. "God, am I going to die?"

Please no. Was the guy having a heart attack? Or some kind of embolism? All she had was her voice. "John, listen to me. You're okay. Stick with me. Just keep breathing. Everything's going to be fine." She kept up the prattle, aware of the milling crowd behind her, until she caught a flash of red and white out of the corner of her eye as the ambulance turned into the street.

It pulled up beside them, dispersing the onlookers. Two paramedics climbed down, an older man and a young woman with short-cropped hair.

Christina patted John's shoulder. "These guys are here to help you now, okay?" She twisted around to the female paramedic. "This is John," she said. "Hit by that truck, there, I saw it across the street. I think he might have been unconscious for a second or two. He's reporting chest pain and leg pain."

"Okay, thanks," the paramedic said. "You a nurse?"

"Med student." She stepped back reluctantly, feeling oddly territorial as the two paramedics got to work. They pulled out a portable ECG and pulse-ox. Soon they'd taken a heart trace, applied a neck brace and were examining John's leg. Christina rubbed her arms, feeling useless, until the police turned up. As she told them the few details of what she'd seen, her attention kept wandering back to what the paramedics were doing.

Soon John was on the stretcher, wincing as they moved his leg. Most of the onlookers had drifted away, although a few were still speaking to the cops. As her colleague settled John in the ambulance, the female paramedic turned to Christina. "Thanks for sticking around. Heart looks okay on the trace so far. You doing terms at the hospital?"

"The base, actually," said Christina, distracted. Glancing over the paramedic's shoulder, she noticed John staring at her, his eyes intense, almost pleading, as though begging her to stop them taking him away.

The woman nodded. "Maybe we'll see you around."

When Christina stepped back into the Belmont, her free hour for essay work was half gone. She stared after the ambulance.

Ten minutes later, she paused outside the hospital's emergency room, wondering what she was doing. She didn't know John. He was in expert hands now; she had nothing more to offer. And yet she wanted to know what would happen to him.

On a Thursday night, the department seemed expectant, as if already preparing for a busy weekend ahead. Staff moved with purpose, their eyes on charts or forms, trolley wheels rumbling across the hard floor. Here was the working world she so wanted to join.

The triage desk nurse looked up when Christina approached.

"I was wondering about a man who came in a few minutes ago by ambulance," she began. "John. He was in an accident."

"Are you a relative?"

"No, I was just at the accident. I'm a medical student," Christina added, then wished she hadn't. The department was probably busy enough without a nosy student poking around.

The nurse glanced over her shoulder. "You have a supervisor here?"

"Ah, no."

"Well, they're pretty busy," the nurse said dismissively.

Blushing, Christina took the hint and was soon back outside, reminding herself she didn't have the right to claim patients, not yet. But the rebuke still stung, and she couldn't shake the concern she felt, having seen the way John had looked at her.

Chapter 5

Aiden spent most of Saturday taking reports from up and down the east coast on the status of the equipment for the Solomon Islands, chasing more drivers, and getting creative with the budget to allow for more support soldiers. But responses were slow over the weekend, and by late afternoon he found himself back in his room. He paced around, unsure what to do with himself, before grabbing his field pack and sitting on the edge of the bed to pull out the contents. He'd do a quick check of his gear ahead of the upcoming exercise. Yawning, he rubbed his face.

The next thing he knew, someone was banging on the door. The window was dark. The kit was still where he'd laid it out on the floor. How long had he been asleep?

"Aiden? You in there?"

Only one voice was that penetrating. The bed creaked as Aiden rolled off, the concrete floor hard under his feet. He stubbed a toe against a full water canteen and swore before reaching the door.

"Such pretty language," said Travers, inviting himself in. He sat backwards on the desk chair and eyed the mess of equipment. "Love how you're keeping the place. Reminds me why I don't live on base."

"You don't live on base because you can't bring women here," Aiden said.

"Also true. Speaking of which, you're coming out tonight. Everyone's waiting."

"That's tonight?"

"Yeah, it's tonight."

Aiden stretched his aching shoulders. "I don't know if I can. The first contingent is supposed to ship out this week and there're still gaps to fill."

"What? Everyone's expecting you. They know you're not here for long and they want to see you. You can't pike."

"Still got a job to do."

"And that job can be done from your mobile right now if you have to. I'm timing you. Ten minutes to shower and change and then we're out the door."

They caught a cab from the base gate and the taxi emptied them out in town right in front of the Mad Cow, which was already bustling, the bouncers manning the door with strained faces. In the queue, they spotted Charlie, Mick and Shane waiting. On seeing them, the men all broke into huge grins. "Aiden, mate! Been too long!"

Deciding to avoid the crowd at the Mad Cow, they jogged across the street to Jack's, a sports bar with wood-paneled walls and pricier drinks, which kept the atmosphere marginally more sedate. They commandeered a corner table, among three sets of Cowboys supporters preparing to barrack the game at eight.

"Travers said you're working the Solomons thing. When'd you get in?" asked Charlie.

Soon they were all swapping stories of their recent postings. Charlie and Travers had been in Townsville for the past year. Mick, whom Aiden had worked with years ago, had just ended a stint training recruits at boot camp in Kapooka. "It was good to begin with, but I'm sick of it," he said. "Too many jubes. Ready for the real world again now."

"What, and you reckon that's here?" said Charlie.

The pints sank, and voices rose over the music. At the bar,

two girls in short dresses were eyeing off their table with interest. Aiden could smell the mix of perfumed bodies and beer. He kept one eye on his phone, but there were very few calls. Still, he felt himself drifting away from the conversation, from the familiar pattern of a night out: getting drunk and having a great time. When he was younger, he'd enjoyed all the female company that a fit young military man tended to attract. He'd woken up more than once in a strange flat, in every state in Australia. But he'd tired of all that in his late twenties, found a girl, and, well … now he had work to do.

The other guys were easily besting him in the beer drinking as Aiden tried to stay sober in case someone called. What did surprise him was that Travers seemed to be lagging too, the medic displaying none of his usual stamina.

"Check that out," said Shane.

Aiden followed Shane's gaze to find three heavily made-up girls squeezing between the tables towards the bar. "Go for it, if you want to be orange tomorrow," he said. "That fake tan must have gone on with a roller."

Travers squinted but said nothing. That was another surprise, given his reputation with the ladies.

"I guess," Shane said. "Nice smiles though. I feel very lucky tonight. It's my birthday."

Charlie shook his head. "It's your birthday every week."

"So it is. I'm going to go invite them over. Another round?"

Aiden leaned back from the table, catching Travers' eye. "What's up?"

"Nothing, why?"

"You're not going hunting?"

"Nah. Was hoping you might, though."

Aiden ignored this. "Everything cool at work?"

Travers rotated his pint glass, watching the liquid swirl and foam around the sides. "Yeah, same old. Students started this week, that's all."

"Students?"

"Med students. Doing their term at the clinic."

"And?" he asked, sensing something left unsaid.

Travers shook his head slightly. "And nothing. Just extra work, you know, teaching them how to do things."

"But you enjoy that, right?" Aiden pressed, but Travers wouldn't be drawn. Then the girls joined the table, giggling, and the game kicked off, and they had to raise their voices over the din, so he moved on. "Thought any more about this dive thing?"

"Yeah, actually," said Travers, brightening. "I've got a lead on a boat."

Half an hour later, Aiden had heard a detailed rundown of the potential boat's pedigree, and Travers had listened to Aiden's problems with the Solomons job, offering the odd knowing smile or sarcastic joke.

"Yo, Aiden!" called Shane from across the table. "You remember that time we got lost out in front of the sentry post?"

"I think you had the compass," Aiden fired back.

Shane gave the girl on his lap a knowing grin. "No, sir, I think that was you."

"Oh, 'sir'," said the girl, giving Aiden a wide-eyed look. "Is he important?"

"Well, he's an officer. I don't know about important." Shane winked. "As I was saying, Aiden had this map …"

Aiden shook his head. The story was fifteen years old, from when he and Shane had been on a navigation course. He watched with a kind of voyeuristic fascination as Shane, Charlie, Mick and the girls tried to impress each other. A crooked line of spent shooters soon snaked across the table, even while Aiden and Travers both nursed their second pints of beer. Aiden could already tell that the evening would end messily and there would be some sore heads tomorrow.

Sure enough, just after eleven, he and Travers found themselves half carrying the three girls outside, none of them in any state to go anywhere but home. "Lezgo to The Bank now!" slurred one, staggering against Aiden.

He had seen the size of her heels and hoped she wasn't going to break an ankle. He felt the soft touch of her hair against his chin, smelled the remains of her perfume. She looked about twenty. Sticking out a hand, he flagged down a taxi, thinking he should catch one himself – back to the office.

"Aw, come on, man," Shane objected. "They don't want to go home."

"You won't be saying that in fifteen minutes when you're all sick everywhere," said Aiden as he bundled the girls into the cab and made sure they had money for the fare. He turned back to Shane. "I'm calling it a night too. Work to do."

"But we haven't had a chance to catch up," complained Shane.

"Next weekend," said Aiden, not really meaning it.

"Yeah, party at my place," said Travers. "That's better anyway. Cheap beer, fun and games."

Soon the group had split up, and Aiden and Travers were standing on the strip amid the bustle of the Saturday night crowd. Music pulsed from pub doorways and balconies, while bodies still crowded to be admitted.

Travers scratched his head. "Well, that wasn't quite the plan. I just didn't feel like it."

"Happens to the best of us." Aiden checked his watch. "Time to find a cab?"

"You need some food before you get back to it. Come on."

After the long day, and no dinner, Aiden's stomach betrayed him with a rumble. So they walked east, vaguely towards a kebab shop that Travers thought was the best in town.

"Oh, wait, *pizza*," said Travers as a garish sign appeared ahead for a takeaway and home-delivery joint. As they approached, an old white Holden Belmont pickup pulled up out the front, large magnetic stickers on the doors proclaiming *Carlo's Fine Pizza*.

Aiden whistled. "Wow, I used to have one of those—" He broke off as a girl threw open the door and climbed out, her blonde hair in a rough ponytail swinging behind her head, a pizza box warmer shoved under her arm. She strode across the sidewalk, her face intent below her cap, and disappeared into the shop. He didn't know what it was about her, but he stopped, unable to remember what he'd been saying. Wow.

"What's wow?" asked Travers.

"Nothing," Aiden said quickly. He hadn't realized he'd spoken aloud.

Inside the pizza store was a small sitting area and a bright busy kitchen. Large menus covered two walls. Travers was instantly distracted by the drinks fridge, while Aiden's attention was focused on what was going on in the back.

The counter was manned by a lanky teenage boy, currently on the phone, taking an order. An older man who resembled the face on the shop's sign stood at the assembly bench throwing toppings on a base. And there to one side was the Belmont girl, counting out her change bag on a wide steel bench. Aiden watched how she laid out the piles of coins with swift, sure movements, even while her eyes darted to the counter. Seeing him waiting, and the lanky boy still on the phone, she tipped the change back into the bag and strode over.

"What can I get you?" she asked, picking up a pen. She had green eyes, her face natural and smooth, her expression serious. After the painted and pretentious girls he'd been around all night, he found it refreshing. Then she spotted Travers and her face fell. "Corporal Travers," she said, a little warily.

"Dr. Price! What a surprise." Travers turned towards Aiden. "Aiden, meet Christina. Med student in the clinic. She can do a mean cannula, too."

Christina. So, that was her name.

Her cheeks reddened. "Thanks to you," she said, with a

quick smile that Aiden wished was for him. She eyed them both, and there was something about her appraisal that told him she was more mature than she looked. Old soul, or something like that. "Been having a good night?" she asked.

"Sort of," said Travers. "Starving now though. What's good?"

"It's all good," she said, with the tired inflection of someone who just wants to get the job done. Aiden noted the fatigue in her face. Her blinks were slow and deliberate, the tiny muscles under her eyes cramped with the effort to focus. Exactly how he got when he was dog-tired. "But you're going to be a minute choosing, so I'll leave you to the others. My shift's over."

"Hey, wait a minute, I've got a better idea," said Travers, grinning. "Give us a ride back to the base. We'll order a pizza to deliver there, and you can take us along with you."

Christina glanced over to the man at the bench. "Even if I was allowed to do that, I don't want to have to come back here."

"Leave her alone, Travers. We'll get a cab," said Aiden, but in truth he was hoping she would agree.

"How about this?" said Travers. "We'll get takeout and you can count your till while it cooks. Then we'll give you the cab money to take us back to the base. Deal?"

Christina bit her lip, then glanced quickly over her shoulder. "Okay. But you better tell me fast what you want."

Christina suppressed a yawn as Travers directed her to the base through the Townsville streets. The Belmont's cab smelled strongly of cooked cheese and pepperoni, a scent she was eager to scrub out of her hair.

"I do know the way there," she said at one point. This did nothing to deter Travers, who had crammed his friend into the middle of the bench seat and then had twisted round against the passenger door as if it was a lounge seat to keep talking.

"Is that why you have this thing?" he asked, picking up the dog-eared map book, which Christina had tagged with Post-its in the relevant pages. "Why don't you just use GPS?"

Christina glanced across and caught the other man's eye. Aiden, Travers had called him. Broad-shouldered and watchful, he exuded an air of quiet authority, but in an attentive way, so that she suspected he missed nothing. Christina had no idea what to say; she didn't want to explain she couldn't afford a GPS, and that an app on her phone used too much data. Fortunately, Aiden spoke instead.

"Travers hasn't had his meds today," he explained, displaying a sense of humor. Was it that, or something about the curve of his smile that made her own lips tingle?

"Hey, I have too," protested Travers.

Soon they'd reached the entry gate to the base, where the guard eyed the delivery stickers on the pickup before checking the men's passes.

Travers stuck the half-empty box out of the Belmont's window. "Personal delivery, how's that? Want some?"

The guard declined but waved Christina through. She glanced at Aiden. "Normally I have to sign in. Is this okay?"

"Yeah, I know. You're going straight out again though."

"Luff," said Travers, mouth crammed with pizza.

"What?"

"Left," corrected Aiden.

Christina followed their directions through the winding streets until she pulled up outside an accommodation block. Cars were parked underneath the building. Most of the windows in the block were dark, but a few yellow squares indicated life.

"Thanks for the lift," said Travers, stuffing a ridiculous number of notes into Christina's hand and fishing a set of keys from his pocket as he exited the Belmont, leaving her alone with Aiden.

They watched Travers half trip down the bank towards a bright yellow Monaro. "He's not going to drive, is he?" Christina asked in alarm.

"Don't worry, he's sleeping on my floor, but I actually think he's pretty sober. He's just a little hyper. And he always checks the car before bed."

"I've never seen him like this before," Christina said. Travers was normally so serious and intense at work; she was having trouble accepting him as a hyperactive-when-drunk type.

Aiden paused, his gaze on her steady. Then his eyes dipped to her lips before he quickly looked away. Christina's heart pounded in her ears. No one had ever looked at her like that before.

"Well," he said. "Thanks for the lift. I hope it didn't put you out."

Christina managed to nod. He hesitated, as if he wanted to say something else, then pushed the door open. The Belmont's suspension rocked as he stepped out. Christina admired his easy muscular grace as he climbed the stairs. She shook herself. Her eyes were scratchy with fatigue. She really needed to get to bed.

She eased off the handbrake and drove up the road, made a U-turn, and headed back to the front gate. But after a minute, when the road swung unexpectedly to the right, Christina realized she must have missed a turn. She turned back. There, that was it. But the road soon ended in a cul-de-sac, dark buildings looming around her. Streetlights made pools of yellow light on the asphalt.

"Dammit," she muttered, yanking the Belmont's wheel around again. The base looked nothing like it did in the daytime. And by the time she'd glided down yet another wrong street, she had to admit it: she was lost.

She pulled over, batted at the cabin light and fumbled for the map book. But when she found the page, the base was nothing but a huge yellow rectangle with only the main roads shown. Looking around, she noted the bulk of Mount Stuart rising to her left, crowned with lights. Okay, she'd try taking roads that led away from Mount Stuart. That would have to get her back to the gate, right?

But after a few more turns, she was no closer to finding a way out. She tried not to imagine camouflaged men leaping out of the buildings to demand who she was. Finally, though, she found herself driving down a street that seemed familiar. The surge of hope was quickly dashed when she recognized the accommodation block.

Christina gave a frustrated sob as she hauled the Belmont to a stop outside. What did she do now? There was no bloody way she was driving around for another twenty minutes. She might end up somewhere she really wasn't supposed to be, like the shooting range. Or the place they kept the tanks.

"For *Pete's* sake," she muttered, killing the ignition and pushing her door open with a creak. This was all Travers' fault, for convincing her to drive them back here. He could bloody well show her the way back to the gate. She noted that one of the rooms that had been dark was now lit. Hopefully that was where her passengers had gone. Praying no one saw her, she snuck up the stairs to the room.

Before she lost her nerve, she knocked. Inside, she heard footsteps and a moment later the door opened, revealing not Travers but Aiden.

He stood in the puddle of porch light, shirtless, his hair spiky wet from the shower, a pair of dark blue boxers low on his hips. A tattoo covered the left half of his chest and shoulder, curling from the furrow in his chest muscle across his pec and into jagged edges on his upper arm. Below, his stomach dived flat into the midnight-blue waistband. Christina's mouth fell open. Oh, he was perfect. He really did look like a plate from her anatomy book; she could see the origin and insertion of every muscle fiber. Hastily, she averted her eyes, pretending to find the wall behind his shoulder absolutely fascinating.

"Hi," she said, trying to suppress the flush that was building in her cheeks.

"Hello again," he said, looking a tad bemused. "You forget something?"

"I got lost," she blurted.

He cracked that amazing smile. "I won't tell Travers."

"Is he here? I need him to show me back to the gate."

Aiden stood back. Beyond him, Christina could see a light making a ring on the hard floor, a simple desk against the wall, and the edge of a bed. "He went to the gym, if you can believe it. It's all right, I'll show you the way. Come in for a sec. I need to get a shirt … and some pants."

"You must think I'm a complete idiot," she said five minutes later, when Aiden had her heading on the right road back to the gate.

"Nah," he said, bunched in the passenger seat as he tied his shoelaces. "You wouldn't be the first person to get lost here. My sister did, the first time. The directions only make sense if you know what you're looking for, and it's worse at night."

The yellow-lit gatehouse with its cloud of hovering insects came into view ahead. As Christina pulled up, Aiden reached for the door handle. "This is my stop. You'll be fine from here."

"Let's hope so," she said.

The guard looked out the window, a sly grin on his face. "Hope it was a good pizza," he said.

Aiden served the guy a look that made him lose the grin and disappear back into the booth, then paused with his hand on the door. "We weren't introduced properly earlier. I'm Aiden Bell."

"Christina Price," she said, shaking the hand he offered, their fingers lingering on the warm touch.

"You're at the health center during the week, right?"

"Yeah, most days. Why?"

His look lingered, a fraction too long for just friendly interest. "Drive safe." Then he was gone. Christina watched the reflective flashes on his shoes disappearing into the night as he jogged away. A great rush warmed her veins, as though her tired blood had been replaced with something fresh and vital.

"Gate's up," called the guard impatiently.

She fumbled for first gear and turned the Belmont out of the base, remembering Aiden's gray-blue eyes ... and what he looked like under his shirt.

Chapter 6

That night, Christina dreamed about the accident, arriving at the hospital after John only for the doors to close in her face as he was taken away. She woke with a start. The dream faded fast, but it left a sense of cold spreading panic: that she was an impostor and would never graduate. Struggling to fall asleep again, she didn't rise till nine.

Feeling guilty about sleeping in, she measured out cereal as the kettle boiled, one eye on the pile of textbooks and notes on the kitchen table. Since Carlo had recently lost a driver, she was picking up a lot of shifts, which didn't leave much time for study or working on her essay. Today, she'd better get stuck in.

Having eaten, dressed, and put on a load of laundry, she'd just sat down when the phone rang in Harriet's study. Christina debated whether to answer. It wasn't her house. Then again, what if Harriet was calling? Bracing herself, Christina ran into the study and grabbed the handset.

"Hello?"

"Harriet?" A man's voice. Deep, older.

"No, sorry," Christina said. "She's not here."

"Do you know when she'll be back? It's important," he said. Christina pictured him as looking like Dr. Vaughn, with graying hair, but no sense of humor.

"She's overseas. I'm just looking after the place."

"Do you have a number for her? There's been … it's

important," he repeated.

"I'm sorry, who are you?" She didn't want to give Harriet's emergency contact to just anyone.

"Just a friend. I'm sorry to have bothered you," he said, and hung up.

Christina replaced the handset. Odd. She walked back through the house, unsettled, and opened the front door to let the breeze in. It was probably a telemarketer, she told herself. Though he hadn't asked the usual questions about whether she was the householder. She stepped outside and plucked a rolled-up newspaper from the lawn, still thinking. Maybe he was a debt collector. Christina had had a brush with them once before, and they were prickly about only identifying themselves to the debtor. But then Harriet had always been so good with money.

Christina was still mulling when a red Honda rolled up, its horn cheerfully tooting.

"Hi!" called Katie, erupting from the driver's seat with a satchel over her shoulder and two grocery bags. She looked so fresh with her sunglasses perched on her head, her long hair framing her face.

"Oh, hi," said Christina, groaning internally. Her plans were about to get derailed again. "I was just about to—"

"Study, I know." Katie rolled her eyes and guided Christina back into the house. "You said you study on Sunday, so I'm here to help. And I've brought brunch." She waved the bags, from which wafted the scent of roast chicken and fresh bread. "You never eat lunch at the clinic. You have to take care of yourself."

"I'm just never hungry at lunch," Christina lied. Two meals a day was cheaper than three. But she slid into her chair at the kitchen table, swayed by the aroma and by the force of Katie's will. "But not yet, okay? I need to get some study done. How about we work for a couple of hours, and then break to eat?"

Katie grinned. "Fine with me." She dumped the bags on

the bench and took the chair diagonally across from Christina, pulling her laptop out of her satchel. "So, what topic are you thinking for the essay?"

Christina glanced down at her notes, the kitchen clock making soft ticks. "I'm writing about painkiller prescription in acute sports injuries," she said. "We've had a lot of those on the base this week. One sore knee and two ankle sprains in one day. And I had no idea what to give the first guy."

Katie sat back, her blue eyes thoughtful. "Mmm, I guess." "What?"

Katie twitched her lips. "Sounds a bit specialized, don't you think? More sports med or emergency department than family practice?"

Christina twisted her fingers around her pen. "Painkillers are pretty basic," she pointed out.

"I guess. But trust me on this, I'm really good at the essays. You want something more relevant."

Christina didn't have a good academic history; maybe Katie was right. She scrambled to think of what else she could write about. "What are you going to do?"

"Effective preventative health strategies for general practice," Katie said proudly. "I'm going to take five things like pap smears and skin-cancer checks, and come up with a ranking for which is the most effective. Use research data to justify the list."

"Wow, that does sound really practical," said Christina. Her own project seemed so small in comparison.

"I know. It was my brother's idea – pretty cool, huh?"

"It's not a bit big for the assignment?"

Katie shook her head. "Nah, I'll be fine. He's going to help me with it. Do you want to brainstorm a different topic for you?"

Christina wavered, but she was already invested. "I'm going to stick with it."

"Suit yourself."

Soon the kitchen was filled with the sound of tapping keys.

And for all her fears that Katie would prove a distraction, Christina had to admit that having someone else there really kept her bum on the seat. By the time they broke for lunch, Christina had written an essay outline and found several papers on the topic. With her anxiety momentarily chased into a corner, she enjoyed the break.

"So why did you come back for this rotation?" Christina asked, feeling mildly social. "I thought you loved Brisbane."

"My brother convinced me," said Katie from around a mouthful of chicken sandwich. "It's much cruisier here. The base isn't half as busy as a normal family practice clinic. He's a doc in the air force now, did I tell you? He's so awesome. Helps me out a lot, which is cool."

"That's great," said Christina, her throat tight. Her memories of Sebastian Prior and his mates didn't allow her to imagine him being *"so awesome"*. Quite the opposite. "It might be quiet, but the base is really good," she went on. "I've never had anyone teach me things like Travers. I sucked at needles, but he made me practice until I got it right."

Katie smirked. "Yeah, he's not bad either."

"He's a pretty good teacher, even if he is a bit intense."

"No, I mean he's all right to look at. I'm going to ask him out."

"Why would you do that?" Something small but unmistakably territorial flared inside Christina. She wasn't interested in him like that, but he was *her* teacher. The idea of Katie dating him was icky.

Katie shrugged. "Could be fun, right? And I know he's been looking at me."

"I wouldn't know," Christina said, returning the butter to the fridge. Her only experience of boys at university – a couple of unfortunate early encounters – was that they drank a lot and quickly lost interest in her when she proved unready to party. In any case, study came first; there simply wasn't time for anything else.

Katie had moved on, however, again playing with the pile of mail at the end of the table while she licked mayonnaise off a finger. She picked up a postcard. "Oh, lovely – is this where your aunt is?"

Christina glanced over. The picture on the postcard was of a rustic fishing boat moored off a beach of pure white sand. "Dunno." She took it, turning it over to find the photo credit on the other side. The reverse was blank but for Harriet's address and two words in the message column: *I'm sorry*.

"Oh, juicy. Who sent that?" asked Katie, her voice sparkling with intrigue as she looked over Christina's shoulder.

Christina frowned, inspecting the spiky letters. "No idea."

"Come on, no one sends that on a postcard," said Katie, whose fingers were now riffling through the mail pile, where she quickly found another, this time of Uluru. She flipped it over and showed Christina the back. *Forgive me*, it said. "So? What's the deal?"

A ripple of emotion coursed through Christina. For a moment, she'd wondered if the postcards were from her aunt, apologizing for the argument they'd had all those years ago. But she knew the handwriting wasn't Harriet's.

"I really have no clue," Christina said. "I don't know my aunt that well."

"You're staying in her house," Katie said.

"Come on, we'd better get back to it."

But that evening, after Katie had left, Christina sat at the table looking at the two postcards. Harriet's life was a great mystery to her now, and contemplating what it contained was painful. Firmly, she tucked the postcards away at the bottom of the pile of letters. Strange mail was none of her business. The argument with Harriet was in the past, and it wouldn't help her finish her essay.

On Wednesday morning, Christina found herself in a curtained bay at the base clinic, peering into the face of a young man with bits of grass in his hair and a good deal of sand stuck to the collar of his fatigues.

"So, explain to me again what you were doing?"

"Grenades. On the range," he said. "It was *awesome*."

"And you think something hit you in the face?"

"Yeah. There was, like, this puff of dust up ahead, like something smacked the ground, and I got hit in the face."

"Hmm." Christina had been looking pretty hard but could find no damage at all. Certainly no blood. All she could see was a superficial scratch on the side of his nose. Gently she prodded across the cheekbones. "Any pain?" she asked.

He shrugged. "Feels weird. Like there's something in there."

Dutifully, Christina trekked off to report to Dr. Vaughn. "I can't see anything," she finished. "But he thinks there's something there."

Dr. Vaughn brought in a bright lamp and a magnifying glass and was soon prodding, eventually focusing on the side of the nose. "Christina, we need to do a little exploration here. Do you want to draw up some local anesthetic?"

"Sure," she said, selecting a syringe and needle tip from the wall bins.

"What are you going to use?" Dr. Vaughn asked.

Christina paused. They used two forms of local anesthetic in the clinic: one with adrenaline, and one without. Adrenaline constricted blood vessels, reducing bleeding, but in some parts of the body, that was dangerous. And the nose was one of them. "Lidocaine, straight," she said. "No adrenaline for the nose."

Dr. Vaughn nodded. "Excellent. And I'm going to show you something else. Here, watch." He unwrapped a needle tip and turned the beveled edge in the light. "This is a really small site, much too small for a scalpel. But the edge of a needle tip works brilliantly."

In short order, the anesthetic took effect, and Dr. Vaughn

deftly made a tiny cut over the scratch Christina had seen. A little pressure, and a moment later a dark sphere the size of a peppercorn appeared in the cut.

"Oh, wow," said Christina as Dr. Vaughn dropped the object with a *metallic tink* into a sample pot. She held it up to the light. "What on earth is that?"

"Ball bearing. Grenades are full of them. You're very lucky," he added to the patient. "A fraction further left and it would have been in your eye."

"Huh," said the soldier, squinting at the sample pot unperturbed. "Can I keep it? I wanna show my mum."

Christina exchanged a look with Dr. Vaughn. "Maybe wait until she's in a good mood," he said.

After the patient was patched up and discharged, Christina emerged to see Katie with Travers in the second resus bay. He beckoned Christina over. "How many cases have you seen this morning?" he asked.

"Three so far," she reported. "We just dug a ball bearing out of the side of a guy's nose."

Travers gave Katie a look.

"All right, fine, I'm going," she said, and stomped off to collect a clipboard and a patient.

But Christina noticed the smile Travers gave the back of Katie's swinging ponytail, before the doors opened and two men appeared in dirty fatigues, one guiding the other, who seemed to have a large rectangular box on his head.

"Uh, we need some help here," said box-free man. "He's kind of stuck."

Christina looked at Travers. "Oh no, don't look at me," he said, holding up his hands. "This one's all yours."

Half an hour – and half a jar of Vaseline – later, when Christina had pried the ammo box off the private's head, she returned to find Travers leaning on the front desk. "What is it with today?" she said.

"Freak day," he supplied. "Happens every so often. And the privates have to amuse themselves somehow. Now, back to real work. Anything you want to go through?"

"How about another go at a cannula?"

Travers gave a mock groan. "Created a monster, that's what I've done." But he cheerfully grabbed the phlebotomy trolley and stretched himself out on the gurney, still talking. "So, we're going to have a party this Saturday at my place."

Christina half listened while she gloved up. Hovering over Travers' vein, she tried to imagine what it would be like if she had been the one seeing John in the emergency room, if she had to do this for real. Then Travers stopped talking and she caught a movement from the corner of her eye. She glanced up to see a man in fatigues standing at the head of the bed. Christina absorbed the authority as her eyes tracked up: three pips on his chest, wide-shouldered, strong jaw, commanding gaze. With a jolt, she realized it was Aiden.

"Bad time?" he enquired.

"See, freak day," Travers stage-whispered to Christina with a grin. He tipped his head back to address Aiden. "Sorry, sir, you'll have to wait in line. Now, Dr. Price, imagine you've got your OC breathing down your neck. No pressure. Take your shot. What can I do for you, sir?"

Unexpected nerves tangled in Christina's chest, knowing Aiden was watching, but she really was getting rather good at this. A moment later she finished the line, her hands barely shaking. Quickly, she removed it and taped down a cotton ball on the site.

"Actually, I came to see Christina," said Aiden. Christina nearly dropped a kidney dish. Travers raised an eyebrow, but got up and moved out of the bay. Aiden smiled. "Did you get home all right the other night?"

An image flashed unhelpfully into her mind of Aiden in his boxers. She bit her lip as the heat reached her cheeks. "Yeah, thanks."

"How's the clinic treating you?"

"Not too bad." Christina then noticed Travers, who was

watching this exchange with keen interest. "Well, I'd better go and see the next patient."

She scampered away to the desk, where Katie stood peering, patient file in hand. "Who's *that?*" she asked, nodding to where Aiden and Travers were now talking.

"One of Travers' friends," Christina said, trying to sound casual. "I gave them a lift back to the base on Saturday."

"Really?" asked Katie as, for the third time in a minute, Aiden glanced in their direction. "Hang on a second, he's a captain. What's he doing being mates with Travers?"

Christina tried and failed to look somewhere else. There was something about Aiden that was compelling, that put a current under her skin, and it bothered her that she couldn't find a word for it. It was almost a relief when he left, that straight-backed walk carrying him out through the back door.

Travers wandered over, picking up their earlier conversation. "So, as I was saying, party on Saturday. How about it?"

"Me?" asked Christina.

"Yeah. You're all right."

"I don't—"

"Of *course*," answered Katie, nudging Christina in the ribs. "We'll be there."

Later, when they were leaving, Christina pulled Katie aside. "I don't want to go to a party. You go, though."

"You've got to be kidding." Katie scowled. "I said you should have some fun and I meant it. Besides, you *have* to come. I can't turn up by myself."

"But I've got heaps of study to do. And I'll probably be working." Christina didn't mention that she'd never much enjoyed parties, what with the drinking other students did. She remembered only loud occasions where it was impossible to talk to anyone, and she shied away from dancing, sure that she would look idiotic. She'd never been cool.

Katie wagged her finger as they plunged from the air conditioning out into the harsh winter sunshine. "No you don't. You're coming. You'll just have to work harder on Friday."

When Aiden finally reached his room that evening, he dropped his pack inside the door and sank onto the bed. He stared at his boots, knowing they had to come off. He just needed to find the energy to do it. His phone was ringing again in his breast pocket, as it had been all day, but the first wave of equipment had deployed; that was something.

"Aiden Bell."

"Hey, it's me."

Aiden let himself fall back on the bed. "Hey, Dani. Sorry I haven't called—"

"I know, you're busy." He detected only the slightest reproach in her tone. "But did you remember we were supposed to have dinner tonight?"

Aiden sat bolt upright. "We were? Shit."

"Yeah. That's why I thought I'd call. I was worried. Do you want to reschedule again?"

Aiden rubbed at his gritty eyes. God knows he'd worked in a much more wrung-out state than this before. Sometimes it couldn't be avoided: plans fell apart, disaster relief ran around the clock, and he kept going on the reserve tank that he always found at the apparent end of exhaustion. But he knew Daniella did exactly the same thing in her role, and she always found time for him.

"Yeah, I really need to sleep," he admitted reluctantly. "But I promise I'll make it up to you. How about next week? What day are you free?"

He heard pages shuffling as she checked her roster. "Well, Monday, maybe, if you could come by the hospital?"

"Monday it is." Aiden silently hoped that another crisis wouldn't come up.

Daniella sighed. "You know, Aiden, don't take this the

wrong way, but it's been a long time since we were both in the same place like this. I miss you. It's too good an opportunity to let pass."

"I know." Aiden pulled at his bootlaces, feeling every one of those years apart. His little sister had grown up without him. He still had trouble seeing her as a grown woman with a life of her own, a flourishing career, and a fiancé whom Aiden had met just once, when Dani and Mark had made a trip across to Perth during his last posting.

"Please tell me you remember I'm getting married in less than three weeks," said Daniella, as if she could hear his thoughts.

"Of course I remember. I booked the leave months ago."

"Are you bringing anyone?"

"I have a great idea for a gift," Aiden hedged.

"All I want is to see you there," she said, her voice catching on the edge of tears. "I mean, I'd postpone if you weren't going to make it."

Aiden's throat constricted as he recognized again her loyalty towards him, even when his job had separated them for so much of their lives. She never forgot a birthday, and she'd sometimes waited hours to see him. But he'd chosen this life; she hadn't.

"No, you won't," he said gently. "Mark would have my head, and it's not fair to you. But don't worry. I'm going to be there, okay? And I will see you on Monday."

After hanging up, Aiden stared at the pile of work on his desk. A busy week awaited. But in the midst of it all, he unexpectedly thought of Christina. Images of her had stuck fast in his mind – her purposeful stride the first time he'd seen her, her amused tolerance of Travers on the drive back to the base … the relief in her face when he'd opened the door of his room to see her standing there, her focus in the clinic. He toyed with the idea of calling Travers, to ask about her. The idea lasted for ten seconds before he pulled himself up. He didn't have time for this. There was too much work to do.

Chapter 7

If Christina had thought she was going to get out of the party, she quickly realized that Katie had other ideas. Her fellow med student had suddenly found a burst of motivation to attend the clinic, showing up for a full day on both Thursday and Friday, and then coming around on Saturday morning to work diligently and wordlessly at Christina's kitchen table. Christina tried several times to say that she needed Saturday evening to work on her essay; she'd been delivering pizzas on Thursday and Friday nights.

Katie was unmoved. "You'll have Sunday to study. Besides, what are you worried about? You're already working on the essay and we only have to present our topics on Monday. The essay isn't due for six more weeks."

"That's not long really, when I've got weekly readings, clinic and work," Christina replied. She didn't mention that other things were preying on her mind: Lena hadn't phoned about her mother all week, and Christina had intended to use this evening to call and make sure there'd been no more unplanned excursions, and then be alone to deal with any emotional fallout, which might involve watching something mind-numbing on TV and going to bed early.

"Too bad," said Katie. "You've been here two weeks and it's time to go out. Otherwise …" her brand of evil eye drifted towards the mail pile, "I'll just have to start going through your aunt's letters. Must be some good stuff in there. Aha!" Katie laughed in triumph at Christina's shocked expression. "Come on, don't tell me you're not curious about those postcards."

"I'm not," said Christina firmly.

"Great. Then we're leaving in an hour."

Christina bit her lip. "Your brother's not coming tonight, is he?"

"No. As *if*."

So it was that at precisely seven, Katie and Christina were creeping down The Strand in Katie's little Honda, looking for the turn to Travers' apartment. During the day, The Strand was lined with a strip of lush carpet grass separating the road from the beach, where tourists baked themselves red in the harsh sun or tipped a volleyball across the nets. Now, on dusk, Christina saw joggers in singlets running along the beachfront path. Opposite, the craggy peak of Castle Hill was backlit in the fading light, a line of ascending climbers like ants. The temperature suggested palm trees and sitting by a pool.

"Should be able to hear it by now," Katie said.

Christina peered at the apartments in some alarm. "Will it be noisy?"

"Probably. These army guys know how to party. Ask my brother."

"I thought you said he was in the air force?"

Katie swung the car around a small roundabout. "Yeah. But he works with them."

Finally, they found the party, up a long flight of stairs in a stuccoed apartment block that looked like holiday resorts Christina had seen in magazines. She hung back. She could hear music leaking through a door, on which number twelve glowed in a burnished gold.

With a burst of volume, Travers opened the door, a grin on his face, the collar of his red Hawaiian shirt turned up at the back. "It's the med students," he shouted over his shoulder, standing aside and gesturing them into the apartment and down a long hallway. With no choice but to obey, Christina tried to keep Katie between her and the noise and strangers.

At the end of the hall, Travers' living room sported two plush couches and open glass doors onto a balcony, which was already filled with a dozen people. She spotted girls in tight mini-dresses. A cooling breeze played with the edge of the curtains, and the sound of rattling ice came from the kitchen.

"Sit, sit, we're playing Six Degrees of Kevin Bacon," said Travers, helping a girl in a tight blue dress to shove across. Katie instantly dropped into the sliver of vacant space, leaving Christina to stand with her fingers coiled into the sofa back. She could smell the prickly tang of beer. She wrinkled her nose, craving fresh air and quiet. Outside, the night was settling, snuffing out the last of the sun in a slick of orange across the horizon. Against this seam between the indigo water and steel-gray sky stood two palm trees in black silhouette.

"Okay, okay," said a guy on the other couch, holding up his hands for quiet. Someone turned the music down a notch. "George Clooney and Christina Hendricks." A whoop came from one of the guys.

"Katie, you're up," said Travers, who'd managed to conjure a drink from somewhere into Katie's hand.

"Clooney was in *The Ides of March* with Ryan Gosling," Katie was soon saying. "And Gosling was in *Drive* with Christina Hendricks."

"No way! Hendricks isn't in that."

"Yeah, totally," said Katie, bouncing forward on the sofa. "She does the job that goes wrong at the pawn shop."

"Hey, she's right."

"Wow, two links, nice one!"

Katie preened. Christina sank back against the wall, hoping she wouldn't be called on next. She had no idea what this game was, and she certainly hadn't seen enough movies to be any good at it.

"Christina, your go," said Katie.

Christina spotted the empty kitchen through a doorway.

Escape.

"Chri-is?" Katie's voice stole after her, but Christina kept going.

"Hey, let her get a drink," someone said.

Christina leaned her hands on the edge of the sink and stared out the window, which gave the same view of the evening ocean, dotted with shipping lights. To anyone else, that would be an uplifting scene, no doubt: gentle breeze, balmy air, the restfulness of night. But right now, with the party chaos, all it reminded her of was the awful past.

The fridge door snicked closed behind her. Christina turned, then started when she found Aiden Bell, in board shorts and a snug white t-shirt, holding a milk bottle.

"Hello. Again," he said.

"Oh, it's you," she said. His hair had been cut since she'd last seen him, and that the shorter shaved sides lent his commanding air a harder edge. Then that smile curved his mouth, softening the angles of his face.

"Want a beer?" he asked.

Christina made a face. "Ew, no thanks."

"How about coffee?" Aiden set the milk down by the machine.

His look warmed her. The fingers that she'd clamped against the sink unclenched, one by one. "Okay."

"How do you like it?"

"White," she said, watching him work the machine.

Katie burst into the kitchen. "What's taking you so long? We need you, come on!"

She dragged Christina out into the living room, where the group were now leaning forward on the couches around the coffee table. Sheets of paper and pencils had appeared, some already wet in the condensation dripped from beer bottles.

"Pictionary," explained Katie. "It's our turn. And we're going to beat everyone."

"Less talk, more game," said Travers, brandishing a box of cards.

The room seemed to be the center of some kind of whirlwind. Christina glanced towards the kitchen, wishing she could return to the calm, quiet space, and to Aiden's easy company, but Katie began drawing and at least someone had further turned down the music. Despite her discomfort, Christina made herself focus on the pencil lines. "Frisbee," she guessed as two concentric ovals appeared, but Katie shook her head and drew lines downward. "No, table ... um ... yoghurt?"

"Yes!" declared Katie. "My drawing's terrible – you must be some kind of savant."

"Right," said one of the boys across the room. "That's the warm-up. Now, we're playing strip rules."

Christina assumed they were joking, but as the next pair drew and guessed, it became evident that she was wrong: running out of time, they both shed their shoes. All right, that was enough. Asking for the bathroom, Christina instead found the front door, and the stairs. She needed a few quiet minutes, alone.

The complex had a pool ringed by a fence, the surface glowing soft blue from underwater lights. She eased through the gate, wondering why on earth she had agreed to come tonight. To make up for it, she pulled out her phone and dialed Lena's number, letting the night shield her.

"Everything's been fine," Lena said after they'd exchanged greetings. "We've been out today, and the physiotherapist was here this morning. Actually ..." The sound became muffled, and Christina could hear Lena talking to someone in a low voice, before she returned. "Your mum wants to speak to you. Hold on."

Christina stiffened as the phone was handed over. Her mother didn't speak at first; all she could hear was breathing.

"Hi Rita," she said.

"Why didn't you tell me you were going to Townsville?"

Christina silently cursed Lena, who must have let this information slip. Then she felt bad; Lena's job was hard enough. "I'm not here for long," she said.

"But *I* wanted to go. I need a holiday."

"It's not a holiday," Christina said quickly. "I'm working."

"Are you running away again?"

"What does that mean?"

"Like you did when you left school. Don't make me come find you again."

"For Pete's sake, I wasn't running, I was trying to …" Christina stopped and took a deep breath. Against her will, she could feel her mother worming through her defenses; Rita's loneliness and dependence had always triggered Christina's automatic need to support and bolster, to reassure. To trust. Even the knowledge that Rita always disappointed didn't diminish the power of Christina's instinctive response. It was this reaction she had tried to escape when she left Townsville. Now, that same response only left her angry – she wanted Rita to grow up, but arguing and reasoning were pointless.

She tried to hold her voice neutral. "Rita, listen. I had to come here at short notice for school. There's no time for holidays. I'll be back in a few weeks." Even as she spoke, she heard the phone being handed back to Lena. Rita wasn't listening.

When the call ended, Christina's mobile was slick with sweat where she'd pressed it tightly to her ear. She put it aside and slipped off her shoes. As her feet broke the water's surface, a cooling pool spread through her thoughts. Leaning back on her hands, she let out her breath, swirling her legs in the water and trying to dissipate the lingering ripples of frustration in her mind.

She heard footsteps, and the pool gate opening behind her.

"There you are." The next moment, Aiden had set two travel mugs down between them. "White, I guessed no sugar," he said, pushing one of them towards her.

After a moment's hesitation, Christina accepted the mug. "Thank you."

"Not enjoying the party?"

"I draw the line at Strip Pictionary – oh, that's good," she said as the silken coffee slid across her tongue.

"Travers is a coffee snob – only keeps the good stuff." Aiden eased his own feet into the water, settling in.

"Aren't you going back upstairs?"

"Strip Pictionary is also not my thing. I'm much better at strip poker," he added, giving her a quick grin. "Besides, Travers won't shut up about this boat he has a lead on. He's got a picture of it in his pocket like it's his girlfriend. I needed a break."

Christina snuck a look at Aiden, acutely aware of him next to her. She only reached five-feet-three; he must be six-feet-something, and even in a t-shirt and shorts he reminded her of the charity fireman calendar that hung in the student common room back in Brisbane, permanently displaying the ripped torso of Mr. February. His thigh must have measured two of hers, and his commanding presence was not at all diminished out of uniform. She wondered if that was something he'd learned in the army, or did it just come naturally?

All of this pointed towards a type of man who never normally spoke to her, however much he made her feel shiny inside. Christina looked back down at the water.

"Travers did mention something about a boat," she said finally.

"Uh-oh. You're in the vortex. But I'm glad he's making a plan."

Curious about Travers outside the clinic, and noting that Aiden still showed no inclination to leave, Christina took the chance. "How long have you known him?"

"Since we were eighteen. We got off the bus together at Kapooka, fresh grunts."

Christina let that sink in. She'd never had a friendship that had lasted so long, couldn't imagine a connection standing the test of that many years.

"Of course we're often posted to different places," Aiden went on. "But sometimes we end up in the same base for a while. Did he tell you why he's getting out?"

"His shoulder," said Christina. "And knees and ankles."

"Right," said Aiden. "Did you know he was a sniper? A very good one, and he can't do that without full function, that's why he retrained as a medic a few years back. I was luckier." He tapped his knee, on which Christina now spotted the twin-eyed marks of a surgeon.

"You've had a knee reconstruction too?" Forgetting herself, she touched the marks, his skin warm under her fingertips.

Aiden caught her eye with a small smile. "A few years ago. Snapped my anterior cruciate and had to have it stitched back together. Luckily it came good."

"How did that happen?"

"Something really simple. I was out for a run. It was raining. I hit one of those little valve pits that had a cracked lid. My foot stuck and I kept going."

In her mind, Christina visualized the anatomy, picturing the knee's anterior cruciate ligament running diagonally through the joint, connecting the femur to the tibia, preventing the latter from sliding too far forward on the former. A moment passed before she realized Aiden was staring at her, his cup halfway to his lips.

She blushed. "I'm sorry, did you say something?"

He gave a short laugh, shaking his head. "You had the doctor look on your face just then."

"The doctor look?"

"Yes. The one that says you're trying to put things together in your head. I know that look really well."

Christina's brows drew together.

"Yes, like that," said Aiden, and laughed again.

Christina tried to relax her face, which only made it worse. A bubble of laughter escaped her own lips. "Fine, I'll just look at the water." She raised her mug and stared at the light-dappled surface of the pool.

"Nah, don't do that," said Aiden. "I didn't say it was a bad thing. When did you decide you wanted to be a doctor?"

Christina glanced at him, suddenly on guard. "Ah, a while ago."

"Doctors in the family?"

"No anything in the family," she said quickly. "I mean, my aunt was a nurse. But that's it. How is it you know this doctor look so well?"

"My sister's a doctor. My dad's a surgeon. My mum was a nurse. And I've injured myself or needed shots or medicals enough times. I think that qualifies me."

"So how is it that you're not a doctor too?"

Aiden set his mug down. "Never was my thing." He pulled his feet out of the pool.

Thinking he was heading back to the party, Christina extracted her legs too. "Thanks again for your help the other night," she said. "I guess I should go back up."

Aiden took her empty mug. "Don't mention it. And you don't have to go back up if you don't want to. How about a walk?"

Aiden led her out of the complex and across the road, until they met the path running along The Strand. He could hear the laughter and music from Travers' flat, slowly diminishing in the rhythmic shush of waves running in to shore. He wasn't entirely sure what he was doing, only that he was more interested in being out here than back at the party.

Christina glanced back at the flat. "What was the game they were playing before Pictionary?" she asked.

"Six Degrees of Kevin Bacon. Someone chooses two actors, and you have to connect them through other people they've been in movies with."

"Who's Kevin Bacon?"

Aiden stopped. "You're kidding, right?"

"No. I don't watch TV much. Pretty hopeless with pop culture."

Aiden stepped off the path and sat down on the grass, beneath two palm trees on the edge of the sand. "You'll have to have a Kevin Bacon movie night. *Footloose, A Few Good Men, Tremors, Apollo 13* ... just avoid *Hollowman.*"

Christina sank down beside him. "I better just watch the previews. I have too much study to do. I shouldn't even be here tonight."

"That makes two of us," he said. "I should be at work too."

She looked him in the eye then, and he saw understanding. He stared back, trying to work her out. She wasn't like other girls he'd known; there was a reserve about her, but some energy ran under her skin, a passion that would put study ahead of parties. He was drawn to it, and he wanted to know how deeply it ran. Wanted to know everything about her.

"Travers said you grew up here," he prompted her.

She glanced down at the sand. "Yeah. But I left a long time ago. I only came back because my placement in Brisbane fell through. I'm looking after my aunt's house while she's overseas."

"So it feels weird to come back?" he guessed.

She gave him another look, and he knew he'd struck a sore point.

"Actually," she said slowly, "I promised myself I wouldn't ever come back. And yet here I am."

"I know that feeling," he said. "In my job, you can't always choose. I never stay long in one place, but I often end up back again later, even if I don't want to."

Christina gave a small nod, the lines between her brows smoothing out. "Is that the kind of life you wanted?"

"I didn't think about it." Aiden leaned back on his arms as the waves washed in. The night sky was clear and star-pinned. And then, without thinking, it all spilled out of him. "I only ever wanted to be a soldier. I didn't fit in with the other kids in school, kids who were going to be accountants or lawyers or whatever. I didn't want Dad's career. An army recruiter came to the school when I was ten. He was there for the high schoolers, but something about him grabbed me. I cornered him in the car park at lunchtime. I thought he'd brush me off, but we talked for half an hour. He'd been overseas, all around Australia, clearly loved the job. I knew it was right for me then, never looked back."

Christina was picking at the grass, slowly running her fingers along the blades as she listened. "I feel like that about med," she said slowly. "When you asked earlier, when I decided? It was like that for me, too. I knew I'd found my place."

She smiled, briefly, and Aiden saw a flash of her passion, dedication, determination. Everything she was. His heart tripped. When she asked him a question, he had to ask her to repeat it.

"I said, what do you do?"

"Oh … operations stuff." He heard his own hesitation.

"Is it classified or something?" she said.

He chuckled. "No, it's just that when I say I'm in the army, not everyone reacts well. I think some people have the wrong idea about what we do."

"I've seen the ads. You don't put on war paint and jump out of choppers every day?"

"Well, some days. And sometimes it is classified."

Her eyes rounded, as if she had been joking and now realized he wasn't, and was trying to imagine it. "Wow."

He smiled. "I started out as a combat engineer. Lots of work with explosives, and heavy earthmoving equipment. Our job was to either disrupt enemy paths, or make ours secure." He shrugged. "But gradually I did more and more disaster stuff. I'm coordinating the Solomons flood recovery operation right now."

She looked confused.

"You might not have heard about it, since the floods were weeks ago. But there's still villages covered in mud, roads out, clinics and schools unusable. We need a heap of heavy equipment and boots on the ground to fix it. I make that happen."

"I had no idea we were involved."

A spark of pride kept Aiden talking. "There's always ops like that going on. Last month it was clearing munitions in Papua New Guinea. Year before last, the Cyclone Fletcher recovery in Western Australia. A few years before that, cyclones Larry and then Yasi. And next month, we have a training exercise out west … Sorry, I'm probably boring you."

"No, you're not. You must end up in a lot of interesting places. But it sounds exhausting."

"Can be," he said. "When I was younger, I could burn the candle at both ends. Now I feel it more."

Aiden thought about the hours he'd spent in transport planes, or freezing or baking somewhere out bush or overseas. The times he'd been at the edge of his endurance and somehow kept going. But here, with the calm night sky overhead, and the breeze freshening in the palm fronds – even with his eyes gritty from too many late nights – those times seemed part of some other life.

"How old are you?" she asked abruptly.

"Guess," he said.

"Dunno – twenty-nine?"

He laughed. "I don't know whether to be insulted or flattered. I'm thirty-four."

Christina's gaze flitted over him, her cheeks darkening. "Oh. Well, everyone under sixty is young in medicine. I'm pretty bad at guessing. I just look at the chart."

Silence came down on them again, and this time Aiden was aware he'd been doing most of the talking. He'd come out here curious about her, and he still knew nothing.

"Then I'd guess you're maybe … twenty-three?" he asked.

"Twenty-seven."

"Really?" he said. "I'd never have thought."

She paused. "You know, when I met you the other night, I thought you were a quiet type but we've been talking for an hour."

"Probably am quiet, compared to Travers."

She laughed. He looked at her again – her blonde hair tucked behind her ears, her quick eyes that were watching the waves roll in. His chest stirred again, like a feather was brushing over his heart.

She dusted her hands. "I think I should go back. Unless …" she stopped, as if struck by a thought, "they're all going to be naked."

"I somehow doubt it. They're not drunk enough yet." Aiden laughed, but he couldn't help his disappointment. He couldn't remember the last time he'd had a conversation like this, where he lost track of time – even forgot about work – just sitting with someone else.

When they arrived back at the party, Strip Pictionary had been abandoned. The group had split in half, one side deep in a video game while the others played a drinking game, flicking a casino chip off a tall beer bottle. Katie was perched on Travers' lap, which told Aiden that Travers must be very drunk. Christina was looking around, clearly keen to go.

"You don't have to stay," he said.

"Katie drove. I said I'd wait," she said, clearly torn.

Aiden took his keys from his pocket. "Do you want a lift? I don't think she's going anywhere for a while."

A moment later, when she agreed, he couldn't deny the surge of pleasure he felt at walking out the door with her, even if it was only to drive her home.

Chapter 8

The following Monday afternoon, Christina perched on a chair in the hospital's teleconference room for the weekly tutorial link to Brisbane. On the screen was Professor Green, the imposing clinician who kept a strong grip on the tutorial timetable, leaving room for hard questions and squirming, even from hundreds of miles away.

"All right, well, you have some study left to do, don't you?" he was saying now to one of the Brisbane-based students, who'd failed to give a satisfactory answer relating to angina management, the discussion from last week. Christina had studied it like a demon, as the chances of seeing cardiovascular cases in the army base clinic were remote.

"Katie," boomed Professor Green through the video link. "You had the task of researching medications for hypertension. Please give the group a summary."

Beside Christina, Katie brightened. "Actually, Chris and I both researched this, right, Chris?"

And somehow, into the vacuum, Christina found herself giving a summary from her notes. "Diuretics, uh … beta blockers, ACE inhibitors … uh, angiotensin-two receptor blockers …"

Slowly, by pretending Professor Green wasn't there, she managed to outline how each drug worked. Still, when she'd finished, one look at his face struck her with terror. "That's wonderful," he said drily. "But I asked Katie."

An embarrassed pause seemed to affect everyone except Professor Green and Katie. On the teleconference screen, the students in Brisbane looked down at their notes. "Katie, give me an analysis of ACE inhibitors and ARBs – which would you prescribe?"

Katie didn't even blink. "Well, they have about the same effectiveness, but some patients on ACE develop a dry cough, which might reduce their compliance. On the other hand, ARBs are more expensive. I'd start with an ACE and switch to the ARB if the cough became a problem."

Just like a pro. Professor Green grunted. "All right," he said. "Our last item of business this week is to assign pairs for the case study."

Christina felt an icy sensation between her shoulder blades. What case study? She tried to flick surreptitiously through her notes to the assessment page.

"Each pair will take a system theme," Professor Green was saying. "Katie and Christina will obviously work together. And I'm going to give you the *neurological system*."

As Professor Green continued to allocate themes, Christina found it – the last lines of the assessment section that in the chaos of her trip up here she had completely missed because they'd wrapped onto the next page. In pairs, they were supposed to find a case to follow through the term, with a written report due in the last week. The cold sensation had now wrapped itself around her. "Professor Green," she blurted. "We're on the base here. Most of the patients are young and fit. I'm not sure we'll even see a neurological case we can follow through the term …"

Professor Green was already gathering his notes. "Then I expect you'll need to use initiative. That's all. See you next week."

After the screen went dead, Christina pushed her chair back and put her head in her hands. "Shit," she said.

"Hey, don't worry. I'm sure my brother can help out," said Katie. "Or we could just find a case at the public hospital."

Christina peered through her fingers. Katie seemed to be immune to anxiety; Christina wondered if she'd somehow been vaccinated. Christina's own thoughts were scrambled just by the idea of an extra assignment to do, and she absolutely did not want Sebastian's help.

It wasn't until she and Katie had left the hospital, walking out under a wide awning with the afternoon scent of sun-warmed grass filling her nose, that she moved past the panic and began to think about how to tackle the case study. She was due at Carlo's in two hours, which would mean another late night. Then back to the base clinic tomorrow morning. When would she find the time to hunt down a neurological case? She caught the eye of a paramedic, sipping coffee with her partner against the external wall. And immediately she thought of John.

She stopped, glancing up at the hospital rising behind them. Would he still be here? He'd hit his head in the accident; that qualified as neurological, didn't it?

Katie had already walked on ahead, so Christina jogged to catch up, trying to work up the nerve to go back in. It would be perfect: she could find out what had happened, finish the case she'd started and the assignment. The only problem was, her placement wasn't at the hospital.

"What's up with you?" asked Katie, as Christina took an age to open the Belmont's door. "Is this still about Saturday night?"

Christina re-pocketed the Belmont's keys. "No, I just had an idea for a case."

"That's great," said Katie, pulling at the locked passenger door handle. "Open up and tell me on the way."

"Come back with me," Christina said. "There might be a patient here I know already. MVA with a head injury. Maybe he'll talk to us."

Katie folded her arms. "Oh no, I'm *done* today."

"It'll take ten minutes. Please."

"I know your version of ten minutes. Let's go."

Christina threw the keys to Katie. "Wait here, then. I'll be back soon."

Christina took a punt and went for the surgical ward, figuring that if John was still here he'd probably needed an operation on his leg. She found the two nurses staffing the ward's station, one wearing half-frames and a weary expression and surrounded by stacks of paperwork, and the other seated behind a computer screen, her long brown hair pulled back in a ponytail and her finger trailing down a results list. Christina tried to affect confidence as her eyes ran down the patient board mounted on the wall. Three Johns were listed. One, a John Hunt, was notated with *MVA #femur right*. She couldn't be that lucky, could she?

Christina introduced herself at the desk in a rush, her fingers worrying at the end of the stethoscope about her neck. "… And so I was wondering if I could talk to John, possibly for a case study assignment," she finished.

The weary nurse glanced across at the other woman. "I'm not sure that's the best idea."

Christina paused, unwilling to give up. "Oh. It's just that I'm at the army base clinic and I need a neurological case—"

"Didn't one of the other students tell you?" The nurse's expression was grim and Christina slid her ID back into her pocket, ready to leave and drag the shreds of her assignment-saving plan behind her. But then the other woman pushed away from the computer and beckoned to her. She had a kind face and quick gray eyes, despite the tired-looking shadows around them. Edging past the other nurse, Christina followed her into the office. The woman pulled out a second rolling chair, and it was only then that Christina noticed her ID badge. This wasn't a nurse; this was a doctor.

"I'm Daniella, the registrar," the woman said, her smile warm. "So, you saw Mr. Hunt before he came in?"

Christina's voice found strength again. "Yes. And I thought he might be good for a case study."

"It's not just that, though, is it?" asked Daniella. "I see that look. You're curious, right? It feels unfinished, after you were there at the start?"

Christina nodded, surprised.

"I haven't let any students see him," Daniella went on, "because he's difficult – very difficult. But you did see him first. Look, he's about to go to x-ray, which will be an ordeal in itself. But you can go and see if he'll talk to you. If he will, you can come back tomorrow."

So Christina noted the bed number and slipped down the hall, her shoes silent on the floor, conscious of Katie waiting down in the car park. The smell of surgical tape and hand soap was in the air.

Entering the third room, she quickly spotted John nearest the window in a group of four beds, the curtain pulled forward to shield him from the next patient. His head was tipped towards the view out the window: Mount Stuart, rising gray-green against the endless blue sky. His leg was under a tent. He sported a healing welt on the bridge of his nose, and patches of yellow and purple beneath each eye, but his gray hair had been neatly brushed. Christina tried to process his features: the crooked nose, strong jaw and heavy shoulders. He looked like a man who'd worked hard all his life.

She cleared her throat and approached his bed. "Ah, Mr. Hunt?"

His eyes swiveled towards her. At first his expression was openly hostile, all steel-cold eyes. Then, slowly, it changed, a line pulling between his brows. "What are you doing here?" he asked, his voice rough.

"You remember me?"

"Christina," he said.

"Good memory," she said, surprised. "I wasn't sure if you'd

remember anything from the accident." In fact, she was a little disappointed. This didn't bode well for making a neurological case study. "Actually, I was wondering if I could talk to you about the accident."

"Did they bring you in specially?"

"Specially?"

"To make me talk."

Christina took another step forward. "Not if you don't want to. But I'm a medical student, you see, and we talk to patients to learn. At the moment—"

"You're a medical student?" He pushed himself higher on the pillows, peering at her.

"Yes. I'm doing my rotation on the army base."

"And they didn't ask you to come here?"

"Who?"

He jerked his chin towards the door and the nurses' station. "*Them.*"

She shook her head. "It would just be me, and another student I have to work with. We'd start tomorrow and come back a few times while you're here."

His jaw worked as he considered. "Fine. But only because you helped me out. I don't forget that." He turned back to the window, but as Christina went to leave, she could have sworn he was staring at her reflection in the glass.

When she reappeared at the nurses' station, Daniella was back at the computer. "How did it go?" she asked.

"Well, he remembered my name and said I could come back tomorrow."

"He actually spoke to you?" Daniella looked amazed.

"Yes. Why?"

The doctor shook her head. "I'm usually pretty good with difficult patients, but I've had barely a word out of him the whole time he's been here. He won't tell us if he has a family doctor, or anything about himself, and he has no records here. So we have no idea if he has any relevant medical history. At first we thought he might have a serious head injury. But now I'm not sure. Maybe he's had a bad experience, or he's just a tough guy finding dependence hard. He doesn't ask for pain relief. Let me tell you, getting consent for procedures has been a nightmare. I've been dreading his x-ray trip all day."

Christina tried to think of anything useful. "After the accident, he had chest pain, and he was worried he was going to die."

Daniella nodded. "I saw that in the paramedics' notes. From what we can tell, it was a panic attack. No cardiac pathology at all. In fact, apart from his leg, he seems to be in fantastic shape. But if he'll talk to you tomorrow, it'll be immensely helpful. This is his chart." She pulled a slim file from the wall unit. "Come and see me if you have any problems, okay? I mean it – anything at all."

Christina didn't get far down the hall before the ward doors opened and a man came striding through. She took one look at that straight-backed walk, the broad shoulders, the familiar face, and stopped, a pleasant shock going through her. Aiden. The last time she'd seen him was when he dropped her home two nights ago. They'd sat in the car talking for several minutes before she'd finally said she had to go, and then he'd waited, making sure she was safe inside before pulling away.

He spotted her and his steps slowed. "Christina," he said, smiling.

"What are you doing here?" she asked.

"Taking my sister to dinner."

Looking into his face now, with the warmth in his eyes, the same gray in the iris, Christina put the puzzle together. "Daniella?"

Aiden glanced past her. "You've met?"

"Just now … but she's the nicest registrar I've ever known. I can't believe she's your sister."

Aiden's smile widened. "I'll try not to take that the wrong way."

"Oh, that's not what I meant—"

He laughed. "Don't worry. I've been called much worse things than Dani's unbelievable brother."

Her cheeks burning, Christina glanced at her shoes, crushing her nails into her palm. "Well, I better go."

"Wait."

She turned back, dragging her eyes up. Aiden's smile was in a different shape; more tentative. "Would you like to join us?"

"Oh, no, thanks." She couldn't imagine invading their plans, especially after Daniella looked so tired.

"I enjoyed our conversation the other night. We should do it again sometime," he said. "How about dinner on Friday? I can even lend you a Kevin Bacon movie."

Christina suddenly found her heart thumping, wondering if he really meant it. "I work most nights," she said finally. "And I'm just here for a couple of months. I don't really have time for dinner and movies. No offence."

"None taken. Are you working Friday night?"

"Yes."

"What if I navigate for you? I'm good with a map. Make sure you don't get lost."

Christina looked at him closely. His face was perfectly straight, but something impish glittered in his eyes. "Cheeky bastard," she muttered. "I can read a map just fine." But she couldn't deny the idea of seeing him again was exciting.

"What time do you start?"

"Seven," she said weakly.

"See you then." He waved as he strode off down the hall. Christina stared after him before jogging to the lifts. He couldn't be serious, could he?

When Christina reached the car park, Katie was sprawled across the Belmont's bench seat, windows down, radio on and talking on her mobile, a call she ended when she spotted Christina. "So, have we got a case?"

"Yes," said Christina, tugging open the driver's door. "We can go back tomorrow and interview him."

"What now?" asked Katie as Christina, thinking about Aiden, failed to even slide her keys into the ignition.

"I think I might have been asked on a date."

"Ewww!" declared Katie, screwing up her face.

"Oh God, not the patient," said Christina, chucking a discarded candy wrapper at Katie. "Aiden Bell. He was up in the ward."

Katie sat up straight, instantly alert. "Really? Oh, you must tell me *all* the details. I bet his body's fantastic. You talked to him at the party, didn't you? I thought you were gone a long time. Tell me everything!"

"Nothing to tell," said Christina firmly, backing out of the space, regretting she'd said anything. "Besides, he can't possibly be interested in me."

"Don't be such a noob," Katie said. "He's a guy. Of *course* he's interested."

"Well, I'm not. I'm only here a few weeks and I have too much to do." Even if every response within her disagreed, she didn't have to tell Katie.

Katie shook her head. "Fine, whatever. I have something much more exciting to tell you."

"What?"

"Travers just called. There's a group trip up the coast on Saturday."

"I have to study," Christina said automatically.

"This is Crystal Creek, Chris. You can set aside a few hours for rock pools, can't you? Chris?"

Christina hardly heard, feeling a momentary glitch in the turn of the earth, as if she had been sucked back in time. Crystal Creek was one of *those* places, the ones at the end of the road trips her mother promised and never delivered. All the other destinations her mother had mentioned, she had decided that perhaps they didn't exist. But her school class had gone to Crystal Creek without her, her mother having no cash for excursions. Seb Prior had been particularly savage about her missing out, citing it as clear evidence she was a loser for life. To emphasize the point, he put rocks and sticks in her bag for a week, then laughed when the dirt shed off her books. Since then, it had become a fabled place in her mind, something kept from her by circumstance. To miss it again would be too cruel.

"I've always wanted to go there," she whispered.

"See, perfect. We're leaving Saturday morning at eight, be back in the afternoon. Plenty of time for studying all night. You'll be a social butterfly after all, Chrissy."

Christina shook her head as she steered them out of the car park. That was something she'd never expected to hear.

Chapter 9

The next morning, Travers greeted Christina's arrival in the clinic with a broad smile. Since the party, Christina was enjoying even closer attention from the medic, though she didn't know what she'd done to deserve it.

"Morning, doc," he said.

"Will you stop?" Christina hissed, taking the top clipboard from the pile. "I'm still a student. The docs will think—"

"What? They don't care."

Christina glanced over at Captain May, scrutinizing a computer screen, while Dr. Vaughn stirred a coffee with his finger. "Well, I don't like it. It's presumptuous. You're tempting fate. I haven't graduated yet. So cut it out."

"Yes, ma'am." He gave her a salute.

Giving him a suspicious glare, she headed off to collect her first patient, whom she found in the waiting room, bending forward in his seat.

"Pain in my gut," he supplied, once she'd maneuvered him into a curtained bay. Christina took a quick history; he'd been out bush with his unit for the past two weeks. The pain had started overnight after they'd arrived back, and now it was worse. Christina examined the man's belly with growing concern; the pain was in the lower quadrants and he looked distinctly green. Mentally, she went through possible explanations for abdominal pain, looking for reasons to rule each one in or out. Pleased that she was getting the hang of this, she found Dr. Vaughn at the reception desk and quickly relayed the details. "I'm concerned about appendicitis," she finished.

"Absolutely," he agreed a minute later when he'd seen the patient himself. "So what do we do now, Dr. Price?"

Christina hesitated, but her confidence had grown enough not to panic, and to think about the options. She knew the unit wasn't equipped for surgery; maybe it was time to transfer the patient to the hospital. She suggested this to Dr. Vaughn.

"Well, before we do that, let's organize an x-ray, see what that shows."

Christina then had to wait. Travers found her loitering by the front desk. "Possible appendicitis," she explained.

The next moment, Katie appeared with her own clipboard. "Tetanus booster," she said, heading towards the cold store.

"Captain May okay that shot?" Travers called after her.

Silence.

"Katie?"

She appeared again, reading the date off the pre-packed vaccination syringe box. "Yes, of course," she said. "Double-check the date for me?"

Christina watched as Travers stepped over, tilting the pack. "It's good," he said, then, "You know those pre-pack needles are blunt, right? Let me show you a change-out. Kinder."

Katie rolled her eyes, but followed him back into the store feigning a smile. Then Christina spotted Dr. Vaughn standing in the hall holding a film and trotted towards him.

"Come and look at this," he said with amusement, throwing the x-ray up on the light box. "See."

Christina peered into the dark field with its bright white shapes of bones: the base of the ribs, the stacked column of the spine, the curve of the pelvis. The fainter whites between them were internal organs. She ran her finger over the different regions, not really knowing what she was looking for. "Wait, what's this?" she asked, pointing to the faint, knotty loops across the abdomen.

Dr. Vaughn grinned. "That," he said. "Is stool. Your patient's backed up from here to Sunday. Probably a combination of ration-pack food, low water intake and not wanting to take a dump outdoors. There's no troubling history. Enema should fix it. You want to give it?"

That afternoon, as Christina was replacing her last chart, she described the case to Travers. "He went to the bathroom within half an hour. An hour later, he felt great again. I'd have had him admitted for appendicitis and evacuated over to Townsville General." She shook her head glumly.

Travers grinned. "So, potentially serious problem turns out to be just something jammed up the back passage? Sounds about right. Actually, sounds like a few commanding officers I know. But you're learning. What else do you expect? Better to be overcautious. And you haven't seen what things are like out field."

Christina glanced into the waiting area. No more patients. "What are things like out field?"

"Well, imagine you get up at dawn, in your pit for clearance. That's the defensive point around your position." Quickly, he sketched the arrangement on a notepad. "The pits are simply points around the camp, dug in to provide some cover. You're eating ration packs, and the food's all right, but you don't get much time to eat – maybe ten minutes in the morning and a few minutes here and there through the day. It's stinking hot and you're carrying ninety pounds, maybe more. You might be patrolling all day, setting ambushes, or practicing attacks, so you have trouble keeping up your water intake, and you've only got what you can carry – maybe four liters. You're on alert all the time. Once you stop for the night, you have to set up your camp and pits, and then you'll be on sentry, and probably on a few hours' piquet overnight – that's a rotation through watch, who stays up to keep an eye out for the enemy. There's not much time for thinking about what you're eating or drinking.

You're focused on the mission. Then the next day, you do it all again."

"Sounds intense."

He nodded. "The only thing worse is being an officer. Because while the rest of the guys are sleeping, the officers are preparing orders, trying to hold everything together so they can get the best out of everyone. Don't tell Aiden I said that, though. The official line is that we grunts are the awesome ones."

Christina rubbed her face. "Puts my bad days in perspective."

"Come on, you're doing all right. You better be – I'm putting in enough effort."

"Not here. I meant work last night."

"Bad how?"

Christina hesitated. She would never normally talk about such things but she knew Travers wouldn't let it go. "Two drunk guys ordered ten pizzas, then refused to pay for them. So I had to ring my boss, whereupon they decided the delivery was wrong after all and they didn't want it. Carlo was furious." She didn't mention that after covering her rent in Brisbane, she was low on fuel money and not sure if she'd make it through her shifts before payday. And that her mother had called at midnight, wanting to *talk*, but then became bored after five minutes and hung up.

"Well, that's crazy," Travers said. "You need a bouncer to come with you."

"What's crazy?" put in Katie, who'd just reappeared from the minor procedures room.

"Nothing," said Christina, checking her watch. "Are you done? We should go and interview John before visiting hours are over."

Travers raised an enquiring eyebrow.

"We have to do a case assignment," Katie explained. "Chris found a patient over at the hospital."

"Why aren't you doing it here?"

Christina shrugged, picking up her bag. "We have to do a neurological presentation, and I haven't seen one here yet."

"Just wait for sports day," said Travers. "I'll find you a few concussions. Pity it's not on busted knees. I could find you heaps of those."

Christina smiled. "Coming, Katie?"

"Actually, Captain May's removing a lesion and said I could suture. But you go," Katie added.

"It's a pair assignment," Christina complained.

"And I'll totally pull my weight in any follow-up, I swear. I'll come over on Friday."

By the time she reached the ward, Christina had tamped down her annoyance, determined instead to make progress with the case study. She found John in much the same position as on the previous evening, still watching Mount Stuart through the window. This afternoon a haze had descended over the blue-green hide of the mountain. His leg was raised, the tent gone, a backslab-cast now visible running from hip to ankle. He looked uncomfortable but resigned. She glanced at his bedside table for clues about him; other patients had flowers from relatives, books they were reading. But John had nothing.

"Mr. Hunt? It's Christina. I said I'd come back today."

"Yeah. I changed my mind. I don't want to—" He frowned, and tipped his head to look behind her. "Where's the other student?"

"Not coming," said Christina.

"Scared of me?" asked John hopefully.

Christina laughed. "Scared of work, I think."

He grunted. "Gone Jack on you, then?"

"I'm sorry?"

"Gone Jack. Pissed off and let you do all the work."

"She decided to stay in the clinic." Christina sat, eager not to miss her opportunity. "Um, how's the leg?" she tried.

"Broken in five places," he said, curt.

Christina winced. "I can't imagine how painful that must have been. Do you remember anything about the accident?"

"Just waking up."

She waited. When he said nothing more, she tried something simpler. "Do you have any allergies, to food or medicines?"

"No."

"Any medical history you could tell me about?"

"Nothing important."

"Any family come to visit you?"

"No."

And so it went on. She'd soon exhausted a long line of questions without learning anything. The faith Daniella had in her was clearly misplaced. She wasn't going to get anything out of him. Finally, she put down her pen, casting around for another direction. Unconsciously, her fingers had found the scar on her palm. She caught him looking and hastily picked up the pen again.

"Have you ever been to Brisbane?" she asked.

"Where did that come from?"

Christina shrugged. "I'm from Brisbane. I was trying something different."

"You're not from Brisbane. I know a local when I see one."

Surprised by his certainty, Christina took a moment to form her response. "I only grew up here. Brisbane's home now."

"Really?" He seemed interested now. "Why'd you come back then?"

"I needed somewhere to do my rotation."

"Staying at a hotel?" he pressed, his focus intense.

"No, at my aunt's."

"Ah. And does—"

But suddenly Christina didn't want to play anymore. She was the one meant to be asking the questions. She got up and crossed to the window, looking out on the mountain just as he'd been doing when she walked in. The western face was golden as the sun descended, deeper swathes of green showing the shadowed spurs. She rubbed at the scar on her hand and took a deep, silent breath. Just a few seconds, that was all she needed to compose herself.

"Making it hard for you, am I?" John asked from behind her.

Christina shook her head.

"Hazy day," he went on. "Been a dry winter, after two wet summers. So there's two years of bone-dry fuel load out there, just ready to go up. Something's burning already." He paused. "The smell sets my teeth on edge."

Christina glanced back. He'd screwed up his nose, his hard eyes fixed on the mountain, as if daring it to combust right then and there. Something in that look told her he'd just skimmed the surface of something large and lodged in his psyche.

Then he nodded at her. "What happened to your hand?"

Christina dropped her worrying fingertips. "Nothing."

She took the chair again but didn't pick up her notebook. She would have to leave soon. Frustration prompted her next question. "Mr. Hunt, are you sure you don't remember anything about the accident? Were you on your way to meet someone, anything like that?"

He sighed. "Look, I saw a beat-up old Belmont across the road. I used to ... Well, they're good to do up that's all. So I thought I'd take a look. Next thing I was waking up, and you know the rest."

"I have to admit, the Belmont's my ride."

"I did wonder," he muttered, his lips pulling at the apparent irony.

"Do you restore cars, then?" she asked.

But John refused to say more, the discussion shut down.

"Okay," she said finally. "Thank you ... for your time."

She trudged back to the empty nurses' station and peered

into the office. Daniella's head rested on the desk, her long eyelashes closed.

"How did you go?" she called, as Christina was attempting to creep away.

Christina turned back apologetically. "I didn't mean to wake you."

"You didn't." Daniella straightened up, clutching her coffee mug. "I was just resting my eyes. So?"

Christina leaned against the doorway. "Nothing, really. Doesn't remember anything about the accident, nothing about family. He mentioned that he'd restored cars, but I couldn't get any more from him about that. I think I'm just wasting your time."

Daniella stood up. "Why don't you come and have a cup of coffee with me? I want you to go through everything he told you."

A few minutes later, Christina was stirring the instant brew with a plastic spoon in the staff kitchen while she went back over the scant information John had given her. "So, you see, nothing," she finished. "He can only remember seeing my car across the road before the accident. He was crossing the road for a closer look. I feel really bad about that."

"Anything else?" asked Daniella, warming her hands on a chipped china mug.

"Oh, he said he didn't like the smell of smoke. You can see the haze outside today," she explained. "I'm sorry, I hate to sound selfish, but he doesn't have any neurological signs. I can't make a case report out of him. I'm going to have to find another patient for my assignment."

"That's a tough one," Daniella admitted. "But Christina, you've honestly no idea how little he's said to anyone else. Give it some time, okay? I know you have to pass exams, but it's more important to learn how to really do this job. He's easy to brush off. But there's something there, I'm certain of it. We had to pin his leg, and the consultant's not sure about how it's healing yet. Give it a few days and try again. He's going to be here for a while. You don't have to find a perfect neurological case and giving you neurological is arbitrary anyway. You can write about trying to establish the history. Why don't you run with it?"

Daniella's faith held Christina's broken confidence together like a thin thread of spider silk. And for a second, it was fifteen years ago, a different doctor, but the same kindness and support. A white bandage on her hand. *It's all right, you don't have to go back there.*

Tears prickled her eyelids. Christina blinked to clear them. "Okay."

Daniella sipped thoughtfully. "You know my brother, don't you?"

A warmth crept up Christina's neck. "Ah, sort of."

"He was asking about you at dinner last night."

The flush reddened her cheeks. "Oh. He's friends with the medic at the base clinic, and he gave me a lift home after a party one time. Seems nice though," she said carefully, not wanting to say more and give herself away.

Daniella beamed. "Oh, he's lovely. Just very hard to reach at times." She laughed. "I'm afraid he'll forget to come to my wedding, or, you know, have to run off and do something important instead. It has happened before. I shouldn't complain, because that's his job, but I do miss him."

Christina's eyes drifted to the engagement ring that hung on a gold chain around Daniella's neck. "I'm sure he'll be there," she said, hoping it was true. Daniella was so kind, she didn't deserve to be disappointed.

"I'm going on," said Daniella, making a shooing motion. "Take your coffee and go home. I've got discharges to do. See you another day."

Christina paused at the door. "Daniella … did Aiden tell you about me getting lost on the base?"

Daniella laughed. "You too, huh? No, he just said to be nice to you because you have to put up with Travers."

Chapter 10

The rest of the week sped past. On Wednesday Travers drilled her on first-aid scenarios, before an afternoon working on the essay and a long shift at Carlo's. Thursday was filled with blood-test requests, including one patient with suspected Ross River fever, which turned out to be regular flu. Christina then spent a reasonable portion of Friday cleaning up an army lawyer who'd come off his pushbike and managed to score a deep puncture wound to the back of his calf from the sprocket, and who'd waited a few days before coming in to have it checked out.

"I couldn't really see it," he explained.

"It didn't hurt?"

"Oh yeah, and it kept on bleeding. But I figured that would clean it."

Christina shook her head as she inspected the deep red-rimmed, angry wound, which still sported a ring of grease. Later, after he'd been patched up and bandaged, had a tetanus booster and limped out with an antibiotic script, she and Travers spent ten minutes trying to work out the mechanics of the accident.

"I mean, did he get tangled in the chain?" asked Travers, twisting his leg around an imaginary bike.

"Said he couldn't remember. Just that he was on the ground with his leg bleeding, and you can see the imprint of the sprocket."

Travers shook his head. "Lawyers. Who knows."

"Would it be wrong of me to have hoped he'd hit his head?" she asked.

"As long as you don't say it out loud," Travers said, tapping his nose.

For despite Christina's prayers to the gods of med students and neurology, no suitable patient had presented themselves for the case study. So when she arrived home early that evening, she wrote up her limited notes on John Hunt, and tried several times to reach Katie – who, despite promises to come around and talk about their assignment, hadn't showed to the clinic or at Harriet's. Giving up, Christina crammed down a dinner of crackers and cheese before her shift.

She was locking up the house at quarter to seven, her driver's cap on crooked and her bag in her teeth, when she heard a car pull up in the street behind her. She twisted to look, and found a sun-bleached green Holden Commodore. The driver pushed the door open. Christina only needed to catch the rhythm of his walk to recognize Aiden. She dropped her bag as he approached.

"Bad time?" he asked.

"Oh, hi. I'm just …" Christina stopped, taking in his worn jeans, white t-shirt, and the pair of dark aviators tucked into the neck of his shirt. Man, he looked good. "I'm on my way to work," she finished.

"Nice hat," said Aiden. "This is going to be fun."

Christina tipped the hat down to cover her blush as she walked to the Belmont. She'd thought he was kidding about coming along on her shift. She didn't want him to leave, but neither did she want him to see her in her awful red uniform, and in the horrible Belmont all night. She pulled open her door, torn.

He saw her expression. "You don't want me to come?"

"It's not that," she said quickly. "I just think … you'll be bored."

Aiden laughed. "I doubt it. Would it help if I told you it's been a really long week and I don't want to sit in my room tonight? I'm happy to drive around and talk. But I'll leave if that's what you want."

She hesitated, imagining how she'd feel if he drove away. "Okay, then."

With a satisfied grin, Aiden folded himself into the Belmont's bench seat and pulled the map book onto his lap, the Post-it notes fluttering like flags.

Christina had to admit, after the first delivery with Aiden directing her through the winding streets in the foothills of Castle Hill, that it was much easier than finding her way alone, which involved trying to memorize where she was going, and making sideswipes at the map when she inevitably got lost. Aiden had slipped into some kind of work mode, relaxed and companionable rather than talkative, one long arm along the Belmont's open window, the other spreading the map book on his knee. He took the odd work call, which with all the army jargon Christina found largely incomprehensible.

His presence seemed to accelerate time, probably because she wasn't so panicked about finding addresses or that people might refuse to pay. As they headed back to Carlo's after the first three double runs, the Belmont rattling, windows down to catch the evening breeze, Christina's mood was much lighter than usual.

"Sorry the ride isn't so great," she said.

"What do you mean? This is nostalgic. I used to own a Belmont and I'm sorry I sold it. And I've been in a lot worse."

"Don't know about that," she muttered, as the Belmont's CV joints clunked alarmingly around a corner and the fuel light blinked on.

Aiden glanced at her. "Well, sixteen hours in the back of a Herc isn't great. Neither's fanging across country in a Bushmaster with a lunatic driver. Done a fair bit of both. Turn right, here."

Christina made the turn. "Where does sixteen hours in a Herc get you?"

Aiden looked away. "Somewhere you probably don't want to go on holiday."

The conversation was interrupted as Christina picked up her next delivery. When she returned with the boxes, her stomach growling at the smell, Aiden was flicking through a stack of white cards from the glove box.

"What are these?" he asked.

"Anatomy flip cards," she said. "I tell myself I'll look at them between deliveries, but I never seem to have the time."

"Aha." Aiden rubbed his hands. "How about some multitasking then? What is the origin and insertion of the rectus abdominis? That sounds dirty, by the way. Next left," he added.

Christina suppressed a smile, sneaking a look across at him. "Er, origin …"

They fell into an easy rhythm of cruising and quizzing, winding through the suburban streets as the moon rose and the night deepened. But increasingly, Christina's eyes flicked to the light on the dash. She chewed her lip, her anxiety rising as she wondered whether the fuel supply would last the night.

"What's the nerve supply for the gluteus maximus?"

"Shit," she mumbled as they headed downhill and the fuel light refused to go off. She had no cash for petrol. She'd never been approved for a credit card, not that it would have been a good idea anyway. She'd been hoping to hold out until she got her pay from Carlo on Monday.

"I'm pretty sure that's at least a few inches off. You got this one before." Aiden tapped the card on his forehead, miming psychic transference.

Without warning, in the face of Aiden's relaxed attitude, Christina snapped. She pulled into the curb, stopping the car with a jerk. "Why are you doing this? Did Travers put you up to it?"

Aiden turned to look at her. "Put me up to what?"

"Coming to work with me, quizzing me on stuff, being ... *nice*."

"Being nice?"

"Yes." She stared out at the road, feeling exposed in the glow of the streetlight above, the scar on her palm palpable under her grip. She hoped he'd just get out and she could deal with this problem on her own.

Aiden's tone now carried the burred edges of command. "I do something wrong?"

"No. Just ... no."

He took a breath. "You know, your fuel light's on. There's a servo up ahead. If you're going to chuck me out, can it wait till then? It's a long enough walk back as it is."

"Fine." Moodily, Christina encouraged the Belmont back onto the road, then into the service station, her hand lingering on the keys after she killed the engine. She'd have to put in five bucks of tomorrow's food money, and if he asked why she hadn't filled it up ... well, she'd think of something. Then, turning, she realized that Aiden had already vacated the passenger seat. Jumping out, she found him pumping the petrol, the total already past fifteen dollars.

"What are you doing?" she demanded, horrified.

"Being *nice*," he shot back.

Christina felt the grimy fear trickle through her gut. A full tank cost close to a hundred dollars. She'd be late with her rent. Or have to ask Carlo for her pay early. She reached her hand out to the door post, feeling sick. Aiden glanced up and saw her face. "You feeling ill?"

Christina leaned against the Belmont, her hat dangling from her hand, her limbs weak as the adrenaline ebbed away. "No," she managed. The breeze tickled a tendril of hair against her cheek. If only he knew what he'd just done. She just wanted the shift to be over, so she could go home and somehow sort this out. She eased her wallet from her pocket, ready to take the hit.

He shook his head. "Already done." He gestured to the autopay. "I swiped at the start. My shout."

"Why did you do that?" Christina didn't feel any better. The panic proved difficult to shift.

"Hoping it would improve my chances of not being chucked out. Can I get a ride back to my car, at least?"

She stared at him, looking for traces of mockery, or pity. Nothing. He simply seemed ready to accept whatever fate she'd decided for him. "I suppose," she said.

"Good enough for me," he said as they climbed back in, the mood tense. As Christina restarted the engine, he said, "I mean, I'd rather know what I did. Though it make a better story to kick me out. I could say, there was this girl once in Townsville, real nice good-looking girl I just enjoyed hanging out with, and she suddenly went nuts and kicked me out of her Belmont. Had to walk all the way back to my car. Never did work out what happened."

"You enjoy hanging out with me?" she asked, pulling out of the service station. *You think I'm good-looking?*

"Yeah. You're interesting. Especially at moments like this." Aiden was looking out the window now, his fingers playing on the seat. "You know, once, years ago, long before I went through officer training, Travers and I got left out in the field. We were on exercise, in full gear – webbing, pack, weapon, everything. Stinking hot summer, and the CO thought it would be a great joke to leave us stranded. He didn't like Travers too much. Travers had been rubbing the guy up the wrong way for weeks."

"What did you do?" Christina asked, intrigued in spite of herself.

Aiden gave a sly grin. "We navigated back to camp overnight. They were searching for us by then, but we holed up when we heard them coming. We snuck in just before dawn and Travers found the CO's tent—" He broke off. "I probably shouldn't tell you this."

Christina pulled up outside Carlo's. "You can't stop there!"

Aiden laughed. "Travers had this chemical stuff that stank like a sewer, and he sprayed it all over the CO's gear. The guy had to put up with the smell for the rest of the week until we went home. It was pretty funny watching the other brass avoid him."

"Didn't you get caught?"

"No, that was the best part. We snuck out again and circled back to the searchers a few miles out. For all anyone knew, we were out all night."

Christina laughed. "And why shouldn't you have told me that?"

"Firstly, because I wouldn't want you to get a false impression of the incredible integrity of the Australian armed forces." He gave her a wink. "And I wouldn't want you to think I'd have done that to you, if, you know, you'd chucked me out back there. But I can be sneaky. I've got skills. You didn't even see me swipe my card, did you?"

Christina snorted, reaching for her door handle. "Don't worry, I'm taking you back to your car. My shift should be done now, anyway."

"I know," said Aiden, climbing out.

"What does that mean?" she asked, catching a tone.

"You'll see."

When Christina had finished counting her till and signing out, she found Aiden leaning against the Belmont, holding a pizza box. "You know, Carlo's a pretty nice guy. How about a trip up there for dinner?" he asked, tipping his head towards the dark shadow of Castle Hill.

Christina glanced towards the looming mountain. "No, I don't want to go up there. And don't talk to Carlo again. I don't want him liking you more than me. I need this job," she said, making a joke to soften the rejection.

Aiden only looked amused. They ate the pizza perched on the Belmont's bonnet in Harriet's driveway. Christina ate in the exhausted relief that came at the end of the day when there was nothing more to do. No longer occupied with worrying, she couldn't ignore the effect Aiden had on her.

He leaned back against the windscreen, his long legs stretched out on the hood, one arm behind his head. He looked like the kind of man who knew how to relax on command, despite the after-hours work calls. And he didn't seem to think less of her after the incident in the car. She was suddenly aware that she'd never done anything like this before, or known anyone like him.

"You and your aunt must be close," he said. "Lending you the house while she's overseas."

"I haven't seen her in years," Christina found herself saying.

"Really?"

Christina let silence ebb the pressure from the topic, then neatly steered away. "Aiden, do you know what 'going Jack' means?"

"It means being lazy and making it hard for someone else. Very army term. You hear that from Travers?"

"No, a patient at the hospital. I was talking to him for a case study we have to do this term. Katie and I are supposed to do it together."

"Dani told me."

"She did?"

"She says you're extremely dedicated."

Christina looked away. "Do you want a drink? There's bottles of water in the house."

Aiden paused. "I'm fine. I should go anyway."

Disappointment twisted in Christina's chest. She hadn't made sense of him yet, begun to understand why he was hanging out with her. All she knew was that she enjoyed it. She closed the pizza box and climbed down from the bonnet, resigned to the idea that it would be the last time.

"Are you coming on this trip tomorrow?" Aiden asked suddenly.

"You're going on that?" she said, surprised.

He gave her an easy smile. "I wasn't going to, but we sent

off a deployment today, and Travers is insisting. But Crystal Creek is beautiful. If you're only here a few weeks, you should see it. Can I persuade you?"

He slipped off the bonnet, and Christina caught the scent of aftershave on his skin. He was looking at her as if she was the deciding factor in his plans. She found herself nodding.

"See you tomorrow," he said.

Chapter 11

"What are you doing here?"

The next morning at eight, Christina opened the door expecting Katie and instead found Aiden and his battered Commodore.

"Travers sent me," Aiden said. "We're meeting the others at the petrol station near the airport. Travers likes their pies."

Overnight, clouds had rushed across the sky, bringing depth to the greens of Harriet's garden and abating the intensity of the morning sun, but Christina could still feel warm air on her legs as she folded herself into the car's deep, comfortable seats. The Commodore was old but well maintained; such a novelty to travel in a car that didn't smell of stale food delivery, or have parts missing from the dash, or an oil light that lit up like a strobe.

When they pulled into the petrol station a few minutes later, the others were congregating around Travers' Monaro and a RAV4 with an open top. She recognized three faces from the party, all with the same clean army look she'd been seeing for three weeks now. Among them, in a floaty pink sundress, was Katie.

"Hey, you actually came!" Katie exclaimed as Christina reluctantly climbed out of the car. Several sets of eyes swiveled in her direction.

"This is Charlie, Nathan and Mel," said Katie, pointing

around at two men – one tall and sandy-haired with a crooked smile, the other dark and stocky – and a woman, who was petite but athletic-looking, her thighs toned in a pair of denim shorts. Travers himself was sculling an energy drink.

Aiden called across, "So, are we all just standing around?"

"No, sir," said Travers, crushing the can in his fist and opening the Monaro's door. Christina watched as Katie slid into the passenger seat, winding down the window. "See you up there." The other three climbed into the RAV4.

Christina turned back to the Commodore, and found Aiden watching the departing Monaro, his eyebrows raised. "You know anything about what's going on there?" he asked.

She shook her head. "No idea."

They were soon on the highway, Townsville falling away behind as Aiden drove with sure hands on the wheel. Christina had never been this far north and she rested her head on the window, watching the changing landscape. She still had trouble accepting where they were going.

"Would you like to brave some conversation or shall I put on some music?" Aiden asked after a few minutes.

"Will you be offended if I choose the music?"

He laughed, and flicked the dial, finding a soft instrumental tune that melded the country twang of a steel guitar with a flowing rhythm that suited the unending road. Christina sighed, her body relaxing. Blue hills rose in the distance, and she watched eagles lofting over the grass, tails steering in the breeze.

When they eventually turned west, the hills had crept into the near distance, their edges sepia-brushed where fire had licked them, and by the time they turned again, onto a narrow dirt track, the land was undulating in the lee of the mountains. Driving through gums and grasses, they bounced over corrugations, and pale clouds of dust billowed in the air from the cars ahead. Finally, the three cars pulled up in a cleared space beneath some trees. As the dust settled, Christina spotted tents and campervans in the distance to her right.

Slowly, she pushed her door open. Air moved across every leaf and blade of grass, smelling clean and faintly of resin. Somewhere ahead, she heard running water. Christina's heart swelled, nine parts with anticipation for this place and one with the fear of it evaporating.

She was finally here.

To steady herself, she braced a hand on the Commodore, aware of Aiden beside her. She smiled, shyly, caught in wonder. His responding smile was warm, unselfconscious, and sent a thrill through her heart.

"Let's go!" Katie broke the restful quiet. She had a beach bag over her shoulder and was dragging Travers by the hand towards a break in the trees.

Grabbing her own bag, Christina followed. Down a short wooden boardwalk, the bush opened up and she found herself on a slope above a rocky outcrop rising from a flowing creek, the water so clear that she could see the ripple pattern on the sandy bottom. Travers led the way into the water with a whoop while Katie and the others stripped down to their swimsuits. Two other pairs of swimmers were waving and shouting welcomes from the water, their German accents carrying.

"Come on, Chris!" yelled Katie. "I'll race you to the other side!"

Standing back from the rock, Christina winced. She had pictured herself floating in the water, in the quiet, imagining she really was in some distant and magical kingdom.

Aiden briefly touched her shoulder. "You want to swim?"

Christina shivered, wanting to feel the warmth of his hand again, and trying to think of a way to explain that Crystal Creek was a mythical place in her mind, and she didn't want to share it with Katie. Didn't want the moment spoiled.

"I'm just not feeling the group vibe today," she said, feeling lame.

Aiden looked over to where Nathan was trying to pass Travers a beer, the big man evidently distracted as Katie stood on the rock in her tiny white bikini, barracking for encouragement to dive in. He turned back to Christina, and dropped his voice. "I know somewhere better."

"Like where?"

"Up the track a bit." For a moment his hand rested in the small of her back, turning her towards the road.

Christina licked her lips at the thrill of his touch. The noisy group seemed to fade; Aiden had tapped some instinct inside her, one that was powerful and brave, that wanted to discover the magic she knew was here. "I don't know," she managed to say, to quieten the fear that she might not find it … or that she might just find magic with him, too. "You might be some kind of axe murderer."

Aiden's mouth twitched. "Well, it is a state forest, and there *are* a lot of backpackers around …"

Christina laughed. "That's in very poor taste."

His smile was playful. "You think *that's* poor? You've clearly not spent enough time with infantry." He gently pulled her hand. "Come on. You haven't seen the best part yet."

Back in the Commodore, they rattled up the track for a few more minutes, Christina feeling the thrill of having left the others behind. The road ended at a fence along an old, rusty water pipe. The place was deserted, only the low buzz of insect noise disturbing the quiet.

"I've actually seen plenty of infantry guys at the clinic," Christina was saying as they climbed out.

"I'm sure you have." He led her through the gate and across a ford in a shallow, rocky waterway. "Travers says you've become good at sticking needles in them, too."

"Did he tell you how terrible I was to begin with? I'm just glad I've stopped bleeding people everywhere." The sandy path led them up the hill now, then left, weaving through eucalypts. Christina could hear water ahead.

"He's impressed with you," said Aiden.

"He said that?"

"Not exactly. But I can tell. He's usually pretty hard on the students." He looked at her. "What, you don't believe me?"

Christina kept walking, a frown pulling at her eyebrows as she tried to understand why the idea bothered her. She was so used to doing poorly; the expectation she could be good brought pressure, and the fear she'd disappoint not only Travers, who'd been so kind, but herself as well. Her experience had taught her to expect the worst – then there were no surprises.

The sound of tumbling water drew closer. And then, suddenly, the bush gave way to a monolithic rock, part of a seam of stone that formed the hillside. Through this, the creek had carved a pale blue pool. Christina then saw another pool above, and another, each linked by a gurgling waterfall, as though the water were the thread of life in this mountainside. An oasis amid bush so often ravaged by drought and fire.

"Oh," she breathed, goosebumps prickling on her arms. This was magic.

Without a word, Aiden started down a carved stone staircase towards the first pool. Christina followed him, and soon stood beside the water, the sun hot on her back. Aiden pulled off his shirt, and Christina's attention caught on the edges of his tattoo before he dived into the depths.

Self-consciously, Christina peeled off her t-shirt. She didn't have a swimsuit, making do with an old black sports top and a pair of quick-dry shorts. But she forgot this as soon as she slid into the cool water. The worn rock slabs were smooth under her hands, the surface of the pool rippling from the waterfall's entrance. She floated in the shallows, surprising two striped fish with eye-spot tails, who darted away.

Aiden surfaced and drifted over. "Was I right?" he asked with a grin.

"Yes," she admitted, her voice soft. "This is the best part."

He propped himself on a nearby rock. "Can I ask you

something?" he said casually.

Christina turned over, buoyed by the sublime water. "Mmm?"

"Last night, when you were going to chuck me out of the car, did you have money for fuel?"

Christina stiffened, and focused her attention on the rock in front of her. "Why are you asking?"

"You were watching the fuel light for at least an hour. And we passed a petrol station about five times."

Christina snuck a glance at him. His head was tipped back against the rock, as if speaking to the sky, his eyes closed. She didn't detect judgement in his tone, only curiosity. And whether it was his manner or the soothing water, for the first time in her life, Christina didn't feel the need to lie about money.

"I burned a lot of cash coming back here for the rotation, and pizza delivery doesn't pay as much as my job in Brisbane," she explained. "I still have to cover rent and books and things like that. But don't pay for fuel like that," she added.

"Can't stop me," he said. "I could get a squad of guys to go over to your place and fill it up every night if I wanted."

"Are you serious?" she asked, alarmed.

"I'm always serious." Then Aiden opened his eyes, turned towards her and smiled. "Okay, joking. Really. But I did enjoy your company. I didn't want the night to end with you pushing the car home."

Christina saw something tender in his eyes before he looked away.

"Come on, there's a natural slide in the rocks, two pools up," he said.

They stayed in the pools for what seemed like hours, then dried out on the flat rocks in the shade, watching the striped fish circling lazily in the azure depths.

"Now I know why all the kids in my class wouldn't shut up about this place," Christina said. "But I'm glad I never knew what it was really like. I'd have been too jealous."

"You never came up here on a rebellious teenage road trip?"

Christina made a face, but here among the beauty of the rocks and trees, there was no sting in the question. "I didn't have friends like that. And I didn't get my license until after I got to Brisbane."

"When did you leave Townsville?"

"Right after high school. I went to Brisbane to try to get into university."

"You didn't want to go here?"

"Never. Besides, I didn't get good enough results to apply for med right away. I had to re-do senior, then science and lift my grades plus working in between. There's an entrance exam. It took me three years just to get in. That's why I'm older than the others." Absently, she rubbed the oval scar on her palm, its puckered surface faded to white.

"That's a nice one," Aiden said, gently tilting her hand towards him. Christina quickly closed her fingers. "I've got these, which you know about," he said, running a hand over his knee. "And these, too," he said more softly, twisting around to show her the pale grooves of deep scars hiding below his ribs.

"What's that from?" she asked.

Aiden chewed his lip. "How's this: I tell you mine, you tell me yours?"

Christina shrugged. "Fine."

"Afghanistan. We were in a convoy heading to a checkpoint. Car in front stopped suddenly, we didn't know why. I think I was climbing out. Next thing I remember is white, just a whiteout. Roadside bomb went off. Copped some shrapnel."

Christina's arms crawled with gooseflesh, and her stomach felt as though it had dropped into the pool below. She couldn't imagine Aiden, sitting beside her so warm and vital, being in such danger, and so matter-of-fact about it.

He took her hand again and traced the outline of her scar. "And you?"

She came right to the edge of telling him. Then, firmly, she closed her hand again. "I can't," she said.

He shrugged. "Another time, then."

Relief flooded through her, almost as sweet as the world around her. It was a perfect day. On the rocks over the waterfall, someone had scratched their initials. In a thousand years, she thought, the water and the wind would have worn the letters but the evidence would probably still be here. She knew her memory was more fragile. So she tried to fix every aspect of this day in her mind, every rock and splash, every detail of Aiden, in case this never happened again. He watched her curiously.

"What are you thinking?" he asked, as she was staring at the dark lines of his tattoo.

"Taking a mental picture. Does that have a story too?"

Aiden peered down at the tattoo, as if he'd forgotten about it. "I was in Bangkok," he said. "On R and R with a mate who liked to draw. He designed it."

"It's so unusual," she said, her eyes following the pattern. Over his chest the lines were delicate and swirling, interlocked with vines, but then the design gradually hardened, becoming jagged shards down his arm, raw and primal.

"At the time, I thought it was a bad idea," he said. "But then my mate was killed a year later, and that changed it for me. Now it's how I remember him."

Christina met his eye. He gave her a small smile, so sad it turned Christina's heart. "I'm so sorry," she whispered. "Can I?" She reached a hand towards him. He caught her fingers in one hand and steered them to the jagged lines on his shoulder.

"Hard edges," he said, moving her fingers slowly across the warm skin into the center of the design, over his chest. "Soft heart."

His attention seemed fixed on her. She could see the depth

of blue in his eyes, the way it grayed at the edges, like the rocks at the edge of the pool. Her lips tingled. The muscles of his chest were smooth and firm under her hand. She was aware of the clean air in her lungs, the hot blood under her own skin, his heartbeat under her fingertips. Her usual caution vanished; there was nothing but this moment. And within it she found herself driven, as if it were natural and easy, to lean in and kiss him.

His lips were soft under hers, so good it was a shock to her senses. In an instant, he deepened the kiss. Christina's breath became short as his hands pulled her closer, her arms sliding around his neck until her fingers stroked the muscles of his back. For a moment she worried that she had no idea what she was doing, and that he would know how inexpert she was, but the fit with Aiden felt perfect. Exploring her mouth, he kissed her upper lip, then her lower, his tongue caressing hers, his arms strong and sure around her.

When they finally broke apart, breathing quickly, his arms cradled her from hip to shoulder, and their foreheads pressed together. Christina had lost herself, only wishing for time to pass at the slowest possible rate.

"Wow," he murmured, releasing his grip.

As reality rushed back in, Christina's cheeks burned and she drew away. "I'm so sorry. I don't know why I did that. I'm going back to Brisbane in five weeks."

"I know," he said. "And I'm … not right for you either. Too old, for a start."

They stared at each other, regret palpable between them, and Christina hastily blinked away tears. Much as she knew it couldn't go anywhere, she still wished he hadn't agreed with her so readily. She scrambled to remember what mattered. Study. Graduate. She would have to return to Brisbane, to her responsibilities there.

Aiden kissed her forehead, his lips lingering on her skin. "You are so lovely," he said. "It can't work. But I wish it could."

His eyes reflected the water. Then a shock of blue above them caught her eye. A Ulysses butterfly, trailing its black wingtips. They watched it together, the urge to kiss again spoken only in how close they sat, though neither moved to act on it, both restrained by their agreement.

Then Aiden stiffened, glancing towards the bush above, at the top of the carved steps. "Do me a favor and stay here?" he said in a low voice.

"What are you doing?" she whispered.

He shook his head, and rose casually, wandering back down to the pool as if he was checking on the gear they'd left under a tree. Then he turned onto the stairs. Halfway up his gaze fixed on something in the trees. "You bastard, Travers," he said loudly.

For a moment, nothing moved. So Aiden picked up a rock and chucked it into the bush. It landed with a solid *thunk*.

"Ow, fuck!" declared a voice. Slowly, the undergrowth shifted and Travers, Nathan and Charlie all emerged, dressed in nose-to-tail camouflage suits, faces painted, grass stuck in their hats, as if they'd sprung into existence from the scrub. Christina blushed, wondering how long they'd been there.

"Shit, Travers, we must be losing our touch," said Charlie, rubbing his side.

"Nah, you can't sneak up on Captain Bell."

"Didn't have to throw a fucking rock, though. Especially when we brought the beer."

At that moment, Katie burst from the top of the path, still in her white bikini, laughing. "What do you reckon, Chris? Is this cool or what?"

And all Aiden could do was turn back, a look of regret and apology passing between them. They both knew the moment was over.

Chapter 12

At ten o'clock the next morning, after one of the worst night's sleep of his life, Aiden groaned and pulled the pillow over his head. His unrested brain felt stuffed with cotton wool, the sun streaming in the window like rays of murder.

Dragging himself vertical, he checked his phone, expecting to see missed calls from his boss, and from Travers. Of the first, he found three. But nothing from Travers. And if he allowed himself to think about it, nothing from Christina either.

"Shit," he muttered, throwing off the sheets. It was probably a good thing. She'd been in his mind all night, sweetly stealing his sleep, his brain replaying the kiss over and over. And as the night had gone on, his mind had taken him past sweetness, imagining what would have happened if he hadn't been so quick to say it couldn't work. Then, in the logic of dreams, Christina became Tracey, the past replaying itself. Each time, Aiden had woken in a sweat. He'd calm himself, remember where he was, and then it would begin again, back at Crystal Creek with that amazing kiss. It was a change from the darker dreams he sometimes had, but no more conducive to rest.

Trying to distract himself, he returned calls, then pulled together his gear for the next day. He had range practice, then the training exercise starting the day after. Plenty to focus on.

And yet he found himself playing with his phone, contemplating calling Christina. He wished they hadn't been interrupted yesterday afternoon; once the rest of the group had turned up, Katie had dragged Christina away, and she hadn't said much on the drive back. Aiden felt a restless energy in his chest. The friendship that had been forming between them now felt uncertain. Possibly, he might never see her again. He didn't like the idea.

But maybe it was better that way.

So he made a different call and Travers answered on the third ring.

"What happened to you?" Aiden asked. "I thought you were hot to see that boat today."

"Nah," said Travers vaguely.

"I was expecting harassment. Quite unlike you."

Travers laughed. "I figured you'd be sleeping in."

Picking up on Travers' innuendo, Aiden sank onto the bed, staring at the plain white ceiling, trying to stop the memories of Christina playing themselves out again. Is that where things could have gone if he'd let them? And would it have been so wrong if they had?

"You still there?"

"Yeah," Aiden said, shaking himself back into the present. "You having second thoughts about this dive thing?"

"No. I was just busy."

Travers was definitely being evasive, and Aiden had only seen him this way once before. And that had nearly gone very badly wrong. A shiver of worry shot through him. "Travers, this is me you're talking to."

The big man snorted. "Appreciate you looking out for me. But I *was* busy. And what's the deal with you and Christina?"

"No deal. She's going back to Brisbane soon anyway."

"Didn't look like that from the long grass. Thought you might be finally moving on. She's a nice girl."

"Give it a rest, Travers. So, have you gone cold on this boat?"

"No way. She's got a twin outboard, already fitted with an air compressor. It's perfect."

"Just remember that's only the first part," Aiden said. "You need new gear, and the business will need to be set up – registered, insured. And you want a contract for that work you've been promised."

Travers grunted. "I don't suppose I can convince you to join the business?"

"You know I can't leave."

"I know you don't really want to. But what would you do if you didn't have a choice?"

Aiden was suddenly aware of the disparity between them. He was still doing what he loved. For the first time he found himself considering: could he do something else, if he had to? "I don't know, Travers," he said honestly.

"Fair enough. So what about next weekend?"

Aiden sat back up on the edge of his bed. "I can't. It's Dani's wedding. I'm driving out Saturday morning."

"Are you serious? You're going on a three-day exercise, where you'll be run off your ass, coming back Friday on almost no sleep, then driving out west on Saturday to a huge family event that will go all night, and driving back Sunday?"

"Don't suppose you want to come along and keep me awake?"

Travers laughed. "Couldn't drag me off the water. Although if there's going to be drama …"

"Drama?"

"Did you tell your sister about your next job yet?"

Aiden's chest tightened. "No. And I won't be telling her on the weekend. Shit, she doesn't need that. It's—" He stopped, hearing a female voice in the background, asking who was on the phone. The sound became muffled as Travers put his hand over the receiver, but he caught: *It's Aiden.*

"Sorry about that," said Travers a second later.

Aiden guessed. "That Katie with you?"

"Yeah." A pause. "I took her with me to see the boat this morning."

"Travers … you sleeping with a student?"

"Aiden, she's twenty-three. And I've got nothing to do with her sign-off."

But after he'd hung up the phone, Aiden sat there for a few minutes, motionless with surprise. Despite noticing Travers' interest in Katie, he hadn't expected him to get involved with her. Travers had always had strong opinions about dating at work. But Travers was a big boy. Aiden shook it off and looked over his gear. His pack and webbing were battered, the camouflage pattern faded. There were nicks in the plastic of his water canteens, worn spots where he'd carried the gear against his body in a dozen places at home and overseas. Every pocket and piece of hardware was as familiar as his own hands; and yet now it seemed foreign, as though his mind hadn't quite returned from the other-world tranquility of Crystal Creek. Frowning, he stood up. He just needed some sleep, to forget what had happened yesterday, and things would be back to normal.

But thoughts of Christina refused to fade, even after two hours at the range on Monday morning. Then Aiden walked into his office at around ten and found a stack of urgent documents in his in-tray, and a backlog of emails on his computer.

Corporal Stratton knocked on the door a minute later. "The major's been looking for you, sir. One of the excavators is bogged."

Aiden groaned. "How did that happen? It's the bloody dry season."

The corporal shrugged. "One of the Bushmasters is in the shop, too. It's meant to go on the exercise this week." He handed over another three phone messages.

With almost a sense of relief, Aiden knuckled down to

work. The unit was a den of activity before the next day's exercise, and he seemed to spend the day marching back and forth between the office and the depot keeping across the action. When the sun had dragged itself across the sky and seventeen hundred hours had come and gone, he was still knee-deep in his to-do list. Another hour passed. But the shorter the list became, the more restless he was. He played with his phone, checking for calls or messages. His office light was the last on, but the after-hours quiet in the unit didn't soothe him as it usually did.

And then he was dialing, his heart lurching.

"Let me guess," he said a moment later when she answered. "You're about to leave for work?"

Christina paused, and for a moment he wondered if she didn't want to talk to him. Then she laughed. "Don't tell me you want to drive around with me again?"

Relief. "I think I've proved myself useful," he said, a smile spreading across his lips.

"I'm not working tonight, sorry. I've got study to do."

"I won't keep you—"

"It's okay—"

They both broke off, their newfound awkwardness a legacy of the kiss. Aiden shook his head; he hadn't been hung up on a girl like this since high school. A new email blinked into his inbox. He averted his eyes and tried to be an adult. "Listen, Christina. We didn't get the chance to talk much on Saturday afternoon. I didn't want to just leave things like that."

"Okay," she said slowly. "But I didn't know what to say to you. I felt like an idiot."

The knots eased in Aiden's shoulders. "Don't. Really. In a different time and place—" But even as he said it, a stab of longing struck, right down in the base of his gut. And then he knew why he'd backed off so fast: he could never be casual about her. He sensed the edge of a high cliff ahead and he was in danger of going over it. And he couldn't. Not again. He had no idea what to say, just that he couldn't let things end this way.

Christina sighed. "So what happens now? Why did you call?"

"Would you talk to me for a while? I'm still at work and I'm going to be away on exercise for the rest of the week. I want to think about something else."

This seemed to surprise her. "Sure, I guess. What would you like to talk about?"

Aiden realized he was smiling. He leaned back in his chair. "Anatomy. Physiology. Pharmacology. I don't care. Why don't you start with what you're working on?"

Chapter 13

The next morning, Christina walked through the doors of Townsville Hospital with a light step courtesy of her conversation with Aiden the night before, but also feeling a little guilty that she'd left it a whole week before coming to see John again.

The ward's weary nurse nodded Christina through with a motion that revealed how tired the staff were of this patient. "Refused to have his blood test this morning," she said wryly.

John himself seemed improved, however; there was color in his rugged features and the bruising had almost completely faded. He was peering at a square of paper in his hands, and Christina noticed a half-finished game of solitaire abandoned on the bedside table, a barely touched meal tray pushed to the side.

At her approach, he glanced up and tucked the paper in his top pocket. "I thought for a second you were that nurse coming to stick me again."

"No, I'm just here to talk," she said.

"I didn't think you were coming back."

Christina looked down at herself with a mock confused expression. "All evidence points to you being wrong about that. Is this a good time?"

"My leg's broken in five places," he replied. "Pins and everything. Not going anywhere." But he gave her a crooked expression that could have been a smile.

"You sound like you want to, though." She sat down in the chair beside the bed and brought out her notepad and pen.

"I hate how I feel in here, like being in jail. I've done more than enough time with hospitals and nurses—" He broke off and glanced at her, his expression suddenly guarded.

"I thought you said you didn't have any medical history."

"Very clever," he grumbled.

"Mr. Hunt, do you work on the base?"

"What makes you think that?"

"Last time I was here, you mentioned 'going Jack'," she said. "I believe it's an army term."

He nodded grudgingly. "Gave myself away, didn't I. I used to. Not that it's really surprising. Townsville. Army. Must be Friday."

Christina laughed. "I'll take what I can get."

He smiled back, just briefly, and in that moment he was a different man. She glimpsed the person he must have been before the accident, someone with vitality and humor; someone with a life outside of here. Encouraged, she pressed on. "So, what sort of work did you do?"

He shrugged. "I'll give you the short version. I started out as an apprentice electrician. Worked on a heap of different gear, everything from trucks to radios and radar. Really important stuff. Posted all over, worked my way up the chain. Now I'm semi-retired and back here again. That's it."

Christina absorbed this. "What sort of places did you go?"

He looked up at the ceiling, and his voice was very quiet when he spoke again. "Listen, Chris. I don't want to talk about this, all right?"

"Okay, that's fine." Christina paused. The mood had turned on a right angle. Maybe John had some kind of post-traumatic stress disorder from his service. She made a note to come back to it, and looked around the room. "So who brought you the playing cards? I don't imagine it was the nurses."

John caught her tease, and gave a conspiratorial look. "A mate. He came by yesterday, when the coast was clear."

"That's good. What's his name?"

A pause. "Stash. We used to work together."

"Stash, really?" she asked. "How did he get that name?"

"Don't really remember," said John. "And it probably isn't a story suitable for young ears."

After some of Travers' stories, Christina gave him that point. "Is he an electrician too?"

"Mechanic."

"Is he coming to visit again?"

This time John said nothing, and the silence drew out for a long minute. Christina was just forming a new question in her head when he got in first.

"How did you hurt your hand?"

"What?" She looked up from her notes, surprised.

"Your hand. Last week you said it was nothing, like it didn't matter. But that scar looks bad, and you play with it all the time."

"Just a flesh wound, nothing serious," she quipped. But her fingers had already crept protectively over the thick skin of the scar. She parried back, "Why don't you like the smell of smoke?"

His expression darkened. Feeling herself on the edge of a breakthrough, Christina rushed on. "Smell's the most primitive sense, you know. It hooks into memory and emotion without any filtering. When I left Townsville eleven years ago, I remember the sky being all hazy. Fires everywhere. I'd had a shitty time at school, and the day I graduated I had an argument with my ... I had a fight with someone, and now when I smell smoke that's what I think of. I can't help it. It's wired in my brain. Is that how it is for you? Something happened and you relate it to the smell of smoke?"

"What was the problem at school?"

Christina realized she'd revealed more than she intended to. But to her surprise, she found herself opening up to him, the way she never could with someone she knew. "Bullies, mostly," she said. "There was this one kid called Seb – Sebastian. In elementary school, he called me Chrissy-Lice. In high school, it was Chrissy-No-Tits or Surfboard Girl. Stupid kid stuff, but it still hurt." Christina tried and failed to forget the worst things, like when she'd had a blood nose in eighth grade and Seb had told everyone she had AIDS; or when he'd spread a rumor in their senior year that she was sleeping with Mr. Ryan, the math teacher. Every term, there had been something for the other kids to talk about behind their hands. "In senior, he said he looked forward to the day I was bagging his groceries at the supermarket."

"Did you punch him?"

Christina laughed. "Yeah, I did once. All that happened was that he looked smug and I landed in the principal's office, terrified I'd be expelled."

John grunted again. "Well, joke's on him, Miss Medical Student."

Christina sighed, wishing it were that simple. For all Seb's horrible points, he was the one who'd graduated medicine four years ago and was presumably busy establishing his career.

John glanced out the window. Today the sky was brilliant and clear. In his fingertips, he turned the ace of hearts. "There was a fire," he said. "A long time ago."

"I'm sorry," Christina said automatically, hearing the unspoken loss his words surely implied. Possessions, lives; a deep wound she didn't know how to explore. Eventually she asked, "Were you hurt?"

He shook his head. "I'd rather not talk about that either."

Christina put down her pen. She'd hardly written any notes, and what he'd just said felt too personal to document. "I'm sorry if I upset you. Would you like me to go?"

"Just sit a minute," he said. He reached for his deck of cards on the table, squaring the edges, and gave her a half-smile. "I need someone to guard me against that bloody nurse."

Christina glanced back towards the hall, where she could hear the tapping of the keyboard. "What did she do to get on your bad side?"

"She always tells me it won't hurt, and then it bloody does," he complained. "I bet all you medical people do that."

"Actually, I spend a lot of time apologizing to patients. I'm getting better though," she added. Then she told him about Travers teaching her, and some of the cases she'd seen in the clinic, including the soldier she'd thought had appendicitis, but who'd turned out to be constipated. John unexpectedly laughed.

"I should go," she said finally, noticing the time, and with some regret: for the first time she felt as though they'd made some kind of connection.

She'd almost left the room when he called her back. "Tell the nurse you can take the blood test," he said. "You can't be any worse than her."

Christina was worried that the nurse might be offended that John had requested her, but the woman only seemed relieved. Ten minutes later, with the blood taken and sealed for the lab, Christina excused herself again and went looking for Daniella.

"I made a little progress," she told the registrar, who was stacking files for the morning ward round. "He mentioned something about a fire, and he was in the army, too. It's not much, though, and he doesn't really want to talk about it. And I still don't know if there's anything neurological."

"Keep trying," said Daniella, putting an encouraging hand on Christina's arm. "I'm worried about him; he was so closed off when he first came in. And I think he enjoys your company." She glanced down the hall, where a man in a suit had just pushed through the doors, glasses perched on his nose and a stethoscope around his neck. "Look, we're about to start rounds, but come back again soon. We can't send him home until we're sure he can cope."

As she left the ward, Christina was still wondering about

John Hunt. Who was this man who had crossed her path, who didn't want to talk about his past, but who had clearly lost so much? She was bothered by unsketched parts of him, like tendrils at the edges of her mind, light and flickering, and refusing to be caught.

In the base clinic several hours later, still mulling over the enigmatic patient, Christina picked up her next chart and saw a familiar name. Sammy, her patient from three weeks ago with the injured knee, only this time he was evidently in a much worse way. His knee badly swollen, he limped across the floor. After a brief examination, which he grimaced through, Christina gently lowered the leg onto the exam table.

"So, you woke up this morning like this?" she asked.

"Yeah." He stared at the ceiling, his body rigid with pain and worry.

"What was happening yesterday?"

A pause. "We had PT in the afternoon."

"Was that your first one back?"

Another pause. "No. I only took a few days off. It seemed okay."

"Has it been hurting?"

"Yeah, a bit," he admitted.

"All right," she said, peering out to see if Captain May's door was open. "Wait here, okay?"

Twenty minutes later, after Captain May had performed his own assessment and Sammy had been sent back to his room under orders to rest, Christina was distractedly unpacking a training bag with Travers. Concern itched under her skin; Sammy would be sent for imaging tests, suspected of rupturing a cruciate ligament. She imagined surgeons in his future.

"Something on your mind?" Travers asked, laying out the resuscitation doll.

Christina paused with the ECG cables dangling from her

fingers. "It bothers me. If he'd just kept off it and had his physiotherapy until it was healed, he might have been okay."

Travers grunted. "That's how it works a lot of the time."

"Why? He was supposed to avoid stressing it."

"You have to understand the psychology. No matter what the medical orders are, your sergeant might be on your case. And you don't want to fall behind everyone else. Even if something's hurting, a lot of guys will keep pushing to keep up. It's weak to do anything else. Weak to admit you're not a hundred per cent. And you feel like you're not supporting your mates. You understand that, right?"

Christina frowned. "I'm not sure I do."

He laughed. "Yeah you do. You do the same thing every time you don't know how to do something medical. It doesn't feel comfortable to ask for help, especially if you think you're supposed to know it already. You want to be as strong as everyone else."

Christina stared at him, feeling as though she were an insect, caught and mounted. "They do expect us to know," she argued.

"Who's 'they'?"

"The school, the supervisors," she said testily, thinking of the intimidating Professor Green.

"I'm sure they don't. They're putting on an act too, you know. Conditioning you for how work's going to be. You have to fake it till you make it, true, but you still need to know when to ask for help."

Something inside Christina curled tight. "Are you saying I can't do that?"

"No, I'm saying you don't."

Irritated, Christina folded the manikin's bag and changed the subject. "Where's Katie today anyway?"

"Why are you asking me?"

"Because we're supposed to work on our case report, and she hasn't put in any time yet." *And because you were together on the weekend.*

Travers straightened. "Well, that rather sounds like your problem."

Christina bit her tongue. A tense silence grew between them as they finished assembling the materials. Travers had promised to run through several emergency scenarios, but Christina had lost her enthusiasm.

Finally, Travers stepped back and leaned against the wall, his uniform blindingly white against the gray paint. "You want to slug me one, don't you?"

Christina scowled. "Maybe."

"I tend to have that effect on people. And I pushed your buttons pretty hard."

"I don't have buttons."

Travers grinned. "Of course you do. Allow me to demonstrate. Do you like him?"

"Who?" But the red flush was already burning on her neck.

"You know who."

"Are we going to do this or not?" Christina demanded, turning back to the manikin.

Travers reached for the scenario cards, tapped them against his hand. "You told him you're going home in a few weeks. That right?"

"Doesn't sound like any of your business. But yes. I'm only here for this term. I'm heading straight home when it's over."

Travers hesitated before he said, "Sorry. He's my friend. And he's been done over before. I'm just looking out for him."

"What does that mean?" she snapped.

"Just be straight with him, okay?"

Christina gave Travers a look. Nothing was going on between her and Aiden. He'd said it himself, and geography would soon intervene. "Well, like you said, that's my problem, not yours. Now, shall we get on with it?"

Travers shrugged. "Fine. You're a medic with the 1 RAR, and you're deep in country."

"RAR?"

"Royal Australian Regiment. Your lieutenant wandered off and got bitten by a snake. What do you do first?"

Christina sighed, reaching for the bandages. "First, I make a mental note to tell the story to all the other grunts later. Then I move to help."

Travers grinned. "Correct. Now, let's see your compression bandage technique."

But later in the afternoon, despite telling herself she'd brushed off Travers' words, Christina arrived home in an intractable bad mood. When the key stuck in the lock, she kicked the front door in frustration, then realizing she was angry over nothing, told herself to calm down. She would be in no state to study like this. Travers didn't understand what had happened between her and Aiden, and she *did* know how to ask for help.

She could hear running water; the next-door neighbors must be sprinkling their garden again in the heat. She listened, soothed, until she realized that the sound was coming from inside. The key finally turned in the lock; as she threw open the door, the sound became a rush.

"Oh no!"

The noise came from the laundry. A giant puddle was spreading down the tiled hall, and a dark wet circle had crept halfway across the lounge room carpet. Christina hotfooted through the water in the hallway, soaking her shoes, and found a geyser erupting from the washing machine hose. With water spattering her eyelids, she blindly groped for the tap. Thank goodness it was the cold one. After her hand slipped twice, she finally shut off the flow, then stood dripping into the spreading puddle, her body momentarily frozen in horror at the damage.

A minute later, her fingers shaking, she waded back to the hall cupboard and grabbed a stack of towels.

"Hello?"

Christina glanced up from her impromptu dam

construction in the lounge to see Katie coming through the front door.

"What on earth are you doing?"

"Leak from the laundry," panted Christina. "Can you grab more towels from the cupboard?"

Katie dropped her bags outside and slipped off her shoes, then picked her way across the carpet, laughing. "What happened?"

"Washing machine hose is busted." Christina spotted the water disappearing under one of the cardboard archive boxes alongside the display cabinet. Squelching across, she pressed the towels to the carpet, then lifted the box to move it away. It had the dead weight of dense paper, and the wet cardboard tore. "Dammit," she muttered.

"You want me to unpack it and lay out whatever's in there to dry?" asked Katie, moving a wet towel around with her foot.

"Would you mind? I'll try to call Harriet." Christina hoped fervently the house was insured as she dug out her aunt's emergency mobile number. The phone rang three times before diverting to voicemail. Christina left a message, hoping that Harriet would pick up her messages soon.

She collected the first round of sodden towels and shoved them into the washing machine to spin. Wondering what to do next, she trudged back out to the lounge to find Katie laying sheets of wet paper on the backs of the lounge chairs. "It's only the bottom inch or so," she said. "I don't know why anyone would keep this stuff. It's all pay slips and boring stuff like that."

"Don't read it," said Christina reflexively.

"Kind of hard not to. This stuff is ancient, anyway. Look." Katie held up a page printed on a dot matrix. "Box is ruined though."

Christina picked up the collapsed cardboard. The rest of the contents would have to be stacked on the sideboard for now.

"Oh, look," said Katie. Christina glanced up to see her holding the photograph of Harriet, the one she'd found her first day here and left on top of the boxes. It had fallen onto the floor, and dripped water as Katie turned it in her fingers. "Is that your aunt?"

"Harriet," said Christina, avoiding her aunt's face in the shot, with its high round cheeks and flowing blonde hair.

"Who's the guy?" asked Katie. "Looks sexy."

"Jeez, Katie."

"What? Looks like an army guy."

"Thomas. Harriet's husband. He was a major," Christina said quickly. "He died last year."

"Oh." Katie looked at the photo again. "Is she your mum's sister, or your dad's?"

"Mum's."

"Are they very different?"

Christina took the photo, wiped off the water with her shirt, and turned it face down on the sofa back to dry. "Could we not talk about this?"

Katie tilted her head. "Hey, didn't mean to pry. I was just interested."

Christina looked at Katie's earnest expression. "I haven't been in touch with my aunt in a long time, and I just want to get this rotation done and go home again."

"All right, then. Sorry."

But despite what she'd said, Christina's thoughts did dwell on Harriet and the one memory she always returned to: the last time they'd seen each other, just as Christina was leaving Townsville and Harriet was returning from down south. They had only met by chance, up at the top of Castle Hill. Christina had tried to tell herself that Harriet meant nothing to her anymore. But all the awful things that had happened since Harriet left had made her angry, and when Harriet had smiled – delighted and unaware – Christina had lost all resolve to be cool and nonchalant.

Christina could still hear her own voice, full of sorrow-sown anger, screaming at Harriet, hurling blame and reproach for abandoning her. Her aunt hadn't fought back; she'd seemed too shocked. People had stared at them. So Christina had left, feeling as though she'd been the one in the wrong. Not for the first time, Christina wondered if Harriet had deliberately planned this latest trip away to avoid a repeat of that day.

Eventually, with the towels on another spin cycle, Christina and Katie sat down at the kitchen table, Katie thumbing through an anatomy app on her iPad. Worried about the water-soaked house, Christina found it impossible to concentrate. Finally, she opened her notebook. "Can we talk about this case study?" she began. "I've been interviewing John Hunt."

Katie looked up. "Wow, you've made a lot of notes."

"I need to talk to him again, but can you do the research stuff? Just some papers on acute head injury, I think. Strategies for assessment, especially for taking history in a challenging patient. It would be good if you could meet him too. The nurse and the registrar said we could come in on the weekend—"

"I have plans."

Christina paused. "Katie, we both need to work on this."

"I know, absolutely. I can do all the background stuff. But you know this patient now, right? It might be confusing for him to have another person come along."

"Just come and see him, that's all I'm asking," said Christina.

"All right, fine. But next week, okay? I'm going out on Travers' boat this weekend."

For a second, Christina wondered if Aiden would be going along as well, then pushed that thought away to the same place she'd put the flooded house, her memories of Harriet, and her mother. She looked up to find Katie scrutinizing her expression.

"What?" asked Katie.

"Nothing."

"Are you jealous?"

"Of what?"

"Of me and Travers."

Christina laughed. "No. But don't you think it's a bad idea?"

"Why? It's just a bit of fun to make the time go quicker. It's not like he's assessing me. It's fine."

Christina was just searching for words to respond to this when the house phone rang in the study, sending a jangle of nerves through her chest.

"It's Harriet." Her aunt sounded crisp on the line. "You mentioned a problem?"

Christina relayed what had happened, then followed Harriet's directions to find the insurance documents in the study's filing cabinet. Once Christina had read out the policy and phone numbers, Harriet said she would organize the rest and not to worry. Moments later, Christina found herself with an empty phone line. All very pragmatic.

She slotted the insurance documents away, then sat with the drawer open, her mind turning over. Each of the files was carefully labelled, except for one right at the back, which was at least an inch thick. Christina pulled the cream folder open with her fingers, and caught the edge of a familiar-looking paper. The next moment, she'd yanked the file from the cabinet and spread it open on the desk.

On top was a printed report on the opening of the new hospital. Christina's name was written on the front in her halting teenage hand, the photos and text laid out with the help of Harriet's word processor, the teacher's grade, a B+, penciled in the bottom corner. Next in the file was a birthday card she'd made for her aunt, with a childish portrait of Harriet on the front, wearing her blue nursing uniform. She paused with the card in her hand, remembering making it in her eighth grade art class, hunched over it to protect her work from Seb Prior.

Christina flicked on, through her school essays and projects, items she'd made, all carefully preserved in plastic sleeves. Some of it she couldn't even remember creating. When she'd finished, she slowly gathered it all back into the file, holding back the tears that were threatening to fall. She hadn't thought Harriet had cared so much. Hadn't realized that these things were important to her. Or maybe, Christina told herself, her aunt had simply forgotten they were there.

She replaced the file, and was briefly contemplating calling Harriet back when her mobile rang. For a moment, she thought it was her aunt again – the voice was so similar, although older and tired-sounding. But the confusion was momentary, and Christina sat up in the chair.

"You said you'd be back soon," said Rita.

"Not yet."

"I want to know where all my money is."

"What do you mean?"

"My money from my pension. Did you take it?"

"Lena has your purse. You can spend whatever's in your account."

"Where's the rest of it?"

Christina rubbed her forehead. They'd had this conversation before. "It gets spent on rent there, and to pay the care staff, and your prescriptions. Lena can show you—"

But her mother had hung up. Christina listened to the empty line for five heartbeats before she put the phone down, trying not to let this affect her. But it was too late.

She remembered a sunny Saturday morning when she was nine, excited as she strapped herself into the car.

"We're going on a trip!" Rita said, her eyes shining.

Christina was beside herself. Their bags were on the back seat. It was finally going to happen – a weekend trip, just like the other kids at school talked about. She was finally normal. They drove down the road, Rita in high spirits, her thumbs drumming on the wheel as she sang along to the Spice Girls, encouraging Christina to join in.

Christina stopped singing abruptly when they pulled over

ten minutes later. "Why are we here?" she asked. The pub loomed over them like a specter, destroying her hopes.

"Just getting some cash from the machine," Rita said. "And I don't like that tone from you." The door creaked open, slammed shut. The keys were still in the ignition.

And so Christina waited. And waited. An hour later, she slid out of the car and sneaked to the door of the pub. Her mother was at the bar, drinking from a tall glass and chatting to a man on another barstool. Christina slunk back to the car and turned the key one click, then turned the radio down low. The song playing was "Tubthumping". Curled on the seat, her bony knees up to her chin, she waited. Something died inside her that day. She knew there would never be a road trip. And she would never again trust anything her mother said.

Coming back to the present, Christina firmly closed the filing cabinet drawer, and went back out to study.

Chapter 14

The next day, in the training field forty minutes west of Townsville, Aiden stood over his plans in operations, one ear on the radio calls from across the tent. The camouflage net made disrupted shadows on the dusty earth, the same dirt that was inside his clothes and stuck to his face. His pack sat two feet away, his rifle ready within reach. The air smelled of cam paint and eucalyptus.

"Dozers are making a second pass now," called the signalman.

"Heading out in ten, then."

Ten minutes later, he stepped out of a vehicle to survey the earthworks, alongside the unit's major and lieutenant colonel. His team of armored bulldozers and graders had recut a damaged road, working in tandem with two sections of engineers sweeping for fake IEDs. This might have been a training exercise, but Aiden had done it for real in many of the places he'd worked. And tomorrow they'd leave the training area and repair public roads damaged in last summer's flooding.

"Looking good," said the major.

"Got to hand it to you, Bell," said the lieutenant colonel. "You know how to run these things. Excellent work."

Then Aiden noticed a roller moving back along the canted road edge, fixing a patch of spall. The machine was far in the distance, but Aiden felt a qualm and reached for the radio. "Alpha-two-zero, this is zero-alpha. Your roller on the north face looks steep on the angle. Acknowledge, over."

"Ah, zero-alpha, acknowledge. On it. Over."

The last thing they needed was a rollover. Then there would be casualty evacuations, and pain for everyone, not least the poor driver.

Seeing the roller adjust its position, Aiden breathed out, but he could never fully relax, not when he always had to be across where everyone in the unit was, and where operation requirements were deviating from the plan. It was long after stand-down when he finally felt sufficiently prepared for the next day's work to leave the ops tent and haul his webbing, pack and weapon to the shell dugout under his hoochie.

Maybe it was simply his mind escaping from the dirt and sweat but during those quiet steps, he thought of Christina. He wondered what she was doing. When or if he would see her again.

These thoughts ended as he reached the hoochie's canvas shelter, where he smelled hex burning from a canteen heater and saw a shape sitting in the darkness. Aiden knew that thirty meters away to his two o'clock, two men were posted on piquet, and another four in tents nearby. But none of those men would invite themselves into his space.

"Who's that?" he asked softly.

"Tea service," said the padre from the dark. "Want a brew?"

"God, yes." Aiden unslung his webbing and rifle and sank down in the hoochie's lee, the prospect of hot tea making his mouth water.

"The exercise is going well, I hear," the padre said, handing across a steaming canteen.

"So far."

"The CO tells me you're being deployed again soon, too."

"In about six weeks," Aiden said into the darkness. "I'm handing over the Solomons job, and heading to the MEAO to do an operations role for the security and recon forces – lots of long-term planning and engineering support after the Iraq flare-up. Things are a mess over there."

"Ah," the padre said. "It sounds like exactly what you do best. Are you looking forward to it?"

"Definitely," Aiden said, but a thread of doubt pulled at the edge of his conviction. He thought again of Christina. And then about his empty house in Brisbane. The two emotions – desire and apprehension – were on a collision path.

"How's the family feel about it?" the padre asked. "Must be an emotional time."

Aiden was grateful for the darkness. "I … haven't told them yet. It's my sister's wedding on the weekend, and—" He stopped himself before he mentioned Christina. "Well, it hasn't seemed the right time."

"Worried about how they'll react? I remember what you said happened with Tracey."

Aiden scalded himself on the tea. He'd forgotten he'd mentioned it to the padre; it had been on that terrible night with Travers eighteen months ago. "You've been serving a long time, right, Padre?"

The older man nodded. "Twenty years in the regular infantry, fifteen more as an officer, then ten years in this job."

"And you're married?"

"Yes, with two beautiful daughters and my son in the special forces." The padre fell silent; he seemed to be waiting. The pause stretched full of tactical night silence, begging to be filled with the question that Aiden couldn't quite ask.

When he spoke again, the padre's voice was kind. "Do you want to ask me if it was hard to be married through all that?"

"How did you know?"

"I do a fair bit of wedding preparation with couples these days. That's the question the girls always ask. The guys think it's all going to be fine, and usually they're wrong. Look, in my experience, it's pretty hard to tell who's going to cope better than others. But people who trust each other and expect there'll be some hard times, they seem to do better than the ones with rose-tinted glasses." He clapped Aiden on the shoulder. "New girl in your life?"

"Don't know. Seems like a bad time to be starting anything."

The padre chuckled quietly. "It's always a bad time when it's something important."

Three days later, Christina stood among the mounds of uprooted carpet. The insurance company had been swift, sending in assessors and two burly tradesmen, who'd whistled as they pried off skirting boards and ripped the carpet back to sodden underlay. Now they were plugging in industrial dehumidifiers and fans.

"It's pretty hot and noisy," yelled the foreman. "But we have to dry everything out, then they'll check the walls, make sure all the water's gone."

"How long is it going to be like this?" asked Christina, leaning in to make herself heard.

The guy shrugged. "The weekend should do it. You can turn them off Sunday night. Usually people go stay somewhere else."

Great.

She'd passed the day in the university library, checking off reading for the week's topic – dermatology – until she was cross-eyed from poring over photographic plates of rashes. Within five minutes of returning to the house, her skin was slick from the sweltering heat, and her arms became stuck when she tried to pull on her delivery uniform. The dryers and industrial fans droned oppressively, rubbing her nerves raw.

As she tried a second time to pull on the shirt, she heard a seam rip. Well, that was just perfect. Even when she escaped outside, the hum still leaked through the walls. She would have to find somewhere else to sleep tonight. The Belmont had a good-sized tray, or maybe she could camp on the grass in the backyard. She made a dash inside for her keys, her hair already lank and sticky.

As usual on Fridays, the pizza oven was on overdrive, all three baking tiers working. The cutter stood at the end, retrieving and boxing each pizza with practiced skill. The other student staff had phones to their ears, taking orders, and Carlo himself was madly assembling at the bench.

"Christina!" he bellowed. "Two orders there to go, right now. Let's move."

Christina pulled down her cap and headed out with the order, trying to read the address on the delivery ticket as she dodged pedestrians on the sidewalk. It took a few minutes to find the street in her map book; when she arrived there fifteen minutes later, she found a dark house and no one home. After she'd paced up and down on the sidewalk for a few minutes, she was about to give up when someone called over the next-door fence, "Hey, pizza guy, it's this one!"

The evening progressed in similar fashion: two run-ins with large scary dogs, two wolf-whistles, and one ten-minute delay when she was stuck in roadworks north of town. She'd just offloaded what she hoped was her second-last delivery when her phone bleeped with a text.

Christina opened the message. *Are you up?*

Aiden. She hadn't seen him since the day at Crystal Creek, and they'd only exchanged the one phone call since. Now her heart raced. She texted back: *Thought you were away?*

Just got back. Can I call you?

A moment later, her phone rang.

"I thought you might be at work," he said, sounding tired.

"I am," she said. "Just on my way back to the store now."

"Any chance you want some navigational assistance?"

Christina chewed her lip. "Aiden, I'm not sure—"

"I'm not up to anything," he said quickly. "I just got back

from three days out field and I can't sleep. I promise I won't pay for anything."

Christina glanced at her watch: ten past ten. "I've probably only got one delivery left."

"That's okay," he said. "It might be a hard one."

He was waiting at the store when she got back, leaning on the counter and talking to Carlo, who was laughing now the rush was over. Aiden's hair was wet and he wore clean clothes, but she noticed scratches on his left cheekbone and on both of his hands, and dark circles under his eyes.

Carlo handed Christina the last order with a smile: five pizzas and three bottles of soft drink. "Big one for last. Lucky you have help."

"Nice guy, Carlo," said Aiden with a slightly teasing tone, as they piled into the Belmont.

Christina paused before she turned the key in the ignition, suddenly playful and ridiculously happy to see him. "You look terrible, Aiden."

He laughed. "Yeah, I bet. Haven't slept much."

"How did you get those?" She nodded at his hands and cheek.

"Lantana," he said. "That's a kind of shrub. Battle to the death, it really was. Now, what's the address?"

Soon the Belmont was chugging up a steep road near Castle Hill. Christina slowed and peered at the house, a sleek slab of pale cream render with wooden fittings and big windows lit in candle yellow. Voices and music bubbled out. A sleek black Audi was parked in the drive, the rest of the street choked with guest cars. The twinkling lights of The Strand, the port, and boats on the water were just visible down the side of the house. It would have a stunning view from the back.

Christina left Aiden on a work call in the double-parked Belmont and, balancing the five boxes, pushed the doorbell with her elbow. The light above the door was stark as sunlight, but held no warmth. She rocked from foot to foot, keen to offload the awkward boxes.

"Pizza's here!" came a call from inside.

The door was thrown open and a tall man appeared, a half-empty Corona in his hand. With a flash of instinctive warning, she took in his golden-brown skin and smooth brows, the short sharp haircut. The unease tore through her before her mind had a chance to catch up. His gaze was slipping easily down the length of her body before she finally realized who he was.

Oh, God. He might be more than ten years older, but she'd recognize Sebastian Prior anywhere. She tipped her head down, hiding under her cap, her eyes on the order docket, her stomach in free-fall.

"Well, hello," he said, his voice smooth. "Another one to join the fun. It's not a costume party, but for a hot thing like you, maybe we can make an exception." He laughed and swigged the beer.

"Two supreme, one pepperoni, one chicken, one Hawaiian," Christina rushed out, desperate to leave before he recognized her.

"Oh, all business. I like that," said Seb. "Now I definitely want you to join us."

"No, thanks," she said, trying to hand over the boxes.

But Seb wasn't having it. "Sorry, darling, my hands are full. How about bringing them inside? Come on, we're having a great time."

No way in hell was Christina walking through that door. "Can you just take them, please?"

"What, no service?" he returned. "Come on, clock off for a few and live a little."

The next thing, his finger had hooked under the peak of Christina's cap. It tumbled to the ground, her ponytail whipping around her neck and sticking to her skin. So there was nothing to shield her as she looked up at him. The playful smile stayed on Seb's face for two seconds, then his eyes widened and a different kind of grin spread across his lips. "Holy shit, it's Chrissy-No-Tits," he said loudly.

And just like that, the years since school were wiped away and Christina was back in the playground again, in the dust and desperation of it. He was very close to her now, a large, heavy male body that smelled of beer and aftershave. Sweat trickled down her back.

"Well, well, Chrissy," he said. "I'm going to have to think of a different name, aren't I? Who'd have thought you'd fill out so nicely. And you were just going to duck away without saying hello – tut, tut."

"Will you take these boxes, please?" Christina said, hunching to pull her chest in.

"Tell you what," Seb said, leaning closer as voices approached down the hall behind him. "I'll take the boxes, and you come join us. Then you and me can go for a drive in the Audi later. Show you a real car." He smirked past her, probably spying the Belmont's bonnet at the end of the drive.

Not on your fucking life, Christina wanted to growl. But by now, other people were clustering around the door. She recognized many of the faces, all Seb's buddies from school. One woman had perfect blonde hair tucked behind her ears, which held tiny pearl studs. Steph Morgan, thought Christina, remembering the girl's acid tongue.

"Why did you order *Carlo's*?" Steph complained. Then she laughed. "Oh my God, it *is* Chrissy. How're you doing, Chrissy? Moving up in the world, I see. Crazy Rita must be proud."

A cold stone formed in Christina's throat. She stared at all of them, caught in their bullying scrutiny, mortified. With a grin at another man, one of the guys made a fist in front of his mouth and stuck his tongue suggestively into his cheek.

Then Katie appeared between them. "Hi, Chris, you came! I hoped they'd send you when I ordered!"

Christina registered this slowly. How could Katie be so stupid? Desperate to escape, she pushed the boxes in Katie's direction, but Seb put an arm out to stop her, warming to his audience. "So, what's it going to be? Coming in?"

His audience sniggered. Time to go.

"Can you pay for the pizzas, please?"

"You know what, I think you're late." Seb made a show of checking his watch. "I think maybe these should be free. What do you say, Chrissy?"

Christina looked to Katie for support, but she was leaning on the doorframe, not meeting her eye. "They're not late," she managed to say. "You have to pay for them."

"Oh, do I?" asked Seb. "Well, maybe I'll just call your boss and see about that. Unless, of course, you want to come and join us. I'll be happy to pay you for your services."

He took out his mobile and began dialing. The others watched him, caught up in the fascination of whether he'd go through with it. But as he put the phone to his ear, something inside Christina tore loose from its moorings. She shoved the pizzas at him. The boxes connected with Seb's solid middle and thumped to the ground, disgorging hot cheese. "Fuck you," she spat, and turned on her heel, just as the first tear splashed onto her cheek.

"Hey!" Seb yelled behind her, but Christina kept walking. Her bravado was spent. Halfway down the drive, she met Aiden coming up, a bag of drinks in his hand, his expression very different to anything she'd seen in him before. Intense, calculating, and mad as hell. She wondered what he'd overheard.

"What's going on?" he asked.

Christina swiped at her eyes. "Nothing."

"Christina, wait!" Katie came running after her. "Hey, you know he's just trying to be funny. Lighten up, okay?"

"Like hell," Christina said. "Take your damn drinks." She snatched the bag of bottles off Aiden and pushed it into

Katie's arms.

"Don't be like that. Look, come back and join the party when you finish work. It'll be fun, I promise."

Christina wasn't listening. Her eyes were on Sebastian and his mates, who were now coming down the driveway.

Katie glanced over her shoulder, and a moment's uncertainty crossed her features. "Hey, I've got the drinks," she said. "Let's just go back up."

"No, this isn't finished," said Seb. "I want replacements for those pizzas. And you're going to fetch them, Chrissy. Then you're going to say you're sorry."

Christina stood, frozen. Part of her wanted to crush him with her voice, but another part was still in high school, helpless under the weight of his scorn. She was too aware of her greasy hair, her flushed face, her humiliating uniform. She may as well have been bagging his groceries. The energy in the group was intimidating. Then Seb's gaze shifted, and she realized that Aiden had stepped up beside her.

"What the fuck are you doing?" she heard him say.

"Hey, it's Bell, right?" said Sebastian smoothly. "Party's inside."

"Oi, Chrissy darling, why don't you come in and sit on my face!" called one of the men, slow to register the change in the situation.

Aiden's eyes flicked towards him. "Why? Is your nose bigger than your dick? You really brag about that? Shut up, you stupid ass."

The titters died. Suddenly, none of them knew what to do.

Aiden snapped his attention back to Seb. "And it's Captain Bell to you," he said. He looked around at the group of men, his eyes daring them to speak. A few lowered their eyes. Aiden's tone was low and dangerous. "This a display of moral courage, is it? You should all be ashamed. Every one of you."

"Look, this is a private thing," returned Seb, shifting uneasily. "Sir."

"Look around," Aiden said. "You're a serving member, and

you've got five men standing off against one woman. That tells me you're a coward, and a bully. Now, back off or you're going to have a colossal problem with me. Who wants a go? You, Private? How about you, Corporal?" His eyes flared with fire, the gouges on his cheek adding a dangerous edge. One by one, the group slipped away like shadows, until it was just Seb and Katie on the driveway.

"Just jokes, you know, Chrissy," Seb said, pulling out a bunch of banknotes. "No hard feelings."

Christina said nothing, just plucked the money from his hand without touching him. Her head and chest felt hollow as Seb stalked away, trailed by Katie, who glanced back over her shoulder, mouthing, *Sorry*.

Christina felt sick as she got back into the car and started the engine.

"What was all that about?" asked Aiden, pulling his door shut.

"Don't ever do that again," she said. "I don't need you coming to the rescue." But her voice wobbled, and something within her was fiercely grateful he'd been there.

She headed back to the store, trying to forget Seb, but damn it if the bastard's face didn't keep appearing in her thoughts.

Aiden kept quiet until they arrived at Carlo's, but she could see his reflection in the windscreen. Could feel his conflict. When she'd killed the engine, he put a hand on her arm.

"Sorry if I got in the middle," he said. "I'm not saying you can't handle yourself. But I can't stand a bully. It makes me crazy. Don't ever think that I'll stand by when shit like that is going down." Then he smiled.

"What's the grin for?" she asked suspiciously.

"I'm not sure if you're brave or stupid, but I do admire your nerve."

"Hmph."

"… and I'm thinking about the guys I'm going to send

round there later."

Christina's mouth dropped open in alarm.

"Kidding," he said, then added in a low voice, "Wish I wasn't."

As she was about to step out of the car, Aiden said, "I don't suppose you want dinner now? I'm happy to sit on the bonnet in your driveway again. I reckon I can go home and sleep after that."

Christina twisted a loose thread on the Belmont's steering-wheel cover. She pulled, but the thread refused to break. The smell of pizza in the car stuck to her skin like the stink of Sebastian Prior. She wanted a shower.

"Actually, the house is full of industrial fans," she said.

"It is?"

"And dehumidifiers." She then had to go over the story of the water leak.

"Where are you staying tonight, then?" Aiden asked when she'd finished.

"I'm thinking of camping in the backyard. It's warm enough."

He paused. "No, you're not. I'll pick you up at your place in half an hour."

An hour later, Christina glanced furtively over her shoulder and slipped into Aiden's base room. "What if someone sees me?"

"They won't, trust me," he said.

She looked around. His room was just like the first time she saw it: rudimentary – a double bed and plain white walls, a pine cupboard and a desk. A beaten camouflage pack leaned in the corner, two water flasks neatly stacked to the side as though he'd been in the middle of unpacking it. Carefully, she sat on the edge of the bed, pushing her bag between her feet. She licked her lips.

"Don't worry," he said gently. "I'll sleep on the floor."

"You can't do that – it's your room. I'll sleep on the floor. It'll be ten times better than sleeping in the Belmont."

"Christy, I've slept on the ground for the last three days, what bit of it I actually did sleep. We were running almost around the clock. I caught a few hours on the trip back, but trust me, I'm going to be out like a light. And I'll ask Travers if you can crash at his place for the rest of the weekend. I have a long drive tomorrow."

"Where are you going?" she asked, liking the way he shortened her name.

"My sister's wedding. It's near Ryders Ridge – about six hours west."

"You can't be serious, Aiden," Christina said, aghast. "Do you know how many people crash driving fatigued?"

He sank down next to her, and Christina's stomach fluttered. The memory of their kiss at Crystal Creek was a tingle in her lips, just as the idea of him driving so tired made her weak with worry.

She stood up. "You are definitely having the bed."

He caught her hand. "I've got a better idea. Come with me."

"What?"

"Come with me to Dani's wedding. You know her and she really wanted me to bring someone. You can make sure I stay awake on the drive."

Christina stared at him, her stomach twisting. She'd never been to a wedding before, and the prospect of being social with unfamiliar people was daunting. But concern for Aiden had lodged in her chest, and then there were the damn fans at Harriet's.

"I don't know," she hedged. "I have to study."

"Can you work in the car?"

"I guess … Don't you have someone else you can take?"

He shook his head with a small smile, as if at some joke she didn't understand. "Well, I did ask Travers, but that might create the wrong impression. Christina, I enjoy your company. And I'd like it if you'd come. Family events aren't really my thing."

"Why not?" she asked, sinking back down beside him.

"I've moved around so much that I missed a lot. I haven't actually seen Dad in a few years. We get along, just, but we're very different people. I don't live in his world and he doesn't live in mine. Dani's the intermediary most of the time."

Christina plucked at the bedspread, a thick blue fabric that reminded her of hospital blankets. "I want to ask you about something Travers said – you know, after last weekend."

"Shoot."

"He said you'd been done over before."

Aiden took a moment to answer, then nodded. "I was engaged a few years ago. She broke it off when I was deployed overseas."

"I'm sorry," said Christina.

Aiden shrugged. "Long time ago now. But listen, Travers is the only one who knows that it happened while I was away. I didn't tell Daniella and Dad. They just know that we split, and I'd like it to stay that way."

Christina frowned. "Wait a minute … did you just assume I'm coming with you tomorrow?"

Aiden smiled. "Put it this way. In return for a road trip, country shindig and a bed without fans, all I ask is that you keep me awake, and keep my little secret. Deal?"

Christina was tempted. "But I haven't got anything to wear to a wedding," she protested.

At this, Aiden acquired a thoughtful look and pushed up off the bed. He paced across to the wardrobe and, after some rummaging, turned up a slinky black dress with delicate lace running over the top into a halter neck. He held it up. "I do apologize in advance, but what about this?"

"What's the apology for?" asked Christina, thinking he was going to say it belonged to some ex-girlfriend.

Aiden scratched the side of his head, peering at the stitching along the back zip. "We had a fancy dress function last year," he said. "I borrowed it off a female colleague who said she didn't want it back – bridesmaid dress I think, and she hated wearing skirts. Travers took one look and bet me a slab I couldn't wear it. I just hope I didn't damage it. I could only get it half on and the back wouldn't do up. But I kept it, wondering if Dani would like it. For the party I ended up with some hideous eighties formal dress from an op-shop."

After a moment's pause, Christina collapsed laughing, which was only made worse when Aiden produced a photo on his phone as proof, showing him in a jewel-blue dress with puffed sleeves complete with a strawberry-blonde wig. It was a few minutes before she got her breath back. "All right, fine," she said. "If you can sacrifice your dignity like that, I suppose I can come. I'll see if Harriet has some shoes I can borrow."

Aiden laid the dress out on the back of his desk chair and pulled her towards the bed. "Absolutely. And you don't have to sleep on the floor. The bed's big enough, and I'm a gentleman."

He was asleep in ten seconds. Christina lay awake watching him in the faint light from the window, trying to make sense of the hot, exciting feelings he stirred inside her. And then she wondered about him, about all the places he'd been, the things he'd done, all the layers that made him who he was.

Chapter 15

They left the base early the next morning, looping south around Mount Stuart while the rising sun was still painting the mountainsides golden. Christina sat in the passenger seat, her laptop on her knee, but found herself staring out the window at the passing countryside. A smoky haze hung over the mountains again, and as they turned further west, the blue-green hills stood out above vivid lime-colored pastures. Then the bright palette gave way to the red-tinged dust, golden grass and dark scrub of the Flinders Highway, which saw them all the way to Charters Towers.

After that, in between reading and rearranging paragraphs of her essay, Christina watched the countryside slowly change, until by around midday the land had no more discernible hills, simply a vast plain of grass and occasional knots of scrub, all under the great dome of sky. Through the middle of it all, the road cut a straight ribbon.

She glanced at Aiden. "Still awake?"

"Absolutely."

In fact, Aiden had been a machine behind the wheel, steering them westward without interrupting her progress or putting on music. He turned his neck from side to side, stretching. "How's it going?"

"Actually, I'm stuck," said Christina, letting her head fall back against the headrest. "I've just read the same paragraph three times, and my battery's low."

"We need to stop, then. Leave it for a while." He pulled the car over onto the shoulder and they climbed out.

With the engine off, the silence was endless. They were so alone out here, and the wide open space felt … comforting. Aiden was just in the edge of her vision, staring into the distance, his face tired but calm.

A minute later, he reached into the car and produced a bag of dull brown packets. "Hungry?"

"What's this?"

"Rat-pack I didn't eat on the exercise. Always prepared."

The one Christina chose was full of bright chocolate candy, sweet and delicious. And suddenly, all this – the trip, Aiden – seemed natural and easy. Exciting with possibility.

By the time they climbed back into the car, the tension had left her shoulders. When she returned to her essay, it appeared closer to completion than it had before. She could take the evening off without worrying.

After another hour, Aiden slowed, consulting his GPS as they passed a road sign announcing Ryders Ridge. "If we keep going we'll hit the town, but I think we take the next turn," he said. In the distance, they spotted two bunches of white balloons tugging on their strings, tied to posts either side of a narrow bitumen road. So confirmed, Aiden took the turnoff. After a few hundred meters the bitumen gave out, and the road became a smooth dirt track through the grass.

Christina gripped the seat, thrills of anticipation sparkling in her heart as they cruised towards a distant rise, which resolved into a spur of land, then, in the cradle of the spur's curve, a homestead. Aiden leaned forward in his seat with a soft whistle. "Wow, look at that."

To Christina the house was like something from a painting – the pale roof stretching protectively over the deep verandas, the honey-colored stones and wide windows. Today the veranda posts were dressed in gauzy white bows with flowing tails, and as they drew near she could see rows of trucks and cars parked along the spur.

A gangly young man in a suit and a cowboy hat, bowtie undone, knocked on Aiden's window. "Hi, sir. You can park there on the end of the row. Or I can do it, if you want," he added hopefully, standing taller in his oversized tux jacket.

Aiden grinned. "Thanks," he said, leaving the disappointed teenage valet behind and easing the car around to the indicated parking space. As they climbed out, Christina glanced nervously at the people crowding the veranda. She looked down at her jeans and t-shirt, then at the dress laid out in the back seat, wondering where she'd be able to change.

Aiden was beside her, shading his eyes as he looked at the house, his other hand braced on the car. She read in his stance his own hesitation. At least she wasn't alone.

A wiry woman in a green dress and a wattle corsage met them on the path to the house. "Good afternoon," she began, and then she paused, looking Aiden over. "Oh, you must be Aiden! Daniella will be so excited you're here. I'm Kath. This way."

Christina trailed behind Aiden through the beautiful house, the hall opening into an expansive lounge with a brick fireplace and antique furniture. A wedding dress hung from a curtain rail, and three women sat on the sofas, their hair done but wearing bathrobes and sipping champagne.

"Oh, a man!" said one of the women, spotting Aiden. She had tight jet-black curls piled on her head and a merry expression. The two other women looked up. One had dark hair trailing down her back and quick, intelligent eyes. The other was Daniella, her light brown hair that Christina had only ever seen pulled into a hasty ponytail now caught up in an elegant twist and fixed with diamond pins. She looked unspeakably beautiful, far from the tired registrar Christina had met on the ward.

Daniella was on her feet instantly. "Aiden!" She rushed over and hugged him. "You didn't drive all the way today?"

"You look wonderful, Dani. And it's all right. Christina kept me awake."

Daniella turned her smile on Christina, who hung back, her hands clasped before her. "I'm so glad you came. We're ready far too early and we've been trying to pass the time. The men are down at the cottages, except Dad, he's in the kitchen. Why don't you come and sit with us for a while?"

She led Christina over to the women on the sofas. "This is Aiden's date, Christina. She's a med student in Townsville. Christina, this is Jackie, my best friend." The woman with the curls raised her glass. "And this is Beth. She's engaged to Will, Mark's brother. She's a doctor too. And Jackie's a nurse, but she's starting med school next year."

"Wait, you're all doctors?" asked Christina, taking in their welcoming expressions as Daniella turned back to talk to Aiden.

"Well, not quite," said Jackie. "But I'm working on it."

"Which rotation are you on, Christina?" asked Beth, offering her a champagne flute.

Christina took the glass, but glanced back to where Aiden and Daniella were now in conversation by the door. "Family practice. I'm doing it on the army base."

"Ah," said Beth, brightening. "That will make a change from sick children and diabetes." She and Jackie both laughed.

"Christina's very keen," said Daniella from the doorway. "She came to the hospital chasing a case study."

"Ugh, assignments," said Jackie. "I was hoping I could avoid them."

"There's an essay, too, I'm afraid," Christina said, encouraged by their high spirits.

"Oh no," said Jackie in mock horror. "What topic have you chosen? Entertain us!"

"Um, appropriate analgesia for acute sports injuries," said Christina. She shrugged. "Hardly entertaining."

"What, no testicles or feces?" asked Jackie. "Surely on the

base you could have found plenty of both?"

Christina heard Aiden snicker from the doorway.

"She's only kidding, Christina," said Daniella, walking back to the sofas and poking Jackie with her toe. "Analgesia is very important. And Christina's fine with us," she added in Aiden's direction. "You can pick her up later, so shoo. Now, Christina, tell us your findings."

Christina smiled at Aiden reassuringly, trying to look braver than she felt, and he gave her an encouraging nod and headed away down the hall. Sitting on the sofa next to Beth, she tried to quickly summarize her essay, thinking how inappropriate this was in the middle of a wedding day. But after a while she realized that all three women were genuinely interested.

When she'd finished, Daniella gave a satisfied nod. "Sounds like you're going to do fine."

"So," said Christina shyly, as she carefully put down her untouched glass. "How did you and Mark meet?"

Daniella's eyes slid to Jackie. "Have we got enough time to go through it all?"

Jackie laughed. "Maybe, but Christina's going to need something stronger than champagne."

Daniella rolled her eyes. "The short version is I came to Ryders to work, and stuff happened. The longer version I'll have to tell you later."

Without a word, Jackie replaced Christina's champagne with a glass of sparkling water. "Oh, thank you," Christina said, while Jackie gave her a kind smile. "Is there somewhere I can get changed? I feel out of place in jeans."

Jackie jumped up. "Of course. How rude of us. I'll show you to the bathroom. And when you're dressed, make sure you come back," she added.

Christina closed the bathroom door and leaned against it, a swirl of emotions behind her breastbone. The women were kind and welcoming, but she couldn't help wondering where Aiden had gone. Her connection to him seemed temporarily severed, and she felt like a small boat drifting from the pier, longing to find the way home again.

Aiden's footsteps down the hall accompanied the drumming in his chest. He'd been anticipating this in-person moment with his father for more than six months, and each time it had been put off in some way: Daniella's birthday falling when he was away on an exercise; his father's promotion celebration when he was on a course. But now, here they were.

The kitchen had a huge scrubbed table as its center, a deep pantry in one corner, and windows on two sides facing both the path into the house and the farm buildings down the spur. Standing by these windows looking out, in his waistcoat and suit pants, and sipping a single malt, was Peter Bell.

"Dad."

His father looked around, his austere face splitting into a relieved smile. "Aiden." He placed the glass down on the bench, and crossed the space between them, capturing Aiden's hand. He held it longer than Aiden expected, his eyes searching his son's face. "Been a long time."

"I guess it has." And with those words, Aiden felt the weight of it. Nearly three years. He hadn't seen his father since before his stint in Victoria. Three years that had made Peter Bell's cheeks leaner, and put new lines around his eyes.

His father released his hand. "I'm glad you made it. Have you seen Dani? She was anxious to see you."

"She looks wonderful."

"Doesn't she?" His father stepped back. "Hard to imagine she's so grown up," he said, then raised a wry eyebrow at Aiden. "Although she tells me I sound old when I say that. But her mother would have been proud."

They avoided each other's eyes, looking towards the window, though Aiden knew his father would be feeling the loss of Aiden's mother afresh, just as Aiden was. "Yes," Aiden said softly.

His father cleared his throat. "I had no idea how they were going to make it work, back at the beginning – Mark living out here, and her starting the surgery training program – but they have."

In the face of Dani and Mark's success, Aiden found his thoughts automatically turning over what had happened with Tracey.

"Drink?" his father suggested. "This stuff is rather good. Never manage to have it in Brisbane. I seem to be always on call."

Aiden saw his opening and took a deep breath. "Speaking of being on call, I have something coming up."

His father was focused on pouring the drink. "I saw you were involved in the Solomon Islands recovery. Good thing, that. Poor buggers. Did you know Beth was over there with a medical team a few weeks ago?"

"I didn't. But it's not that. Something else."

Peter Bell's eyebrow twitched, just a fraction, as he handed Aiden the scotch. Otherwise his expression remained controlled, the way Aiden imagined it did when he had to tell families bad news about their loved ones. "Where are you deploying?" Peter guessed.

"Middle East," said Aiden. "I can't say much more than that. This situation in Iraq is bad, and it's not the only thing going on."

"How long?"

"Six months, maybe seven."

"And when do you go?"

"A few weeks. I haven't told Daniella."

"Don't tell her today, whatever you do." And he unexpectedly pulled Aiden into an embrace. "Be careful, you hear me?"

Then the moment of emotion was over and Peter Bell pulled away. "So, who's the young woman you brought with you?"

Aiden felt his lips tug. "You saw that?"

"I've been standing at this window for a while. William Walker was very good about it. He has a daughter too – just handed over the bottle of scotch and said to come down to the cottages when I felt like it." He sighed. "Mark's a good man, but Dani's still my little girl."

Aiden glanced down the hall as a peal of laughter spilled from the lounge room. He hoped Christina was enjoying herself. When he looked back, his father's expression had grown serious, his gaze on his scotch.

"Aiden, we all get older and I don't want you to think that what I'm about to say is any comment on your abilities. You're still a young man, and you've done some incredible things. Survived some incredible things. But priorities change. What about when you find a girl you want to stick with? I know it didn't work out before, but you were away a lot. And you still are. It makes a big difference. I should know – I spent half my life in hospitals when you and Dani were small. And it was a huge strain on your mother. You might want to think about doing something else."

"Sure, Dad." It was Aiden's standard reply. He didn't know how to explain to his father how much he loved what he did, the knowledge that he could be the difference between a completed mission and a botched one; that he could move proverbial mountains if the situation demanded it. That he could save lives, put them back together, just as surely as Peter Bell's surgical skills did. He wondered if his father could ever see it that way.

"Right," said Peter, draining his glass and rinsing it in the sink. "Can't put this off forever."

As five o'clock rolled around, the atmosphere in the lounge became more charged. Christina was amazed that Aiden's dress fitted her so well, and the other women admired the way the stretchy material clung to her waist. She'd never worn anything like it. She'd been especially surprised when Jackie had offered to fix her hair and do her make-up. Christina was on the verge of declining, not wanting to be in anyone's way, but Jackie assured her that there was still plenty of time, and besides, she wanted to ask Christina more about med school.

"How do you find the contact hours?" asked Jackie. "No, keep your eyes closed."

Christina obeyed, trying not to flinch as a brush touched the sensitive skin of her eyelid. "They're okay," she said. "Only half-days sometimes, and most of the resources are online."

"What about the school facilities?"

"Pretty new. They re-did the anatomy labs not that long ago. The tutorial rooms, too."

The discussion went on for a while until Jackie pulled her up, giving her a shrewd look. "Okay," she said. "What I really want to know are the things other people won't tell me. What's hard? What might I struggle with?"

Christina looked at Jackie, who was poised with an eyeliner pencil, her expression earnest. She hesitated, then admitted, "I feel lost a lot of the time. I have no idea how much I need to know about a topic. And there's not much practical teaching. I was picking things up by trial and error – mostly error – until I came to the base and this medic taught me a few things. Though I imagine," she added hastily, "that being a nurse you won't have any of those issues."

Jackie's lips twitched wryly. "Maybe. But I'll have different problems. My son, for a start. You can't imagine the destructive powers of those sticky fingers. And I've never been good at book learning."

"I'm good with it, if I can get the time. I'm just slow on the practical."

Jackie gave her a warm smile. "It's always something. But, for now, I think you're done." She handed Christina a mirror, and Christina had to look twice; she hardly knew her own face. With her hair in an elegant French twist, expertly shaded eyelids and a soft coral lipstick, she looked like someone else –

someone confident, mysterious.

After that, it was time for Daniella to dress. Feeling that she was intruding, Christina edged away from the three friends and escaped outside. Two men in cowboy hats balanced on the veranda railing at the back of the house, attempting to straighten a crooked arch of white chiffon and flowers over the stairs. Below, where the spur gently sloped down towards the grass plains, straw bales had been covered in hessian and set in rows on either side of an aisle. Children ran between them, trailing lofting streams of white gauze, stolen from the decorations. Christina skirted the area, wandering down towards the yards where horses flicked their ears at all the activity. In her borrowed shoes, she picked a path through the dirt then leaned on the fence, breathing in the animal scent. One of the horses ambled over and sniffed her fingers. Christina gently offered her hand, enjoying the horse's hot breaths even as she heard voices begin to gather up the hill.

"Hi there."

Christina started. A tall young man wearing a new-looking white shirt, slightly too large dress pants and a broad hat leaned in beside her. He grinned. "I'm Simmo. Are you one of Daniella's friends?"

"Ah, no, I came with her brother," she explained.

"Looks like Rocket likes you."

Christina stroked the velvety muzzle. "So soft." She glanced up the hill. "I suppose I should head back."

"Yeah. The boys are coming over now. I've been sent to round up." And he offered his arm.

Christina laughed; Simmo looked about eighteen but already had the manners of a country gentleman. As they walked back, Christina noted his slight limp, and by the time they'd reached the bales, she'd extracted from him that he'd been in a bad accident just a couple of years ago, a car wreck outside Mount Isa that had kept him in hospital for four months. He and his friends had been on their way to a rodeo.

He found her a seat halfway back and sat beside her, still chatting as the throng of guests took their own seats.

Christina saw a group of men in dark suits and cowboy hats step up onto the veranda. The first two men had a similar bearing; probably brothers, she thought, the first one slightly taller and fairer. He had a lovely open expression; confident and happy, at home as he listened to something his brother was saying. An older man followed. "Which one is the groom?" she whispered.

"Oh, the taller one in front. That's Mark. He's my boss," added Simmo. "Next to him, his brother Will. And their father, William Walker, the big boss."

Aiden came next, straight-backed and powerful in his suit, and she guessed that the older man beside him, not as powerful but with a similar dignified posture, was the legendary surgeon Peter Bell. Father and son shook hands and then Aiden stepped down off the veranda, running his eyes over the crowd.

Christina's heart had time to skip before he found her, and relief settled his expression.

"You look amazing," he said when he reached her. Christina blushed, and gave Simmo a look of apology as Aiden claimed her and drew her towards the front row.

In what seemed like no time, the sun had sunk until the sky was a mass of apricot-touched clouds. The groom and his best man, a dark-haired and serious-looking man listed in the program as Dave, stood together. Two violinists appeared on the edge of the veranda and Pachelbel's Canon rose sweetly into the evening air. The crowd hushed, turning in their chairs. Then Daniella and her father stepped down the aisle. A murmur of admiration. Daniella's dress was exquisite white silk, a sweetheart neckline flaring into a full skirt. She had no veil to obscure her expression, which told Christina she'd been waiting for this moment for so very long. Christina twisted back to face the front.

Mark was clearly trying to keep his face impassive, but a

grin broke through, then tears tracked down his face. They watched each other the whole way down the aisle and through the ceremony, as though nothing could separate them, not even the distance of their daily lives. Christina wondered how people ever came to feel so certain about each other. Then as the vows were being exchanged Aiden took her hand. For a moment, his skin rested warm against hers. Christina wanted to lean against him, but when she glanced up, he let her go, though she wasn't sure if is look was apology or regret.

The reception swung into full country party as the sky darkened to deep blue. Christina found rose petals in her hair as she followed the crowd towards a giant marquee nestled in flat ground between the stables and a shingled shed. Inside was a huge parquetry floor, the tantalizing scent of roast beef in the air. Straw bales had been stacked around the edges of the marquee, some with saddles. She found her place card on a table in the front corner of the room, where she sat watching the party as Aiden, a member of the head table, was kept busy with speeches.

She found she couldn't shrink away, no matter how foreign this land of happy families and joyous celebration seemed. First, it was the man seated next to her, a wiry local called Hugh who regaled her with tales about the district, including the history of Ryders Station, such as he understood it. Then, on finding out she was a medical student, he beamed, and proceeded to show her all his skin cancer scars and tell her all about Dr. Harris, the local family doctor everyone loved. Christina laughed despite blushing as two older ladies at the table joined the conversation and added a few too many intimate details to their own medical stories.

After this Simmo had come and chatted to her about the horses for half an hour, then winking slyly and saying that he knew the cook, gallantly fetched her a plate of superb roast beef when the line looked too long. And suddenly Christina realized she no longer felt shy, and actually struck up a conversation with a young woman at the next table, who was quite happy to chat about her two kids, her sheep property, and even Daniella from when she'd been working in Ryders.

When the speeches were over and everyone was on the dance floor, Christina sat on a straw bale to the side of the speakers, taking a moment to herself but enjoying watching the children cavort around to the live band's upbeat country tunes. She hadn't spotted Aiden for a while, and when she finally did, it was just as Beth and Jackie came to drag her on to the dance floor. She grinned at him and waved. When "The Gambler" came on to cheering, Christina found herself singing along, even though the tune was one she usually associated with pubs and her mother.

Half an hour later, she sank gratefully onto a straw bale with Beth to rest her aching feet.

"Now this is my idea of a good time," Beth said.

Christina grinned, wondering where Aiden was. It occurred to her she had no idea where she was meant to sleep. She scanned around, trying to spot him.

"He's talking to Daniella before she has to go," said Jackie, who boogied in at that moment and caught her looking. "Now, the Nutbush is next, so come on!"

Christina declined, letting Beth and Jackie head back into the dancing, where Will and Jackie's partner, Dave, were beckoning to hurry them up. She couldn't deny it had been a lovely day, and a happy party. But she missed Aiden and didn't feel like dancing anymore. Finally, a song ended and the bandleader spoke into the microphone. "It's that time of the night when we have to farewell the happy couple. So for the last dance, everyone on the floor for a little 'Desire'."

There were a few whoops from the crowd and the guitarist strummed the Ryan Adams ballad softly, slowly, building the rhythm of an achingly tender love song that raised goosebumps on Christina's skin. She rubbed her arms, feeling hollow as the bandleader began to sing the words, full of longing. She'd never felt like crying to a country song before.

A warm hand touched her shoulder. "Hi," said Aiden.

"Hi," she said, and the hollow feeling was gone, replaced with relief and something warm and gentle that only he could bring.

"Would you like to dance?" he asked, a smile on his lips.

Christina glanced at the dance floor, where the whole party was swaying to the music: Daniella, her head on Mark's shoulder, Beth and Will entwined – even Jackie, dancing with the best man who was trying to balance a little boy on his shoulders.

Christina shook her head, overcome. Many times in her life, she'd wished to belong – to a family, a circle of friends – but she'd never before wanted to belong to *someone* like she wanted at this moment to be Aiden's. And that couldn't be possible. "I don't know how to slow dance," she said.

Aiden pulled her up. "Then you'll have to let me lead."

Soon Christina found herself in the midst of the crowd, held firmly within Aiden's embrace as he led her across the floor in flowing steps. His jacket smelled faintly and deliciously of hay and aftershave, and his skin was warm where he pressed his cheek to her hair. Gradually, as the music washed around her, she relaxed. *Desire*, sang the bandleader, the notes tunneling deeper under Christina's skin with each drumbeat. Desire. Desire. And her cheeks were pink with it, as she realized how she was trying so hard not to fall in love with him.

"Did you have a good day?" she asked, trying to put some space between them, searching for the reluctance he'd voiced at Crystal Creek.

"Mmm," Aiden said, his eyes focused on her.

"Daniella looks very happy," she tried again.

"Mmm." His lips spread lazily into a smile.

Christina's heart was racing. The way he was looking at her

... something new was in his eyes, as if he believed this song was theirs, that they belonged to each other. The music wound to an end, and everyone in the crowd loudly cheered the band and the happy couple, who were waving from the marquee doorway. Christina expected the spell that had settled over her and Aiden would slowly ebb away, leaving only a pale brush mark of a once-possible romance.

But Aiden wrapped Christina's hand in his. "There's something I want to show you."

With the lights and noise of the marquee retreating behind them, Aiden guided her through the dark, his hand warm around hers.

"Where are we going?" Christina asked, as they turned left and headed along the ridge away from the house. They passed sheds and outbuildings, small lights glowing above the doors then they walked through a knot of trees. On the other side, the land opened up, the sky pricked with a million stars and hung with a near-full moon. The grass here was thick, swishing past Christina's legs, until they came out onto open ground. There, the vast stillness of the land stretched to the jeweled sky.

"Beautiful," she whispered.

"Will tipped me off about this spot, so I staked it out earlier," Aiden said as they stopped at a darker square on the grass. He looked at ease, his tie loosened, his collar unbuttoned, but his words caught in his throat as if he was breathless. Guided by his hand, Christina sank down beside him, and felt a blanket under her fingers.

Overhead, stars sparkled in the deep indigo night, but it was Aiden who had her attention. Without a word, he slipped an arm around her and drew her close. Christina's blood thrummed as he leaned towards her. Feeling the heat of his skin, she finally dared to look up at him. His gaze was fixed on her, his eyes coal-dark in the moonlight. He raised a hand to gently tuck a strand of hair behind her ear, and his fingers lingered, sliding gently down her jaw to tilt her chin towards him.

"I shouldn't do this," he murmured, his breath hot against her cheek. "But I can't stop."

His lips came against hers, gently at first, as if seeking permission. But she felt the urgency behind his restraint. Christina had a moment of panic; hadn't he said he didn't want this? Then any fear burned away in the flame his mouth ignited inside her. She returned the kiss, reveling in the softness of his lips, then parted her own, wanting more of him.

And suddenly he was kissing her with a white-hot passion, his arms strong around her, his hands like firebrands on her back. Now she had no doubt that he wanted this as much as she did.

Her hands slipped beneath his shirt, his skin velvety smooth over the muscles of his chest. The next moment, he turned her easily, lifting her into his lap. She gripped his arms to keep herself from falling, but then realized that he held her firmly, he wouldn't let her go. One of his hands gently traced a line from her throat down over the dress, coming to rest where the fabric had bunched up at her thigh.

"I think this dress has done a stellar job," he said against her mouth. "How about taking it off?"

Christina's pulse raced harder in her chest, her face flushing at the thought of touching her naked skin to his. But he didn't rush, simply nuzzled at her cheek and mouth, kissing her breathless until she found herself scrambling to her knees and tugging the dress up and over her head.

"You're so beautiful," he murmured, his hands on her thighs, stopping her there so he could look at her in the moonlight.

She looked up into the starry sky, pleased and embarrassed, until he pulled her back down to him on the blanket. And before his hands could remove the last of her clothing, she set her fingers to his shirt buttons. Knowing that he was watching, encouraging her with the hand he stroked over her hip and back, she managed to undo them. When she looked at him again, he had such a satisfied smile on his face, she stopped.

"Why are you grinning like that?" she whispered.

His smile only widened. "I've been thinking about getting naked with you all day."

Mildly scandalized, Christina laughed, pulling his shirt off his shoulders. Soon there was only skin between them, and she forgot everything besides his touch.

Much later, when the air temperature had dropped and the Milky Way had turned through a fair arc of the sky, Christina lay in the crook of Aiden's arm, his body like a furnace warming her, the mood between them close and tender.

She plucked at the dress, discarded beside her. "This has taken some punishment," she said. "The back side's all crushed and there's some kind of spiky prickle that will have to be surgically removed."

"As dresses go, I have to say it's seen better treatment tonight than I gave the other one."

"Is cross-dressing a regular army event? I would have thought that was more for the navy."

"Oh, she makes a joke," said Aiden, and chuckled.

"What was it like, seeing your sister get married?" she asked.

"It was wonderful to see her so happy," Aiden said carefully. "It's funny, most of the time I feel like I'm outside the world she lives in ... that most other people live in. Being in the army, I seem to run on a different clock. But today ... I feel like I'm part of the same world. We even managed to have a good conversation, and it felt completely normal."

He hugged Christina closer, not saying anything for a long time. Finally, a wistful note in his voice, he said, "Mum would have loved this. And she'd have loved Mark too, though I think she'd have had some reservations about Dani marrying a guy who lives on a cattle property and them spending so much time apart."

"Are your parents divorced?"

"Mum passed away when Dani was really young."

In the dark, Christina squeezed him, sensing old grief not yet resolved.

"I'm not sure how well Dani remembers her," he went on. "I'm six years older. Mum was lovely. Tough, but kind and fair. Dad was always keen for me to go to university, study, probably be a doctor too. But I didn't want that, and she accepted it long before he did."

He paused. "I know my sense of what's important is different to other people's. Sometimes I wonder if that's why I don't connect with people outside the military so well. I wonder why I do with you?"

Christina felt his eyes move over her as a shooting star streaked overhead. She wondered what she'd done to deserve the perfection of this night with him. But maybe it was something to do with this place, with its huge sky and kind, happy people, the magic of the wedding. A different kind of Crystal Creek, a place where troubles faded away, where anything seemed possible.

Christina enjoyed the moment, until she felt the long day catching up with her.

"We're not sleeping out here, are we?" she asked eventually. "My clothes are back in the house."

"No," he said, the resonance of his deep voice raising goosebumps on her neck. "I made other arrangements. Of course, if you want to stay out under the stars, I have all my field kit in the car, but it might be cold later."

"You must have done that more than a few times," she said.

"Slept out? Sure. I like it out field. It's where the heart of my job is. Actually—"

Christina rolled onto her side to look at him, sensing him

about to share something deeper. Then he exhaled heavily. "Doesn't matter. Anyway, space was at a premium in the house, but there's a hayloft in the stables. I hope you don't mind horses. What's so funny?"

For Christina had burst out laughing, and couldn't stop. When she finally got herself under control, she said, "Four weeks ago I was living in a horrible share house in Brisbane. Now I'm at a wedding with a drag-wearing soldier and I'm going to sleep in a hayloft!"

Aiden's teeth gleamed white in the darkness. "I guess it is a bit weird, when you put it like that. Tell me about this place in Brisbane."

"Share house from hell, on some days," she said. "You wouldn't believe it."

"Dunno about that. I've lived in barracks for a long time. Although I suppose you don't have a sergeant to maintain standards."

"I wish," said Christina, and told him about the all-night parties, washing left to grow musty in the machine, the constant tardiness with rent and bills.

"Why do you stay, then? Why not get a place on your own?"

"Money," said Christina. Although out here, under this magnificent sky, the daily struggle she had to fund herself seemed so inconsequential. "A place alone in the city is expensive. I also have to put petrol in the car and buy books and my equipment. We're encouraged to buy an ophthalmoscope – do you know what that is?"

"Yeah, an instrument your sister uses to blind you," said Aiden.

Christina chuckled. "Yeah, well, that instrument of blindness costs hundreds. I haven't managed to afford it yet. Last time I had the cash, the car needed new tires."

"What job do you do?"

"I'm a research assistant. I work at one of the hospitals for a doctoral student. I find patients and give them a questionnaire and tests, then enter the data in a program. I do a shift on Friday night, then early and late on Saturday and Sunday. It's not great, but if I get enough patients, it pays okay. Some of the other med students are lucky – they did physiotherapy or pharmacy beforehand, so they can work professionally part-time."

"Couldn't you get some kind of scholarship?" Aiden asked. "I mean, the army would pay you to study. They're always after doctors. Beth's thinking about joining – she rings me now and again to quiz me about what might be involved."

Christina shook her head.

"Isn't there something else to apply for? And don't you qualify for assistance?"

Anger gathered inside her, born of her desperation. "You don't understand," she said, folding her arms across her chest. She tilted her head away from him, trying to banish feeling angry on this night.

The grass crackled under the blanket as Aiden shifted, drawing her back towards him. "I offended you," he said. "I get that it's a touchy subject. I remember the fuel thing. So, want to tell me off for being a nosy prick?"

"No," she said, the heat going out of her ire. He didn't deserve it, and she was tired of keeping these secrets.

"I'm going to tell you something I've never told anyone," she said, hardly believing she would tell him at all. "When I was growing up in Townsville, Rita – that's my mother – never had her life together. No job, no money. Lots of boyfriends. Lots of booze. She'd forget about meals. I was washing my clothes myself when I was eight. Sneaking food out of neighbors' bins. Sometimes when things were bad enough I'd do it at school too. Jeez, the other kids loved it when they caught me. Everyone thought I'd end up a useless welfare case. I feel I'm always running away from that life, that world. And yeah, some other students have scholarships, but they're also bonded to practice in certain places. No way am I doing that."

"So, you don't want to owe anyone?" he said.

Christina nodded. The fire of her anger had gone out. She took a deep breath, full of the scent of clean grass and midnight's coming cool.

"That's not all," she said quietly. "She followed me, Aiden. Six months after I left Townsville, Rita turned up on my doorstep in Brisbane. Said she just needed somewhere to stay for a few days to find her feet. A few days turned into months, sleeping on my couch, eating my food."

"She freeloaded off you?"

"I guess. I was working in a burger joint, trying to pay the rent. My housemates were annoyed she was hanging around. Now and then she'd be sober for a while, but otherwise she was always drunk and out of money. Then, just when I'd decided she had to go, she had a stroke. She'd had accidents for years when she was drunk. Falling down stairs and hitting her head, that sort of thing. I think she'd had seizures long before the stroke. But afterwards they got worse, and she couldn't take care of herself. There was no one else. I was trying to study, work and look after her, living in this awful granny flat at the time. It took me three years to get a place for her in residential care. I was barely scraping by until four months ago but that care house changed everything. I finally got some time back."

"That's ... amazingly huge to have done all by yourself."

Christina fixed her gaze on the stars. "I'm her guardian because someone needs to do it. But she hasn't been my mother for a long time. I do what I have to, that's all." But as the barrier in her mind wobbled, she knew some part of her didn't believe the detachment.

"Do you mind if I ask – what about your dad?"

Christina laughed, the idea was so ridiculous. "Never knew him. Rita told me all kinds of stories. I'm not sure I believe any of them. He didn't want to stick around, anyway. Why would he?"

A long silence drew out, and the breeze rustled in the grass.

Aiden spoke again, his voice gentle. "But you only have, what, a year and a half to go? Then you'll graduate and you'll never worry about money again."

"Don't jinx me," she said quickly. "I still need to pass."

Aiden laughed. "Honey, you studied in the car on the way to a *wedding*. You're going to pass."

His fingers brushed her hair, then her shoulder. Christina sucked back the silent tears his confidence evoked and curled against him, unguarded and clinging to the security his faith offered. The sounds of the distant party had long ago died down, and into the silence, Christina said, "Aiden, I want to tell you now. About this." She opened her palm, the scar silver in the moonlight.

"Mmm?"

"When I was ten, I lived with my aunt for a while," she said quickly, keen to get over this part. She briefly recalled her carefully preserved work in Harriet's filing cabinet, then pushed the thought away. "But after that, I ended up in a foster home. The woman was okay, I guess, but her husband was nasty. He watched me all the time … made me nervous. He was a prick about everything – strict rules and lots of punishment. I often went to bed without dinner. Anyway, one day when I got home from school, the house was empty, and I found a pack of his cigarettes. I was fourteen and I'd seen some older kids smoking at school, and they looked like they didn't give a shit about anything. So I took one and tried it."

Christina stared at the bright stars while she pulled the next words together. "I didn't hear him come home. He caught me outside the back door. He didn't say anything, but he had this look on his face. Like finally he had the excuse he wanted. So he took it off me, sucked it hot … and then he put it out on my hand."

Aiden winced, and Christina felt the gooseflesh run up his arms. He tightened his arm around her.

"When I tried to pull away, he held me down, closed my

hand around it. Made sure it went cold before he let me go."

"Dear God." Aiden folded her hand in his and brought it to his lips, his voice harsh. "I would have killed the fucker."

Christina shivered; she'd thought many times about what she'd like to do to that man, but Aiden sounded dangerously intent and capable, and she suddenly wondered if he'd ever actually killed someone.

"It was a deep burn," she went on quickly. "But I was too scared to show anyone. I didn't know how to explain it, or what else he might do if I told. I tried to clean it, but it hurt too much, and of course it got infected."

"Holy shit, Christy."

Christina shook her head, and even though there were tears on her cheeks, her voice was fierce. "That's the thing. This is how I got out. This is the part I didn't tell you before, about why I decided to be a doctor.

"When I turned up at school with a fever and I couldn't hold my pen, one of the teachers finally noticed. They took me to the hospital. And there was this doctor who saw me. She was the first person in a long time who'd treated me like I mattered. She was so gentle and had so much conviction. She told me she could make me well again and that I didn't have to go back to that house. That I was brave and things could be better for me. She stayed past her shift until she was sure I would have somewhere new and better to go to. And I decided right then that I wasn't going to end up like my mum, like everyone thought I would. I was going to be like her."

In the aftermath of telling him, Christina waited for the regret to flood in, at having revealed to him who she really was. But Aiden simply hugged her tighter, his chest warm under her cheek as she silently cried. He didn't say anything, try to comfort her or describe his own experiences, just let it be exactly what it was, have the weight and time it needed. And after that weight had settled, he helped her dress, pulled her up and guided her back to the loft above the stables, where they fell asleep together on the straw.

Chapter 16

On Sunday, after a long and rowdy morning-after breakfast around the station's barbecue, Aiden and Christina re-joined the road to Townsville. Christina had been very quiet all morning. Aiden understood; he'd have felt raw too, telling someone his darkest secrets. So he left her alone to flip through her notes as the Commodore ate up the highway, focusing his thoughts on work so he wouldn't be tempted to interrupt her. And so he wouldn't feel as though that different world they'd occupied last night was now receding in the rear-view.

The insurance people had said she could turn off the fans today, and she wanted to go back to her aunt's house before she went to work. So he dropped her off with a long hug, a gentle kiss and a promise to talk soon, then headed back to base. A sickly sensation crawled through him when he was back in his room. He didn't know what to do next.

Maybe it was better to do nothing. She had made it clear that she was going home at the end of term, while he had only two weeks left at work, then three of enforced leave before he headed overseas. He sat in his plain desk chair, so like dozens of others he'd sat in, and put his head in his hands.

He would have to move on again. Same as usual.

Only this time, he suddenly wondered if he could.

Christina dragged herself out of bed early the next morning, exhausted after yesterday's long drive and a delivery shift last night. The house still smelled of damp and chemicals, but at least after today – if the fans had done their work – the carpet would be put back.

The workmen knocked on the door at seven, and soon had the equipment carted away. They promised that the carpet layers would turn up in the afternoon.

So, normality would return. Well, whatever passed for normality. Aiden was constantly in her mind but she had no idea what the future could possibly hold or what to do about her feelings for him. It was already week five of the rotation, past halfway – in a month's time she would have to return to Brisbane. She couldn't afford to be thinking about Aiden all the time. She needed to start studying for the end-of-term exam, but first she had to finish the essay, and the case report.

That was what brought her back to the hospital ward. She stifled a yawn as she trekked down the long hall. Daniella was away on her honeymoon, but the nurse recognized her and waved her through. "He let the social worker talk to him yesterday," she said. "See if he'll see her again. Then he can go home and we'll all have some peace."

John's cast was no longer elevated, but he looked tired. He had a notebook in his lap, and was studying it with a pen in his fist.

"It's the physiotherapists trying to kill me now," he said when Christina pulled up a chair.

"I think they're trying to send you home," said Christina. "The nurse said you spoke to the social worker."

John grunted. "A bloody social worker. As if I need one." He paused. "But I do want to go home. Nothing to do in here, except blood tests and x-rays and battles with physiotherapists."

"What will you do when you get home?"

"Back to my projects," said John. "I was wiring up a trailer, and Stash needs some work done on a new bathroom."

"With a full leg cast?"

"Well, maybe in a few weeks. The plumber's got to do his bit first."

"Don't mention plumbing," said Christina. "I've had enough of water pipes for one year." She told him the story of the broken hose and the house flood, the fans and the dryers.

"Make sure you get the wiring checked," John said when she was finished. "It's probably fine, but best to be safe."

"Oh no, that's all right. The insurers—"

"Are all scummy bastards. Can't be sure they'll do the job right. I'll get you someone who'll do it properly. Aitkenvale's just round the corner from him."

"But I can't let you do that—" she began, then frowned. "How do you know I live in Aitkenvale?"

John's face was a mask. "Lucky guess."

Christina fell silent. She was sure she'd never mentioned it to him, not once. Discomfort drifted through her body like a feather, landing softly in her gut, where doubt took over. Maybe she was wrong.

She pushed on. "So, can you tell me some more about your projects?" she asked.

"Actually, I'd like to rest." John turned his gaze towards the mountain again. The smoke haze was back, a light veil over the treetops.

Christina knew she was being dismissed. "I bet you know the mountain really well," she said, wondering what had just happened. "Isn't it part of the base?"

"I need to sleep before that physiotherapist comes back."

Flustered, she gathered her things. "I was meant to ask if you would talk to the social worker again. So you can go home."

"If that's what it takes."

Christina returned to the nurses' station, confused. She'd

thought she was doing much better with him. He'd mentioned his friend again, and his interests. And then …

"How'd you go?" asked the nurse.

"He said he'll talk to the social worker again," said Christina.

"Good. We're trying to track down this friend of his, see if he can help out at home, with some extra support from a community nurse if John will allow it. The leg's healing well now, so there's no reason to keep him here."

The rest of the day passed slowly. With few patients in the clinic and no Katie, Christina took a textbook down from the shelf in the tearoom and read through the section on cardiac emergencies. But her thoughts kept wandering. First to Aiden, reliving the weekend, wondering what life would be like if such a time could last. And then her mind kept returning to John, to all the things he didn't want to talk about … and how it was that he knew where she lived. *Lucky guess.* But Christina didn't believe in luck, except maybe the bad variety.

As if to confirm this sentiment, Lena called the moment Christina arrived home after the teleconference tutorial – another Katie no-show – just when she was about to resume work on her essay.

"We're at the hospital," she began, sounding harried. "Your mother had a fit this afternoon. She cut her leg in the fall, and they want to do an x-ray to make sure there's no fracture."

"Okay," Christina said, feeling jolted back to earth.

"But she's refusing. Doesn't want the x-ray, or the stitches. She says she won't speak to you, but you're her guardian. The doctor wants to talk to you so you can give permission. She's right here."

"Put her on."

Christina was soon speaking with a resident, who seemed shaken that someone was refusing to have a leg wound treated. "The x-ray isn't absolutely essential," she said. "But given the medical history, I think it's a good idea."

"What about the stitches?"

"Well, that's the best option. But she's pretty emphatic and I don't want to have needles in my hands if she starts kicking. Still, the wound needs closing. We'll do our best to clean it, and then use glue and strips. We'll sedate her if we think she might do herself more harm."

Christina blew out a long breath, thinking simultaneously what a crap day the resident must be having and how helpless she was from hundreds of miles away. "Do what you have to. If you need me to sign something, I'll give you a fax number." She'd seen a machine in Harriet's study, the number stuck to the side in typical organized-Harriet style.

But even when Lena rang back an hour later to say that the wound was finally dressed and Rita sleeping off a Valium, and not to worry, Christina found herself staring at the kitchen wall, trembling, and trying to rebuild the barrier to her old life in her mind. Parts of it were crumbling dangerously. Maybe it was Aiden and the weekend, forgetting her responsibilities; or maybe it was just being in this house again. Evidence of Harriet was everywhere – the orderly filing cabinets, the labels. Everywhere, that was, except in person.

Long after the sun had gone down, after a full day's work, PT and a shower, Aiden found himself caught in no-man's land, and inside his own goddamn room. He'd only managed to put on his shorts, his regiment t-shirt still on the chair. His field gear was half-unpacked, his mind half made up as he paced. He had to see her. Had to tell her. And yet his shirt stayed on the chair, his keys on the table.

Finally, he thought about what Travers would say, and gave himself a mental uppercut. He just had to man up and get in the car. Five minutes later, he was behind the Commodore's wheel, driving out the base gate.

By the time he arrived at her house, his heart was thumping as though he were a schoolboy on a first date. Emotionally, he had one foot pressing on the accelerator, while the other one was trying to slam on the brakes. He sat in his car outside her house, trying to pull himself together. Told himself that Christina was going home in a few weeks. That it didn't have to go anywhere. He should just lay things out, have an adult conversation. None of which did anything to quiet his nerves as he got out of the car and knocked on the door.

"Just a minute," he heard faintly.

"It's me," Aiden said through the security screen.

"Door's not locked," she called. She was somewhere deep in the house, and sounded distinctly distracted.

"Where are you?" he said, walking past the empty kitchen and down the hall around the lounge. Action was helping to dull the nerves. The house smelled strongly of industrial cleaning products, but at least the equipment was gone.

"Here," she said, appearing in a doorway at the end of the hall, her eyes on a slim navy-blue booklet in her hands. She was dressed in a pair of cut-off track pants and a singlet, her blonde hair knotted behind her head and a frown on her face. At the sight of her, something inside Aiden gave way, as if his heart had been strung on a tight wire that had suddenly broken. He had no idea where to begin.

"Sorry I didn't call, but I wanted to talk … What is it?" he asked when she didn't look up.

"This is a passport," she said, holding up the booklet. "My aunt's passport."

"Didn't you say she'd gone overseas?"

"Exactly. She talked about Kokoda. So why is it here?" Christina paced past him into the kitchen. She turned once in a circle, as if looking for something she'd missed.

"Maybe it's expired," Aiden said. At this, Christina showed him the picture page. "All right, so it's current. Maybe she thought she lost it and had it replaced. How did you find it?"

"I was trying to file the documents the insurance people left," she said, sinking into a kitchen chair. "The passport was in the cabinet. No way Harriet would have lost it in there.

She'd have turned the place over looking for it."

Christina still hadn't looked at him, her gaze fixed in midair beside the table. "I thought it was a bit odd – her trip matching up with me coming here. I wouldn't blame her for avoiding me."

"Why would she avoid someone who's staying in her house?" Aiden asked reasonably.

Christina folded her arms across her chest. "We had a bad argument the last time I saw her." She finally looked up then, her deep green eyes fixing on him, full of regret. A spot of color crept into her cheeks. "I'm sorry, what were you saying before?"

"Doesn't matter. Tell me about this. You haven't said much about Harriet. I didn't think you were close." He pulled her out of the seat and steered her through to the lounge and onto the couch, where he sat beside her. And after a quiet minute, he felt her relax against him, as she had on the spur at Ryders Station.

"Harriet's my mum's younger sister," Christina began softly. "I was always scared of her when I was little. She's tall and imposing, and she was an army nurse. If she visited my mum, sometimes in her uniform, I'd watch her from the end of the hallway, terrified and fascinated." For a second, a smile touched her lips. "Her visits usually ended with Mum yelling at her for being a nosy bitch. They didn't get along well. So I was surprised one day when Harriet came to pick me up from school. I was ten, and Mum was going through a particularly bad patch. Drunk all day, every day. I was taking myself to school, looking after everything. Anyway, Harriet asked me if I wanted to stay with her during the week, and just go home on the weekends. I didn't dare refuse. That's when I first came here."

Aiden cleared his throat. "Do you think they'd worked out an arrangement?"

"I have no idea. Mum wouldn't talk about it. But life

changed overnight. I couldn't believe how clean Harriet's place was. I had a room of my own, and a desk. Hot meals, and packed lunches for school. In the evenings, we played Scrabble and Monopoly – Harriet taught me. Funny thing is, I was actually really difficult at first," Christina admitted. "I was used to being left alone, so it took me a while to accept her rules. Doing homework. No swearing. Eating greens."

Aiden chuckled.

"After that, it was great. When I went home on weekends, Rita would quiz me about what Harriet and I had done all week, and I learned to keep my mouth shut. She didn't like hearing that Harriet had taught me how to check the car oil, or that we'd made cookies. Harriet even took me out to this farm once to see goats and chickens – friends of hers owned it. She had friends. I hated going home, and always looked forward to Sunday night."

"So what happened?" asked Aiden.

Christina shrugged but Aiden saw hurt under her attempt to be casual. "When I was nearly fourteen, Harriet suddenly changed her mind about it all. I know she was stressed – she was having the whole downstairs closed in and renovated, so there were walls down, problems with builders, things like that. She'd sit at the table at night looking at the paperwork. Then one day, out of the blue, she told me that my mum wanted me back, and that she was getting married to some army guy called Thomas. So I went back to Rita's full time. Soon after that, Harriet went with Thomas when he posted away."

"Just like that?" asked Aiden.

"Harriet told me she wished I could go with her. But Rita told me Harriet had just had enough of me and wanted her life back."

Feeling the fine tremor in Christina's body, Aiden could see how deeply that statement had burrowed in and hurt her. He rested his lips on her forehead, wanting to comfort her.

"You know some of the rest," she rushed on. "Mum had been sober for a while then, even had a job, but a few months later it fell apart again. She set the kitchen on fire and the department intervened after the police saw the state of the house. I ended up in the foster home. When that went bad, a different one before Rita had another dry spell and I was back at her place for senior year. Then later, I ran into Harriet out of the blue."

Christina closed her eyes. "I was leaving town. So I went up Castle Hill for a last look, a good-riddance I guess, and there she was. I was so angry. At the time I didn't even realize how much. I called her horrible things, blamed her for everything that had happened. And I told her I never wanted to see her again.

"Later, when I'd calmed down, I felt bad about it, but I hadn't spoken to her again until a few weeks ago. I never expected her to take my call, but still, I wouldn't be surprised if she doesn't want to see me again."

"You think she might have taken off just so she didn't have to see you?"

"Why else would she tell me she'd gone overseas?" But she frowned and Aiden wasn't sure if she really believed it.

"If that's true, then I'm sorry," he said. "But it doesn't make sense that she would let you stay in the house if she was holding a grudge."

"I guess ..." she said. Then she stood up. "I want to show you something."

A minute later, they stood at the filing cabinet in the study, Aiden's fingers flicking through the file she'd produced, pages and pages of Christina's childhood work, all lovingly preserved.

"This was put together with a lot of care," he said at last. He looked at Christina, who was biting her lip. "Hey, she must still care about you. Otherwise why keep this stuff?"

"Maybe she forgot it was there."

"Maybe," Aiden said doubtfully. "But what are you going to do about it?"

"Nothing," Christina said firmly, tucking the file away.

Then she glanced at the clock. "I really should get back to my essay."

Aiden nodded, knowing his chance had passed. "Listen, Christy, I'm going to be stupidly busy for a fortnight. Early starts, late finishes, until I've handed over this task. But I want to talk about some things, after the weekend. I'll call you in a few days?"

When she nodded, and hugged him so warmly that he couldn't help a long, slow kiss, Aiden reproached himself for his cowardice. He could only hope things would become clearer before the next time he saw her.

Chapter 17

Christina arrived at the clinic on Tuesday to find Captain May, Dr. Vaughn and Travers finishing up their morning meeting in the lunch room.

"Back again," said Captain May when he saw Christina.

"Why does he always say that?" she asked Travers when both doctors had disappeared back to their rooms.

"Because most of the students aren't here as much as you are, as you can see. Want a patient?"

Noting the absence of Katie for a second day, Christina took a walk-in patient form off the rack and stepped out. The waiting room contained only a handful of people, one man sitting by himself, and another with a woman and two small children by his side. Unusual. She hadn't seen someone come with a family before.

"Josh Roche?"

The man with the family stood. His eyes were sunken, as if he hadn't slept in a week, his skin sallow, and he moved as though he had sand in his joints.

"This way," she said quickly, opening the curtain to a bed bay.

"I'm sick," he said, sitting stiffly on the bed.

"I see that." Christina noted the yellow tinge in his eyes. "Tell me what's going on."

"Been hugging the toilet all night, just can't keep anything down. My gut's aching. I feel like I've gone ten rounds in the ring."

Christina scribbled frantically. "Anyone else sick at home?"

"No, everyone's okay for once. Wife made me come down. I just got back from deployment last week and she thinks I must have picked up something over there."

Christina's thoughts churned, but she felt calm, and the questions seemed to come to her more easily than ever. "Any change in your urine or stools?"

"Piss is dark, but like I said, I can't keep anything down. Haven't taken a dump in three days."

"Where does your stomach hurt?"

"All over," he said, but his hand moved to the upper right, near his ribs.

"Ever been sick like this before?" Christina asked as she stood and pulled on a pair of exam gloves. Sweat was trickling down the side of Josh's face as she tested his nail beds.

"Feels like flu, or gastro," he said, swallowing audibly. "Nausea's terrible."

Gently, Christina palpated his abdomen, feeling for the liver, which normally evaded her, being tucked up under the ribs in a healthy patient. But this time, she definitely felt something. Was his liver enlarged? "Josh, sit tight. I'm going to fetch one of the doctors."

She found Dr. Vaughn at the front desk. "I have a sick one," she said. "Thirty-four-year-old lieutenant, recently returned from deployment with a three-day history of nausea and malaise, and twelve hours of vomiting and anorexia. On examination, scleral icterus, slow capillary refill, abdominal tenderness and possible enlarged liver."

Dr. Vaughn nodded curtly. "Let's go."

In the ER bay, Christina hung back as Dr. Vaughn made a quick assessment. Then he turned to her. "Christina, could you please get a line started? Josh, we're going to take care of that nausea first, all right? You look like shit."

"Thanks, doc," said Josh with a ghost of a smile.

As Christina grabbed the cannula trolley, Dr. Vaughn put a hand on her arm. "We'll give him ten milligrams of metoclopramide. Draw it up, but check it with me first. I have to make a phone call. He needs to be admitted."

Christina set to work. For the first time, she felt more than just a student. She laid out the materials: a cannula, tourniquet, cotton balls, tape, alcohol wipe. After all Travers' training, it was automatic. The stilette was in the vein and she was releasing the tourniquet before she remembered that this had once been frightening. She secured the line port in the cannula and taped it down.

"Not long now," she told Josh. She strode across to the drug store and retrieved the metoclopramide, checked the concentration and drew ten milligrams into a syringe. She found Dr. Vaughn and showed him the dose.

Christina locked the syringe into the port and, after Dr. Vaughn's nod, slowly pushed the drug into Josh's vein. Like magic, she watched the color returning to his face. By the time she'd given the full dose, Josh had stopped sweating.

"How do you feel now?" she asked, hanging a bag of fluid that Dr. Vaughn had brought in.

"Better. Don't wanna spew anymore."

As she began to pack up the materials, a sense of accomplishment glowed warm inside her. She was grateful she'd been able to make a difference, even a small one.

Dr. Vaughn sat on the edge of Josh's bed. "We're going to admit you until we work out what's going on. Could be that you've picked up hepatitis, but we need to rule out a few things. I'll bring your family in. You'll need to tell them it will be a few days at least."

After the arrangements were made, Christina and Dr. Vaughn sat at the desk as he signed off the last of the paperwork. "Thanks for your help today," said Dr. Vaughn.

Christina later related the story to Travers. "I can't thank you enough for your teaching. I didn't even have to think about it. Got the cannula first time."

"You'll be all set for the wards next rotation, then." He paused. "Listen, have you seen Katie since the weekend?"

"No. I was expecting her to be here. She's supposed to come over to study tonight." Though after what had happened on Friday night with Seb, Christina wasn't sure she wanted Katie to turn up.

Travers' face was unreadable. "Having trouble reaching her, that's all. Could you … Nah, don't worry about it. How's things with the captain? You went to the wedding, right?"

Christina tried not to smile, but she couldn't help it. "It was nice," she said, trying to sound offhand. "Big cattle farm out west. And you'll enjoy this: his sister's a doctor, and the groom's brother is marrying a doctor, too. The maid of honor is a nurse, starting med next year. And Aiden's dad's a surgeon too."

Travers grinned. "Yeah, I know. So Murphy's Law says not a single person was sick the whole weekend, right?"

Christina laughed. "Right." She reached for her bag. It was time to head home.

"Don't think I missed you not answering my question," said Travers.

"Which question was that?"

"How things went with Aiden." Travers' gaze was locked on her.

But Christina was prepared this time. She pushed the idea of her and Aiden behind her protective barrier. "It was nice," she repeated, and walked out the door.

To Christina's surprise, Katie turned up on her doorstep at five thirty with her textbooks and a contrite expression.

"Hi," said Christina coolly when she opened the door.

"Are you mad?" asked Katie, screwing up her face as though waiting for a blow. When Christina said nothing, she relaxed and cracked open an eyelid. "Okay, look, I know Friday night wasn't cool. I should have asked you if you wanted to come."

"So?" asked Christina, rather thinking Katie was missing the point. After all, it had been her brother causing the issue.

"So, look, I know Seb was a complete dick. It's no excuse, but he's under a lot of pressure. And I'm here to make it all better – I have study notes, and in an hour, I'm buying us Chinese."

"I don't know, Katie …"

"Oh please, come on. You need to eat more."

Grudgingly, Christina had to admit she was right: her funds were critically low, the delivery shifts covering little more than her rent. The wedding weekend meals away had helped, but there were going to be many packets of two-minute noodles in the next few weeks. Knowing that, the oily, salty glory of fried rice was hard to turn down.

"Fine, okay," she said, standing back.

Katie beamed as she came inside. "I was so worried you were pissed at me," she chattered. "And Seb is all wound up because Dad's visiting this week. He always gets like that, just like when we were kids. What do you want to do first – reproductive system or next week's reading?"

Later that evening, the table ringed with Chinese takeout containers, Christina felt her eyes crossing as she read a paragraph on scrotal masses for the third time. "I can't do this anymore," she said, reaching for a cold dim sum.

"Reproductive health is the worst," Katie agreed. "Imagine if you got a case like that in the exam? I was at this dinner in Brisbane once, and that author Nick Earls told this hilarious story about a scrotal exam he had to do as a student."

"Mmm," said Christina, her eyes burning from being held open.

"I think it involved the Pope. The room was in stitches."

Christina closed her book. "How's the case study research

coming? Do you want me to take over any of it?"

"I'll have it by the end of the weekend."

"Are you sure? I know you like the weekend to do things."

Katie looked up with a smile. "Do you want to come out? We'll go clubbing. It'll be fun."

"I don't think so."

"Why not? Too busy with Aiden?"

"Don't be silly," Christina said quickly.

"Well, what then?"

Christina stood up and flicked on the kettle as a diversion. "Because I don't want to. Anyway, I'm not coming out with you and Travers."

"Who said anything about Travers?"

"I just assumed …"

Katie shrugged. "Nah. I'm going to dump him."

A dark sinking sadness plucked at Christina's heart. "I thought you liked him."

"Yeah, I did. But I thought he was different, you know? I was just looking for a fun time, and he's taking it way too seriously."

"What do you mean?"

Katie rolled her eyes. "You know, talking about what happens from here, how we keep seeing each other, like he loves me or something. Besides, he's all messed up underneath. And he talks about army stuff all the time, like stuff he's seen overseas, army this, army that. Might be his life, but it's not mine."

"You don't find that interesting?"

"Not really. Plus he's so fixated on this stupid diving business. He's got all these brilliant medical skills, but he doesn't want to use them. He could do med if he wanted."

"Maybe he's just done with those things, Katie. You can tell the diving business really excites him."

Katie began gathering her things. "Well, whatever, it doesn't matter. Like I said, it was supposed to be fun and it's not anymore. Best to be done with it."

Christina didn't know what to say. This was between Katie and Travers, and none of her business. But all the same, she felt awful for Travers. She'd seen the way he looked at Katie. He couldn't help who he was, and she hated to think that he was going to be hurt.

When they reached the front door, Katie spun around and leaned on the doorframe, her brow creased. "Hey, Chris, do you ever, you know, think about doing something else? Other than med, I mean."

It took Christina a few seconds to process the question, to realize it was one that could even be asked. "No," she said. "I never thought about it. Why?"

Katie shrugged again, like it hadn't meant anything. "I'll see you tomorrow, yeah?"

At three p.m. the next day, Aiden exhaled into air that smelled of dust and sweat, adjusting his stride to take the pressure off his shins. He had forty kilos of pack and webbing on his back, a Steyr rifle slung across his chest. Behind him he could hear the other officers breathing, the crunch of trail dust under their boots. Usually he'd have marched with them. But in the final physical assessment test before his assignment, he needed to prove what he was made of. He remembered being a grunt and seeing officers who weren't as fit as those they commanded; he never wanted that to be him. He wanted to be sure that all the men he led knew that he could still do what they did.

He shrugged his pack, easing the ache in his shoulders. Already today he'd carried barrels and gone over obstacles. He'd left his own CO far behind. His heart was pounding, his lungs sucking the air, but he still had energy to burn. There were just a few miles between him and the end of the course.

Ten minutes later, amid the rising heat and the roar of insects, he was picking his way downhill when his foot slid on a loose patch of dirt. He caught himself just before the weight on his back pulled him over, but as he stood recovering, he felt pain bloom hot around his knee.

Shit, his good knee.

He took a step forward and the pain flared. Several more steps and he found a rhythm again, but the stabs of pain kept coming. He finished the march in good time, but he couldn't enjoy the accomplishment, having to concentrate not to limp.

As soon as he was back on base, he went to his room and packed his knee with ice. Then, holding it on with a bandage, he drove straight to Travers' place.

"Come on in," said Travers, who had a stubby in his hand. Then he glanced down. "What's that on your knee?"

"Can you look at it? Slipped in the pack march and jagged it." Aiden sat and watched the joggers along The Strand below as Travers took a look at the joint.

"You haven't gone to the med center?" asked Travers.

"No."

"Why not?"

"You know why. If it's nothing I'll just create a heap of trouble over deployment."

"So you're not avoiding Christina?"

Aiden felt a qualm. "Why would I be avoiding her?"

Travers sighed. "Look, the injury might be nothing. You were able to keep going on it, you've had it iced, and I can't find any bad signs now. But if it's not one hundred per cent in the morning, you go in, deal? I'm not a doctor."

Reluctantly, Aiden agreed, propping his leg up on the end of the couch.

"Now, I'd offer you a beer, but you need all the healing you can get, so you'll just have to watch me drink."

Aiden caught a tone. "How many have you had?"

"A few."

"You want to talk about the dive business?"

"Nah."

Aiden twisted around to look at his friend. Travers wrinkled his nose as he downed the beer, putting it away faster than usual.

"What's going on?" Aiden asked.

Travers took another swig. "Got my ass handed to me, that's what."

"At work?"

"Nah. Katie. She dropped me pretty hard."

"Shit, mate." Aiden examined Travers' face. "When did it get that serious?"

Travers swung the beer bottle between his knees, his forehead creased, face pinched. "Hell, I didn't even know. She seemed so into me. She wanted me to meet her parents, she was talking about transferring up here to finish her study. I thought it could really go somewhere. I trusted her. And then I made the mistake of telling her about … well, you know, about Victoria. She said … she didn't want to be with someone with baggage, and some other stuff I don't want to repeat."

Aiden was floored. He'd known Travers a long time, but he'd never seen him so downcast over a woman. Travers had never been the type for commitment. Now, finally, he'd fallen hard, opened himself up, and she'd trashed him.

"You know what's worse?" asked Travers. "If she knocked on my door now and said she didn't mean any of it, I'd take her back. How sad am I?"

Aiden grunted. "Let me guess, she say you could be friends, too?"

"Yeah, don't they always." Travers rolled his eyes.

"Well, then," said Aiden. "You better give me the phone so I can call for a pizza, and put something on the TV."

"Yeah, okay," said Travers. About to hand over the cordless, he paused. "Calling Carlo's, are you?"

"She's not working tonight," said Aiden, scanning through the movies on Travers' hard drive.

"That right?" said Travers.

Aiden ignored him. "*Platoon? 300?*"

"Nah, I don't need to see my bullshit past life up on

screen."

"*Starship Troopers?*"

"Yeah, okay."

Aiden laughed. "All right, your bullshit past life *in space* then."

Soon they had demolished two pizzas and Travers four more beers, as Johnny Rico and friends destroyed the bugs. Travers said nothing throughout, until the brain bug was captured and the closing credits were rolling. He hit mute, and reached for his bottle with deliberate slowness. Aiden realized he must be absolutely hammered.

"How did you pull it back together after Tracey left?" Travers finally said, slurring slightly. "I mean, that was a hell of a thing. A hellavathing."

Aiden tipped his head back and adjusted the ice pack on his knee. The ice was melting and needed replacing. "Well, the manner of her leaving helped. There wasn't much time to feel sorry for myself when I was just trying to survive."

"Hell, yeah." Travers paused. "You didn't want her to come back, even then?"

Aiden laughed. "No. I mean, I drove myself nuts for a while trying to work out what I could have done differently. But I never wanted her back. Not after that."

Travers was quiet as the credits came to an end and the title screen reappeared. Then he glanced across. "You worried about it happening again? Is that why you haven't told her?"

"Haven't told who what?"

"Why you haven't told Christina that you're being deployed. I know you haven't."

Aiden let the statement fall through him like a red hot anvil. "It's not like that," he said. "We're not ... She's going home before I leave anyway."

"So it doesn't matter if you tell her, then," Travers pointed out. "You don't think she'll want to stay in touch with you? You know how much it means when we're over there – having letters, someone thinking about you."

Aiden couldn't answer him. Up till now, it had all made perfect sense in his head. That he'd tried but the timing wasn't right. But as he tried to assemble words around his reasons, they collapsed.

Travers nodded. "That's what I thought. You should tell her, Aiden. If she really doesn't want to be serious, how can she be mad?" He staggered up, collecting the empties. "Remember, no courage without fear."

Aiden grunted. He knew Travers was right, and yet he fought against the idea all the way back to the base. He was so preoccupied that he didn't notice that his knee felt fine until he'd climbed the stairs to his room. Inside, he paced back and forth, scrolling through his phone contacts for someone to call. Maybe he should try the padre, but he suspected the advice would be the same as Travers'. He had many friends; that was one benefit of moving around so much. The flipside was that he'd been out of touch with many of them for a good while. They'd been close at one point, but he still didn't want to call, so late at night, and lay out his problem. Daniella was the one person he'd have rung without hesitation, but she was on her whirlwind honeymoon, somewhere on a tropical island.

He chucked the phone down on his bed. He didn't need to get worked up about this. It was a non-issue, just as he'd told Travers. He just had to talk to Christina. And he would … once the week was over.

Chapter 18

By Sunday afternoon, Christina seemed to be on top of her university work, but as the hours went by, her frustration with Katie mounted. Finally, she called her.

"I really need that research to put in the case report," she said. "It's due Wednesday. I have clinic during the week and I'm working every night."

"I'm sending it now, jeez," said Katie.

Christina's relief was short-lived. The file Katie emailed through contained almost nothing of value – three study abstracts on concussion, and half a paragraph of woeful analysis, nothing she could include with the case report on John. Christina had emphasized in her own part the examinations for neurological signs, and the challenges in developing rapport, but she needed Katie's part to support that they understood acute brain injury, even if John didn't turn out to have it. Christina could barely contain her ire as she stabbed at her phone, calling Katie back. But Katie refused to pick up.

Christina was left with no choice. If she wanted to pass, she would have to take up the slack. She downloaded papers until she had to go to Carlo's for her shift, then resumed when she returned home, skimming and searching until she could no longer keep her eyes open. She forced herself to get up early the next morning, to compile the data and write up an analysis. In her sleep-deprived state, the anger bubbled up on so many things. Why had Katie dropped the ball? What had happened with Travers? … And why had Harriet lied to her?

"For Christ's sake, go home and sleep," said Travers when Christina showed up at the clinic at nine o'clock, looking like a zombie. "You've already won the gold star for attendance."

Christina went, but not home. Instead she found herself driving to the hospital and dragging her feet along the ward floor, determined to round out the case study with John. If she was honest, she was still troubled by the strangeness in the last visit and wanted to see if John would be more forthcoming this time.

"You missed him," said the desk nurse. "He went home yesterday. But the community nurse is doing visits. She'll probably let you tag along if you want. Be good for you to see community practice like that."

And so, after that afternoon's tutorial in the conference room and another non-appearance from Katie, Christina found herself standing outside a plain brick house in the nearby suburb of Annandale. The bubbly nurse, who clearly thought an interested medical student was a prized rarity, ushered her inside. Christina checked her watch; she was on the early shift at Carlo's.

"Mr. Hunt is pretty well set up for now," the nurse said. "He says his friend is dropping around later. I'll just be in the kitchen, putting his meds together for the week. You go ahead."

Christina found John sitting in a desk chair in the lounge, his leg propped on a stool. The house was neat but sparsely furnished, and the top of a nearby dining table was covered in a tarp and the pieces of a disassembled motor. On his lap was a stable table, on which he'd balanced a soldering iron, wires, and the innards of a machine Christina didn't recognize. John nodded towards the kitchen and rolled his eyes.

"She kicked me out of my shed yesterday," he said by way of hello.

"You were using a circular saw," complained the nurse from the kitchen doorway.

"They're still pushing drugs on me, too," he added.

"I heard that," the nurse called.

John gave Christina a small smile. He certainly seemed happy to be home, relaxed in a way he'd never been in hospital. Without a scowl on his face, he looked ten years younger. Christina pulled a stool over and asked what he was fixing. He explained that it was the motor from a water pump.

"I made the nurse pull it out of the pond," he added, when he'd finished going through all the parts, naming them for her. "So I guess we're getting along. And she has to earn a living somehow."

The nurse made a noise from the kitchen. Christina smiled, but she was too tired for banter.

"John, I actually want to ask you something."

Very carefully, John put his soldering iron back in its cage. A thin wisp of smoke escaped from the tip. "What's that?"

"How did you know where I lived?"

"You must have mentioned it. When you were talking about your rotation."

He seemed so genuine that Christina let it go. She was starting to feel unhinged for dwelling on it. "All right. I have to hand in my assignment soon, so there's just a few things I wanted to make sure I got right."

She spent ten minutes going over the details of the accident and what John remembered afterwards, and he answered everything as he had before. Finally, when she was preparing to go, he said, "Is everything all right at the house? You know, after the flooding."

"Seems fine. The carpet's back now, and the insurers said they'll check the wall moisture in another week."

"Your aunt overseas for a while, then?"

Christina put her notebook into her bag. "Seems that way. You know what's funny? Sometimes I don't think she is overseas. I found her passport. So, now I wonder if she's just avoiding—" Christina stopped abruptly. She was rambling, revealing these stupid feelings that had just lodged themselves within her and now bubbled over in a careless moment.

Glancing down, she noticed a tremor in John's hand. "Are you feeling okay?"

"Fine," he said, making a fist. "Just not used to this detailed work. Bloody solder points are made for pygmies."

"Had something to eat today?"

"Oh, he's going to eat," called the nurse.

John made a face. As Christina said her goodbyes, she tried not to feel despondent. She hadn't realized how much John had become part of the fabric of this rotation.

Only when she'd driven down the road did she wonder: she knew she'd told him she was living at her aunt's place, but had she said Harriet was overseas? She frowned. She must have. But that feather of suspicion again tickled in her gut.

It was nearly six when Christina reached the house, with half an hour to spare before her shift. She whipped around her room, stuffing clothes from the bed and floor into the washing basket. "Behave," she warned the machine as she tipped them in. Returning to strip the bed, she immediately thought of Aiden. A week, and he hadn't called. But he'd said he would be busy.

As she started the machine she heard her phone ringing from the bedroom. Maybe that was him now. But after scooping up the handset, she saw it was Lena on the line.

"I'm so sorry, Chris. Your mum's leg's developed an infection. The doctor's been round and given her antibiotics, but she won't take them. She picks them out of the other pills."

Christina leaned her shoulder into the wall. "Did she say why?"

"No. Probably she just doesn't like the change, but she's

shut down, ignoring me."

"Do you think she'd notice if you put them in something else?"

"That's what I was going to try, if you're okay with it. But she might notice – it could be bitter."

"Try it," Christina said. "If that doesn't work, see if the pharmacist can compound it some other way, maybe in a syrup?"

"Of course. Okay. I know you probably have to go to work."

"Oh, Lena? If neither of those things work, tell her that she might have to go to hospital and have a drip instead. She can't suffer a terrible infection for the sake of two weeks of tablets."

Christina put down the phone and took two deep breaths. She hated forcing things on Rita, even when it was for her own good. She'd just begun to change for work when her phone rang again. Expecting it to be Lena calling back, she instead heard a strange woman's voice on the line.

"Christina Price? This is Anne, the PA for the dean of the school. Can I connect him through?"

"Sure," she said, perplexed. Why would the dean be calling her? She only knew him from a few lectures in first year, and his photo on the wall in the school office.

"Christina." The dean's voice carried authority. "I want to say at the outset I would have preferred if this was a face-to-face meeting, but as you're away on rotation, this will have to suffice."

"Okay."

"I'll dispense with pleasantries. We've been made aware of some serious irregularities in the surgery rotation exam, which we're looking into. The school is taking it very seriously, and during exam week we'll be meeting with all the students. There's reason to believe some students accessed the test ahead of time. Is there anything you know about this? If you do, the earlier you tell us, the better."

"I don't know anything about it," she said blankly.

"All right," he said, sounding tired. "Please call the office if you want to at any time."

Christina hung up the call with shaking fingers. She'd done well in the surgery written exam, because she'd studied hard. But she hadn't done well in the vivas, or in any previous exams. Was that an irregularity? Failing an exam was one thing, cheating was quite another.

She needed to get dressed for her shift. As she pulled the work cap down on her head and grabbed her keys, she pushed away the anxiety and tried to focus on the hours ahead.

The Belmont still had a quarter-tank of gas, so at least she didn't have to worry about that, and during the evening the orders were steady but not too rushed. During the last hour, she debated with herself whether to try to stay up and finish the case report, or go straight to bed and get up early instead.

On her second-last delivery, Christina had just taken a turn when she heard a siren behind her. Glancing in her rear-view mirror, she saw flashing red and blue lights.

"Oh great, what now?" she muttered. She pulled over and wound down her window, her heart thundering. In the wing mirror, she watched the officer step from his car with a flashlight and stalk towards her door.

"Hello," he said curtly. "Do you understand why I've pulled you over?"

"Not really, no," she said, peering up. He was wearing a cap too, his features shadowed under the brim.

"You took a turn back there and you didn't indicate."

"I didn't?" She blinked a few times, feeling caught in a dream. Surely this wasn't happening.

"Think what could have happened if there'd been a cyclist behind you."

"Was there?" she asked, appalled.

The officer ignored that. "You also failed to indicate left at the last roundabout. Is there any reason you didn't do that?"

"No," she admitted. There was nothing more to say. She'd

been driving on automatic. She couldn't even remember a roundabout.

"Do you have your license with you?"

Christina fumbled with frozen fingers, eventually extracting the card from her wallet's cracked plastic sleeve. Then the officer made her verify that her indicators did indeed work.

"Wait here, please," he said. He made a circuit of the Belmont, then reappeared. "Is this your vehicle, Christina?"

Christina's tongue felt thick and foreign in her mouth. "No. It's my aunt's. Harriet Reed. I'm staying at her house," she added.

The officer flipped the license over. "Is this your current address?"

"Yes. I mean, no. Sort of. That's my Brisbane address. But I'm living here for a few weeks before I go back there."

"What's your address in Townsville?"

Christina gave it to him, watching the shifting patterns of red and blue reflecting across her bonnet. A few people wandering up the sidewalk stopped to gawp. She hunched down in her seat, wishing that the Carlo's magnetic stickers on the car weren't quite so huge and yellow and that there wasn't two pizzas rapidly cooling on the bench seat beside her.

"Are you working at the moment?" the officer asked, as if he could read her thoughts.

"Yes," she said meekly, feeling ready to cry. "Second-last delivery."

"Right, here's what's going to happen. You're going to receive a ticket for both failures to indicate a turn. So I'm going to go and write that up. Wait here." He paced back to his car.

Christina sat numbly for a second, then reality hit. Fines. "Shit," she whispered, ashamed at her stupidity. Her hands lay limp in her lap. She hadn't wanted to come back to Townsville. She'd nearly escaped the life everyone had expected of her. And now, look, here she was. Returned. And a felon.

The officer darkened her window again, handing across two sheets of yellow paper. "Here are the notices for failing to indicate a change-of-direction signal. That's a sixty-six-dollar fine each. Your full legal rights are printed on the back. You have twenty-eight days to pay the fine or respond. Do you have any questions?"

Christina shook her head, her throat closed and her lip quivering. She wished he would just go away.

"You have a pleasant evening. Remember that signal." He strode off.

Christina waited until the police car had pulled around her and disappeared down the road. Her cheeks were wet; she hadn't known she could cry without noticing, but there was the evidence. She folded the yellow tickets, the bend crooked. A hundred and thirty-two dollars. She couldn't pay it. She would have to ask for more time, eat more noodles.

And there was a bigger problem.

When she arrived back at the store after completing the delivery, she wiped away any trace of tears before she went inside. Carlo was counting out a till. "Last one for you, there," he said.

"Carlo, I need to tell you something."

"When you get back."

"No, now, please."

Carlo tipped his cap up. "Okay. What is it?"

"I just got a ticket. From the police." She was going to be fired. She knew the policy; she'd worked enough delivery jobs in Brisbane.

"You speed?" asked Carlo, frowning.

"No, I didn't indicate when I turned left. Twice." She held out the tickets so he could see.

"Pfft!" Carlo made a dismissive gesture. "They give you ticket for that? These cops, they are bored tonight, Christina. They are little generals swinging their sticks. Don't worry about it."

"Really?" She couldn't believe it.

He shrugged. "Hey, you're my best worker. You always

come to shift, never piss off early. Levi is sick this week, you take his shifts. This means a lot to me. Of course is okay. Here, you give to me." He made a tearing motion with his hands.

Christina backed away. "Ah, that's okay, Carlo." Two fines were bad enough, but she imagined how much worse it would be if they were in pieces in Carlo's bins.

She was painfully careful with the next delivery, indicating at every opportunity and pausing extra long at any stop sign. At the end of her shift, she crept home again, not feeling like driving for another month.

In the kitchen, she stared at her books and notes piled on the table, any enthusiasm for work now missing without a trace. First the medical school, then the cops. If she didn't get back to Brisbane soon, somehow she'd end up in a lock-up. And when Aiden finally sent her a text, asking how she was, she couldn't do any more than tell him she was exhausted, and turn off the phone.

Chapter 19

By Wednesday morning, the sting of the fines had dulled to a creeping anxiety. Christina still had no idea how she would pay them, but the assignments were more pressing. The case report she submitted on the web at lunchtime; she still had until the end of the week for the essay, but it was nearly done. Even when she discovered in the early evening that she'd forgotten Monday's load of washing in the machine, she didn't lose her temper. She tipped in more powder and started another cycle to wash out the smell.

She was sitting at the kitchen table, reading through the essay draft again, when a knock came at the front door. Katie, again looking contrite. "You've been ignoring my calls," she said.

Christina held the edge of the door, barring entry. "Because you did hardly any work on the case report. I did pretty much the whole thing myself."

"Look, I know, I know. That was bad of me. But it's been a rough time. There was all that stuff with Travers. Then my brother had to go on a trip, and my mum's been sick. But I promise I'll make it up to you. We're pretty good study buddies, right?" Katie gave a hopeful smile.

Christina's grip on the door slipped. She supposed that was true; Katie had spent a lot of hours at the table with her. "How are you going to make it up?"

"Can I come in?"

Christina hesitated, then turned away, leaving the door open. Katie followed her into the kitchen. "I don't suppose you'd accept a shopping and movie day? No, well, I thought not. What about we study together for the family practice exam?"

"I study on my own," said Christina. The traces of annoyance had barbs that were clinging tight.

"Yeah, I know. You're really dedicated. What are you working on now?"

"The essay." Christina leaned on the back of a chair.

"I'm really sorry, Chris. It's truly been a really bad week at home. Forgive me? Please?"

Christina sighed. Down the hall, the washing machine beeped to signal the end of its cycle. "I'll think about it. Wait here. I have to put the washing out."

She trudged down to the machine and hauled the clothes into a basket. The screen door snapped shut behind her. Outside, in the cooler night air, the sky full of stars, Aiden came into her mind. With the end of term looming, she had to face the fact that she was leaving soon. And that meant leaving him behind. Her heart squeezed. She closed her eyes, her hand finding the wall to hold herself up. Two deep breaths. She had to focus on what mattered. But she couldn't help seeing possibilities, like bright new stars in the darkness of the night. All she'd wanted when she'd first arrived in Townsville was for this term to be over. Now, the realities of Brisbane seemed pale and uninviting compared with how much she wanted to see him.

She pegged out the washing, longing for him. All the while tiny moths bashed themselves against the overhead light, and she wondered if in the morning the dust from their wings would cover her clothes.

Ten minutes later, when she padded back to the kitchen and sank into her chair, Katie had her head down over her notes. Christina tapped her laptop's keys to wake it up, but nothing happened. Come on, she thought, tapping again. But the screen remained dark.

"Crap."

"What?" asked Katie, not looking up.

"My laptop's dead."

"It's probably just sleeping. Try pushing the power key," said Katie.

Christina did. A moment later, she was greeted with a line of text. "'Windows did not shut down correctly'," she read. "What the …"

Katie got up and came around to hover over her shoulder. "It did make a beeping noise a little while ago. Maybe it crashed. Maybe you should—"

"Don't talk," hissed Christina.

"Okaay," muttered Katie, returning to her seat, affecting hurt.

The system was an age coming back up, and the task bar was blank. Christina's blood turned icy; she'd had four files open – the essay, her planning notes, and two papers. Dread gripped her as she reopened the word-processing program. Her essay was right there at the top of the document history. She clicked on it, holding her breath, and the file opened. Oh, thank God. Then she scrolled down and saw that the file was full of junk symbols, nothing readable at all.

"Oh, God. It's gone." Christina sat back, her hands jammed between her knees.

"It can't be." Katie reached for the laptop.

"Don't touch it!" Christina frantically closed the document and reopened it. Still the screeds of nonsense symbols. The cold feeling had vanished now; her blood pumped hot into her face. "Jesus, it's all gone. It's due in less than two days."

"Are you *still* not backing up?"

Christina squeezed her eyes shut. She knew that she was supposed to. She knew other students used external hard drives with fancy software that backed up their computers without them thinking about it. Katie had showed Christina hers a few weeks ago. But those drives were another expense. She'd been using a USB, but when was the last time she'd used it? The days had slid by so fast, she couldn't remember.

"No, I'm not," she whispered.

Katie laughed. "I told you weeks ago you were meant to!"

Christina leapt up. "I know what I'm supposed to do. This isn't helping."

"Hey, it's not *my* fault. It's an old laptop. Jeez."

Christina slowly sat again. She looked down, and clenched her fists until the pale blue veins stood out on the backs of her hands. She traced the blood paths, automatically selecting which one she'd choose for a cannula. She'd been so close to doing well this time. So close. Snatched away by a stupid mistake. "Can you please go," she said. "I … just want to be alone." So she could fall apart without any witnesses.

"What are you going to do about the essay?"

"Katie. Just leave. Please."

After the front door had clicked shut, Christina stared at the document. She expected tears to roll down her face, but all she felt was the heat pulsing in her cheeks. Maybe her blood had boiled her tears dry. She checked the rest of her essay folder. She still had the papers she'd downloaded. She plugged in her USB, just in case she'd backed up recently, but all she had was an outline from weeks ago; almost nothing. With a sob, she pulled out a notepad, closed her eyes and tried to remember. Then she began to write, fast as she could, before she forgot everything.

Around eight thirty that evening, Aiden pushed his phone into his pocket and grabbed the Commodore's keys. He had two days of work remaining before he went on leave, and too much to do, including the Solomons handover. But he couldn't go another day without seeing Christina. He knew she was busy —

she had assignments due this week – but he also knew how she neglected herself when she was working hard.

When he arrived, the house was quiet, the garage closed. He knocked under the porch light, his heart thrumming in his chest, wondering if she was at work. He heard a chair scrape and soft footsteps. She cracked the door two inches, her expression angry. Then relief washed across her face.

"Aiden! Sorry, I thought you were someone else."

"Everything all right?"

The facade cracked and she turned away. "No."

"What's going on?"

She opened the door wider but didn't invite him in, rubbing her eyes before she'd look at him again. She was wearing an old t-shirt with a ripped collar, her blonde hair twisted behind her head with a pencil stuck through it, and shorts a size too big. Aiden thought she looked adorable, and very tired.

"I lost my essay," she said. "I'm trying to remember what I wrote, but I'm running out of steam. I don't know how I'm going to get it done by Friday."

Aiden reached for her but Christina caught his eye and stopped him. "Please. I'm only just holding myself together."

Aiden held back. He'd seen it before, many times, people up against the edge of their endurance still with a long way to go. The ones who got through knew which parts of themselves to shut down so they could press on. "Do you have to go to work?" he asked.

"No, I called Carlo. I felt terrible about it after he was so good about the tickets, but he gave me the night off."

"What tickets?"

Christina groaned. "You don't want to know."

"Had dinner?"

"I can't eat right now."

Aiden stepped inside and shut the door, then gently took her hand and led her back to the kitchen table. Papers were strewn in every direction, some lying on the floor in crumpled waves. A black mug stood empty to one side, the laptop screen a glowing square. "Tell me what happened to the computer."

She filled him in on the details, all the things she'd tried. When she'd finished, he said, "You can't ask for an extension?"

She laughed bitterly. "No, absolutely not. We're expected to keep backups."

"Okay, how about this. Give me the computer. I've got a mate I can ask. He might be able to recover the file."

"Before tomorrow?"

Aiden shrugged. "Probably not. But he can check that's the only thing that was affected. I'm sure you've got other work on there, too, right? I'm going to get you an old laptop of mine to use — it's reliable and just gathering dust. I'll be back in fifteen minutes. In the meantime, keep working on paper." He grabbed the mug and filled it from the jug of cold water in the fridge. "I'll organize dinner after that."

He set the mug back on the table and retrieved the crumpled sheets from the floor. As he laid them on the table, he saw the look on her face, the one that was trying to think of how to tell him to bugger off.

He gave a low chuckle. "This isn't optional. I've got resources at my disposal and I'm giving them to you."

"Yes, sir," she said weakly, sinking back into her chair.

But as he was leaving, she called out across the kitchen, "Aiden. Thank you."

By eleven thirty, Christina was stifling yawns. Aiden had cleaned up from their dinner of toasted sandwiches and retreated to the lounge where he wouldn't disturb her, returning intermittently to fill up her mug, at first with water, then tea, then strong coffee. When the mug had been empty for at least half an hour, she felt his hand slide warm onto her shoulder.

"How's it going?"

Instinctively, she leaned back against him. "I don't think I can do any more. I've put most of it back together, but I'm missing parts. I'm just staring at the screen, trying to remember what I've forgotten."

"Is it time to stop and come back to it fresh in the morning? It will look better after you sleep." He pulled her up. And Christina found her arms sliding around him, catching her breath at the thrill of feeling him against her.

Feeling his hesitation, she pulled away, ashamed to cling to him, her eyes on the table. "I'm sorry. I'm just really tired."

"Don't be," he said. His voice was so soft, she had to look back up. The intensity in his gaze was enough to set her blood on fire. Slowly, he pulled her back into his embrace. They stood there, caught between the heat of their attraction and the uncertain future. Christina tried several times to find something to say, but no words came to her tongue. Aiden seemed to be having the same problem, but in the end it was him who steered her to bed. She lay down with her clothes on, unsure of what would happen next. Aiden crawled in beside her, and they stared at each other in the glow of the bedside lamp. Suddenly, the words were bubbling on Christina's tongue, the ones that asked how this could work between them. She wondered, from the look in his eye, if he was thinking the same thing.

Then he smiled, as if none of it mattered.

He kissed her. A lingering, soft, sensual kiss that left her aching with joy. Unhurried, he pulled her closer to him, until they fitted together along their length, Christina feeling the heat of his body from her lips to her toes. They were both exhausted, and yet in their fatigue, the embrace was deeper, more connected than before. Aiden removed the pencil and slid his fingers through her hair, traced his hands down her back and over the curve of her hip, while Christina stroked the solid muscle of his shoulders. His heart beat against hers as he tipped her chin to deepen the kiss, drawing a sigh from the depths of Christina's heart.

Finally he pulled away. "I should let you sleep." But from the way his hands lingered, he wanted to do anything but.

"No, don't go. I've had too much caffeine anyway. Beyond the Ballmer Peak."

"Ballmer Peak?" he asked, pulling her close again.

"Increased performance from a substance, but I think it's usually used for alcohol. Either way, I'm way past it. Tell me what you were doing all evening."

"Putting out metaphorical fires. I had a stack of call returns to do. Sorted a part supply problem that had grounded some of the dozers. You know, that sort of thing."

"So, you just solved problems for the Solomon Islands … from my aunt's living room?"

"It's the modern world. Besides, it wasn't all work. Your aunt has some pretty interesting military history books in her collection. I spent the last half-hour reading."

"She used to take me to the library every week," Christina said, remembering how much she'd enjoyed it. She tucked herself into Aiden's side and listened to his heart thudding inside his chest. Slow and steady, with a clean *dub*. She counted, trying to guess the rate. Forty-five beats a minute, maybe. He must be very fit.

"Who did you think I was?" His voice was distorted with her ear pressed to his skin.

"When?"

"Earlier, when I got here. You said you thought I was someone else, and you didn't look pleased."

Christina sighed. "Katie. I thought she might be trying to apologize again and I didn't want to hear it."

"What for?"

So Christina told him about the case report she'd had to complete on her own. "She came over today to apologize. But I kicked her out after she was so superior about backing up the essay. I was still mad about the assignment."

"I should think so. Bloody hell, leaving you with all that work? I thought she was your friend."

"She means well, but she's just so … young. I guess I hoped we could be friends. But it's less trouble on my own. Besides," she added, tiredness loosening her tongue like drink, "I didn't like what she said about Travers."

"What did she say?" Aiden's voice was tight.

"Um, that she just wanted some fun, that he was messed up or something. She was so casual about it. Travers is the first person who ever took the time to teach me. He seems like such a good person. What she said made me angry."

Aiden rubbed a hand through his hair. "Yeah. Travers was hurt. I've never seen him like that before."

Christina sighed heavily. "What a shitty week."

"What else happened? You said something about tickets, too."

"No, I'm too embarrassed." She turned her face into his chest, hiding.

"Hey, come on," he said. "This is me. Tell me about the tickets."

Wrapped in his arms, Christina shook her head. "No," she whispered.

"How bad can it be? Do I have to tell you a story to make you feel better?"

"Probably." She raised her head a fraction.

He sighed dramatically, feigning deep thought for a few seconds. "We were out bush one time, out in the middle of nowhere. I was dared to streak through the camp with an empty ammo box on my head, past where the commanding brass were having a meeting. So I did. Most exhilarating twenty seconds of my life. Couldn't really see where I was going, which was probably a good thing. But I was lucky I didn't trip and go ass-up. Literally."

"That didn't happen."

"Did too. I have witnesses. Getting the ammo box off

again was a bit of a problem, though. Those things are narrow."

"I know. I had a guy in the clinic with one stuck on his head just the other week."

He laughed. "Well, they are handy. If a bit heavy."

"But you didn't get caught," she pointed out.

"No, true. But there was this other time when I went for a nude surf, also for a dare. Got caught that time. Fortunately it was early, and pretty cold, so there was no one much around. The lifeguard had a good laugh, I reckon, after he told me to get lost."

Despite herself, Christina laughed. "Do all your stories involve being naked?"

"No ... but some of the best ones do." He gave her a cheeky grin.

"And where's this brazen man gone?"

"He grew up ... mostly."

"All right, fine," she said, rolling over to extract the tickets from where she'd stuffed them into the bedside table. She handed them over.

"Failure to give change-of-direction notice ..." he read. "Really? The cop must have been having a slow night."

"That's what Carlo said. But it happened after I had this call from the med school." She briefly told him about the concerns with the exam in the previous rotation. "I mean, I don't know anything about it, but it felt like the dean thought otherwise. I have to talk to him when I go back to Brisbane for the exam."

"You have had a bad week, haven't you?" he murmured.

"Not the best. And after the lost essay, and the case report, I've got washing backing up, dirty dishes in the sink. The lawn needs mowing. I've become my housemates. It's awful." She made a face.

"When is the exam?"

"Week after next, last week of the rotation."

"I'll be on leave then," he said.

"Mmmm." Sleep was falling leaden on her now, crushing

insomnia under its weight.

The next thing she knew, it was morning, light streaming in; Aiden was still there, fast asleep, still with his arm around her. She stared at him, a hollow feeling opening inside her as she thought about going home to Brisbane without him.

Aiden left early, his phone pressed to his ear. Christina planted herself in front of his laptop, space-aged compared to hers, the crappy reality of rewriting the essay slamming back into her consciousness. Thank goodness she'd done so much work last night.

When she next looked up, it was eleven o'clock, and she had a new version almost done. Aiden was right, more things had come back to her after a night's sleep. She could do a half-day at the clinic for some mental space, then come back and do a final read before handing it in.

"Why are you even here?" asked Travers when she showed up. Christina thought he looked pretty rough himself.

"I need time away from it," she argued, checking the waiting area for a fresh case.

"Well, don't leave yourself short of time. When are you going home?"

"You trying to get rid of me now? Am I getting too good? Your job looking shaky?"

"Confidence, I like it," he said. "But, please. As if they would turn away *this*—" he gestured up and down his crisp whites "—for a good-looking young medical grad. Oh wait …" He paused, pretending to think. "Again, what time are you leaving?"

"Another couple of hours."

"Fine," he said, disappearing into the lunch room. Christina stared after him. Travers seemed in an odd mood, even for him.

Despite his concern, she had the paper finished within forty minutes of arriving home. She was just double-checking the submission receipt, when a knock came at the door.

"Aiden," she said, grinning in her relief. Then she noticed the eight men lined up behind him. "What's going on?"

"I called in some favors," he said. "Did you get the paper in?"

"Yes …"

"Do you trust me?"

Christina peered past him. Every one of the men had army-short haircuts, and some wore regiment t-shirts. She recognized one face from Travers' party and the Crystal Creek trip. Three trucks were parked in the street behind Aiden's Commodore. "I … guess."

He turned. "Tony, Bazza – lawns, front and rear. Socks, wait a sec for the kitchen. Foxy, Charlie, Shane – check the gutters."

Five of the men broke for the pickups and began unloading mowers and ladders.

"How's the oil in the Belmont?" asked Aiden.

"To be honest, I haven't checked it in a few weeks."

"Okay, you have the keys?"

Christina handed them over, and two other guys sprang into action.

"Don't worry, they'll be gentle. They're both mechanics," he said. "And this is Socks. He's a chef, so he'll sort out the kitchen. Don't worry, I'm not going to get anyone to touch your laundry, but I'll do it, if you like."

"Why are you doing this?" she asked, amazed, as Socks went past her into the kitchen and began clearing dishes from the sink.

"Because you looked exhausted last night. And because I can. There would have been ten of us, but Trent's working on your computer. Now, show me to the laundry and go take a load off."

Five minutes later, Christina paced back into the lounge. Lawn mowers were running front and back, and she could hear the men up on the roof. Aiden had said they needed to check the gutters; having tinder up there in the fire season wasn't a good idea. She leaned on the back of the couch, overawed. Although she was initially uncomfortable about having things done for her, she had to acknowledge that it would take her a week to do everything they could do in an hour. Still, it didn't feel right to do nothing.

A book with a thick green spine rested on a side table, and she picked it up. This must have been the one Aiden was reading last night. She pried open the slot to re-shelve it and a fat envelope fell down behind the row of books. Retrieving it, Christina's hands fumbled, and the heavy packet fell to the floor with a thud, disgorging a sheaf of cards and papers. Christina bent, then stopped. They were postcards, just like the ones that had arrived the first week she was here. *I still love you*, said the top one.

Christina picked through the pile. Card after card, the same messages: *Forgive me. Please call. I still love you. I need to talk to you.* Persistent. Christina looked at the postmarks: all in the last six months.

Underneath the postcards were a stack of pages that looked much older, their edges yellowed, one side ragged where they'd been torn from a book. Looking closer, Christina realized they were diary pages, each short entry in Harriet's careful handwriting. She scanned the dates: 1988 through to 1995. No wonder they looked old. The early entries all began the same way: *It's been three weeks since he left. I tried to write again, but I can't bring myself to finish a letter.* Then: *It's been five weeks since he left. I've started three letters, and thrown them all away.*

Gradually they changed. Perfunctory entries about work, a difficult colleague, a holiday to the Northern Territory. But then she read: *His letter arrived this week. I tore it open, but couldn't read it for an hour. Then I couldn't stop reading it. I'm being an idiot, but I managed to write back, and actually posted it this time. I felt sick all the way home from the post office.*

The entries ran out. All Christina could discern was that someone Harriet had loved had moved away, and she'd tried with difficulty to forget him.

She gathered the pages and cards and pushed them back into the envelope, but met resistance. Pulling the stack out again, she looked inside and saw another piece of paper scrunched down in the bottom of the envelope. Fishing it out, she realized that it was a newspaper article, the paper thin and stained with age. She smoothed out the wrinkles. Above a faded photo of a charred house, the headline read: *Fire Destroys Home.*

"Hey."

Christina jumped as Aiden touched her shoulder. She slotted the newspaper back into the envelope.

"Matt says the Belmont's coolant is low. Do you have any?"

"Might be some in the shed," she said, distracted.

Aiden strode off with purpose. As soon as he was gone, she closed herself in the study and picked up the phone. The diary might be old, but those postcards were recent, and troubling.

The line rang, then clicked to her aunt's voicemail. Christina hung up without leaving a message. Probably, on second thoughts, it was a good thing. After all, what would she say? *Hi, Aunt Harriet, has someone been bothering you? A man you used to know — and love?*

Chapter 20

With the house now spotless, and fire-ready, her essay done, and the Belmont purring like the day it left the showroom, Christina felt renewed as she drove to the clinic the next morning. Walking in, she was surprised to see an unusually punctual Katie talking to a patient in the first exam bay. Travers was in the drug store, cataloguing the stock. The frosty atmosphere was palpable.

"Hi," said Christina. "Any patients for me?"

"Check the rack," said Travers.

"Nope," she said a moment later. "Guess it must be a slow day."

"I guess."

Christina leaned against the doorframe. "You all right, Travers?"

"Fine and dandy." He squinted at the expiry date on a vial of saline.

"So did you have a hand in Operation Clean House yesterday?"

A smile flickered on his face. "That's classified."

"Fine." She paused. "Aiden was telling me about your diving business. Are you going to teach people?"

He looked up and his eyes were pinched and dull. Christina found it incongruous that such a large, muscular man, in his crisp white uniform, could appear so vulnerable.

"You don't have to do this," he said.

"Do what?"

"Make conversation."

Christina marched into the room and stood beside him, peering at the list he was holding. "I'll help, then. Which ones haven't you done?"

For five minutes, Christina worked alongside him, doing as he asked and waiting for him to fill the silence. It was an interview technique all med students had been instructed in, but she found it excruciating to refrain from asking questions and hope the other person – usually a patient – would cave first. But just when she thought she could bear it no longer, she was rewarded.

"It's not a teach-people-to-dive business," he said, into the silence.

"What is it then?"

"Some government departments hire contractors to do surveys out on the reef, or university departments hire them to do research. Stuff like that. I'm thinking about getting into salvage too. I have a few mates who've promised contracts. That would be sweet."

"So you'd get to spend all your time on the water?"

"Or under it." He finally cracked a smile. "There's still a bunch of stuff to organize, setting up the business. I want to have it all ready to go when my op's done and I'm recovered."

"You won't miss all this?"

He shrugged. "My heart's not in it. I only started being a medic because I couldn't physically do my other job anymore. But really, I want to be out in the field. And if that can't be on dry land, then on the water. Who knows, maybe I might do search and rescue down the track."

Christina touched him on the arm. "Maybe your heart's not here but it doesn't stop you being brilliant at it. Thank you for all your help. The next group of students won't know what they're missing."

He smiled. "No problem. Happy to help. If you come back

up here sometime, drop me a line, okay?" He looked past her shoulder. "But before this turns into a smushfest, remember you're still here for another two weeks, and there's a patient for you now."

The rest of the day sped past. When she left the clinic, Christina took her books to the local university library to study for the final exam. The air conditioners rumbled as she sat in a nook behind the towering bookshelves and made a study plan, dividing the topics into days. Then she began on the first block, making notes, revising lists of symptoms, drugs and examinations, testing and retesting herself until she knew it backwards. The information gradually seeped in, and stuck. Everything was going well. When she drove home to prepare for her shift, the Belmont still cruised along.

She arrived home at ten thirty with anticipation jangling under her skin. The night sky was starless as she brought in the washing. She showered and changed, washing off the smell of pepperoni, then fussed around the kitchen.

She threw open the door before he could even knock.

"Hi," he said.

She didn't answer, just slipped her arms up around his neck and kissed him. With no hesitation he drew her into him, his hands caressing her back, sliding up under her shirt. His fingers were like fire against her skin, and she quickly pushed his shirt over his head. She dropped her lips to his chest, kissing the warm smooth skin. Aiden tipped his head back in pleasure. "That's quite a greeting," he breathed.

Christina took his hand and pulled him towards the bedroom. She hardly knew what possessed her, simply that she must have him, right now. Her clothes fell with his help, and then there was nothing but pulse-racing passion, her every touch an extension of how much she adored him.

Afterwards they lay together on her bed, Aiden with one arm behind his head, the other holding her against his side. Through the open curtains, a wedge of the night sky was just visible above Harriet's garden.

"Good day?" he asked.

"Yeah, it was pretty good. And thank you again for yesterday."

"Not a problem."

He shifted on the covers as if uncomfortable; he might have been checking his watch, but she didn't want to know if he was. "Do you want to stay?" she asked.

"Up to you." She sensed again his coming to the edge of some disclosure.

But when he made no move to get up, tiny fireworks sparkled in her heart and she relaxed against him, their bond allowable if unspoken.

"Christina ... can I ask you something?"

"Sure." She tensed, wondering what it was.

"Next Friday there's a function at the officers' mess. Would you come with me?"

"What sort of function?"

"A formal one."

Christina groaned. "Does that mean your outfit will get another turnout? I don't have anything else."

"What if I bought you something?"

Christina's good mood dipped. "No thanks."

"All right then. I have to admit, it looked better on you than me."

"I'd want to hope so!"

"That sounds like a yes, then. Aren't you going to fight me, use your study schedule as an excuse?"

She snuggled against him. "My study schedule is under control. Two weeks till the big exam, which is plenty of time, then onward into the internal medicine rotation."

"And goodbye, Townsville."

"Correct," she said slowly. Beside her, she felt him tense again. "Not that I'm dying to get back to the housemates."

"I can't imagine what it'll be like without you," Aiden said suddenly. And in that moment, all his hard edges disappeared.

He looked at her, a question in his eyes.

"I don't want this to end," she whispered.

He hugged her against him, his lips in her hair.

She wanted to ask him how it would work, discuss it, transform her hopes into some kind of substance. Maybe they could visit each other? Townsville and Brisbane weren't in different countries, after all. But now wasn't the time – he seemed so relaxed, and there was more than a week before she had to go. They would have another opportunity.

Christina spent the weekend studying, and took her notes to the clinic on Monday, where she snatched extra time to study in between patients. She was gratified to see Sammy back in for a check-up, his knee recovering. Katie was there too, showing a remarkable burst of enthusiasm, but she kept her distance from Travers. Christina saw him sneaking glances at her when her back was turned. At lunchtime, she ended up drinking coffee out the front with Travers, sitting on the clinic's low brick wall.

"I don't get it," she said as a troop carrier rumbled past. "She didn't want to turn up the whole rotation, and now she's here every day."

He shrugged, looking away. "She has to get signed off like every other student. She's probably logging up hours at the end, making sure Captain May will tick the box. I've seen it before."

"I'd be too terrified to do that," said Christina. "It's hard enough with the amount we have to learn without cramming a bunch into the end."

"It's just a lack of forward planning," he said. "Why do today what you can put off until tomorrow? I would have thought med students were smarter than that, though."

Christina considered. "I don't know about that. In my first-year PBL group—"

"PBL?"

"Problem-based learning," she translated. "In my first-year group, there was a guy who argued with me for two weeks that chewing gum really did take seven years to digest – you know that old myth? He was adamant it was true. I ended up finding papers to prove him wrong, and he still wouldn't give it up. And evidence is the basis of all modern medicine – at least, it's supposed to be."

"Don't you have to go through a selection process for med school?"

"Yeah. An exam, application and an interview. I did it three times."

Travers grinned. "Yeah, well, the army misses some of the crazy ones too. But look, see? I've got you telling stories, *and* you taught me a new TLA."

"TLA?"

"Three-letter acronym. Backbone of the army. My work here is done." Travers dusted his hands, laughing.

At that moment, Christina's phone rang. Seeing Lena's number, she tensed. "Sorry, I have to take this." Travers simply nodded and took himself back inside.

"Good news," said Lena. "We've just come back from the clinic and the infection's clearing nicely. And she's taking the antibiotics without any trouble now."

"Good, that's good," said Christina.

"We have another follow-up in a few days. Do you want to speak to her?" Lena sounded jubilant.

"All right."

Some rustling followed as Lena walked across the room. Christina heard a muffled discussion, but couldn't catch any words. Lena came back on the line. "Ah, sorry, Christina. Her show is starting. Maybe another time."

When Christina hung up, she was amazed at how such a tiny slight could still hurt, even when she expected it, even after so many others before it. It was the never-was kind of hurt, which was somehow worse than the things once held and since lost.

By the time she got home, she'd walled the pain behind that barrier in her mind. At least things in Brisbane were under control. Things here, too, it seemed. When she went inside, only the pile of papers from the water-damaged box on the sideboard disrupted the tidiness of the house. She'd better find somewhere to put them.

Five minutes later, she was transferring the last of the stack onto the top of another archive box. When she went to pick up the photo on the back of the sofa, it caught a gust of air and fell face-up onto the floor. Christina stared at her aunt's face for a second before snatching up the photo and turning it over again.

But before she knew what she was doing, Christina had moved the whole pile of pages onto the floor and was sifting through them, wanting to understand what had happened with Harriet. It was mostly old pay slips, pages of faded print. Peering at the top of each slip, she read: *MAJ Reed, Thomas.* Harriet's husband. Man, she must be insane thinking there was some kind of conspiracy. But she couldn't shake the feeling that she was missing something. She turned to the bookshelf and pulled out the envelope from beside the thick green spine of the military history.

She spread out the postcards on the floor beside the documents. Could Harriet have gone away to avoid the sender? But then where had she gone? Frustrated, Christina pulled out the old news article.

The headline and the photo occupied two-thirds of the page, the story crammed below. Christina began to read.

Fire destroyed a Sydney home last night, with a woman making a dramatic escape. The blaze damaged two adjoining houses before fire crews could bring it under control.

Miranda Hunt, 36, said she woke because a neighbor's dog was barking, and had to climb out with firemen's help from the second-story window.

The article speculated on the cause of the fire and praised the actions of the firefighters and neighbors. Christina reached the final paragraph. *The community have rallied in support, especially as Miranda's army sergeant husband is currently posted to north Queensland. Donations can be made to …*

Christina rocked back on her heels as an electric shock went through her. Sergeant Hunt. John. A fire. A fire that took everything.

But what was this doing in Harriet's house?

Leaving the newspaper article on the carpet, she opened another archive box. More paper: bank statements, bills. All in Thomas's or Harriet's name. She rummaged through the whole box, her former reluctance to pry crushed under a sudden burning need to understand what was going on.

When she ran out of boxes, she started on Harriet's study, flicking through the filing cabinet and desk drawers. Bills and deeds for the house. Insurance. Professional association correspondence. An old shoebox full of stationery – old red pens, paperclips and broken-tipped pencils.

The bottom drawer of the filing cabinet was locked. Christina stood up, shaking her right foot, which had fallen asleep. It was then that she took in the photo hanging on the opposite wall, the one that had been there the whole time.

It was a group shot, the army unit's name printed in faded ink with the date: 1986. The photo was as old as she was, and someone had mounted it on a thin board. Men's faces stared out above crisp dress uniforms, their slouch hats and belts shining with brass.

Christina gently took down the photo and traced her finger along the name block, disturbing dust, looking for Thomas Reed. And there he was, in the second row. But it was a name in the next row that made her pause: John Hunt. She found him among the faces. He was much younger, well built, with confidence in his stance and the jut of his jaw. But it was definitely the same man.

With a gathering cloud of suspicion inside her, Christina

went through the desk drawers again. "Where is it?" she muttered. Harriet had always kept the key here somewhere …

She finally found it in the shoebox of stationery, tucked into the corner. A second later, the drawer was unlocked. Inside she found a wooden box, full of letters. The first, still in its opened envelope, was a folded page torn from a notebook with spiral binding.

Dearest Harriet, I miss you and I've only been gone a day. Thank God this trip is short. Counting the hours until I see you again … Feeling guilty, Christina skimmed through it, all the way to the end: *All my love, J.* The letter was worn at the edges with handling, but it was the date that crashed through her senses. *September 1999.* A month later, Harriet would marry Thomas and leave Townsville. Taking the unit photo, she padded back to the lounge, where she searched the newspaper clipping for a date. She found it at the bottom of the page: 28 September 1999.

With a chill creeping down her neck, Christina reached for the photo of her aunt, still facedown where she'd left it. She stared at the man in the shot, her eyes moving between him and the unit photo. Even out of focus, she knew it wasn't Harriet's late husband. That jaw unmistakably belonged to John Hunt.

"I'll be goddamned," Christina whispered.

The Belmont's engine roared to life as Christina threw the gears and bounced out of the driveway, trying to remember the way to John's house. After a few wrong turns, she pulled out the battered map book.

She pulled up outside the low-set house fifteen minutes later, and sat pensively in the car. What would she say? Finally, she decided to wing it. This wasn't a case report. She was trying to find out about Harriet.

She marched up the path and rang the doorbell, hearing it

shrill within the house. There was no movement inside. Several more rings produced nothing. Maybe he wasn't there. But where could a man with a leg cast go? Knowing John, probably out into the shed to play with the circular saw while the nurse wasn't around.

Gingerly, feeling intrusive, she picked her way down the side of the house to the shed, but no one was there either. As she retreated, she passed a side window. She stopped, shaded her eyes against the glare and peered in, feeling as though she was really crossing a line. The lounge inside appeared empty. She spotted the dining table in the back, still covered with parts from a motor, and the desk crammed with model materials. A few things were scattered on the floor. Then she noticed a chair tipped on its side behind the desk. And there, half hidden by the couch, she could see a dark shape.

She banged on the glass. "John!"

The shape moved.

She turned in a circle, frantic, looking for a way in. The first thing she saw was a garden gnome sporting dark sunglasses and a biker jacket. The next moment, the gnome had gone through the window. Christina wrapped her hand in her t-shirt to protect it from the glass as she lifted the catch, and then the pane slid up, and she was clambering over the low brick sill and hoping she wasn't wrong about what she'd seen, that she hadn't just broken John's window for no reason.

The air inside smelled of pine floor cleaner, motor oil and surgical tape. The stable table, soldering iron and motor pieces were strewn across the floor. John was sprawled beside them, his injured leg stuck out awkwardly, his hand on his chest, gray and struggling to breathe. Christina crouched, fumbling for her phone, then dialed emergency while she put a hand on his shoulder.

"John ... John? It's Christina. What happened? Can you talk?"

John was gasping for breath, and his eyes had lost focus.

"Just keep breathing," she told him as the call went

through.

"Emergency, which service do you require?"

Mashing her phone against her ear as she waited to be connected, Christina checked John's airway, wondering if he was choking, but she couldn't see an obstruction. So she pulled his good leg up at the knee and rolled him into recovery, the motion automatic after all Travers' drills. Maybe he was having a heart attack? She had nothing on hand to deal with that, could do nothing except try to keep him calm, and wait for help.

Time seemed to crawl, her panic rising until finally she heard approaching sirens and then a vehicle pulled up outside. Telling John to hang on, she bolted down the hall to open the front door. A minute later, two paramedics were working rapidly as Christina relayed what she knew. An oxygen mask was soon in place, a pulse-ox and ECG applied, and John loaded onto a stretcher.

Christina stood on the sidewalk as the ambulance pulled away, her chest tight. She returned to the house, where she righted the chair and table and returned the work materials to the desk. She moved around slowly, picking up the discarded plastic packets the paramedics had left. Among them was a dog-eared square of paper.

She was about to crumple it up with the rest of the packaging when she realized it was a photograph. Turning it over, she nearly dropped it in surprise.

The picture was of Harriet and herself, looking awfully alike with their green eyes and blonde hair, both holding sticks of pink fairy floss. Christina knew exactly when it had been taken: at the school fete, the last year she'd lived with Harriet. For a long time the photo had been in a frame on Harriet's desk. This version had been cut down to pocket size, and was faded and creased. It must have come out of one of John's pockets.

"What the hell …?" whispered Christina. She had the feeling of puzzle pieces all around her, without knowing what picture they formed.

Resisting the urge to snoop further, she pulled the front door closed behind her and drove straight to the hospital. The nurse at the triage desk was only able to tell her that he was being seen. Christina sat down in the waiting area, trying to mentally unravel the connection between Harriet and John. After what felt like hours slumped in a chair in a corner, she spotted movement in the hallway. Daniella Bell appeared.

"You must have been here for ages," the registrar began, taking the chair opposite. "Here's what's happening. John's developed a pulmonary embolism. The clot probably started in his injured leg, and broke off before travelling to his chest."

"That's why he couldn't breathe," said Christina.

"Right. We've started him on drugs to thin his blood and hopefully prevent more clot from forming, and we're evaluating now whether we can use meds to break up the embolism, or whether he'll need surgery."

Christina's body sagged. This was serious. "Is there any good news?"

"Yes. We know what we're dealing with now, and early signs are positive. But it's going to be a long night, so you should go home. Check back in the morning. I just wish we knew if he had family to call."

"He only ever mentioned a friend called Stash," said Christina, not ready to admit to any more tenuous connections.

"Maybe he'll turn up." Daniella stood and stretched her back. "The triage nurse said you found him. I was going to say you have unnatural dedication to following your case, but looks like it was lucky you did."

The undeserved compliment made Christina feel guilty. "The stars must be aligned or something," she mumbled.

"That happens sometimes," Daniella said with a small smile.

"I didn't expect you to be back at work yet."

"Yes, well. The honeymoon was lovely, but we'll try to take a longer break later. Couldn't make it happen this time of year." She touched Christina's arm. "How's Aiden?"

Christina couldn't help but smile, then knew she'd given herself away. Daniella patted her arm. "I'm glad. Tell him I love him and I hope to see him soon. I'd better get back."

Christina, too, wanted to see Aiden – more than anything. Friday's function seemed too far away after he'd called to say his handover had been delayed, and would tie him up for the week. But the questions in her mind were gathering like storm clouds.

The rest of the week swept past in giddy repetition. Between her stints at the clinic and long study sessions in the university library, Christina called in to the ward twice. John was being monitored closely for further clots and developing pneumonia; there was no way Christina could speak with him. Only one thing could she know for certain: something had happened between John and Harriet. Something bad enough that he'd never admitted to Christina that he knew her aunt.

She tried to call Harriet several times but could only leave messages. She had no idea what had passed between them – if John was the same man who'd sent the postcards, that Harriet had written about in her diary – but if he was, surely Harriet would want to know he was unwell? But Harriet didn't return her calls, which made her worry more than anything. In the evenings, she worked for Carlo, her head so spinning with questions that she twice misread a street name and knocked on the wrong door. "Hey, you can leave it anyway!" shouted a shirtless man on the second occasion as Christina retreated to the Belmont.

After that shift, instead of returning straight home she found herself on the long winding road up Castle Hill. At the top, she pulled the Belmont into the car park. It was late as she took the path up to a lookout over the ocean. Below, The Strand was lit in puddles of streetlight, the ocean polished black. Distant glitters marked Magnetic Island, and freight ships on the horizon. Harriet had brought Christina up here on her thirteenth birthday, and they'd eaten ice-cream facing the ocean. Then Harriet had told her she was leaving. Christina pushed the memory away, tears burning in her throat.

"Where are you?" she murmured into the soft night breeze.

Chapter 21

On Friday, after studying in the university library for most of the afternoon, Christina packed away her books a couple of hours early and went home. Eyeing Aiden's black dress, carefully cleaned and hanging from the door of her wardrobe, she was suddenly nervous, realizing she had no idea what to expect from this evening. She showered and then stood in the bathroom, peering at herself in the mirror and trying to remember how Jackie had done her make-up at Daniella's wedding. Christina never wore it, didn't even own any.

Feeling slightly guilty, she opened the drawers in her aunt's bathroom cabinet and discovered foundation, eyeliner and mascara, two soft coral lipsticks, and three palettes of eyeshadow iridescent like butterfly wings. Carefully, she applied a light layer of foundation, and edged her eyelids with the liner. She followed with a slick of gold eyeshadow, and then put on some lipstick, which she blotted to almost nothing with a square of toilet paper. Freshly washed, her hair refused to cooperate with any styling, so she let it hang loose. When she was finished, she stood back. It was nowhere near as dramatic as the effect Jackie had created but she still somehow looked sophisticated and she liked the way the gold brought out the green of her eyes. She returned to the bedroom and took the dress down off the hanger.

Ten minutes later, a knock came at the door. Christina trotted down the hall, the dress shortening her stride, and saw Aiden's shadow through the glass. She pulled the door open.

"Oh my …" she said helplessly.

He stood under the porch light in full dress uniform, his shirt and pants perfectly crisp, his jacket black with flashes of red on his waistcoat and cuffs. His epaulettes were studded with gold pips, his shirt finished with a neat black bowtie. As he looked her up and down, a grin slowly spread across his lips.

"Evening," he said, with eyes that were only for her. He stepped inside, seeming taller and more powerful than Christina remembered, the smell of his clean skin and aftershave making it difficult to think.

"Turn around," she ordered.

With a puzzled expression, he slowly turned, and she admired the cut of the pants over his ass. His shoes were gleaming patent leather – they'd give a better reflection than Harriet's bathroom mirror.

"This is very impressive," she sighed, when he returned to the front.

"That is the general idea. Although I haven't worn it in a while. Pants might be a bit tight. What do you think?" He turned again, giving her another opportunity to appreciate the view.

"I think they're just fine," she said, a little breathless.

"Good. Wouldn't want any Captain Tightpants jokes. And you look amazing," he said, catching her hand. "Are you ready?"

"Just need my shoes," she said, but as she turned away, he squeezed her hand, pulling her back.

"In a minute. There's something I need you to do for me first."

He drew her into the living room and dug in his pocket, producing a fold of cloth that he carefully unwrapped. He placed something heavy in her hand. Christina looked down and saw a row of medals, perfect tiny discs strung on colored ribbons.

"They're just the minis, replicas," he explained. "Can you help me put them on? You should see the pin holes in the jacket already. I just end up stabbing myself."

It took her a moment to register what he was saying. "These medals are yours?"

He nodded.

Christina turned them in her hands, feeling their weight. She sank onto the couch, her fingers moving over the steel and cloth that captured the gravity of Aiden's service. "What are they for?" she asked.

He sat beside her. "From the left, active service. The bars are for particular tours." Christina bent her head, reading the clasps across the ribbon. *Iraq 2006. East Timor.* "That blue and brown one is for Afghanistan. Campaign medal. Then long service, for the first fifteen years. And the last one is the UN medal, for Timor."

Christina ran her fingers over the wreath-circled map of the world, the symbol of the United Nations. She felt as though she had glimpsed another dimension of him.

Carefully, she slid the pins through his jacket and snapped the backs closed. She knew that all of this – the medals, the suit, the entire external show of him – was for display, the army projecting the kind of man they wanted the world to see. Christina saw him exactly as he appeared – impressive, strong and with a kind heart. She knew what he was made of, how he acted, how he made her feel. And just then he kissed her, a kiss that demanded nothing, only a gentle benediction, a blessing.

"I have a surprise for you," he said.

She pulled back. "I don't want you to buy me things."

He shook his head. "I'm not buying you anything. I'm coming down to Brisbane next week. So, technically, I'm buying *me* things. Don't you love how that works?"

Christina was speechless. The air around them seemed

enchanted, dense with possibility. She realized what this meant: he wanted their relationship to continue, too. He really meant it.

A frown grew between his brows and he suddenly looked uncertain. "Is this okay? I can cancel if it's not."

"No, it's great," she said, hugging him close until the hall clock softly chimed. "Time to go?"

He nodded, and his relieved smile stole Christina's breath.

When she returned with her shoes, she found him looking at the old unit photo still propped against the bookshelf where she'd left it earlier that week. "Is this your uncle's unit?" he asked.

"Not exactly," she said. "I'll tell you about it on the way."

"So, this guy you did your case study on, you think he's been stalking your aunt?"

Christina stared out the windscreen as they approached the base gate. "I'm not sure. They seem to have been involved before Harriet was married, and before I even lived with her. But then there are these postcards that are much more recent. Looks like the same handwriting, but I can't work out what it all means."

Aiden frowned. "Maybe her husband had some competition."

"She never mentioned it," said Christina, though it occurred to her that her aunt's life might well have been far more complicated than she'd realized as a teenager. "And now she's disappeared and he's in the hospital."

"You said he used to serve – John Hunt, right? Do you want me to see if I can find out anything?"

"Maybe."

They pulled up outside the officers' mess, an unassuming but cheerfully lit brick building with an attendant waiting outside the door. Christina spotted other officers escorting women in sleek cocktail dresses.

"No one's here who will remember you trying to get into this dress, right?" she asked nervously.

Aiden looked sheepish. "Ah, there might be. But don't worry, they won't get past how gorgeous you look."

Soon they were inside, and Aiden tucked Christina's hand into the crook of his arm as they skirted the crowd. Among the throng, Christina spotted some female officers as well, their dates in civilian suits. Waiters in starched white circled with trays of canapés and she soon had a glass of juice in her hand.

"The VIPs will arrive eventually and there'll be some formal introductions before we sit down," Aiden explained. "For now, come and meet some people."

Christina shook many hands, missing most of the names, lieutenants and majors, a brigadier. She was telling one major about her time in the medical clinic as Aiden drifted away.

Ten minutes later, when the major was asking her opinion of the facilities, attention was called to introduce the dining president. The major apologized and said he hoped they could speak again later. Alone in the crowd, Christina stepped back, turning to look for Aiden. She ran straight into Katie.

"Christina," Katie said, evidently surprised. She was wearing a knee-length slip in sparkling sequined blue, the neck low and scooped, her heels tall and transparent, her earrings fine silver. All in black, Christina felt plain and dull in comparison.

Katie reached out and tugged on the arm of a tall man who was turned away, standing with a group of other officers. As he turned and stepped towards them, Christina first noticed his uniform, which was different from Aiden's – white instead of black and red – and then she raised her eyes to his face and felt herself flinch. "Seb's a guest at the head table tonight," Katie said. "Isn't that amazing?"

"Don't you scrub up all right out of the delivery uniform?" Sebastian smirked, acting as though the encounter at Castle

Hill had never happened, though she could almost have sworn he checked behind him before he spoke.

Christina gave him a level stare. "Come again?"

"Well, maybe later," he said with a suggestive wink.

It took Christina a moment to understand his meaning, and when she did, she recoiled. *Gross.* He would probably never change; the way he treated her was fixed. But her own reactions didn't have to be. She felt curiously different, less affected by him.

"Seb, you know what?" she said. "I wouldn't touch you with surgical gloves on. And you should really get some new material. You're starting to bore me."

She almost said more; almost told him what a living hell he'd made high school for her, what a bully he was. But that would have been exactly what he wanted to hear, an acknowledgement of his impact on her. Instead she held her tongue, letting her face tell him exactly how little power he had over her now.

Something uncertain flickered in Seb's gaze. Then he straightened angrily and strode off, muttering something about *effing dykes.* Christina almost laughed.

Katie was still hovering, her eyes wide. "So, I didn't expect to see you here!" she began awkwardly, linking her hand into Christina's arm and steering her away from the crowd. "I'm sorry I've been out of touch this week – busy, you know. So, who are you here with?"

"Aiden," said Christina quickly, disentangling herself and wishing Katie would disappear too.

Katie nodded. "I figured. Actually, I need to talk to you about that."

"About what?"

"I thought you said it wasn't serious, you and him."

Christina was about to protest that it wasn't, but the lie caught in her throat. All she could do was shrug.

"Now, you need to listen to me." Katie lowered her voice and leaned in confidentially. "I know about army men, and I'm really concerned about you dating him. You should stop seeing him now. It's the best thing to do."

"Why?" asked Christina, not bothering to lower her voice. "I didn't think it was your business."

"These guys do dangerous jobs, Chrissy. Move around all the time. As your friend, I'm telling you it's not a good choice."

"Just because you dropped Travers doesn't mean I'm going to do the same thing," Christina blurted. Then came a ripple of panic as she realized she'd betrayed how much Aiden meant to her.

Katie's eyes flared. "Wow, you really are serious—"

A bell rang, and the dining president asked them all to sit for dinner. Christina felt Aiden's arm slide around her as Katie shimmied away.

"What's she doing here?" he asked.

"Her brother's a guest," said Christina. She blew out a shaky breath.

"What was she saying?"

"Telling me to break up with you."

Aiden raised his eyebrows. "Guess that figures," he muttered.

Sitting beside Aiden, Christina tried as best she could to forget her conversation with Katie and instead pay attention to the dinner. They sat at long tables which all met at right angles to the head table. Christina was grateful the other diners blocked her view of Katie and Seb. Aiden was soon introducing her to the other people at their table, and keeping her up on protocol.

"When the port comes around, just make sure you don't let the decanter touch the table," he said.

"Unless you're in the navy," chipped in a major seated on her left. "Then you're not allowed to let it *leave* the table." He laughed.

"What happens if I get it wrong?" she asked nervously.

Aiden's expression became grave. "Terrible, terrible

things," he said. Then he cracked a grin. "You'd probably get away with it." His eyes sparkled, and Christina saw that this was his world, through and through, filled with deep history, tradition and pride.

Soon grace was said, and the meal served. Between courses, members of the head table rose to speak, thanking the mess for hosting, the guests for attending. By the time the dessert, a perfect panna cotta, landed in front of Christina, she had almost forgotten the Priors and was thoroughly enjoying herself.

Finally, the head table rose, and toasts began, to the Queen, the Australian flag, and the corps, before someone snaffled the microphone and began some good-natured slander of the integrity of the ranking officers. The crowd was soon laughing uproariously, drinks trays circulating as the guests made their way into the lounge. Christina went to follow, but Aiden put a hand on her arm.

"It can get rowdy from here," he said. "And I can see you're drooping."

"I'm not," she protested, but had to cover a yawn.

"It's been a huge few weeks, and you still have an exam to pass. Besides," he added, "I'd rather take you home tonight."

Christina watched the tail of the crowd moving into the lounge, the group he knew so well and was prepared to leave for her. The realization set a smile on her face. Screw Katie. She wanted him.

"You know, I love that smile," Aiden said, squeezing her hand. "I just want to whip around and say goodbye to a few people. I'll be right back."

Aiden hadn't been gone two seconds before Christina caught a flash of blue sequins in her peripheral vision.

"You're mad at me, aren't you?"

Turning, Christina took in Katie's expression, seeking approval. Her blue eyes were slightly unfocused, her transparent heels unsteady, a near-empty wine glass in her hand. The dining hall was now almost deserted, just a few staff still clearing the furthest table, no one to overhear.

Suddenly aching with fatigue, Christina longed for escape. "I'm just going home. I'm not mad at you."

"Yeah, you are." Katie's words slurred. "I really am sorry about the case study report."

"That's done with." But she was tired of this charade, and she knew it was time to say so. "Look, Katie. I don't really care about the report anymore. But the rotation's nearly over. We don't have much in common, and we're moving on to other things. I just want to study on my own."

Unexpectedly, Katie laughed, a little too loud. One of the staff clearing looked up. "You're so funny," Katie said.

"Why?"

"You do everything the hard way." She leaned in. "You have to have fun, too."

Christina frowned, too familiar with conversations like this with her mother. "You're drunk."

"But I had a *good* time. I still got all my work done, and I'll pass my exams. So there."

"You know what?" Christina said, her anger unraveling. "I don't care! So you're smarter than me – so what? I'd never want to see a doctor like you. You don't care. You think you deserve it. You think it ends with a pass mark, with a check in your term box. You think you can say bad things about Travers and Aiden and I'll still want to talk to you. Well, you can piss off."

Christina spun around and stalked towards the bathrooms. After a few steps, she realized she should have gone outside, where she wouldn't be trapped, but the blood was thrumming in her veins and she couldn't turn back now. She shouldered open the heavy wooden door. At the sink, she leaned her hands on the cool rim. Her cheeks were burning, the flush spreading all the way down her neck and splotched across her chest, but her head was clear. A shadow had lifted from her mind, and for the first time since she'd arrived, her conviction felt strong, strong enough to deal with Seb, with Katie; with whatever was left in her way.

Aiden re-entered the dining hall and found it empty, so he stepped outside looking for Christina. He'd rarely been this sober on a function night, never needing to drive anywhere afterwards, and now he wondered if he should have had a few more. He still had to have the conversation with Christina, tell her that he was going away. He was running out of time. And every time he thought of starting it, his courage failed him.

Seeing no sign of Christina, he was about to return inside when he heard heels click behind him.

"Hi, Aiden."

He turned. "Katie." Something dark stirred in Aiden's chest. They didn't know each other well, but he'd seen the effect she'd had on Christina, and on his best mate. And now here she was, more than a little drunk.

"Chrissy's in the bathroom," she said, stepping in close.

"Thanks."

"Good night, isn't it?" She put a hand on his arm, to which Aiden gave a pointed look until she removed it.

"It was," he said.

She looked at him from under her lashes, as if she was thinking of what to say, then slowly pulled her wrap up on her bare shoulders. "So … have you seen Travers recently?"

Wow, she was really going there. "What if I have?" he replied coldly.

"How's he doing?"

"I think you can guess."

She pouted. "I feel bad about what happened. I was thinking we could all get together, maybe, for dinner or something. A farewell, before we go back to Brisbane. I want to be friends, you know."

"You're kidding, right?" Aiden glared at her. She looked

absurdly young under her make-up, young and silly enough that he tempered his next words slightly. "I don't know how you think the world works, but you hurt him really bad. Now, it wouldn't be my business if you'd just broken up with him. But I know he told you something really private and you threw it in his face. And then you're telling Christina what to do about me, like it's any of your business."

"Oh, like Travers and me is any of yours!"

Aiden's temper was on fire. He knew he needed to walk away, but not before he told her straight. "I'm making it my business. He's better off without you, so leave him alone. And as for Christina, I know all about how you let her down with the case study and left her with all the work to do." He paused as a scowl creased her brow. "You're pretty young, so this may seem harsh, but you might want to learn a bit about how to treat people. Now, if you'll excuse me." He stepped around her, leaving her in the sickly cloud of perfume she was wearing.

Inside, Christina was just emerging from the bathroom. "What?" she asked, seeing his expression.

"Nothing," he said, bending down to her ear. "But I meant it when I said I wanted to get you home."

The next morning, Christina left Aiden sleeping and padded towards the kitchen. It was already nine, and she set about summoning the motivation to collect her textbooks and make a start on the next topic, the respiratory system. She knew Aiden would be heading out later to see Travers, leaving her to study.

Before opening the textbook, Christina quickly checked her email. One new message. From Katie, sent late last night. The subject read: *Happy studying!* Christina clicked on it, suspicious. The email contained a link, and the browser redirected to a new page. A dun-colored square appeared on the screen, the resolution poor, dark squares inching in a curving line from top to bottom. She frowned. Then the image blurred and refocused, and she could make out the details. It was a road in a desert, seen from some kind of security camera. Pale stone buildings with flat tops flanked the road; it wasn't Australia, that was for sure. Two military vehicles were coming towards the camera, distinctive in their camouflage. The traffic on the road was moderate, mostly cars, and a truck travelling in the opposite lane, away from the camera. Without sound, the scene had a plodding, expectant quality, and Christina's heart thudded against her breastbone. Why would Katie send this?

Suddenly, the scene vanished in a detonation. Christina watched, stunned, as the cloud from an explosion filled the screen. It rushed across six lanes of road, reaching the camera in seconds, erasing the image in a dirty gray smudge.

She'd heard on the news about roadside bombings in the Middle East, about the injuries and fatalities. But in her mind she'd seen a movie explosion, a contained burst with limited reach. She'd never imagined the scale of this. A trembling began, deep down inside her. No one could have survived this.

She jumped when Aiden slid his hands over her shoulders. The image on the screen was beginning to clear now. Nothing was left on the road, not even wreckage. The truck was gone. The military vehicles, gone.

"What are you watching?" he asked softly.

"Katie sent it to me."

Aiden reached forward and very calmly dragged the cursor to play the video from the start. Christina closed her eyes so she didn't have to watch it again. She felt the tension in the hand he left on her shoulder. "VBIED," he said finally, matter-of-fact. "Vehicle-borne improvised explosive device. In that truck." He pointed at the image, freezing it a moment before detonation.

Christina nodded stiffly, her stomach rolling as she remembered the scars on Aiden's side. "Is that like the one you—"

"No," he said quickly. "That was a roadside IED. This is

much bigger."

Christina quickly closed the window. She stared at the kitchen table. "Is that what you do? Travel like that?"

"Not here."

"But you did, when you were over there?"

Aiden pulled her up, searching her face. "Don't think about it. You all right?"

Her mobile started to ring. "I don't know," she said. Fear had shaken the mortar out of her inner wall. Fear for him. From the realization that what he did really was dangerous.

He drew her into him, his body strong and vital and reassuring. She held on even as her phone rang and rang. After it had stopped, she pushed herself away, trying to recover her balance. Her phone rang again and she fumbled answering it.

"Christina?"

Her blood thinned. She recognized the voice – it was the dean's PA, Anne. On a Saturday. She waved Aiden away. This couldn't be good. In another heartbeat, the dean himself was on the line, sounding harried.

"I'm sorry to call you on the weekend, but we're dealing with some issues at this end, relating to my previous call."

"Yes?" Her mouth was so dry.

"I'd like you to come in for a meeting on Tuesday."

"I'm not flying back until Wednesday—"

"The school will organize the flight. Give Anne the details."

"What's this about?" she asked.

"I don't want to delve into specifics on the phone, but there are some serious issues around assessment in your cohort, and we need to reach the bottom of it as soon as possible so that any consequences can be dealt with between rotations."

Issues. Consequences. Christina's stomach twisted.

When Aiden, wearing only a towel, walked back into the kitchen ten minutes later, Christina was still clutching the phone. "Your aunt call back?" he asked.

Harriet couldn't have been further from Christina's thoughts. She shook her head. "They want me to go to a meeting at the school on Tuesday."

Aiden's smile slipped. "What's that about? You look shaken up."

Christina couldn't answer. She paced around the kitchen, trying to decide what to do. She had to study, but the table was repelling her like a same-poled magnet. Time seemed to be running away, and she couldn't keep up. She had to get a hold of herself. "I hope it's nothing," she said.

Aiden didn't seem convinced, but when she wouldn't say more, he dressed. "I have a few errands to run, but I'll call you when they're done. Okay?"

After he'd left, she sat down at the table, trying to concentrate on her notes. When her phone rang again, a brief hope surged that it might be the school, telling her they'd made a mistake. The world would right itself and she could go on. Then she saw the number.

"Hi, Lena."

"Christina."

As soon as the woman spoke, Christina knew something was very wrong. Lena was crying.

"Christina, I'm so sorry," she said. "Your mother, she's dead."

Chapter 22

She didn't take Aiden's first call a few hours later, nor the next. And when he came back in the afternoon and let himself in, Christina was still on the phone. She'd switched into some kind of automatic pilot, a haze she couldn't escape until everything was arranged.

Aiden sat down in the chair opposite her, a concerned frown on his face.

"Yes, fine. But what if we took out those last three items?" Christina asked. She was onto her fourth funeral director. She scribbled down the numbers, then shook her head as she put the phone down.

"What's going on?" Aiden asked.

Christina rubbed her face before she could look at him. "My mother died," she said.

"Oh, Christy. I'm so sorry."

Christina stopped him with a hand when he would have got up to hug her. "I'm trying to organize things."

"Like a funeral?"

She nodded, the numbers swimming in front of her eyes. "I had no idea they were so expensive. I need to call Lena to find out how much is in the house account."

Aiden closed his hand over hers. "What can I do? Can I make some calls for you?"

Christina pulled away. "No, I … just need to do this

myself."

"How about some dinner, then?"

"Aiden, I'd just like to be alone." Somewhere deep in her mind, Christina knew she was pushing him away, but Rita was her responsibility – no one else was allowed in.

His frown only deepened as he came around the table and pulled her up into a hug that Christina couldn't feel. There was a coldness in her limbs that refused to be warmed. She could only think of how many more funeral directors would be open on a Saturday, and how many of them she could call before they closed. She'd tried to call Harriet; however estranged, she was still Rita's sister, but could only leave a message saying it was about Rita and asking her to call as soon as she could.

"I'm worried," Aiden said. "This must be a terrible shock for you. I don't want to leave you alone."

She forced a smile. "Call me tomorrow?"

Reluctantly, he left, and Christina went numbly back to the table as the sun sank and night crept in. And even though the world kept turning, unchanged, somehow Christina knew that nothing in her life would ever be the same again.

She left the sun behind on Tuesday morning and flew into a Brisbane still wearing its winter coat. The wind cut through her thin shirt, and drizzle caught in her eyelashes. She had only enough time to collect her car from where it was parked outside the share house, throwing her bags in the back before driving to the crematorium, a building white as bone against the gray sky. She sat heavily in the chapel's back row, her heart as heavy as the clouds outside.

The funeral director, a graying man in a dark suit, had in an act of compassion booked an unattended cremation but still allowed Christina and Lena to come. Aiden had wanted to come down with her, but she'd refused. She had no funds for a minister, or flowers, didn't want anyone to see the spartan sadness of her mother's funeral. The director read a poem to give some sense of occasion, and Lena another reading.

Christina took in none of the words. Her eyes were fixed on the coffin, which was sleek and glossy and finished with bright silver handles. But no matter how long she stared, the coldness remained in her limbs, and her eyes were dry. Surely she should feel something? This was the end of a life. Her mother's life.

The coffin disappeared through a curtain, and she was on her leaden feet again. The funeral director shook her hand, and offered well-practiced condolences, before telling her she could collect the ashes in three days.

Outside, the weather had worsened. Lena dabbed at her eyes with a tissue. "How are you holding up?" she asked.

"Fine."

"I have to get back to the house, but please come and see me, even if you just need to talk. All her things are still there."

Christina thanked Lena, who'd been nothing but kind and dedicated, but as she walked to her car she couldn't imagine ever picking up her mother's belongings. She pulled the car door shut behind her. She sat, and sat, as Lena drove away.

She had an hour before her appointment at the school office. As rain beat down on the windscreen, the events of the last seven weeks in Townsville seemed part of another world. Some other Christina had lived them, and now she desperately wanted that Christina back.

Forty-five minutes later, with grief closing on her like a slow trap, she climbed the stairs to the school foyer with its dark wooden walls, checkered antique tiles and brass fittings. The first time she'd come here, for her interview three years ago, she'd been sick with nerves, but triumphant at having made it so far through the entry process. The triumph was now gone. She felt her phone vibrate in her pocket and ignored it.

Anne, a middle-aged woman with a dark bob and a jet necklace, looked up over her glasses. "Christina?" she said, surprised. "We weren't expecting you after your sad … I mean, the dean said this can wait."

"No, I want to be here."

Christina glanced around the anteroom, the mood solemn. Sean and Sarah were there, and two other students she recognized. Sarah's hands were pinned between her knees; Sean rocked a folder from hand to hand. Both of them gave her furtive nods of acknowledgement. Christina sat and waited as one by one the other students were called into the dean's office and then left again, until finally it was her turn.

Inside his office, the cool air freshened her skin where rain had soaked her clothes. More dark wood. A heavy imposing desk. A green banker's lamp. An office that spoke of the school's long tradition, of the rite of passage it represented into a respected profession. The dean himself looked just like his portrait in the hall: a large-boned man, his hair thinning, his face carefully set somewhere between benevolence and scrutiny.

"Christina, we don't have to do this today," he said, putting his pen in his shirt pocket.

Christina glanced at Anne, hovering in the doorway. "I want to get it over with. I still have exams to do. I don't want special treatment."

The dean waved Anne away. "All right. Fine. I'm sorry we're having this meeting at all. But in the last rotation, we know that someone gained access to the surgery paper before exam day. We know that it circulated. Quite a few students did very well on that exam. Is there anything you'd like to tell me at this point?"

Christina shook her head. "I don't know anything about it."

"Obviously, a good result doesn't make anyone guilty. But your result is inconsistent with previous performance. I don't have to lay out your past results, do I?"

Christina swallowed. "I know I've done poorly. I had some difficulties. With money, my mother, and where I was living," she said, embarrassed, her voice thick and uncooperative. "But at the beginning of this year, my mother went into care. I had more time. I was slow on placement, but I studied hard for that exam."

"Perhaps you did. But then we come to this rotation. And now we see you hand in an essay that's very similar to another student's. You know that we have software on the submission system that checks these things."

Christina sat up as though she'd been stung. "*I'm sorry?*"

"Another student handed in almost the same essay. The day before yours."

Christina was too shocked to speak. How could this have … but she suspected Katie.

"The school takes plagiarism and cheating very seriously," the dean went on. "There's been too many scandals in other schools the last few years. Students skirting the entry process because of relatives in the school. Disgraceful behavior on celebratory trips. Being accused of abusing animals on rural placements. We're running a respected institution here. We can't have public faith in our training eroded. Not on my watch." He sat back in his seat. "I have to decide how to act."

Christina leaned forward, realizing how much trouble she was in. "Katie could have taken my essay from my laptop. I left it on the kitchen table where we were studying. Then it crashed—" she suddenly wondered if that had been an accident after all "—and I lost the document. I rewrote it in two days. Katie was supposed to be doing a different topic."

"And what was that?"

"Something about ranking preventative actions in general practice, trying to work out which ones were most cost-effective. Professor Green should be able to confirm that."

The dean made a note. "And the exam? I know that you have access to the school computers through your job for the doctoral student."

"I can only do data entry with my login. I did well because I studied hard. And this rotation I was much better at prac, too.

Please, I want to be here more than anything."

The dean studied her, his face impassive. He must have heard the same plea already today. "I need to make some more enquiries. Anyone we catch with enough proof will have to show cause not to be expelled. Is there anything you want to ask me?"

Until that moment, Christina had had a dozen questions running through her head. Now, she could think of nothing but *expelled*. "No," she whispered.

"You can go then."

She pushed herself out of the chair and crept to the door. Once, in school, Seb Prior and his mates had given her a "dead arm", cornering her in the resource room and whacking the same spot. When they left, her arm had been numb, but the damage was done. The purple bruise that eventually showed had taken two weeks to fade. Now, her whole body felt numb like that, waiting for the damage to show through. She stopped in the doorway and turned back. "I really had nothing to do with it," she said.

"I hope that's true." He held her gaze. "And I'm sorry for your loss."

On leaden feet, Christina emerged under the slate-gray sky, the statue of Hippocrates on the school's lawn mocking her with its benevolent expression. Her phone rang again in her pocket, and for just a second she expected it would be Lena. Then she realized she'd never receive those calls again.

The realization shook something loose. She sat heavily on the top step, just out of the rain, letting the phone ring while she breathed deeply, in and out. Finally, she answered.

"Christina? It's Daniella. I hope it's not a bad time?"

Christina had to swallow the sudden surge of emotion that tried to surface at Daniella's warm tone. "No worse than any other," she said, clutching her head with her free hand.

"Well, I'm afraid I haven't any good news, but I wanted to let you know because you're following the case. John deteriorated yesterday and he's been transferred to the ICU. He's developed pneumonia, and it looks bad. If you want to come in and talk about the case, I'm here until four today."

"I'm in Brisbane," Christina said quickly, trying not to picture John, so strong and feisty, lying vulnerable in the ICU. "I had to come home early."

Daniella was onto her tone instantly. "What's happened?"

"Aiden didn't tell you?"

"Tell me what?"

"My mother died. A few days ago."

"Oh no! I'm so sorry. I had no idea. What a dreadful shock. How are you?"

Christina felt her face crumple. "Uh, pretty bad." She paused, trying to compose herself, and then found the rest of her circumstances coming out in a teary rush. "That's not all. The med school thinks I cheated on an exam and plagiarized an assignment. I just got through a meeting with the dean."

"How could they accuse you of such a thing?" Daniella's voice now had an indignant edge.

Christina only wanted to crawl into a very dark recess until the world stopped spinning around her. "I'm sorry, Daniella. I have to go." Hanging up, she saw a missed call, this time actually from Harriet. Christina gave a bitter laugh. But she couldn't face it, not now. She'd call back when she was home and dry.

After the drive to the share house, Christina parked the Corolla back where she'd picked it up that morning, squishing over the arcs of tire-collected leaves and sticks on the road. The rain had eased to drizzle. She dug for her keys, praying that her housemates would be absent so she could unpack in peace.

As she dodged heavy drops from the backyard tree, it seemed her wish had been granted. No lights were on, and the sliding glass door was closed. She slid her key into the lock, but it wouldn't turn. She shoved with her shoulder, trying to shift the sticky catch. Still, the key jammed. Muttering, she walked around to the side door, which also refused to open.

She paced back around past the sliding door. "Hello!" she called into the laundry window. No answer. Perplexed, she circled to the front of the house, the entrance no one ever used. And that was when she noticed the small, sad pile by the front gate.

Christina gave a wail of horror and rushed across to where four garbage bags sagged under pools of water. The two containing her precious textbooks had split under the weight, the volumes soaked through, pages swollen and wrinkled. Two other bags contained her clothes and whatever else her housemates had decided to pack up from her room.

She tipped up the flap of the letterbox and found a stack of uncollected mail, two final notices from the real estate agent among them, citing unpaid rent. Rain spattered down, smudging the ink of the felt-tip pen the agent had used on the form. The eviction date had been Friday. Her things had been sitting beside the fence for four days.

Christina grabbed one bag of books and tried to haul it back into the carport's shelter. The damaged plastic sheared, the knot breaking off in her hand. She chucked it aside, and retrieved the books from the ruined bag one by one, carrying them under cover. Right at the bottom of the stack, she saw that her biochemistry text had at least escaped, protected by those above it.

Christina sat on the hard damp concrete with the book in her lap, reliving the day she'd first come to Brisbane. It had been raining then too, but summer rain – fat droplets and steam rising from the rinsed roads. The heat, which had seemed mild after burning Townsville, had also seemed a promise of better things to come. Now the rain stung like icicles, her body cold and shivering.

She assessed her options. On the plus side, the rent she'd

been about to pay she could keep. And the original plane fare she'd booked to Brisbane she had back in credit. On the other hand, she'd be sleeping in her car. Her thoughts turned quickly to how to make that work. She could shower at the university sports center. And when the exam was over in a few days, she could start looking for somewhere else to live.

The exam.

That was when the full realization hit. If the school decided that she had cheated, there would be no more exams. And her mother, the only family she'd had left, was gone. A shiver of loneliness ran through her. For the first time in her life, she wanted to be back in Townsville, where Aiden was, where Harriet's house had been a refuge. Where she had been different. She couldn't face him now, not pathetic like this.

Before the rain came down again, she moved her belongings into the Corolla, then slid into the driver's seat. The car smelled of cold muddy water, and her drenched shirt and trousers clung to her body. She dialed Aiden's number, desperate to hear his voice and yet bracing herself for what she had to do.

"Cancel your flight, please?" she said as soon as he answered.

"Why?" He sounded amused, as though he was in a place that still contained laughter and jokes, a place that was warm and welcoming, and far from where she was now.

"It's just … I can't see you right now. Maybe in a couple of weeks."

"How did things go today?"

Christina bit her lip. "Fine," she lied. "But I need some time." *I don't want you to see me like this.*

"Christina. What's this really about? When you left this morning you were—"

"When I left this morning, everything was okay," she burst out.

"Honey, your mother died," he said gently. "I'm sure it

wasn't okay."

Christina rushed on, though the words tore at her. "Now I'm sitting in my car, wet through, all my stuff ruined because my asshole housemates chucked it on the sidewalk when they evicted us four days ago, and no one even called me."

She stopped, her breath catching, the cracks in her endurance running together into a chasm. "So, please," she said. "I don't have a bedroom for you to stay in, and I can't afford a hotel. Will you just wait a week or two for me to get through all this before you come?"

"It's a bit late for that," he said evenly. "I flew in an hour ago."

Christina had no idea what to say. Relief and horror tangled inside her, both bidding to be the victor. He was here. Oh God, he was here. Her voice was hoarse. "You're in Brisbane?"

"Yeah. It's just like I remembered."

"Where?" She squeezed her eyes shut, her mind racing. He couldn't see her in this state. She would head into the university and clean herself up … and then what? She just wanted to be off the phone so she could fall apart on her own. He hadn't responded. "Aiden?"

"Can you hold on for a minute?"

Christina waited. Tiny shivers, both cold and fear, were starting under her skin. When she glanced into the rear-view mirror, her lips were blue. Down the phone line, she heard creaking footsteps; Aiden's, maybe on wooden boards. A rustle of keys. Then the whine of a door hinge. A long, long pause. Christina realized she was holding her breath.

"Aiden?"

"I'm going to give you an address and directions," he said finally. "You can drive here in ten minutes."

Two suburbs away, Aiden ended the call. The door stood open into the house, with its brick walls and cream carpet, the same curtains he remembered hating. But apart from the curtains, it looked nothing like it had when he and Tracey had lived here. The two couches had plastic covers, and the rest of the floor space was empty. Right back when it had just happened Travers had told him the moving men had left the bed and the couches, but everything else had gone. Just the memory lingered, of what it had been like to leave with the house full of life, and come back to it empty.

He couldn't quite bring himself to go through the doorway. He'd come here with the idea of exorcising these particular demons, but now he didn't want to walk inside alone. When Christina had left this morning after three days of pushing him away, he'd known she would need someone, and he intended to be that person. Now he was more glad than ever that he'd come. He needed to force himself to do what he hadn't done in four years. And he was glad that he wouldn't be alone to do it.

Chapter 23

Christina coaxed the Corolla through the streets at the foot of the mountain, then across the freeway and up through the hills as the rain pelted down. Eventually she pulled up outside a low wooden fence painted a deep blue; beyond was a ruddy-bricked home with a pale roof, and a wide wooden deck in front.

The house was near the crest of the hill, the city just visible through the rain. The Corolla's engine choked to a stop, and all Christina could hear was the spattering of raindrops, and the gush of water in the gutter. She pushed her door open.

Aiden waited with an umbrella by the open gate. In faded jeans and a plain gray shirt, spotted with rain, he seemed different, vulnerable somehow in the way his shoulders rounded. And for all she'd said she wanted to be left alone, as soon as she saw him the thought vanished.

He held the umbrella over her head, his other arm wrapping around her, a kiss on her forehead. "Anything left at your old place?"

She shook her head. "I think it's all in here." She indicated the bedraggled heap of clothes and books in the back seat. "So whose place is this?" she asked.

"Mine."

Christina started. "Yours?"

"I'll explain. Come on."

Leaving her things in the car, Christina splashed across the grass and followed him up a rough stone path to steps that led onto the covered deck. She abandoned her soaked shoes on the doormat. The hinges squeaked as Aiden swung open the door.

Christina had no idea what to expect. She'd only seen inside his room on the base twice. Now she had the sense of a window opening into his life, allowing her to see deeper inside him than ever before.

The house smelled like every rental flat she'd viewed over the years – industrial carpet cleaner, stale air. Her toes sank into the soft pale carpet of the hallway. A dining room opened to the left; beyond it she glimpsed the kitchen. To the right, another door opened into a lounge, two couches facing each other under plastic sheets. Another hall from there she supposed led to bedrooms. It seemed large, and very empty. Vacant hooks on the walls, dent marks in the carpet.

Then she noticed the exposed brickwork on the far wall, an open fireplace, fresh logs piled and ready.

"You have a fireplace?" she said, warmed by even the idea.

"That's what you noticed?"

She turned in a circle, taking a little comfort. A fireplace was an impossible luxury. "Well, that and it's kind of empty. When did the tenants move out? It smells like carpet cleaner."

"A few months ago now."

Despite the cold, Christina pulled back the curtains, which were mauve with a pink stripe, and slid the window open. A fresh gust of rain-washed air blew in. The windows faced the backyard of the house, an overgrown and dripping green square that clung to the back-sloping hill. She paced around, through the dining room and kitchen, opening all the doors and windows, until they could hear the rain like drumming fingers and the breeze chased the smell away.

"There," she said. "Just needs opening up."

"It's freezing now."

"You've spent too long in Townsville."

"I only moved back there at the start of the year," he argued.

"Well, where were you before?"

He paused. "Perth."

She would have laughed, but he was clearly tense. And so she told him a little white lie. "You know, Aiden, I'm fine. If you don't want me to stay here, I can sort myself out."

He caught her hand. "Don't go. I haven't been here in a while, and it feels strange."

Curious, she stayed, conscious of the water dripping from her clothes onto the floor while he seemed to take stock, "Do you have a towel? I'm making a puddle," she said finally.

He shook himself. "Yes, of course. You're drenched."

By the time Christina returned to the lounge, Aiden had brought in her things. He'd stripped the plastic off the couches and lit the fire, cheerful orange flames licking around the logs. He'd rescued the worst-affected books, spreading them out before the fire and was flicking through the less sodden pages to stop them sticking together.

"I suppose I should give up on them," she said, holding the towel around herself as she searched her bag for dry clothes. "Everyone else reads textbooks on their tablets, but I still like paper. And I paid for them."

"Well," said Aiden, "I guess neither are immune to water."

After pulling on a crumpled t-shirt and shorts, Christina picked her way through the pile of books and sat on the floor with the glow of the fire on her skin. The late afternoon sky was dark and overcast, but she felt cozy and safe in this bubble with Aiden. She tipped open her pocket *Oxford Handbook of Clinical Medicine*. Its plastic cover had protected the fine pages inside. Another survivor. She put it to one side and sighed.

"Do you know, I've never seen a real fireplace before," she said, leaning back against Aiden who sat on the couch, both of them watching the flames. "Only in movies, or magazines."

"They're not really the thing to have in Townsville."

"Unless you count when Rita set the stove on fire. I guess we had one for a few minutes then." Christina tried to laugh, but then she found tears streaming down her face.

Aiden pulled her up beside him. "Hey, it's all right."

She shook her head against his shoulder, leaning into him until he was the only thing holding her up. Everything else in her life had washed away, and he was the last island on the river to cling to. He stroked her hair.

"You didn't tell me what happened," he said. "With your mum."

Christina closed her eyes. "She … had a massive bleed. Lena found her unconscious. The hospital tried to transfuse her, but it was too late."

"I'm so sorry, Christy."

"It was always going to turn out this way, I guess," she said. "She'd had cirrhosis for years. It creates all these thick veins around the esophagus. It was just a matter of time before one of them broke. Or she had another stroke, or a bad fit. She was never interested in helping herself."

"And now she's gone."

Christina nodded.

Aiden sighed. "What did the dean say today?"

Christina sat silent for a long minute before telling him what had happened.

"Katie handed in *your* essay?" Aiden asked, outraged. "But she can't possibly get away with that!"

Christina shrugged. "I can't prove it wasn't me who copied. Strictly speaking, the school would have to punish both of us if they thought it was plagiarism, but there's the surgery exam thing too. I don't know what's going to happen."

"I spoke to my mate before I came down. The one who's looking at your laptop. He says recovery can take a while and he's been delayed getting to it, but he's hoping to start soon, and I'll make sure you get the computer back."

Christina stared into the flames. "Are you going to rent the house out again?" she asked, trying to think about something else. She caught the tortured expression on his face. "Oh … This is the place, isn't it? When your ex—"

"Yeah," he said quickly. "This is it. Travers cleaned it up for me. Rented it out for me, too, but I've never been back until today."

"What happened to your stuff?"

Aiden laughed and gestured at the couches. "You're looking at it. I'd been in Afghanistan three months when Travers called to tell me she'd split. I'd been in country for weeks, out of touch, so she was long gone by then. She only left the bed and the couches."

"And those curtains I bet."

"Yeah and those, because she knew I hated them."

"I'm so sorry, Aiden."

He made a sound deep in his chest. "I've done some pretty nasty things in my time. Pulled bodies out of rubble and been out in the field in impossible conditions, and none of it compared to knuckling down to my job for another four months while being utterly unable to do anything about *this*." He gestured around again. "She never returned my calls. She left a note, saying she'd had enough. And that was all I got. To this day, I don't really know what tipped it for her."

"Do you want to know?"

"No," he said firmly. "It's done. It's four years ago done." He rested his head back against the couch. "What do you say we head out for dinner?"

"I don't really feel like it."

"Nothing fancy. I'm saving that for after your exam. And besides, I don't know if you noticed, but there's no fridge and the cupboards are empty. If you want to eat, out we must go."

Aiden took her to a little Italian restaurant nestled between a convenience store and a laundromat called The Dirty Sock. On a Tuesday night, the place was quiet, and the two of them sat by a window eating woodfired pizza while the rain kept falling outside. Christina found herself telling him tales of all the share houses she'd lived in since coming to Brisbane, from the one where she'd acquired a tiny old TV set (before losing it again to thieves) to the one where her twenty-year-old flat mate's mother had beaten down her door at seven o'clock one morning.

"I was moving out," Christina explained. "It was early in my share-housing, when I still thought I might find normal people to live with, before Rita turned up. So I advertised my room to replace myself. My flat mate's mother got up me because I didn't offer the room to her son first. In her world, that was how it worked, apparently. I don't know why she cared so much; they were both tiny little rooms. But I did have a window into the back garden."

"This is the mother of a twenty-year-old, right?" said Aiden.

"Yeah."

"Few weeks in basic training would sort that out."

Christina grinned. "Well, much as it would benefit all my housemates to go to boot camp, sadly, normal people appear to be out of my price range."

Despite her housemate horror stories, Aiden's presence, the night and the rain soothed her, and the sting of the day's events faded to a dull ache. After they returned to the house, Aiden raked up the fire again and they lay on the floor before it, kisses replacing words. The night deepened. Aiden's skin was golden in the firelight as she pushed his shirt off his shoulders, then relieved him of his belt and jeans.

"Commando, really?" she said, taking in the lack of underwear.

"I packed in a hurry," he said roughly, trying to catch her shirt hem, and missing as she twisted away.

"Just wait," she said. "I want to look at you." She trailed her hands along his chest and abs, her fingertips detecting the tiny dips and bumps of his scars, ever downwards until his skin was goosebumped under her touch and his breathing short and heavy. Never before had she been so bold with him.

So when, a minute later, he said, "Now your turn," she didn't even hesitate. And soon they were both bare before the fire, its heat on their skin, their attention only for each other.

The words were on her tongue as they moved together, those three words she'd never imagined saying to anyone. But as he drew her around him for the deepest embrace, it was Aiden who whispered them in her ear, so softly and urgently she wasn't sure if he'd actually spoken or if the thought in her own mind was so intense it became voice.

When they were both just recovering their breath, the warm orange of the fire burned down behind black coals, Aiden pulled her against him and gently kissed her neck, where her pulse was still strong.

It felt so natural to be with him, so complete, as though there was nothing outside this room. Christina felt herself slipping away into sleep, just conscious of Aiden's hands on her skin.

"Christy," he murmured.

"Mmm."

"After your exams, I need to talk to you about some stuff, okay?"

"Mm-hmm."

Christina let herself drift, warm and safe. She knew that when she woke, the world would still be imperfect. But she had him. And it was almost everything she needed.

Chapter 24

Thursday came around all too fast. Christina had spent the previous day cocooned with her notes in the university library, testing herself until she was sick of her own handwriting. In the evening, Aiden took over, quizzing her or acting as a patient, and then she tried to sleep.

The next morning, for the first time in two months, the cohort completing their family practice rotation were all assembled outside the exam hall. There seemed to be a lot of them, and Christina had the uneasy feeling of being just a number in a large crowd.

She also felt prepared. She spotted Toby and Sean from a distance, both revising from index cards. Sarah was standing with another group, chatting nervously.

Seeing her, Toby jogged over. "Christina, how was Townsville?"

"Okay," she said cautiously.

"We're having an end-of-term party next week. Want to come?"

"Not right now, Toby, okay?"

"Sorry, yeah. Exam first. Catch you later."

The students were called into the hall. Christina tried to focus on what was ahead. There was a three-hour written exam today, then the practical tomorrow. As she filed in to take her numbered seat, the question of what would happen *then* ran tracks in her thoughts. The exam paper was a thick booklet on the desk before her. With an effort, she packed those other questions behind the barrier in her mind.

"Stop work."

Christina blinked. Her fingers were crabbed from gripping her pen, her test booklet creased, three hours gone in a blur. Only now did her pulse pick up, her stomach fluttering as the examiner collected her booklet. Then chairs were scraping back and the students stampeded for the door. Christina sat still and took three deep breaths before she rose and gathered her pens. By the time she reached the door, the students had largely dispersed, only a few groups commiserating under the awning outside. The rest of them had probably headed straight back to the library, the confident ones to the student bar.

"So, how was that? Pretty easy huh?"

Christina jumped as a familiar voice addressed her from the side. Katie was wearing a new pair of jeans, and a soft pink jumper over a white shirt. She looked clean and fresh and carefree. Christina turned and walked away.

"Wow, not even going to talk to me, huh?"

"No."

"Come on, Chris. No hard feelings, right?"

Christina whirled on her. "No hard feelings? After everything you did?"

"What did I do?"

Faced with having to lay the ugly truth out in the open air, Christina hesitated before stating baldly, "You stole my essay."

"I stole it?" Katie's brows rose, her mouth open, a perfect picture of disbelief.

"Yes. From my computer."

"I never touched your computer. Anyway, I thought you said you lost the essay. You didn't have it backed up."

Christina ground her teeth. "I had to rewrite it. But it was similar enough that the school plagiarism program picked it up.

You're in trouble too, you know. If they decide one of us copied, both of us will be stuck with it."

Katie just shrugged. "We studied together. Of course we ended up with something similar."

"They're not going to believe that."

"Sure they will." Katie crossed her arms but didn't move away. She had the kind of bulldozer courage that was unaffected by disapproval. Christina wanted to leave, but Katie's gall compelled her to hold fast.

As the silence became uncomfortable, Katie leaned back against the brick wall. "You helped me out a lot this semester, Chris, and I appreciate that, I do. We had some good times, didn't we? I know you'll need a bit of time to cool off and everything, but internal medicine's the next rotation and it's really tough. I'll make it worth your while if you study with me again."

Christina laughed. "Study with you? After the essay, the case report, and how you treated Travers?"

Katie pushed herself away from the wall. "I see. No time for anyone else but him."

"Who?"

"That soldier boy you're fucking."

Christina winced. "Don't say that."

"Well, you are, aren't you? Ha, it's so funny," she said, her expression earnest, almost pitying. "You really love this guy. Well, enjoy it while you've got him. In a couple of weeks, he'll be on a plane and then overseas for *seven months*. How much fun will you be having then?"

Christina stared at Katie. Her phone vibrated in her pocket, but it seemed far away. "What are you talking about?"

Katie looked momentarily puzzled, then a smile pulled at her lips. "He didn't tell you." A laugh bubbled out of her. "I can't believe it."

"Tell me what?" asked Christina.

Katie gripped her shoulders. "Christina. Aiden is deploying

overseas in two weeks. He's been preparing for the last two months. Medicals, courses, fitness assessments. Travers told me all about it. What did you think I was talking about at that dinner?"

"Bullshit," whispered Christina. It wasn't true. It couldn't possibly be true. Aiden would have told her. She knew about his ex who had left him, about his mother's death. She'd been to his sister's wedding ...

Yet something told her Katie wasn't making this up. Katie was peering closely at her face. "Chrissy?"

Christina pushed her away, Katie's jumper ludicrously soft under her fingers. "I have to go." Then she was running towards her car, her pens still clenched in her fist. She couldn't do this by phone; she needed to stand in front of him and have him tell her it wasn't true.

By the time Christina reached Aiden's house, her body was still damp from the long run to her car in the drizzle, her face flushed. Pools of water made mirrors on the porch, reflecting the gray sky. The front door was ajar, every window open. She stepped inside; what had been light and fresh when she left was now cold. The faint tang of old fire ash was in the air.

She found Aiden in the kitchen with a fresh mug of coffee, a stack of shopping bags on the bench. He looked up as soon as she appeared.

"How did it go?"

"Fine." Christina leaned her hands on the breakfast bar. "Aiden, I ran into Katie afterwards—"

"Uh-oh." He made a face.

"—and she tried to tell me that you're deploying overseas in two weeks."

The coffee paused on its way to Aiden's mouth.

"Tell me she's just making trouble," said Christina. "Because I know you would have told me about something like that."

Later, Christina considered that perhaps she should give him credit for the fact that he didn't attempt to lie or diminish the impact. He set the mug down, his eyes resigned, his mouth a thin line. "Yes," he said simply.

"Yes?" She pushed up off the counter, folding her arms before her like a shield. "Yes, what? Yes, she's making trouble? Or yes, you're going overseas? What?" But she saw the look in his eyes. She already knew what he was going to say.

"Yes, I'm deploying in less than two weeks." He stepped around the counter, approached her. "And I was going to talk to you after your exams were over."

Christina stumbled backwards, away from his hands, until her back met the wall. "How long have you known?"

"Nearly six months."

"Six *months*?" Christina felt a rip through her chest, and all the feelings for him that she'd wrapped around her heart – trust and love and desire – unraveled. What was left was an aching void that quickly filled with acid sickness. "Six months. Don't touch me," she added as he tried to put his arms around her. Because he wasn't Aiden anymore. He was another person who'd made promises and then abandoned her.

"Christina, please, I never intended this to happen. I didn't plan to fall in love with you. I wanted to talk about what we do now."

The word *love* was like a slap. "Don't you dare say that to me, not now," she hissed. Her cheeks were flaming, her throat raw. She hadn't realized how much she'd trusted him, how deeply he had slipped under her skin. She saw the edges of his tattoo below his sleeve; he was as indelibly etched onto her as the ink.

And now, and now …

He'd withheld the truth from her, an enormous truth, a staggering lie of omission. All the times he'd told her stories of his army service, the times she'd woken up with him beside her, and never once had he mentioned it. Even when she'd told him about Harriet, even when she'd seen that horrific video …

"Where are you going?" she asked in a small voice.

"I can't say, exactly."

"Of course you can't. Is it the Middle East?"

"Yes."

Competing pictures crowded Christina's mind. The scars on his body. The way he smiled when he was happy. The dust cloud rising from the VBIED blast. Harriet saying she was sorry she was leaving, tears in her eyes. Flag-draped caskets on the news. The dean behind his desk. Fear and shame crashed together, and Christina realized how stupid she'd been. All of this was her doing. She'd invited him in, and he'd done what everyone always did. Screwed her over.

Christina pushed the tears back down inside, to the deepest part of her soul, where she could hold them at bay until she left. She marched around him and picked up her backpack by the counter. Numbly, she went down to the bedroom. The bed had been immaculately made. Her few clothes were stacked on one shelf. She stuffed them into the backpack and yanked the zip closed. As she passed back through the lounge, she paused at the sight of the textbooks. They were ruined anyway. It was all ruined.

Aiden appeared in the doorway. "Christina, please wait."

"Go to hell," she growled at him. Then she was through the front door, splashing across the deck. As she climbed into the Corolla, she threw the bag onto the passenger seat and prayed the car would start. Aiden was at the gate, calling after her in anguish, asking her to come back. She wouldn't make that mistake again. The engine turned over and she pulled away from the curb, going somewhere, anywhere, as long as it was away. Her last view of him was in the rear-view mirror, standing at the gate, watching her go.

Chapter 25

Christina spent a miserable night at the university library, trying and failing to study for the next day's practical exam. She chose a branch she'd never visited before, not wanting to risk Aiden finding her. The branch was open twenty-four hours, so she slept at her desk, fitfully and too briefly.

At six, she got up and went across to the sports hall for a shower, washing with a sliver of soap she found on a windowsill and drying herself with a t-shirt. Thankfully the place had an ironing board, even if the iron had something sticky burned onto it. She managed to get the worst creases out of a shirt and pair of trousers, scraped her hair back in a bun and found an abandoned can of deodorant on top of the lockers. But when she finally looked in the mirror, she saw exactly what she expected to see: an exhausted, angry young woman who could scare children at ten paces. She couldn't go to an exam like this. She tried to smile, and it didn't even reach the edges of her lips. So she tried again: tried to remember why she was here, tried to remember that doctor she'd met all those years ago in Townsville who'd first given her the idea that she could be here at all. This time, her smile was more convincing. She could fool a stranger, even if the hurt told her she couldn't fool herself.

After no breakfast, she arrived at the exam venue at the

medical school at nine o'clock, was given a number and sat down to wait for her turn. There would be two "cases", mock general practice interviews with actors posing as patients. One focused on diagnosis, the other on management.

Christina took her seat for the first interview twenty minutes later in a clinically white tutorial room, across from a gray-haired man. She was so tired, she couldn't even summon nerves. Her eyes felt as though they were sinking into her skull, her thoughts sluggish. The examiner sat off to the side, where she couldn't see him unless she turned her head. She was supposed to pretend he wasn't there.

"So, what can I do for you today?" she began. As the man started to speak, she realized she had forgotten to introduce herself. It was too late now.

"… noticed there was blood on the paper."

Christina had missed half of what he'd said. Panicking, she waited, hoping he would say something to clarify. He didn't. So she said, "And how did you feel about that?"

The man frowned. "Well," he said, "I was worried. I guess it's not a good thing to have blood come out *down there.*"

Ah. She caught up. It was a "blood in the stool" case. A shitty case for a shitty day. In her exhaustion, it seemed a little funny, but she managed not to laugh. Slowly, her mind brought up a list of questions to ask him. Had this happened before? No, all right. What color was the blood, bright or dark? Was it only on the paper, or mixed in the feces too? Did he have any other symptoms: pains in his stomach, vomiting? Was he taking any medications? Was there a family history of bowel cancer?

Partway through the list, Christina realized that the patient had been reduced to one-word answers. That wasn't how it was supposed to go; she was meant to let him talk first. But it was too late for that, too. After what seemed like only a few minutes, she had to present her findings to the examiner. She thought the man probably had hemorrhoids, which could be examined for. She'd certainly seen a few of those on the army base, among the older servicemen. She also told the examiner that tests should be done to rule out something more serious.

"What sort of tests?" he asked.

Christina blanked. Then she said, "Fecal occult blood."

The examiner blinked. "We already know there's blood in his stool. Anything else?"

Christina mentally kicked herself. In her irritation, she couldn't remember the name of the test. Instead she described it poorly. As soon as she was outside, she remembered. Colonoscopy. She said it out loud. But the door was closed. Too late for that now, too.

She fared no better in the second round. Her heart sank as soon as she entered the room and saw that the "patient" was an older woman with a bag of pills in her lap. Her experience on the base hadn't equipped her for patients who were elderly and taking lots of medications. At least this time Christina remembered to introduce herself.

"I'm just visiting my old friend in town for a few weeks," began the actor, "and two of my scripts are about to run out. Can you write me renewals for them?"

"Well, let's see what you have," said Christina, playing for time. She wanted to see the names on the boxes, knowing that patients usually knew the brand names for the drugs, whereas it was the pharmaceutical names Christina needed.

The woman laid out seven boxes on the desk between them. The only one Christina recognized immediately was paracetamol, which was an over-the-counter medication anyway. She took a breath and looked closer, conscious of the clock ticking on the wall. Argh, her eyes were so bleary she couldn't read the boxes. In that panicked moment, she thought of Travers. His patience. His insistence she get things right. Take your time, he'd said, over and over. Think about what you're doing.

Christina's vision cleared. Wait, those two names she recognized. Both were blood pressure medications. "Do you know what you take each of these for?" she asked, pointing to the boxes.

"Oh, yes," said the patient. "Those are for my blood pressure. These ones help me sleep. These ones are for my joints."

"And what about these?" asked Christina, tapping the paracetamol.

The woman shrugged. "Oh, my friend takes them four times a day for her arthritis. I thought I'd try that, too."

Christina sat back in her chair. She knew there was a point to grasp here. Up until now, she'd assumed this case was about "polypharmacy", patients who unnecessarily took large numbers of medications. But this was something specific – sometimes the medications could interact with each other.

"Ms. Price, you're running out of time," said the examiner.

Christina gritted her teeth. "Mrs. Smith, you have a lot of medications here. I think we should look at whether any of them aren't necessary."

"I need them all for my health," complained the woman. "Can't you just write the scripts?"

And even though she knew this patient was an actor, something about her casual attitude to the pills pushed Christina's buttons. It was her mother all over again. She pulled the two blood pressure medications out of the row. "You see these here? Both these medications can affect your kidneys. And when you mix them with this one—" she grabbed the paracetamol "—you can end up with permanent damage."

The old lady's eyes had widened; Christina could see her about to reach for another line.

"It's very important," she went on, cutting the woman off, "that you don't start taking anything new without talking to your doctor first, even if you can buy it in the supermarket. Do you understand?"

The actor glanced at the examiner. Christina knew that her manner was overbearing, inappropriate. She dropped the boxes and slumped. A buzzer went, signaling the end of the session. "I'm sorry," she said in the direction of the examiner. "I – I think …" But she didn't really know what to say.

The examiner slotted his glasses into his top pocket. "You can go now."

Christina walked out, just as reality caught up with her. If she'd done well in the practical, the dean might have believed her when she said she'd had a better rotation this time. But now it would just make her surgery exam result stand out all the more.

Two students she didn't know were sitting waiting, anxiously drumming their feet. They had some kind of future, no matter how badly they did. But she had no idea what next week would bring for her.

Her car was in the street outside with everything she owned inside it. She wanted to run away, but instead came another idea, one that honed her anger into purpose. One last avenue of questions demanding answers. And whatever nightmares tomorrow had in store for her, she was not going to put that one off any longer.

She pulled out her phone and dialed Harriet's number. And for the first time, it didn't go to voicemail.

"Christina?" Harriet answered. "I've been trying to call. What's this about Rita?"

The question hung in the air as Christina noted the ordinariness of the street around her. Other students returning to their cars, birds flitting from tree to tree. She felt so distant from it all, as though the words she had to say couldn't belong in an ordinary day.

"She's dead," she said.

A long silence. Finally, Harriet took a deep shaking breath, as though she might have been waiting for this news all her life. "When?"

"Last Saturday. Massive esophageal hemorrhage." She said it as though it was a line from her textbook.

"Do you want me to—"

"I want to talk to you," Christina said. "I know you're not overseas because I found your passport. I'm not taking no for an answer. So where are you?"

Harriet sighed, but her resistance seemed to be gone. "On the farm, south-east of Townsville."

Christina thought about what else she had to lose, and there didn't seem to be much. "Give me the address," she said. "I'll be there tomorrow."

Chapter 26

Wildfire Farm was nestled in the Mount Elliot foothills, surrounded by rolling grassy plains and fed with water from Majors Creek. Driving the Belmont with the window down, her hair tangling in the warm air, Christina made two wrong turns before she finally spotted the gate and bounced up the long driveway. The farmhouse was a green-roofed fibro shack resting on a rise and surrounded by rambling gardens. In the distance, the mountains rose in shades of blue.

Christina's tires crunched on the gravel, and Harriet was leaning in the doorway as the Belmont pulled to a stop.

She had expected her aunt to look older than the last time she'd seen her, but from a distance at least, Harriet seemed exactly the same. Her blonde hair was still thick, and tied back at her nape, echoing the no-nonsense fold of her arms. She wore a blue work shirt and cut-off shorts, her legs tanned to caramel. Only when Christina stepped onto the veranda did she see the fine lines around Harriet's eyes, the corners of her mouth tugged down.

"What have you done to that car?" Harriet asked. "It never sounds that good."

"It's a long story."

A silence grew around them like a forest, both of them waiting for the other to speak. Harriet found her voice first, and pushed the door open. "You'd better come in."

Christina followed Harriet down a hall. It opened into an open-plan lounge and kitchen with floor-to-ceiling windows that looked out onto the mountains. The air smelled of gingerbread, jam, and roasting duck, several pots crowding the stove and baking trays on the bench.

"I'm cooking," Harriet explained unnecessarily. "Do you want to talk about your mother? Organize the funeral?"

"It's done. Brisbane, last Tuesday."

This stopped Harriet in her tracks. "So that's where she ended up. How long had she been there?"

"I'll get to that. Why did you tell me you were going overseas?"

"I thought I'd give you the run of the house."

Christina studied Harriet, who was turned away stirring a pot on the stove, not making eye contact. Her aunt had never been one to avoid an issue; her approach was always to face the problem in front of her.

Well, Christina was resolved to address the issues head-on. She dropped the photo she'd found at John's on the bench. "Did it have anything to do with John Hunt?"

Harriet stopped stirring. "Who?"

"I found the postcards," Christina said. "And the letter and the article about the fire. And he had this photo of us."

She went on, describing how she'd met John, how he'd known where she lived. Harriet listened with her head bowed. When Christina was done, Harriet was quiet, and Christina realized with a shock that her strong, unemotional aunt was trying not to cry.

Harriet rummaged in the pantry, sniffing, then came back with a small sack. "Let's go and feed those chickens."

Christina trotted down the path after her aunt. The chooks had already spotted Harriet striding towards them and were running up the field. Her aunt stopped at the fence.

"I know I haven't seen you in a long time," Christina said carefully. "But this ... hiding away isn't like you. Please tell me, what did he do?" She reached a hand out to touch Harriet's arm.

"Nothing," said Harriet firmly, but she didn't shake Christina off. When she spoke again her voice was smaller. "Well, nothing that I didn't allow. I should have been smarter."

"If he's harassing you, then—"

"I haven't seen him in fifteen years."

She frowned, confused. "Has he been sending those cards all that time?"

"No, of course not." Harriet cast more grain on the grass and the chooks darted after it, clucking and jostling. "The cards started up after Thomas died. John knew better than to contact me while my husband was still alive. He did have some honor, despite everything else."

"So what happened?"

Two long steps led up into the chook house, and Harriet sat down on one end, looking out over the field and the distant mountains. After a moment's hesitation, Christina sat too.

"I met John twenty-eight years ago, when I was twenty-two. It would have been just before you were born. He was a sergeant then. Very self-assured, confident type, like they all were, those army boys. I'd been in the nursing corps since my registration and we met at a function. He was older than me, but I thought I was in control of everything. Knew what I wanted, all that stuff." Harriet laughed bitterly. Christina hugged her arms around herself, chilled by the sound.

"It went on for two years. He was a strange man in some ways with some strong issues about relying on anyone, but I loved him more than anything." Harriet glanced sharply at Christina. "I know this isn't news to you, but your mother and I had a hard time growing up. Our own mother was a train wreck from Monday to Sunday night – drank too much, hopeless with money, married to a man worse than she was. Your mother took after her like butter on a summer's day. Not me. I decided I wanted out of all that. No husband to chain me to a sink, no family to screw up. I wanted my own life. When John had to post away, he asked me to go with him, but I didn't want to. I'd left the army by then and I liked my job. I had a life there, in Townsville. Friends. I didn't want to be the army wife, moving from place to place. I wanted to stay."

Harriet paused, pulling at a strand of grass. One of the chooks took an interest and sidled over, pecking gently at her fingers. Harriet smiled briefly. "It was the hardest thing I'd ever done, I think, telling him I wouldn't go. He didn't understand. He hadn't grown up in my house. He wanted a family, and with me. He said he would always love me, that he'd be back. But I didn't want that uncertainty. I told him to go, and that it should end. Broke my heart, but time was supposed to heal that."

"So when did you meet Thomas?"

"I'm getting to that," said Harriet. "John wrote to me, the whole time he was posted away. I didn't write back very much, because it was difficult. I'd start a letter and then realize I was just making it hard for myself, and I'd screw it up. I couldn't just be a friend to him. My feelings couldn't be turned off like that. I saw a few other men, trying to convince myself I was moving on, but none of them could compare. Thomas was a good friend, back then. He and John had been in the same unit, but he was an officer, and a calm, gentle sort of man. I knew he wanted more, but I think I was waiting, even though I told myself I wasn't. And then, eventually, John came back. Maybe a year after the new hospital opened. I expected that, after ten years, we wouldn't know each other. But it was like he'd never left."

"I remember that time – you were having the house renovated," said Christina. She'd been living with Harriet for nearly three years at that point. "But I don't remember John."

Harriet scowled. "No, you wouldn't. We kept it very quiet." She looked away then, as if embarrassed. "Things with Rita were tricky enough without her knowing about a man in my life. As it turned out, that was rather convenient for John, though I didn't know it at the time."

"Because of his wife?" asked Christina.

Harriet screwed her eyes shut. "You said you saw the newspaper article, didn't you? You know, I never once thought about what he'd been doing during all those years away. Then I saw that article. His house had burned down in Sydney – oh, it was very dramatic, what with his pregnant wife having to escape from an upper window."

"His—"

"Yes, you heard me," said Harriet, in a rush, as though it would hurt less that way. "And despite the fact that he'd been back here seeing me as though he were a free man, he had no intention of leaving her. I tried very hard, for her sake, to be grateful for that … he said he wasn't going to walk away, and I should have bloody well hoped so. All the same, the shock of finding out about her knocked me over."

Abruptly, Harriet shot up, and paced a few feet across the lawn in her gumboots. "All he would say was that he meant to tell me. For six months, he'd meant to tell me." She leaned on the bowed fence rail, looking down the green paddock, her shoulders drooping like the fence. "I didn't believe him, and I couldn't bear it – how his wife would feel if she knew, how I'd let him back in just to bleed my heart dry all over again. But Thomas was there for me. And so I made a snap decision. I married him and I moved to Puckapunyal."

Christina was speechless for a full minute. She watched the chickens pecking around their feet, the swaying of the grass tips in the warm breeze, the gray haze on the horizon. For the first time since their terrible argument on Castle Hill, she felt no anger towards Harriet. She rose and went to lean on the rail beside her aunt.

"I thought you just changed your mind one day and left," Christina said. She glanced around at the cheerful rambling chook house, across to the big shed and the house, and down towards the orchard. "But why didn't you just tell me you were out here when I rang? Why the story of going overseas?"

A shrill ringing suddenly cut the air. It took Christina a moment to realize it was an alarm. Both of them whirled towards the house, and Christina's attention snared on a shimmer in the kitchen window. "What's that?"

Harriet paled. "Oh God, the oil!"

Then Christina saw tongues of flame in the window. The kitchen was on fire.

Christina ran as fast as she could, but Harriet still pulled ahead of her. Her aunt was fit, the muscles in her legs bunching. She reached the glass door and threw herself inside. By the time Christina burst into the kitchen, flames were leaping from the oil pot to the ceiling, blackening the tiles and the range hood, the scream of the smoke alarm deafening.

"There's an extinguisher in the shed!" Harriet called, darting her hand in to try to turn off the gas while batting at the flames with a tea towel.

Christina knew there was no time to get the extinguisher. Feeling oddly calm, she grabbed a baking tray from the bench and slid it across the burning pot. The heat licked around the sides; she held on just long enough to cover the pot before dropping the tray and yanking her hand back. The huge flame snuffed out, leaving only small puddles of oil and jam from the next pot burning on the stove top. She checked that all the gas taps were off, and grabbed a packet of flour still on the bench, dousing the spot fires with drifts of white powder.

As she was scanning around for any more traces of fire, she felt Harriet's hand on her shoulder, and heard the tap running. "No water!" she said, alarmed.

Harriet pulled her to the sink. "I burned my fingers, and you must have too." And so they stood there at the sink, their hands together under the faucet, letting the water wash away the heat. With it, too, seemed to go the distance time and regret had wedged between them. Suddenly, Harriet began to laugh.

"What's funny?" Christina asked.

"I'm a good cook. I've never burned anything in my life. The first time I do, I nearly burn the house down."

Christina found herself laughing too. "Maybe the kitchen could do with a renovation."

"I've been thinking about re-doing the whole house. Maybe this is a sign." Harriet paused. "You were remarkably calm."

"I learned what to do when Rita set the kitchen on fire one day," Christina said. "She threw water on it and the flames shot up to the ceiling. Then she put a saucepan lid on it, but she took it off too soon and it started again." Christina stopped laughing, gripped with sadness. It could have been a metaphor for her mother's life, the destructive flame of her addiction that she could never quite extinguish. And now it could never be any different. She hadn't realized until now that right up until her mother had died, she'd held onto some tiny hope that Rita would eventually change, become the mother Christina wanted her to be. Now she never could.

Harriet's mirth ended too. She pulled her hands out of the water and sank down against the kitchen cupboards. Christina shut off the tap and sat next to her, inspecting her hands. The fine hairs on the backs of her fingers were gone, the skin red and swollen on her fingertips, but she'd otherwise escaped unharmed. Her eyes followed the black streak up the range hood and onto the cupboards. The air stank of acrid char.

"What happened to the smoke alarm?" she asked, spotting the unit, which was hanging from the ceiling at a strange angle. She hadn't noticed when the piercing sound had stopped.

"I stabbed it with the end of the broom," said Harriet. "It was driving me crazy."

They looked at each other. Christina laughed first, and then, a second later, Harriet followed. When the rural fire unit arrived fifteen minutes later, after a call from a neighboring property about the smoke, Christina and Harriet were still sitting on the kitchen floor.

"Oh, look, just what I need, more men in uniform," said Harriet, and cackled again.

That set Christina off too. They were both still in ridiculous moods, though Christina corrected one of the firemen sharply when he suggested they were in shock. "It's not *shock*," she said. "Shock is a specific, life-threatening medical condition of the cardiovascular system. This is just … *debriefing*."

"Debriefing, huh?" said the man, more amused than offended.

"You should listen to her, she's a medical student," said Harriet.

"Well, you ladies are very lucky."

Christina didn't know about that. It seemed, really, that they were rather the opposite. All she could say for certain was that they were both still breathing, and that, after fifteen years, she appeared to have her aunt back. Tentatively, she put her arms around Harriet, as if she was a child again, and was grateful when her aunt hugged her back.

Chapter 27

T hey talked all night, camped out on the lounge room carpet with the door open for fresh air, around takeaway from the village and bottles of ginger beer. And somehow, in the dim lamplight, though neither of them really wanted to talk about it, Christina was able to tell Harriet about Rita, and the lost years Harriet hadn't known about.

Harriet was very quiet. When Christina finished, Harriet shook her head. "It's so much worse than I thought. I had no idea you'd ended up in that situation, looking after her affairs," she said. "Rita was never much good at life. Someone else always had to mind her. She was lucky that she kept attracting people who would, for a while. But it should never have been you. I wish you'd called me."

"I couldn't," Christina said. "I didn't even think about it. I just wanted …" Actually, as she spoke she realized she had no idea what she'd wanted. Maybe for her mother to turn things around. Or maybe she'd been so focused on medicine she'd neglected anything else.

"How is the study going?" asked Harriet, when they'd moved past the last few years.

Christina drained her bottle. "Not great." She told Harriet about the saga with Katie and her own meeting with the dean, and the uncertainty over what would happen next.

"If you had nothing to do with it, then I'm sure that's what they'll find," Harriet said.

"I'd like to believe that," said Christina, but she didn't, not really. She wasn't so naive as to believe that the world was fair. She had been pushing uphill from the start, the odds against her. Other students had families and resources; most of them didn't have to make decisions about whether to buy food or a textbook. Whether she would make it in the end wouldn't take that into account.

"What about these last exams?" asked Harriet.

"I think I scared the patients," Christina said. She described the two practical tests, how in the pressure of the moment she'd forgotten the word "colonoscopy", and startled the old woman with her blood pressure pills. "When I was studying beforehand, Aiden—" She stopped, but too late.

"Who's Aiden?"

Christina shook her head and stood up, as if the action could keep away the tears. She had no energy to answer. The hurt was too raw. She stepped out into the dark night where the balmy air promised an early summer. She heard Harriet's footsteps behind her.

"You asked me earlier why I didn't tell you I was here," Harriet began. "The year I left, your mother was doing much better. She'd been sober six months, she had that job at the pharmacy. She started insisting you go back with her full time. I wasn't sure about it, but then one weekend, she wouldn't let you come back to me. I didn't want to put you through courts, and she did seem better, so I gave in. Then, three days after she took you back, I found out about John."

Christina turned to her aunt, and saw Harriet's mouth drawn down. Even in the dim light spilling from the lounge, Christina could see the pain in her face.

"I never imagined how much the idea of losing you would affect me," Harriet whispered. "But I wasn't your mother. During those first days, before I told you, I leaned on John to get through it. When I found out his lies, the ground fell out from under me. I thought I had nowhere to turn, but Thomas listened to everything, didn't judge. He was a very different kind of man from John. I figured I had nothing left here, so that's why I decided to leave with him.

"We were married fourteen years, and it was calm. We stayed friends, but perhaps not much more than that. When Thomas became sick with lymphoma, I bought this farm from my friends to give him somewhere peaceful to come. We had five years before he died."

"I'm sorry, Harriet."

"Don't you feel sorry for me," her aunt said, curt. "I'm not making excuses. I should have known better. Your mother had a long history of relapses. I called often at first, but she never let me talk to you, told me to mind my own business. She was always suspicious, and a good liar. She told me you were doing well. I didn't know what had happened, that you'd been fostered out. I tried to visit you at home once, and she told me you would be away on a school trip. I should have known then. The next time I called, the number was cut off. She'd moved, never told me where."

Christina hugged herself, moved by the regret in her aunt's voice. "Harriet—"

"I'm not finished." Harriet's voice shook. "When I finally came back to Townsville and ran into you that last time, I found out afterwards through work what had happened to you. I was horrified." She took Christina's hand. "I'm so sorry, Christina, oh God, I'm sorry. I've never felt so sick as when I found out what you'd gone through. I understood why you were so angry. When you were coming up for this term, I didn't want you to have to see me again. Not after I'd abandoned you to that." She rubbed her thumb across the scar on Christina's palm as if she could erase it.

Christina pulled Harriet into a hug, holding on until her aunt stopped shaking. Then she pushed Harriet away slightly and took her by the shoulders. "It wasn't your fault," she said. "If you believe that you're to blame, it excuses her. And that bastard foster man. And Seb Prior, and everyone else. And if you'd never gone, I don't know if I'd be here. This scar gave me the motivation to leave." She told Harriet about the doctor who'd treated her burn.

Harriet's eyes streamed. "I can't believe that. You were bright. You just needed other people to stop screwing up your life. I could have made that happen. And instead ..." She sniffed. "I deserved everything you said to me eleven years ago."

"Shh," said Christina, trying to soothe her. In that moment, she felt older than her aunt. She understood now why Harriet had made the choices she had; she could picture how convincing Rita must have been, and how shocked and betrayed Harriet must have felt over John. And while she knew that she would always carry the scars of her experience, the pain of them had eased. "Nothing can change it now. It's done."

Harriet was silent for a long time. "Except for one thing," she said finally. "John."

They drove back to Townsville the next morning. Christina called ahead to find out whether John could have visitors. The nurse she spoke to said he was back in the ward and it would be fine.

"Still, might be a good idea to wait until he's home," Christina said, uncomfortable at the sight of the determination on Harriet's face.

"No, this has gone on far too long. Besides, I'm still a nurse. I know when to stop."

Christina hoped that was true; she didn't want to cause any trouble in the ward, particularly when Daniella had been nothing but helpful. But Harriet was as good as her word. When they arrived at the hospital, her demeanor was professional, as though she was simply visiting an old friend, but Christina noticed that her aunt's fingers weren't altogether steady as she pushed the button in the lift.

John was propped in a bed by the window. His eyes shifted dully as he spotted their approach, his first glance was blank and uninterested. Then he looked again, his eyes widening in disbelief.

Harriet stopped at the foot of his bed. "Hello, John."

"Harriet." His voice was rough with emotion.

"No, stay," Harriet said to Christina, who had begun to slip away. "This won't take long."

"You look well," he said.

"Well, you look terrible," she said. "And now I hear you've been making trouble for my niece, too."

John smiled, but it quickly faded. "I never thought you'd come."

"We're not going to do this, not again," said Harriet. "It's been a long time for a reason. Do you remember what I said the last time?"

John scowled. "Of course I *remember*."

"Good. Then you know that it's done. But I want you to stop sending the notes. Stop trying."

"I just want to talk to you. That's all."

"That's how it will start," she said impatiently. "You just want to talk. Talking means remembering, John. I don't want to."

Christina groped for the wall behind her, feeling as though she was intruding. She could see the evidence of their past in Harriet's firmly crossed arms, in the flare of John's eyes, in the way the air pulled tight between them.

"I don't forgive you," said Harriet. "I never will."

He held up one hand. "I'm not asking you to."

That stopped her. "Then why send—"

"I don't want this bad feeling between us. I can't live every day with it. Fifteen years is enough."

He looked down at his hands. "I know what a bastard I

was. What I did to you. I need you to hear that I'm sorry, that I've never had a moment without regret. That I've wished every day for a different life. That I've never loved anyone like I loved—"

"*Oh no*," said Harriet. "Don't." A tight silence settled. Christina felt her pulse in her throat, and wondered whether Harriet would simply walk away.

"I understand," he said. "I lost the right to be anything to you. But I can't let our last conversation be an argument."

Harriet glanced towards the window, then at Christina, her eyes betraying an internal conflict. In spite of everything, some part of her aunt still cared for John, Christina saw that now.

"I'll be all right for a few minutes," Harriet said to Christina at last.

"Sure?" she asked. Harriet gave a quick nod.

Christina walked away feeling awful for Harriet. She leaned against the nurses' station to wait. The ward was quiet this morning, the station currently empty. Across the hall, she could see a nurse through the door of a storeroom.

Then Daniella appeared at the office door, her shirt crumpled, strands of hair escaping her ponytail. "Christina!" she said, surprised. "I thought you were back in Brisbane." She yawned. "Sorry. It was a long night. Did you come to see John? He's doing much better."

"My aunt did," said Christina quickly, feeling awkward around Aiden's sister and not quite knowing what to say. "It turns out they knew each other years ago."

"How amazing!" Daniella's tired eyes brightened. "Finally, some contacts. Although I suppose this town's a small place. Was she in the army too?"

"For a while. She was a nurse." Christina shifted her feet.

Daniella smiled kindly. "How are you holding up?"

"I'm sorry, Daniella, it's just ..." Christina trailed off. Daniella had been so kind to her in the last few weeks, but she didn't know how to separate her from Aiden in her mind.

"Why don't you come through here for a minute?" said

Daniella, taking her arm and leading her into the offices behind the nurses'' station. Inside, she sat Christina on a chair and gently pushed across a box of tissues.

Despite her discomfort, Christina laughed. "Do I look like I'm going to cry?"

"It never hurts to be prepared. Now, I don't want to be nosy, but when I spoke to you a few days ago, you said your mother had just died. I'm guessing you weren't close, but it still must be an awful shock."

Christina nodded numbly. The ripples of that shock were still muddling her thoughts, more than Daniella knew, like sediment shaken up from the bottom of a still pond.

"You also said you had some problems with the school. Is that part of it, too?"

Prepared to be defensive with Aiden's sister, Christina instead found herself disarmed by her kindness. "Ah, in a way."

"You want to tell me about it?"

"Not really ... but I will, if you want." And so Christina had to tell the story again to Daniella, feeling more ashamed, as if she were protesting too much after having already told Harriet and Aiden. But Daniella was the first one who didn't immediately try to dismiss her fears.

"That certainly sounds serious, and I can understand how upset you must feel," she said, frowning. "But the school would have to have very good reasons to be able to follow through and discipline students. What about speaking to someone who could help you, the student union, maybe?"

Inside, Christina baulked at the idea of reaching out. "I don't think it will help. I did poorly in the first two years, so I'm always playing catch-up. I'm weak on prac. My good result will still look like an anomaly."

"Really? That's not what I heard."

Christina sighed. "This rotation was different." And that made her think of Travers, and Aiden. And suddenly, with no warning, the pain of what had happened sliced through her, and she did cry. Angrily, she plucked a tissue from the box, embarrassed to show such weakness.

"What else is going on?" Daniella asked gently. "Is it Aiden?"

Christina covered her face with her hands. She had no words for this, couldn't begin to explain how broken she felt inside and how the jagged pieces seemed to cut every time she moved.

Daniella patted her shoulder. "Don't feel you have to tell me. But you can if you want to, and it might help."

"No, it won't," Christina managed. "He didn't tell me, so I left."

"Didn't tell you what?"

"About him deploying overseas next week. He never mentioned it. I had to find out from Katie, of all people. And I thought he wanted to be with me."

Looking up, Christina saw that Daniella had sat back in her chair, her face suddenly drawn, pale and cold. "What's this about him deploying?" she asked.

"You know, that he's going to the Middle East for seven months."

But it was obvious now that Daniella had been as much in the dark as Christina. "Are you quite sure?" she finally asked.

"Positive. He told me himself."

At this Daniella pushed her chair back and stood. She checked her watch. "I'm off shift in two hours," she said calmly. "And then I'm going to kill my brother."

Chapter 28

Aiden hadn't lingered in Brisbane. After Christina's departure, and her refusal to answer his calls, the house had stopped being the haven it had seemed with the two of them there together, and returned to what it was before: cold, dark, and holding too many bad memories. Being back on base was hardly better, however. He was still on leave, which meant he had to find ways to occupy his time and try to remember that in just over a week, he would be on a plane to a war zone.

On Sunday afternoon, he was searching his room for any laundry that could be rounded up and dispatched to the machine when a knock thumped on his door. He sipped at his beer as he crossed the floor. Expecting to see another soldier standing there, he choked on his drink when he saw Daniella.

"Hello to you too," she said, as he coughed. She stepped through the door while he recovered, and stood just inside, her arms folded. "When were you going to tell me, Aiden?"

"Shit," he said, trying to steer her further inside so they weren't standing by the door.

"No, don't touch me," she said with uncharacteristic heat. "And answer my question."

"How did you even get in here?" he asked. "You need a pass to make it through the gate—"

"Answer my question!"

Aiden looked down. "I didn't want to tell you before the wedding. Afterwards, it … I forgot."

"You *forgot?*" Daniella paced further into his room. "You didn't forget, Aiden. I know how these things work from every other time you've been away. You have to be nominated first, and that happens months before you go. You've known about this for a long time. Do you know," she went on, a slight tremor in her voice now, "what it was like all those other times you went? Thinking about you in some faraway place and not knowing whether you were in danger? Hearing on the news that a soldier had been killed and not knowing if it was you? How do I prepare for that in a *week?*"

Aiden sank down on the bed. "I know. It got away from me. I kept meaning to bring it up and I didn't. I couldn't."

Daniella sighed. She didn't say anything for a while, then she put a hand to her forehead as if she had a fever. "I'm sorry, I didn't mean to yell at you. It's been a long shift and then I couldn't get Mark on the phone … I haven't slept yet."

"It's all right."

"No, it's not. I remember you saying that not everyone thinks our army going overseas is a good thing, and they take it out on you. I'm not one of those people."

Aiden got up and put his arms around her. "I've never thought you were."

"Christina came into the ward today."

"Did she?" Aiden let Daniella go. What was Christina doing back in Townsville? He thought she was still down in Brisbane.

"How do you think I found out? Aiden … I don't understand you not telling me, but I understand even less why you wouldn't tell *her*. You're in a relationship. Did you think she wouldn't mind?"

"We're not in a relationship." He sat back down on the bed.

"But you were."

"I didn't even think of it like that in the beginning. She was always going to go back to Brisbane, and I didn't want to get involved … Later, things changed and I meant to talk to her, I did. I just didn't think that …"

"What, that you'd fall in love with her?"

Aiden grimaced as the pain of losing Christina split him apart. "Something like that."

Daniella laughed.

"What's so funny?"

"You. God, I watched you both at my wedding. You were already in over your head. And so was she. You're both hopeless."

Aiden stared at Daniella. "How on earth did you manage to notice that?"

"Oh, I don't know. The way you were always looking for her no matter who you were talking to. That last dance where you couldn't take your eyes off her."

He shook his head, bewildered. "You were the bride. There must have been two hundred people there."

"Aiden, come on. I idolized you when we were growing up. You were bigger and did everything before me, but you always had time for me, and you were kind, even when I annoyed you. You show your hand with kindness the moment you like someone." She punched his arm. "And I get the feeling Christina's not experienced a lot of kindness in her life. I don't know a lot about her, but she trusted you. No wonder she dropped you so fast when she found out; you did the worst thing you could possibly do to her."

Aiden turned the beer in his hands, no longer thirsty.

"You were never like this before, Aiden," she said softly. "I know your work has become more and more demanding, but I wonder if you know how much it's taken over your life. You would never have kept this to yourself before. I'm trying to understand what's changed."

Aiden wondered if he could tell her the truth. Then he realized in a week he'd be gone, and he didn't want to take the secret with him.

"I'm scared," he said finally.

"Of what?"

He stood up restlessly. "I never told you about what really happened with Tracey," he said.

"Tracey the bitchface? You broke up, I know that."

Aiden felt a twinge of amusement. "Since when do you swear like that?"

"Jackie's been teaching me bad habits. Go on."

"She left me while I was deployed."

Daniella paused and sat on the bed. "I thought it happened right after."

"That's what I let everyone think. But she left when I was three months in. Travers found out and told me. He sorted out a few things until I came back."

"That's awful. I can't believe she—"

"That's not all of it." He was right at the cusp now, of things only he and Travers knew. And until this moment, Aiden hadn't quite realized to what extent those events had changed him.

And so he told her, every detail of what had happened when Tracey had left, and what had come after. By the time he had finished, Daniella was aghast. She put her arms around him. "You know, we would have helped, if you'd told us. Dad especially. You know he'll feel dreadful that he didn't."

"I couldn't ask then. I can barely talk about it now."

"The world has a way of sorting out people like Tracey," said Daniella confidently.

Aiden kissed the top of her head. "No offence, little sister, but the world's a big place and sometimes there's no justice at all. Believe me, I've seen some things."

"I'm not talking about justice. I mean that wherever she is, she won't make it through without people eventually finding her out for what she is. Trust me, I've seen *that* happen."

He loved Daniella's conviction. She believed that goodness would triumph in the end. Aiden wondered whether that kind of belief existed in him still, if it ever had. "Okay, I'll let you have that one," he said, hoping she was right.

"The bigger question, though, is what are you going to do now?"

Aiden leaned against the wall and rested his forehead on his fingertips. "What do I do?" he said helplessly. "She won't talk to me. Won't return my calls. And I'm leaving in a week."

"She's hurt and angry. Of course she is. I would be too."

Aiden looked up. "Man, Dani, what a screw-up. I'm sorry I didn't tell you."

She attempted a smile. "You don't have to protect me, you know that, Aiden. I'm strong enough to take it. And so is Christina. Now, I desperately need to sleep. And later, I want to have dinner with you. We need to make up for lost time."

"I owe you so much more than that."

Her smile turned wry. "Maybe. But we'll have years to make it up, you and me. Just make sure you have the same chance with her, okay?"

When Daniella had gone, Aiden sat on his bed for a long time. He'd thought Christina was still in Brisbane, and one of the reasons he'd tried so hard to contact her was that he knew she didn't have anywhere to go. He hated the idea that she might be sleeping in her car, or on campus somewhere. But he also knew how proud she was, how much she would hate him thinking she couldn't look after herself.

Now, though, knowing she was in Townsville, he had a strong impulse to jump in his car and drive around to her aunt's house. But what would he do once he got there? He came up with different plans; thought of all the things he wanted – and needed – to say to her. But despite his long career in planning and thinking ahead, he knew he was utterly out of his depth.

So when he finally left the base in the early evening, he didn't turn towards Christina's but instead headed for The

Strand and Travers' apartment, where he found his friend working off the excesses of Saturday night on the weight bench of the complex's gym.

Seeing Aiden walk in, Travers completed his set and sat up. "You just get back?" he asked, sucking on a water bottle, his singlet wet from neck to waist.

"Yesterday."

"Thought you'd be staying down there for a bit, lying in bed, enjoying the last days before you go," said Travers.

"Didn't work out that way."

"She didn't take it well?"

"I didn't get the chance. Katie told her first."

"Oh, hell." Travers" face tightened with shame. "Aiden, that's my fault. I told her weeks ago about you going away."

"Doesn't matter now."

"I never would have told her anything if … Dammit." Travers threw down a weight glove. "I should have known better."

"Forget it. It's over. I'm leaving in a week." Aiden shrugged, trying to sound casual, but found he had to lean on the wall for support. "But there's something I want you to do while I'm gone."

"What's that?"

"Look out for her."

Travers laughed. "You think she needs it?"

Aiden paced across the gym, ran his hands across the rack of free weights. "I don't like the idea of just leaving her behind."

"No offence, Aiden," said Travers, rubbing his face with a towel, "but she's not going to talk to me if she thinks I'm going to pass information on to you."

"I don't need to know anything. Just promise me you'll look her up every so often. Make sure she's okay."

Travers narrowed his eyes. "That's it then? You're just giving up on her? Delegating to me so you don't have to do the hard work yourself?" He shook his head. "Screw that officer bullshit, sir. This isn't something you should ask me to do. It's the easy road."

"Easy road? I'm leaving in a week, Travers."

"So, you still have a week. And we've all left before. So many times that we've turned cutting ties and blowing town into an art form. Telling ourselves as we're leaving that those people will always be there when we come back, but then enough time passes and it doesn't matter anymore. Don't do that now. You have a week. Sort it out."

Aiden was taken aback. "You think that's what I do?"

"No, I'm saying we all do it. I've got friends all over the country I almost never see. And in my mind, they're great mates, because that's what I remember. But most of them … it's been too long, right? Everyone who's in the force with us, that tie keeps us together. But everyone outside, their lives move on. Sometimes it moves too far and at some point you find out you only *used* to know them. Look at us, Aiden; we've been friends a long time, but I'm getting out now, and I don't want to find in a year's time that I don't know you. So prove to me that's not going to happen. Don't leave her just because it's too hard."

Aiden chewed this over, remembering what Daniella had said. They were blood; they'd always have the bond of family between them. But Christina wasn't his sister; they had only the bond they'd made together. Even if she forgave him later, if he left for seven months she could make a new bond with someone else. And soon all they'd have in common was that they'd once both been in Townsville.

He looked up to find Travers watching him. "Yeah," said the medic. "Not a nice thought, is it?"

As he paced back across the floor, Aiden found himself picturing Christina with another man. A doctor, perhaps, who understood her work, who didn't need to go away or keep secrets. And he hated that he wasn't that man. He stopped in the doorway, looking out at the palm tree across the street. It only registered now that he would probably never see her again.

"She won't talk to me," he said in a low voice. "It doesn't matter what I want anymore. What can I offer her that I haven't already tried?"

Travers sighed and threw the towel over his shoulder as he walked across to his gym bag. He extracted two beers and threw one to Aiden. "Well, that's the stupidest damn thing I ever heard. But it's your life."

Aiden grunted, opening the can.

"Speaking of which, dive tomorrow?"

Aiden paused with the beer halfway to his lips. "You bought the new boat?"

"Picked up the keys yesterday. No more unreliable outboard."

Aiden figured he owed Travers a day on the water. "Better make it early," he said.

Chapter 29

After their visit to the hospital in the morning, Harriet had been quiet on the drive home, and even quieter once they reached the house. Christina asked if there was anything she could do – she'd seen that Harriet had brought the notebook John was often writing in – but Harriet shook her head and went into the study, closing the door firmly behind her.

Christina spent two hours doing some washing, cleaning the kitchen and bathroom, and making sandwiches; when she knocked on the study door with a plate of them, Harriet didn't answer. Christina pressed her ear to the wood; she could hear papers shuffling, and occasionally her aunt sniffed or sighed. Christina understood the desire to be alone. She covered the sandwiches and put them in the fridge.

Later, when darkness had fallen and Christina was attempting to watch television, she heard a grumbling engine in the street. A minute later, there were footsteps on the path and then a knock on the front door. Warily, she glanced at the study door, still closed. A thrill of fear and longing went through her chest as she wondered if it was Aiden.

But when she opened the door, she saw a big man in baggy jeans and a faded black t-shirt.

"Travers!" She was so used to seeing him in his white uniform, she felt suddenly shy and didn't know what to say next.

"If you're not going to invite me in, care to step outside?" he asked.

Christina recovered enough to stand her ground. "I suppose Aiden sent you."

"Actually, no."

"But he told you where I live."

"Nope. Not that either. I found that out from Katie."

Christina paused. "You spoke to Katie? But I thought—"

"That she ripped out my heart and stomped on it? Yeah. So you know I trashed my dignity for the sake of standing here. Does that earn me enough credit for a conversation?"

Christina let him in. "So, what is it you want to say?"

"Darren?" Harriet's voice came down the hall. "Is that you?"

Christina spun around to see that her aunt had emerged from the study, her trousers creased, face pale, her fair hair in a loose knot with two pencils stuck through it.

Beside Christina, Travers stiffened. "Ma'am," he responded. "I'm sorry, I didn't know this was your house."

"Don't be silly, and I haven't been in uniform for years."

"I'm sorry, you know each other?" asked Christina.

"When Darren was training, he did a couple of terms in the practice where I was working. What brings you here?"

"I was the medic in the clinic when Christina was on base this last term," he said quickly. "I was hoping for a word with her about that."

"I won't interrupt," said Harriet, retreating to the study.

"Oh, all right," said Christina when Travers turned to her expectantly. She went to lead him into the lounge, but all she could see was the place where Aiden had sat working while she'd been reconstructing her lost essay. "Maybe we will go outside," she said.

As if sensing her discomfort, Travers spun his keys around his finger. "How about we go for a drive instead?"

Travers' bright yellow Monaro was ostentatious, complete

with dark leather seats and an expensive-looking stereo with dancing LEDs. Yet somehow even the car managed to appear somber tonight, and Travers threw the gears into reverse with purpose. Soon they were roaring across Townsville and towards the ocean, before Travers took the turn up the Castle Hill road.

"You don't have to go to all this effort," said Christina wearily. "Just say what you have to so I can tell you thanks but Aiden can stuff off, and we'll be done with it."

Travers simply compressed his lips and kept driving up the winding road. After her second objection, he said, "You might think I have this all planned out, but I haven't, okay? I'm still considering whether I should tell you what I'm thinking of telling you. So just let me drive. I'll know if I can when we get there."

Christina fell silent. Soon the road ended at the top of the hill, the car park mostly empty. They climbed out into the freshening evening air, which smelled of smoke and the sea, and Travers led her down the path to the eastern lookout, the twinkling lights of The Strand and the port far below. The same place where Harriet had brought Christina on her birthday all those years ago.

"Decided whether you're wasting my time?" asked Christina.

Travers ignored her and sat down on a bench, stretching his legs out. "I want to make one thing clear," he began. "Aiden didn't ask me to do this. In fact, I think he'll knock my head off if he finds out I told you."

"Told me what?" she asked, sitting down beside him.

"I take it you know what happened with Tracey."

"His ex? She left him when he was overseas." Christina paused, trying to see where Travers was going with this. "If you're going to bawl me out, you can forget it. He didn't even tell me he was going."

"Fair enough," said Travers. "He was a dick about that, and

I told him weeks ago he should have told you, and he didn't. So now you're both burned over it. I don't care about that. I'm not going to defend him, because he was wrong, and dumb. But I bet he didn't tell you the whole story about Tracey. Do you want to know?"

Christina turned her head so the ocean breeze slipped across her cheek and into her hair. She was about to tell him that it didn't matter, but a tiny kernel of hope prevented her. Not that things could be different, but that they might be less inexplicable. Finally, she nodded.

"Okay. Good," said Travers. "Tracey wasn't someone I knew well, but I didn't particularly like her. Aiden must have seen something in her though. They were together a few years. She lived with him wherever he was posted and he seemed happy."

Christina felt the barbs of jealousy catch on her heart. "So?"

"I'm telling you this for context," Travers said, a little apologetically. "Tracey was supportive of Aiden early on, but she grew tired of the lifestyle. Many partners do. She was the one who pushed him to apply for officer training. In a way, that was probably a good thing. He was too smart to stay a grunt. He's talented at what he does, and he loves it. But I had the impression Tracey wanted him to do it so he'd have better prospects when he left. Because she wanted him to leave. And lots of blokes do – they leave the army to please their partner."

Christina rubbed her face. She had no desire to know about the intricacies of Aiden's past relationships. "Get to the point, please," she said.

"Fine. Aiden told you she left while he was overseas, right?"

"Yes. And that was an awful thing to do. But it doesn't change anything."

Travers paused. "Christina, she didn't just leave him. She cleaned him out."

"What does that mean?"

"I mean, she took everything, including all his money. She cleaned out the accounts, took pretty much all the furniture. Maxed out all the loans. She left him in an untenable position, and he couldn't do anything about it. If I had to guess, I'd say she did it as punishment, because he'd told her he didn't want to quit. But that's just me."

Christina sucked in a breath, imagining Aiden's dismay. "But how could she possibly do that?"

"Before he deployed, he gave her power of attorney over all the finances. The house was in his name, but she had the authority to act. Most of the guys do that if they're going away. Did you see the place when you were down in Brisbane?"

"Yes."

"Let me guess – two brown couches, the bed, one set of sheets, one towel, one floor mat. And in the kitchen, one bowl, plate, knife, fork and spoon?"

"Yes—"

"That's exactly how she left it for him. He came back to nothing but the shell of that house, and a mountain of debt. And he's spent the last four years systematically digging himself out of the hole. You look at what I'm driving, and what he's driving. He's proud and he's responsible, and he's had a bad time of it, just like you."

"But I told him all about me," Christina said. The new information was still filtering through her mind, its gravity ungraspable. "I told him everything, things I'd never told anyone, ever."

"So you trust him. That means something."

"But he didn't trust me." Somehow that hurt worse than anything.

"Listen, Christina," Travers said. "He didn't even tell his family this stuff. His dad's a hot-shot surgeon, as you know; he would easily have been able to help. Why do you think Aiden didn't tell him? It wasn't just because he wanted to do it on his own."

"Why then?"

Travers laughed, and spread his hands. "He was embarrassed. Not just because he was in a bad place, but because he'd made such an error of judgement with Tracey. She wasn't the person he thought she was. He didn't want pity. I know you've had a hard road of it, but you're just starting out. You're going to graduate next year and you'll be on your way. He was further down the road. He'd worked hard and he was in a good position. And she took all that away from him. He had to start again. You don't really know a man until you've taken everything off him. Aiden's been there, okay? Many times in different ways, but that was the closest to home. And he's come back from there. That takes courage."

Christina folded her arms. Despite what Aiden had gone through being awful, she didn't know if she could forgive him.

Travers paused for a long time, then he said, "Do you remember what I said about infantry boys? That time in the clinic when you had that rifleman with the busted knee? No one ever wants to ask for help. It betrays you, shows everyone else that you're not as tough as you pretend to be. It's just like telling a girl you like them. Once you've said something, you don't get to pretend anymore. You take that leap, and suddenly your position's betrayed. Until that moment, you can only hope you know which side they're on. And if you're wrong ..."

Travers made a pistol shape with his hand and pretended to shoot himself through the heart.

Christina pulled her knees up to her chest. "I'm sorry Katie did that to you."

"This isn't about me," said Travers. "I'm just giving you information."

Christina laughed, but with no humor. Her heart was weighed down with loss and hurts, both recent and long ago. She hoped that some clarity would condense out of the night air, but nothing came. Simply more stars glimmering into the dark sky, more lights below. After a long silence, she stood up. "I want to go back now."

Travers sighed heavily. "There's one more thing I'm going to tell you."

Something about the tone of his voice made her look at him. "What?"

"This part is about me. It's about Aiden and me, and this is what I was most unsure about telling you. When I first injured my shoulder, we were both posted in Victoria, on the same base. I'd been putting up with small injuries for years, getting by. I'd already coaxed my knees and ankles back into service. I didn't want to do anything else but army, ever. My dad was a soldier, and so was his dad. The green is in my blood. So when they told me I wouldn't be able to do it anymore, that I'd end up discharged because I was injured … that was hard to take. Really hard."

He searched her face, then dropped his eyes, and his voice. "It got bad for me. My career was over. Felt like the end of the world. So, one night, I took my weapon and I walked out into the trees on the base and I put the muzzle in my mouth."

Christina stopped breathing. Her skin prickled across her scalp and down her back.

Travers took a breath, still speaking to the ground. "I sat there for ages, trying to make myself do it. And the only thing that stopped me was Aiden. He was two years into picking himself up after Tracey. He was my best mate in the world. And I didn't want to leave him behind. So, eventually, I got up and I went and found him, and I told him what I'd nearly done. I've never seen him turn so white. And then he took me to see the padre. We sat up all night talking, the padre and me. And Aiden sat there the whole time and every day after. I'm still here because of him. Because he means something to me." He paused. "All right, screw it. That's enough sentimental garbage. We all have bad days, right? But this is a man who comes through for you on your *worst* day. I'm not telling you what to do – that's your choice. And I wouldn't blame you either way. I just want you to know the man I know."

Below, the lights of The Strand glowed warm in the gathering night. Christina rubbed her arms. "I had no idea," she whispered.

"Yeah, well, let's try not to make a thing of it." He stood up and offered her his hand. "Come on, I'll take you back."

During the drive, Christina mulled over what he'd told her. When they were almost back at Harriet's house, she said, "I'll be going back to Brisbane soon. We might not see each other again."

"Well, I don't know about that," said Travers. "Did I tell you I bought a new boat?"

She smiled. "Does that mean your business is ready to go?"

"Almost. Just need my op and the recovery, and it's all set. You'll have to come out sometime. I could teach you to dive."

As she stepped back into Harriet's house, Christina saw that the study door was open at the end of the hall. All the things Travers had told her were still turning over, her mind fatigued from tracing the same thought patterns. *How could Aiden not have said anything? But would I have told him, if it had been me?*

Needing a distraction, she looked tentatively into the study. Harriet sat on the floor, her back against the wall, neat piles of paper around her, her pencil-spiked hair slipping from its knot.

"Are you hungry?" Christina asked. "I made sandwiches earlier."

"Not really," Harriet said without looking up.

"Are you cleaning?"

"You could say that." Harriet glanced up then, and Christina saw that her eyes were red-rimmed and bloodshot. Christina looked at the papers on the floor: neat stacks of handwritten pages. More letters. And she noticed John's notebook on the top.

"I don't know why I kept them," said Harriet, gathering them up into a pile. "No, that's a lie. I could never bear to throw them out before." She gave Christina a hard look. "This might sound awful, but when my husband was dying, in the sadness I let my mind think of John. Some of my memories of him are lovely, even in the blackness of the rest."

"What happened at the hospital?"

Harriet sighed. "I listened, mostly. I let him apologize. Let him tell me about what he's been doing the last fifteen years. Seems things didn't work out with his wife. He's been divorced for ten years. She lives in Sydney still, with their son."

Christina came into the room and leaned against the wall beside Harriet.

"What about that?" She pointed to the notebook.

"I've only read a few pages," Harriet said softly. "He wrote down everything he wished he'd had in his life with me. It's hard to go through, after spending so long trying to get over him. I don't know if I'll ever be able to."

She shook herself. "I'm sorry you ended up involved in this. I didn't answer your calls because I didn't want to see him, didn't want to explain why. I didn't think his mate would end up calling here."

"So that's who that was," Christina said. "It wasn't a big deal, he only called once. I thought he was a debt collector."

Harriet chuckled. "In a way, I suppose. I'm sure he thought that after the accident, I might come and see John."

But however Harriet made attempts to laugh or smile, Christina could see how heavy these old hurts sat on her aunt's shoulders. "What are you going to do now?"

Harriet began stuffing the letters into the corner of a box in frustration. "He never once asked if we could be friends. At least he's not that stupid." She stopped with a heavy sigh. "I can't forgive what he did. I can't forget everything that happened. But he was part of my life. And being angry just sucks the life out of every day. He was right about that. I can't decide what to do. That's why I'm here, looking for catharsis, or an epiphany."

"What are you going to do with those?" asked Christina, nodding at the letters.

"I wanted to burn them, but I'm too scared I'd set something else on fire," said Harriet with a hollow laugh. "Maybe I could sink them in the ocean instead."

Christina lowered herself down beside Harriet. "Travers could probably help you with that." She told Harriet about Travers' boat, and about his plans for after his discharge, Harriet nodding with interest.

After a few minutes, however, Christina found it more and more difficult to concentrate. Finally, she excused herself and got up. "Do you think I could borrow the Belmont? I want to go for a drive myself."

Harriet laughed. "If you've managed to keep that old beast running this long, I'd say you don't have to ask."

After setting off aimlessly in the Belmont, Christina soon found herself back on the street she'd been avoiding for the past two months. She crept past the low-set house and pulled into the curb. A light was on in the front window. Christina rubbed her eyes, trying not to remember the place as it had been when she was young; back then it was her mother's hand that would have turned on the light.

But she had no idea who lived there now, so she drew a shuddering breath and drove away. She soon passed the school; at the sight of it, the familiar sense of dread and shame she'd felt every day as a child once again tightened her chest. She could almost still feel the grit in her shoes, the way her foot had pushed through the thin spot in the sole. And behind that wall were the bins where she'd sometimes gone to find something for lunch.

With another shudder, she drove on, and finally ended up at The Strand. She'd walked all the way home from here once, after watching other, happy families playing together out on the sand. But now that was mixed up in her mind with the memory of sitting with Aiden on the grass verge on the night of Travers' party. And that thought led her to Crystal Creek, and Ryders Ridge, and the times he'd sat with her as she'd studied. Was this what Harriet had meant about beautiful memories in the blackness? Flashes of color, like the Ulysses butterfly that had flown over them at Crystal Creek.

She pulled into a space down the block from Travers' apartment. After getting out of the Belmont, she stepped across the sidewalk, her bare feet sticking to the sand. She sank down on the edge of the grass. Under the night sky, the waves lapped at the shore, the expanse of ocean dark before her.

He could have told her. Always she came back to that. Couldn't move past it. Diagnosis: stubborn.

Professor Green had even complained about it during a tutorial back at the beginning of term. They'd been discussing an ethical quandary, and Christina had been the only person in the group who wouldn't give. The dilemma went something like this: *Two patients are dying of liver failure, and you have a transplant for only one of them. The first patient, who has been waiting longer, is a lifelong drinker. The second patient has a genetic disorder that caused his disease. Who is more deserving of the transplant?* Christina was adamant that it was the second one. The first man had made choices that led to his liver disease; he was partly to blame for it, just as a smoker was if they developed lung cancer. All the time she'd argued her case, she'd been angry inside, thinking of her mother.

But Professor Green was also persistent. What might have led to the drinking? he asked. Might that have been something genetic? Or something that had happened to that man in his childhood? Was it possible that this man was not in fact fully able to decide not to drink? That none of us were fully responsible for anything we did?

Christina had hated his argument, and the slippery feeling it created in her. She had a hard-won sense of control over her own life. Many of her decisions had been difficult, but she'd made them and she owned them. In the same way, she insisted, the lifelong drinker needed to accept the consequences of his actions. But now she thought about that chance meeting with the doctor who'd treated her burned hand. What if that had never happened to her? What then?

Had she just been lucky, after all?

And what then did that make of her experience with Aiden? He hadn't told her the truth. But how much had circumstances prevented him? And what about every other aspect of their relationship? Finding him in the first place had just been luck, too.

The only problem was, Christina couldn't change the fact that he was leaving. Couldn't change the question mark hanging over her future. Maybe her luck had only ever been temporary, and now, just as she was finally realizing it, that same luck was coming to an end.

Chapter 30

The sun was still low in the sky on Monday morning when Aiden found himself twenty meters below the ocean's surface. Above him, only bubbles showed the way back up. He'd come out diving to store up memories before he went away, just Travers and Charlie and him in the depths. Travers gave them the all-okay sign and went up early, leaving Charlie and Aiden to run their air down slowly.

When Aiden broke the surface twenty minutes later and found the boat gone, he thought he'd come up in the wrong place. But no, there was the buoy and the diver's flag.

A gust of air broke the surface to his left. Looking around, Charlie pulled out his regulator. "Where the hell's the boat?"

"No idea."

After two minutes checking their location to distant landmarks, Aiden was just putting together an emergency plan when he spotted the sleek cruiser carving a wake towards them. Travers must be playing some kind of joke.

"Very fucking funny," muttered Charlie.

As the cruiser's engines cut, Aiden spotted a second person sitting at the boat rail and his stomach fell away.

"Here I was thinking you'd left us out here," he said as Travers dropped the anchor. But his eyes were only for Christina. She wore a thin white shirt, blue shorts, and her old Carlo's cap jammed down over her blonde hair, wisps escaping in the sea breeze. Her expression was guarded, as though she wasn't sure why she was there. Even so, Aiden could only stare at her as he bobbed in the water. He'd never been so pleased to see anyone.

"Oi," called Travers, and Aiden reluctantly tore his eyes away.

"What?"

"Weight and tank, for the second time." Travers held a hand out over the back of the boat. Aiden released the weight belt and passed it over, then shrugged out of the BCD and let Travers haul it up with his good arm. Without the gear, he felt weightless as he pulled himself aboard and stripped his wetsuit to the waist.

Having replaced Charlie's tank with a fresh one, Travers was now pulling up his own suit, another tank strapped into the BCD at his feet. "I've got forty minutes of air," he said, hauling the tank onto his good shoulder and pulling on his mask. "That's how long I'm giving you two to work it out. Good luck." With that, he stuffed the regulator into his mouth and stepped off the splash deck into the ocean. A moment later, only a small patch of bubbles could be seen on the surface.

Christina was peering over the side, studiously avoiding Aiden's bare chest. "He's threatened to teach me," she said. "Do you think it's a good idea?"

Aiden smiled, even as his heart twisted. "Well, that depends. He is a good teacher. But he'll be on your case to be out here every weekend."

She looked at him directly for the first time, and he saw the hurt and mistrust in her eyes. He wondered if she was thinking about how many of those weekends would include him.

He exhaled heavily and sat opposite her. Water beads on his neck coalesced and streaked down his back. "I'm so sorry, Christina. I should have told you. Daniella ripped me a new one."

Her lips pulled thin. "Yeah, well, Travers told me a few

things too."

"He did, huh?" Aiden's chest tightened.

"He told me more about what happened with Tracey. I … had no idea you went through that."

Aiden slowly nodded. "Guess I didn't tell you about that either."

"No. But I can understand why." She glanced away.

Aiden sensed that she was giving him a chance. And all he had to do was open himself to her, confess the still-raw details of the most shameful episode of his life. As a soldier, a man who was meant to be able to handle himself under every pressure, he had buried this as deeply as he could. But now as he looked at Christina, it no longer hurt, and that part of his brain that sensed the future, that knew when bad things were coming, for the first time glimpsed something golden.

As the waves made a hollow drumming against the boat's hull, Christina listened while Aiden laid out what had happened. All the water had run off his chest, leaving him brown, smooth and muscled, the jagged edges of his tattoo angling down his arm. He sat hunched forward, as if protecting the swirling parts over his heart, and Christina could tell how much he hated talking about this aspect of his past.

"She took everything," he said quietly. "Cash, accounts, furniture, the car—" He broke off, then gave her a small smile. "Before it happened, I'd have told you that stuff didn't matter, and it doesn't. I'd have easily done without it. It was the act of it – of wiping me out. Still puts the chills in me to imagine what she must have been thinking as she planned it. So deliberate and organized. So cold."

Christina found her hand clenched on the boat rail, and she looked down into the rippling blue water, trying to imagine such a betrayal.

"The house was all that was left – I guess it was too

difficult to sell – it was worth less than the loan at the time, after the market drop. And my scuba gear, because Travers had it." He patted the ageing BCD.

"And you never tried to find her?"

He laughed. "I know exactly where she went."

"Didn't you confront her?"

His smile faded. "In the white-hot moment at the start, yeah, I wanted to. But by the time I got home four months later, I was just ashamed I hadn't seen it coming. I thought I knew her. In retrospect, I can see the signs. But I've come too far, and I don't want to see her face again."

Christina watched the way he deliberately relaxed his expression, removing the taut lines that disclosure had etched in his face. "I can understand," she said slowly, "how what happened with Tracey might have affected your decisions."

Aiden shook his head. "It's no excuse. I'll admit, I wasn't looking for this. But Christy … the only way I could go back to the house in Brisbane last week was because I imagined you being there with me."

Christina bit her lip. Hope had sprung to life between them, a chance to remake something she had thought was over. But what could they make? "What are we doing here, Aiden?" she asked, close to tears. "You're leaving next week. Our lives are moving apart. For all I know I just failed the rotation, and the school thinks I'm a cheat."

Aiden shifted to sit beside her. Very deliberately, he took her hand, his skin ocean-cool. "I'll be away for at least six months. I know I can't expect you to wait, especially when you know I'm worth almost nothing." His laugh was hollow.

Christina squeezed his hand. "You're worth plenty. That's only money, and you and I both know how little of it you really need to get by."

He looked at her then, unable to keep the hope from his voice. "Are you saying you will wait?"

Slowly, she nodded. If she was honest, she wasn't sure about this. He had always made her feel so safe, but now that warmth had been tainted with uncertainty. So much could happen in a few months. But the thought of him going away without an understanding between them was worse, and she would rather try than wonder. They would have to make their own luck.

"I have a condition though," he said.

"Oh, you do?"

"Yes. I need someone to live in the Brisbane house. The place needs new life, new memories to replace the bad ones."

Refusal was on the tip of her tongue. She couldn't abide receiving charity from anyone. If by some chance she came through all of this and graduated, she wanted to know she'd made it on her own.

"I know what you're going to say," he went on, before she could speak. "But hear me out. I'm not letting you live there as some kind of generous gesture. It's a house, and they take work. You'd be the caretaker. You'll need to clean gutters, organize repairs, that sort of thing."

"I still—"

He held up a hand. "There's more. In exchange for the caretaking, I'll give you a discount on the rent."

That stayed Christina's refusal. "The rent?"

"Five hundred a week. Let's say four, if you're the caretaker."

Christina shook her head. "Then it's easy. There's no way I can afford that, even with my job."

"That's why you'll also be managing the tenants."

"Tenants?"

"There's four bedrooms, two bathrooms. You choose who you want to live there. You can sort out the rent how you want. The mortgage isn't manageable with it empty, but with rental income I can do it."

Christina looked out over the water, thinking. In the distance, white puffy clouds were rising from the haze on the horizon, while off the stern, the buoy with its blue and white diver's flag wig-wagged over the wavelets. Four hundred across four rooms was unimaginably low rent for the location so close to university. The lure of a never-before-known autonomy, lit up in her mind.

"Why are you doing this?" she asked him.

"Can't you see why?" he said with a smile. "I'm crazy about you. I know why I'm going away, but I want something to come back to. And I can't bear the thought of you living in another bad share house while I'm gone. It's a deal breaker," he added.

"Oh, you're the one setting the deal breakers?" she asked with an arched eyebrow, but a warm glow was spreading through her. "I promise I'll think about it."

The next moment, the realization that he would be leaving struck her and tears started running down her face. She threw her arms around him, wanting to beg him not to go. Aiden held her tight, his body shaking with emotion.

"I swear," he said, his voice low and fierce, "if I had any other job in me I'd do it, for you. But this is what I am, and what I want you to come back to."

Then he kissed her with all the force of his passion, the kiss of a man who couldn't believe his luck. It was both sweet and urgent at once. They only pulled apart when Christina heard a splash and rush of air from the water.

"This looks like good news," said Travers, bobbing blackly next to Charlie in the water beside the boat. "Is it safe to come up now?"

"Oh, so you think you're getting on board after this stunt?" Aiden shot at him, but he didn't release Christina.

"That's my boat," complained Travers. "Besides, you look happy enough. Come on, take this." He and Charlie handed up their weights and tanks and climbed back on board.

With the engines purring, Christina sat next to Aiden, her heart light and free as they streaked back towards the coast, a smudge of green between the blues of ocean and sky.

As Christina stepped back into Harriet's house at nine thirty that morning, after Aiden had left on an errand, her phone started ringing. She glanced at the number, and recognized it as the medical school. Cold dread gripped her stomach.

Harriet, hearing the unanswered ring, stepped into the hall from the kitchen with her eyebrows raised, a wooden spoon in her hand. Christina braced herself, and answered the phone, walking into the lounge.

"Hello?" Her voice was thick with fear.

"Christina." The dean himself, unshielded by Anne. That couldn't be a good thing. "I understand you're back in Townsville."

"Y-yes. I had a … family issue," she said, wondering how he knew.

"Well, I have some news for you," he said, his voice stern. "Are you able to talk?"

Christina found the couch, her heart pounding in her chest. "Go ahead."

"This whole exam issue has become complex, and I apologize for the time it's taken us to reach a conclusion, and for some of what I'm about to say."

Oh dear God. Unable to speak, Christina put a hand to her forehead, nausea rolling in her stomach.

"We are still resolving the issue from the surgical rotation. It seems that a student obtained draft exam papers that were sent for review. We are tracing all the avenues, but at this stage I am willing to clear you of involvement with it, especially seeing as your written exam this semester was also good. In fact, your mark was exceptional."

Christina opened her eyes in surprise.

"However," he went on, "your practical marks are another matter. Not even fifty per cent for surgery last term – a concessional pass. You have three of those now. So, before I allow you to start the next term, you must complete remediation in surgery."

Christina was still speechless. She'd been so sure that she was out, her reprieve was hard to grasp.

"Are you still there? Christina?"

Finally she managed to say, "Yes, yes, I'm here."

"I don't think I need to impress on you the importance of your learning in this course. If you don't complete the remediation successfully, you may be delayed significantly. Do you understand?"

"Yes," she said, her voice choked with relief.

"Good. Then whatever you have planned for the rest of this week, unplan it. You are to report to the surgery department at Townsville Hospital. Dr. Daniella Bell will be your primary supervisor. I've made it clear to her what my expectations are, and for your own sake, you must meet them."

Christina silently blessed him, before she remembered something else. "Wait, what about this rotation? The essay? The practical exam?"

"The essay we've determined as no fault on your part, which I have to say is unusual in these circumstances. Normally in plagiarism cases, both students are penalized. But we received information that demonstrated yours was the original. I can't say more because it impacts on another student. Your case report was good – not quite on topic, but your follow-up was thorough. The practical you also passed – just. A better performance than previous terms."

"I was so sure I failed," she said, shock making her skin hot and cold. "Are you sure you have the right student?"

The dean actually chuckled, and she heard him shuffling through papers. "I have the results right here, and I spoke to the examiners personally. They said your manner was brusque but you know your stuff, and that's what really counts. We also have records of excellent attendance during your rotation, and exemplary reports from your supervisors, including for hands-on skills. I have to say I've never had a student with so many people willing to vouch for them. I have to consider that some people just don't do well in exams, and the wards are where it counts."

He took a breath. "Christina, I understand that you've had a difficult road through the course, and I'm sorry that this term's issues with the exam and assignments can't have helped. But it doesn't really get easier from here. You still have another year of rotations, and the final exams. You will need to pass those, including the practicals. If you run into difficulties, make sure you contact the school as soon as possible. We can help."

Surprised, Christina swallowed. "Okay."

"All right. Well, I hope that next time we meet it's in more positive circumstances. Good luck."

Once she'd ended the call, Christina let the phone fall onto the couch. Slowly, she rose and walked to the kitchen, where she found Harriet stirring a pot of rich red berries, the thick sugary smell of jam in the air. "I have to go to the hospital," she said.

Harriet turned to her with a look of concern. "Are you sick? Oh, you do look pale. Who was that on the phone?"

"It was the dean." Still not quite able to believe what she was saying, Christina told Harriet what had happened.

"See, didn't I tell you it would be fine?" said Harriet.

Christina could only shake her head in wonder. "I still have to do remediation. But he's right – it's only going to become more challenging. My first- and second-year results were borderline. I know I have to do better."

Harriet gently took Christina's shoulders. "That's behind you now. And you know what you want. Do you know how rare that is?" She smiled. "It's better to be sure you want to do something and take time to achieve it than to quickly reach a place you never wanted to be to begin with. Trust me. I spent my career working with doctors, and you'd be surprised how many of them don't want to be there. You have different problems."

"Oh, I do?" Christina said wryly.

Harriet smiled. "Of course. You find it hard to allow other people to do things for you."

"You haven't seen me in eleven years. You can't possibly know that," said Christina, bristling.

Harriet only laughed. "Every meal we've had in the past few days, you've tried to cook. You replaced anything you ate from the pantry. I see the signs. Now, are you going to take the Belmont to the hospital, or would you like a lift?"

Christina chewed her lip. Harriet was the same as she'd always been: tough, uncompromising. She hadn't always been right before, but Christina knew she was now.

"Maybe I could do with a lift," she said.

Chapter 31

After rushing upstairs, Christina found the surgical ward quiet, but the desk nurse was expecting her. "Dr. Bell is down in theatre. She said to meet her there."

Christina navigated her way through to the unfamiliar theatres, where another nurse pointed her towards the change rooms. By now her skin was clammy, as she remembered how intimidated she'd been by the surgical staff in her last rotation. Once, on a rare occasion she'd scrubbed in to assist an operation, the surgical nurse had yelled at her when she'd put her gloves on incorrectly. That was the last time she'd dared to go in.

Her hands shook as she pulled on scrubs and tugged on the shoe covers and hair net. But when she emerged from the change room, ready to find her way to the operating rooms, Daniella was waiting in the hallway.

"There you are," she said, tipping up her theatre glasses. "The ward just called and said you were on your way." She beckoned Christina to follow her. "Sorry to throw you into it all like this, but the dean was quite insistent, and a week isn't long."

"What's the case?" asked Christina, trying to distract herself from her nerves.

"Appendectomy." Daniella turned into the scrub room, where a long stainless-steel sink filled one wall, topped with boxes of scrub sponges, masks and face shields. She grabbed a plastic-wrapped scrub block, turning on the water with a deft flick of her elbow. So practiced. And suddenly, Christina remembered her first week in the clinic with Travers; she needed someone to teach her.

"I'm really bad at theatre prep," she admitted in a rush. "I always seem to make a mistake and spoil the sterile field. I've only made it to fully scrubbed once, and then I nearly passed out from the stress."

"Oh, don't worry," said Daniella. "I was awful too. The only reason I didn't disgrace myself in med school is that I asked Dad to coach me through the process. So let's start at the beginning. Remember, scrubbing is last. You can't touch anything after that."

"So, mask first?" asked Christina.

"Right. I can't tell you the number of times I carefully scrubbed in and then had to do it again because I'd forgotten my mask."

Soon they both had masks. Then Daniella went through the scrub procedure. "Keep your hands up all the time. You always want the water to run from your fingers towards your elbows."

Christina scrubbed herself from fingertips to elbows and under her nails, then followed Daniella backwards through the theatre doors. A green-draped table greeted her, with a folded gown and sterile gloves. Daniella talked her through how to dry her hands, unfold the gown and shuffle into it; and how to hand the closure tape around her body to finish. Following the instructions, she managed to glove up, wriggling her hands into the cuffs and pulling on the gloves without exposing her hands.

Sweating from concentration, she tried to focus on Daniella's voice. "Now imagine we're priests. Hands always together in front of your chest. That way you don't accidentally touch anything outside the field."

Christina's heart was beating in her ears as she looked around the room. The anesthetist was checking a monitor, explaining the numbers to a younger woman in scrubs. Another medical student, perhaps. The patient was already draped, and a theatre nurse counted out instruments. No one looked surprised to see Christina, and she relaxed a fraction. They all must have been learners at one point, and Daniella seemed to know just when to give her directions.

"Christina, you stand on that side. You can watch the monitor for the laparoscope, and depending on how things go, you can do a closing suture."

Suddenly, Christina was involved in a work flow. She watched and listened while Daniella performed the procedure, talking throughout, explaining what she was looking for, how the instruments were manipulated and what potential problems she was trying to avoid. Soon the angry and swollen appendix had been located and removed, and they were closing. When Daniella handed her the suture instruments, Christina didn't have time for nerves.

"That's very good. Who taught you that?" asked Daniella, after the simple stitch Christina put in the keyhole port incision.

"Dr. Vaughn in the clinic, but Travers had me practice it on a fake skin block for a few hours."

After the operation was finished, Christina felt her energy drain away. She was surprised to see it was only just after twelve.

"Quick tea break," said Daniella, as they stuffed the used gowns into the hampers. "Then back to the list. The consultant is coming down for the afternoon cases. How are you holding up?"

"Fine," said Christina, realizing she was.

As she passed through the patient prep area, the other student — a woman with dark hair in a ponytail and warm brown eyes — caught her eye. "Hi," she said cautiously. "Are you a student too? I'm Wendy. I'm doing anesthetics."

"Yeah, I'm Christina. I'm just here for a week in surgery."

"Nice suture. I totally muffed the cannula before the start. Took me two tries." Wendy rolled her eyes. "I still shake so much, I feel like an idiot."

Christina instantly liked Wendy and she smiled in sympathy. "That goes away eventually. Keep at it. Are you in for the rest of the day?"

"Yep. We better go have that tea before the next one. I don't suppose you have any tips on cannulas?"

Even though they drank the tea scalding, and the biscuits were stale, Christina had never felt more at home. Wendy was keen to absorb any information she could offer, and returned the favor with some tips about anesthetics, which Christina would do in later terms. Once the operation list was finished, Daniella took Christina to the ward for the afternoon round, and then Christina helped draw bloods for work-ups to be done overnight. The next time she looked at the clock, it was seven in the evening.

She leaned back in a chair in the office as Daniella explained how to write discharge summaries. Ten minutes into the session, as Christina was transferring information from a patient file to the computer discharge sheet, she heard Daniella make an incredulous noise.

"What?" Christina asked, looking up.

Daniella shook her head. "I just looked at the clock and realized how long you've been here. They weren't wrong about you, were they?"

"Who?"

"The docs over at the base clinic." Then she stopped, as though she'd given away a secret.

Christina paused. "You spoke to them?"

"Yes, and to the dean," Daniella confessed. "I was the one who suggested you come here for a week. Don't look so surprised," she went on. "I remember you telling me all about your essay project weeks ago at my wedding. I wasn't just going to say nothing when someone else copied off you. And then I spoke to Travers, and he put me onto Captain May and

Dr. Vaughn. All of them said you were there almost every day. They'd never seen someone put in so much time. I don't think the dean had anywhere to go after we all called him."

Christina paled. "You *all* called?"

"I think he might have been a little intimidated at first, when he was told Dr. Bell was calling for him," said Daniella, sitting back with a thoughtful expression. "My father's a pretty big fish around the place."

"But that's not right at all," said Christina, dismayed. "I don't want him changing his mind because someone has influence over him."

Daniella broke out in a grin. "Got you, didn't I? Don't be silly. My father's a respected surgeon, but none of us would ever use that to pressure the school. You impressed people with your actions, Christina. You're the one who turned up. You might be slower than some others to pick up some things; that doesn't matter, as long as you have the skills in the end. In fact, it will make you a better teacher later. You'll remember how hard it was for you. The brilliant doctors sometimes … they don't have the patience for people who take a while to learn. You'll have that. And you'll know a dozen different ways it doesn't work. Trust me."

Something in Christina's chest gave, as though a knotted muscle had suddenly released. She had to swallow and study her discharge summary so that she wouldn't cry. "Why are you so nice to me?" she asked finally.

Daniella laughed, a pure bright sound. "I'm like this with everyone. We just ran across each other at the right time."

She hesitated, then went on. "Christina, there's one more thing I have to tell you – about your essay. Aiden asked his friend to look at your laptop and he found something … interesting."

"What's that?" Christina asked, bemused.

"The essay file you thought was corrupted? It was actually a picture file, renamed. The real file had been deleted. He couldn't be sure if the computer then crashed or was just hard turned-off, but the delete happened only a few seconds before. Definitely deliberate. Anyway, he was able to recover the file, and it exactly matched the assignment Katie turned in. That's what finally tipped it for the dean. She's probably looking at some serious consequences."

Christina sat in disbelief as she put together what must have happened. "I don't believe it," she managed. "I mean, why would she—"

"Wait, there's more – and lord, I'm not supposed to tell you any of this, so make sure you keep it in the vault, okay?"

Christina nodded numbly.

"Katie's original essay topic that you told the dean about, the ranking of preventative actions in family medicine? Another student submitted a paper on that same topic a few years ago, and the tutor was the same one you had this term. Now, this is just my theory, but I'm guessing Katie was planning on handing in the same paper, then realized it was the same tutor – too much risk that he'd remember. So she panicked at the last minute and took yours instead."

Christina's mouth opened, but for a moment no sound came out. "But … how did she think she'd get away with it?"

Daniella shrugged. "She was probably counting on you giving up, or handing in something different enough. I'm glad she misjudged you."

Christina noticed that Daniella's eyes were lit with a curious satisfaction. "Wait, I'm missing something. How do you even know all this?"

"Because I was in the tutorial with the student who handed in that essay. And I remember him pretty well – Sebastian Prior. Awful man. I thought the surname was familiar. Anyway, it's all circumstantial, but let's just say I had a personal interest in seeing this through." Daniella dusted off her hands, as if some long-held grudge had finally been repaid. "I meant it when I said it must stay in the vault. I thought you should know, but no one else can. Now, it's getting late and you'll be back here again in the morning, so what about going home?"

Christina thought about the text Aiden had sent, asking her to come to Travers' place tonight. "I saw your brother this morning," she said.

The smile on Daniella's face faltered, her expression turning sympathetic. "How did that go?"

"Better than I expected. I didn't think I'd want to see him again. But now I think I understand why he didn't tell me."

"So you worked things out?"

Christina bit her lip. "In a way. Daniella …" She paused, searching for the right words. "I don't want him to go away. I'm scared for him. And I don't know what it will be like when he comes back."

Daniella nodded, tears glinting in her eyes. "I know. I feel the same. But that's who he is. And I've learned that even when his attention is on his work, it doesn't mean his heart isn't always here with us."

They sat a moment in silence. As an only child, Christina had never understood the bond other people had with their siblings. But now she glimpsed what it might be like, and the sense of possibility was like the first light of sunrise.

"I know you're going on to the internal medicine rotation next," said Daniella. "If you wanted to stay up here, I might be able to arrange something. Spaces are at a premium with the local medical school, but there could well be someone who'd want to do a rotation in Brisbane in your place."

Christina thought about that. Harriet was here, after all, and Daniella's offer was tempting. "Thank you, but no," she said. "I need to go back to Brisbane. I have history in this town, and I want to move on. I don't mind coming back here from time to time, but not to stay."

Daniella nodded. "I understand." She put a hand on Christina's arm. "But please stay in touch. I'd like to talk to you often. And say hello to Aiden for me."

Christina knocked on Travers' door half an hour later. Her world had been turned upside down today. Her legs and back ached from the day in theatre, and her chest from all the emotions she'd been through. Her eyes were gritty from the early start. But as soon as the door opened, she felt fresh and energized.

Travers stood aside for her to come in, a backpack over his shoulder. "I'm off, then," he said, giving Christina a wink as she walked past him into the apartment. "See you tomorrow."

"Where are you going?" Christina called to the closing door.

"The base," said Aiden's voice from the hallway.

Christina turned. Standing there in board shorts and a singlet, he somehow still managed to look like a man who could run the world. "I'm sorry I'm late," she said. "It was a long day at the hospital."

"Your aunt told me where you were. It sounded like you had some good news. You want to tell me about it?" Aiden asked, drawing her towards the living room.

The balcony curtains were open, the evening breeze ruffling their edges. As she filled Aiden in on her day, Christina could hear waves shushing onto the sand below. With only a lamp lit, the room was cozy and restful.

"So does this mean you're staying with your aunt for a while?" asked Aiden, still grinning at the news.

"No," she said. "I'm still going back to Brisbane after this week. I'm glad I've patched things up with Harriet, but this isn't the place for me. Besides, I've had this offer to manage a rental property."

Aiden suddenly wrapped his arms around her, pressing a kiss into her hair. "Really?" His voice was fierce, as if he couldn't quite believe it. "Are you sure?"

"I am," she said. "The question is: are you?"

He took her face gently in his hands. "I would never have asked if I wasn't."

"Then why do you look so worried?"

In answer, he dropped his lips to hers for a long kiss that left her breathless. "Because I'm going to miss you," he said thickly as he pulled away. "I can't pretend I'm not scared as hell about what's going to happen when I'm away and when I get back. And that I don't feel awful that I won't be here for you for the next seven months. It's a lot to ask you to wait."

"Then let's not waste our time now," she said.

He gave her a cheeky smile. "What did you have in mind?"

"You remember when we were watching the stars from the ridge at Daniella's wedding? Maybe we can drive up the mountain and do that again."

Aiden grabbed his keys, and soon they'd driven to the top of Castle Hill. Getting out, they found a spot against a knoll where the night was spread open before them. But after a few minutes picking out stars, they lapsed into silence. Time was so short, and so much was still unsaid. While they watched, the moon rose giant and yellow over the horizon.

"Tell me again what you do next?" said Aiden, breaking the silence.

"Internal medicine," said Christina. "Then I have a rural rotation. No idea where that will be. That takes me until the end of the year."

"And next year?"

"Obstetrics and gynecology, pediatrics, specialties like anesthetics. Then all the final exams."

"But I'll be back before then."

Christina leaned into his embrace, and took a breath. "What then?"

"I'm trying to get a posting back in Brisbane. But that's not going to last forever. At some point I'll be moving again. Victoria or Sydney or Perth. Even somewhere small, in the middle of get-out nowhere. Or back here."

"That's a while away, though?"

"At least two years."

"Then let's just focus on the next year – that's enough for

now. The rest we can work out."

He smiled at her, seeming oddly shy. "I was hoping you'd say that," he said, and reached into his pocket, drawing out a white envelope and a small velvet bag. He handed her the envelope, his face serious. "This is for you to keep safe for me. Don't ever open it. Not unless you're told to. Okay?"

Christina turned over the plain white rectangle, no address, no notation at all, just a long strip of tape closing the back and down the side seams. "What's this?"

"I'll tell you when I leave," he said. "Just promise, please?"

"Okay. I promise."

The tension left his shoulders. He placed the velvet bag in her hand. "And this is for you."

"A gift? Really? I thought you knew me."

"Just open it."

Christina carefully upended the bag, and out tumbled a fine gold chain, its links interwoven in a stunning pattern. There was no pendant, just the long strand of exquisite craftsmanship. "I love it," she said, turning it in her fingertips, trying to catch the low light.

Aiden deftly undid the clasp and fastened it around her neck. "My sister says that a doctor needs a chain, because you have to take off your rings and keep them safe. I thought this would serve you well."

Christina fingered the delicate necklace, touched by his thoughtfulness, and the promise his words held. Above, the sky was scattered with stars, the same sky that had watched them that night at Ryders Station. Her eyes brimmed as the reality of him leaving made her heart sink, even as his presence lifted her up. "I'll wear it every day," she said, and kissed him.

As the stars turned overhead, Christina fixed this moment in her mind so that she could return to it again and again when harder times came. Aiden returned her passion, warm and strong and sure, and she knew that he was doing the same. That they would weather the coming separation, and love would be waiting for them on the other side.

Fifteen months later

The hotel foyer smelled of floral cleaner and breakfast bacon. A ring of tables had been set up around the function room door, advertising credit cards and financial planning to the graduation breakfast crowd, but there was only one table Christina was interested in. She leaned on it now, writing her details on the short form. She scribbled her signature and the date at the bottom of the page, and pushed it across to a woman who inspected the form.

"You should receive the numbers in a week," she said, and added, "Congratulations."

Provider numbers. The last thing she needed to organize before beginning work. As she stepped away from the table, it finally felt real. She'd made it through the course, and in a few weeks she'd be starting work as an intern.

"Hey, Christina!"

She looked up to see Toby and Mallory beckoning to her from the function room. After returning from Townsville, Christina had taken seriously the job of finding flat mates for Aiden's house. Toby had been happy to leave his parents' granny flat for a house closer to campus, and then on her rural rotation Christina had met Mallory, a thirty-year-old student who'd started medicine after ten years spent helping run her father's sheep station. Both of them were quiet, tidy, and understood the demands of the course. And today, they were graduating together.

"Saved you a seat," said Mallory. "Right in the back corner. Looks like the dean's warming up for a long speech."

Christina smiled, but she didn't mind. She barely heard the speeches through breakfast, the excited butterflies in her stomach competing for attention.

"Aren't you going to eat that?" asked Mallory, as Christina left her sausage and bacon untouched.

By the time the ceremony on campus came around at two in the afternoon, the horizon had filled with ominous clouds, foretelling a Brisbane summer storm. The sandstone hall was ringed with mortar-capped graduates and their families: fathers sweating in suits, mothers fanning themselves with programs. Christina scanned the crowd, one hand on her mortar, until she spotted a familiar figure. She rushed across the forecourt and into Aiden's arms.

He was dressed in a gray suit and pink shirt, and claimed he'd chosen the latter in case Christina was nervous and wanted something funny to look at. She laughed and told him it suited him. In fact Christina was still relieved every time they laughed together. Aiden's time away had been difficult, for both of them.

The day after the night he'd given her the gold chain, she'd returned to Harriet's and idly asked her aunt why Aiden might have given her a sealed letter. Harriet took a deep breath and asked if Christina really wanted to know.

"Of course," she said, confused.

Harriet turned the envelope over in her hand. "This is something he's written for you that he hopes you'll never have to open. Do you understand now?"

Then Christina did. It was a letter he'd written to her in case he was killed overseas. The worry had taken her breath away.

Harriet had known what to do. "Put it in here," she said, opening the drawer of the display cabinet. "And push the idea to the edges of your mind. Keep busy and focus on what you want out of your life. You'll forget about the letter, and what it means, in all but the worst moments. And even then at least you'll know that he cared enough to think of all the things he wanted to say to you."

So Christina had pushed the thought away. Still, she'd missed him horribly, even when they were able to email and talk on Skype. The time seemed to pass so slowly. Even worse was the anxiety of watching the news each day, wondering if there had been a bomb or an accident.

Strangely enough, the worst part had actually been his return. Believing that the hard part was now over, Christina had been knocked sideways by how difficult she found it to have him back in her life in Brisbane. After seven months, she'd grown used to living without him and organizing her life the way she wanted. Wanting him, she discovered, had been easier than having him. It was as though she'd forgotten how to make space for him. The tense few weeks of readjustment had been torture, but Harriet had talked to her often, and Aiden had been patient. Eventually they'd reconnected, and had burned the letter he'd left. Then, together, they'd taken it and her mother's ashes to Crystal Creek, gently committing both Aiden's time away and her mother's death to the past.

Now Aiden kissed her before he released her, his eyes falling briefly to the chain around her neck, a private smile on his lips.

"Congratulations, Christina," said Harriet, appearing beside Aiden carrying a huge bouquet of flowers.

"Harriet, you shouldn't have," said Christina.

"Oh dear, well, you might have to feign delight. There's a few more over there with the others."

The others? Christina followed Harriet's glance and saw a large group standing in the shade. She stared in surprise. "Oh my, what are they all doing here?"

"Waiting to see you graduate," said Aiden, drawing her with him, Harriet following behind.

Daniella was there, and Jackie, who had started med school in Brisbane at the beginning of the year and who often came to study group with Christina and Mallory. As a former nurse, Jackie had been invaluable in helping them with their practical skills; and as her son limited her study time, they'd been able to provide her with crash notes and quizzing.

Christina was speechless when she noticed Travers, who she knew was now living on an island off north Queensland, standing to the side of the group, nearly unrecognizable in dark sunglasses and with his hair growing out. He offered his hand. "Next time I need an op, just remember who taught you to cannulate," he said.

A man laughed behind him, and Christina had the final surprise of seeing Dr. Peter Bell, who also shook her hand. "Congratulations," he said. "So, can I put you down for surgery in a few years?"

Christina laughed. "Dr. Bell took some tutorials in my surgical specialties term a few months ago," she explained to Travers. "He's been trying to sell the virtues of surgery to me ever since. But I haven't decided yet."

"And you don't have to for a long time," said Daniella firmly.

"All the same, I only have two tickets to the ceremony," Christina said.

"Ish, we're not here for the boring ceremony. I'm waiting for high tea afterwards," said Jackie. "Remember, don't trip on the stairs. They're live-streaming it on the internet, so there'll be evidence. We'll be waiting when you come out."

Soon Christina had to take her place in the line-up of students and the ceremony began. Her stomach was tight with nerves and excitement as she took in the elaborate robes of the chancellor and the other academic officials, and the faces of her friends. For a moment she found herself thinking of Katie, who wasn't among them. She'd heard that, faced with the prospect of repeating a year, Katie had decided to leave altogether. Perhaps it had been a relief for her. Christina didn't know; she was only glad to have made it herself.

In her nervousness, she caught only a few lines of the dean's long speech. "You've passed this first hurdle, which is a fine achievement," he said. "But always remember that it's the patients who matter, the real people in whose lives you'll make a difference. Put your focus now more than ever on them, with compassion, with humility, and you'll be the doctors we were proud to train."

When it came time to walk up the stairs to the stage, she remembered Jackie's words and carefully watched her feet. Then, suddenly, no one was in front of her.

"Christina Price," read the university registrar.

As she strode across the stage, she heard Aiden's ear-splitting whistle from the crowd, and broke into a grin; she knew Harriet would be clapping proudly beside him. The dean handed her the degree roll and shook her hand. "Well done, Dr. Price," he said.

Dr. Price. Christina floated across the rest of the stage. She'd worried that she might cry at this point, but the tears didn't come until she'd stepped down on the other side. Even as so much else in her life had changed, the part of her that showed a strong face to the world remained.

The rest of the afternoon was full of friends and celebration, first at the staff club, then back at the house, but Christina was still relieved when she and Aiden finally had a moment alone. The graduation ball began at seven, and hanging on the back of their bedroom door at Aiden's house was a new ballgown that she'd bought herself as a reward for finishing her degree, a simple floor-length satin dress in midnight blue.

"Do you think I'd fit in it?" Aiden asked, as he caught her admiring it.

"Don't you dare!"

"You know I'm only kidding." Fresh from the shower, he

was already dressed in his tux pants and white shirt. The first drops of a summer storm struck the deck outside. Aiden took her hand and pulled her to the glass doors, where they watched the wood darkening in splotches. "I found out my posting today," he said softly.

Hope fizzed in Christina's chest. "Where?"

"Brisbane until the end of next year, so I'll be here for your internship."

Christina flung her arms around him with a whoop. "That's great news! And after that, we'll see what happens."

He nodded. Christina knew how hard Aiden had fought to remain in Brisbane for the next year. After that she would be registered, and then she could find a job elsewhere. She had decided to follow him wherever he was posted next, finding her place where he found his. They both knew this life would come with challenges, uprooting themselves and resettling in each new place, so they'd agreed to review it in five years. But for now, Christina was simply excited for the evening ahead and all that lay beyond.

"I got you something too," he said, reaching into his pocket.

"What's this?" she asked as he placed a small box in her hand.

"Open it."

Christina opened the lid to reveal a gold band with a beautiful filigree pattern; she made out the curve of a beak, a wing, and long tail feathers.

"It's a phoenix," said Aiden, extracting the ring from its cushioned blue bed. "In Persian mythology, the phoenix is reborn from the ashes. You've been through so much to be here today, Christy. I thought you might like it."

"I love it," she said, turning the band, which glowed warmly in the somber light. Then she laughed. "For a moment there I thought you were going to propose."

Aiden gave her a joyful smile. "Well, it's also an eternity ring," he said. "The design goes all the way around. I know that you're supposed to get this one last, but since we started a bit backwards, I thought it seemed about right."

She looked at him, amazed. "Are you serious?"

"Deadly." He took her hand as the rain picked up, drumming on the roof and rushing down the gutters. "Christy, we've had a rough start, and things might not be smooth for a long while, or ever. But I want you to know that whatever happens, I'll always be with you, always love the time we have together. So hang the ring on your chain when you're working, and I'll always be next to your heart."

Christina took his words inside her and held them tight. Lightning flashed and thunder rolled overhead, but here, together, they were safe. And when tough times returned, she would remember this moment, knowing that those too would pass and the sun would come out again.

Thanks for reading!

I loved writing Aiden and Christina's story: having them both face their pasts, and giving them a new future together. If you'd like to leave a review for other readers, please head to Goodreads, or Amazon, iBooks, Kobo – wherever you found this copy.

For more books in this sweet romance series (an excerpt of the forthcoming next, *Great Haven*, follows this section), please visit charlottenash.net. If you enjoy women's fiction with a romantic subplot, you will also find *The Paris Wedding* and *The Lucky Escape* there.

If you'd like to hear when new books are out, or be in the running for giveaways, you can sign up for my newsletter at charlottenash.net. Happy reading!

Erin Jacobs has one huge secret …

Great Haven is the next installment in the Walker-Bell world, due out in August 2018. Read on for a taste of this story, set on a tropical paradise with stormy seas and a turbulent history of love.

Great Haven – coming August 2018

Erin Jacobs has spent the last two years sailing solo from the Caribbean to New Zealand, earning a living racing yachts in glittering foreign regattas. It's a life her father taught her, and where she's escaped after his mysterious disappearance offshore. The truth of that night is one she intends to die with.

But everyone has to go home sometime. Returning to Great Haven, the holiday paradise of Queensland's island coast, she finds a changed place. The resort has long closed, the village in hardship, and people are soon talking about Erin – and whispering blame for her father's death at sea.

But not everything on Haven is unwelcoming. There's Tristan Jackson, a man from her past, who is rebuilding the resort and promises Erin a prestigious role in the new Haven regatta – and a return to their romantic past. And Alex Bell, the visiting doctor who Erin finds insatiably attractive, even as his proximity threatens to uncover the truth of her father's death.

Just as the longed-for prosperity begins rolling back into town, Erin is forced to make choices. Unsure whether to trust Alex, and aware of Tristan's dangerous jealousy, she is left with her reputation and future in the balance, as a storm threatens to wash both into the Great Haven sea.